Riverbay Road

MEN'S DORMITORY

NOVEL

1

Riverbay Road

MEN'S DORMITORY

NOVEL

1

WRITTEN BY
Fei Tian Ye Xiang
(ARISE ZHANG)

TRANSLATION BY
Xia

ILLUSTRATIONS BY
Tamtam

Seven Seas

Seven Seas Entertainment

RIVERBAY ROAD MEN'S DORMITORY VOL. 1

Published originally under the title of 《江湾路7号男子宿舍》 by 非天夜翔 Fei Tian Ye Xiang
Author© 2017 非天夜翔 (Fei Tian Ye Xiang)
This edition arranged with JS Agency
English Translation copyright ©2025 by Seven Seas Entertainment Inc.
All rights reserved.

Seven Seas press and purchase enquiries can be sent
to Marketing Manager Lauren Hill at press@gomanga.com.
Information regarding the distribution and purchase of digital editions is available
from Digital Manager Kristine Johnson at digital@gomanga.com.

Seven Seas and the Seven Seas logo are trademarks of
Seven Seas Entertainment. All rights reserved.

Follow Seven Seas Entertainment online at
sevenseasentertainment.com.

TRANSLATION: XiA
ADAPTATION: Max Machiavelli
COVER DESIGN: M. A. Lewife
INTERIOR LAYOUT & DESIGN: Clay Gardner
COPY EDITOR: ECB
PROOFREADER: Amanda Eyer, Pengie
EDITOR: Harry Catlin
PREPRESS TECHNICIAN: Salvador Chan Jr., April Malig, Jules Valera
MANAGING EDITOR: Alyssa Scavetta
EDITOR-IN-CHIEF: Julie Davis
PUBLISHER: Lianne Sentar
VICE PRESIDENT: Adam Arnold
PRESIDENT: Jason DeAngelis

ISBN: 979-8-89160-891-7
Printed in Canada
First Printing: April 2025
10 9 8 7 6 5 4 3 2 1

CONTENTS

CHAPTER

1

No. 7 RIVERBAY ROAD was a six-bedroom villa covering an area of over three thousand square feet. Situated on the Liujin riverbank, it was south-facing and surrounded by ginkgo and wutong trees. Its neighbor to the east was a café for creatives that doubled as a bar at night, while to its west sat a small private museum.

The owner of this villa was Zhang Yuwen, a single, twenty-seven-year-old film director.

Zhang Yuwen was born into a well-off but dysfunctional family fractured by parental discord. His maternal grandfather was a well-known local doctor, while his maternal grandmother was a pharmacist. They had a beautiful daughter—an only child—but she made bad choices in her love life. Zhang Yuwen had practically never seen his father since he was a small child. His mother finally got tired of endlessly waiting for this man and left her son in the care of his grandparents to embark on a new chapter in her own life.

Despite their disappointment, his grandparents gave everything they had to raise their grandson. Zhang Yuwen grew up with them, and when he was sixteen years old, he decided to take their surname. Deeply moved by his gesture, his grandparents bequeathed him their most valuable asset: No. 7 Riverbay Road.

Zhang Yuwen was a lonely child, and only had books for company—the stories penned by great writers and the lives depicted in them were the best companions he ever had in his childhood. These stories inspired his pursuit of a directing major at the film and television academy, and his eventual choice of career: to put it plainly, he made soap operas for a living.

In the year he finished his college entrance exams, his parents finally got the divorce they wanted and went on to start their own respective families, cutting off all contact with one another. After his graduation from university, his grandparents passed away within a year of each other. Apart from the house, they also left their grandson their life savings—a substantial sum given a surgeon's income at the time.

By the time Zhang Yuwen was twenty-two, he already had a luxurious villa and enough savings to last a lifetime.

Heaven always seemed to favor those who were at peace with the world. A friend of Zhang Yuwen's grandfather recommended him for a job after he graduated, and so a short time later, Zhang Yuwen became the diligent assistant to a respected, talented, and experienced director in the industry and began learning filmmaking under his tutelage.

But life often had more twists and turns than the movies portrayed. After the release of several films, this veteran director took on a big project, but during filming, he was embroiled in a corporate money laundering case and ended up arrested and sentenced to several years in prison.

Alas, the film was nearing completion. So as not to let the investment go down the drain with the mentor behind bars, there was no other option but to let the inexperienced apprentice take over the helm. It was thus, with great trepidation, that Zhang Yuwen completed shooting the film.

His mentor's name was struck from the silver screen following his disgrace, and Zhang Yuwen's name prominently took its place under the director's credit. The film received both critical acclaim and box office success, landing Zhang Yuwen his first big payday.

His family had never known the struggle of toiling for hard-earned money, and Zhang Yuwen therefore came to view material wealth as so much dirt. Once he made a name for himself, people would often pour their hearts out to the young Director Zhang about their entrepreneurial difficulties, and he would offer them funding and words of comfort. Many of these investments went nowhere, but eventually two young directors stood out, rewarding their generous backer with bountiful returns.

Of these two directors, one flopped at the box office but hit the jackpot with the critics and brought home an international award, while the other unexpectedly produced a smash hit and raked in a fortune at the box office.

In both productions, Zhang Yuwen was the main investor. Not only did he recoup his capital overnight, he also earned the title of an ace investor. By the time Zhang Yuwen turned twenty-six, his savings had reached a truly astronomical amount, enough to live off for several lifetimes.

As Jane Austen said, a single man in possession of a good fortune must be in want of a wife. This was a truth universally acknowledged, yet eligible bachelor Zhang Yuwen had never publicly sought a wife—because he was gay, and that was common knowledge. As everyone knew, finding a spouse was harder for rich gay men than it was for rich straight men.

The absence of his father when he was growing up left him with a sense of insecurity, and the way his parents had interacted made him instinctively keep his distance from heterosexual relationships.

It was in his third year of middle school that he realized he was attracted to his own sex. At that time, there was a lively, vibrant junior one grade below him whom he enjoyed spending time with— so much so that it got to the point where he couldn't eat or sleep. When he compared this with the many famous books he had read, he soon came to the realization that this was love, thus confirming his sexual orientation.

Although same-sex marriage was now legal, there was still a lot of social stigma attached to homosexuals. Adhering to the principle that it was better to avoid unnecessary trouble, Zhang Yuwen never publicly disclosed his sexual orientation.

Of course, he hardly had any friends, either.

It wasn't until he was in university that Zhang Yuwen thought about finding the love of his life on campus, someone he could trust to build a life and raise a pet with. However, the open—and even promiscuous—lifestyles of the handsome guys in the academy, straight and gay alike, shocked him.

Top or bottom, it was common for them to switch boyfriends every three months. Occasionally, there were even gatherings where the scenes unfolding resembled the set of a gay adult film. Four years in the academy put Zhang Yuwen through so much shock he almost gave up on the idea of dating, but while honest people might be a rare breed, they luckily weren't extinct. At twenty-two, after graduating and entering the workforce, Zhang Yuwen successfully put aside his misgivings and fell in love.

He wasn't a particularly emotional person, and he adopted a calm and rational attitude in most aspects of life. He was the kind of Pisces who, even faced with rejection for a confession of love, would calmly analyze what he had done wrong. As fate would have it, a junior from the performing arts department passionately wooed Zhang Yuwen and professed his love for him, and he accepted, thinking it was worth a try. After they became a couple, he rented a two-bedroom apartment outside of school and started living with his junior. In this relationship, he instinctively took on the role of the top and assumed more social responsibility, while his junior was the bottom who relied on him for living expenses and even tuition.

Zhang Yuwen found this perfectly natural. The only downside was that he was already employed, working hard. It was inevitable that someone would be busy when their career was taking off like his was. He had the finances but not the time, and he could only make up for the lack of companionship with money.

After the junior completed his four years of university with his tuition fee paid in full, he dumped Zhang Yuwen and found an unattractive middle-aged man who looked richer than him—after all, while water tended to flow down, people sought to rise to the top, and social climbing was a normal way of life. This was perfectly reasonable.

Too bad this ex-boyfriend didn't realize the guy he'd so heartlessly dumped was the greatest financial backer ever. Zhang Yuwen was actually much richer than he appeared; he was just too busy to spend money. By dumping him, the junior was, in effect, ditching a watermelon for a sesame seed.

None of that mattered anymore, though. After several years of single life on the rebound, Zhang Yuwen felt a little empty, though he still held out hope that love would come knocking.

Yeah, he had hope for his future, but not much.

He didn't want to keep toiling as part of a film crew, even though a director was already at the top of the food chain in the film and television industry. Instead, he wanted to be a writer, like Kafka or Dostoyevsky, and leave behind some breathtaking masterpieces. Otherwise, life would be meaningless.

Free from any financial worries, he spent a year writing a masterpiece depicting the many facets of life, and personally sent the manuscript to a publishing house introduced to him by an acquaintance.

But he was dealt a huge blow in return. This publishing house unanimously decided to nominate the deputy editor—the second boss himself—to give a scathing critique of Zhang Yuwen's work.

"How should I put it?" The deputy editor mulled over the right words to say. From the attitude of the man who'd introduced them, the deputy editor could tell that this guy in front of him was no ordinary person. He had done his best to hold himself back from shouting abuse at him or throwing the manuscript in his face and scolding him for wasting everyone's time.

Zhang Yuwen, seated across from him, felt his smile freeze.

"It's too fake." The deputy editor racked his brain. "Right, contrived is the word. People like this don't exist in real life."

Zhang Yuwen wanted to say "but," but the word died in his mouth. He just nodded blankly.

Writers and directors both made a living from storytelling, but they worked in two completely different fields. This deputy editor had a lot of prestige in the publishing industry, so Zhang Yuwen trusted his judgment: His own work must indeed be shitty.

"What's your main occupation?" the deputy editor asked, digressing. "You're pretty rich, right?"

"All I can say is that I don't have to worry about my three meals a day," Zhang Yuwen answered cautiously.

"That's it," the deputy editor said. "I'd guess you have too little contact with other people, and you've never really observed them.

You've no need to eke out a living, so you've no need to take your cue from someone else or guess what other people are really thinking. The motivations and goals of the characters you penned aren't realistic—in other words, it's out of touch with reality. It's like a lot of actors you see performing on a glitzy stage. They look vibrant at first glance, but it doesn't resonate with the audience."

"Oh... Okay." Dejected, Zhang Yuwen accepted the criticism.

"If you want to create good literature," the deputy editor advised, "you'll have to interact with people more and not keep to yourself. You live alone?"

"Yup." Zhang Yuwen had spent the entire year cooped up at home, working daily on this manuscript. The characters in his story were all products of his imagination. He was adept at finding character archetypes from literary masterpieces and reinterpreting them—as a director, he reworked the characters the screenwriters created, making their actions exaggerated and their personalities distinct. Every one of them had their own unique label, like characters straight out of comic books, vividly brought to life with the actors' own reinterpretation. But strip away the glamor of the filming sets and the veneer of the performing arts, leaving just the text behind, and Zhang Yuwen's creative shortcomings were completely exposed.

Indeed, all writers needed to observe other people and have unique life experiences to produce good works.

With that blow to his confidence, Zhang Yuwen went home, taking his manuscript with him. He reflected on his career path since his graduation. Everything had been smooth sailing; money and credentials seemed to simply fall into his lap, and he'd forgotten a crucial lesson his mentor had taught him in his professional creative writing class: The most important aspect of character creation was to connect with people and observe them.

Rather than resent the deputy editor, Zhang Yuwen was grateful to him for his insights. He hadn't given up; he still wanted to be a writer and leave his mark on history. However, those who strove to make history rarely succeeded and were far more likely to achieve infamy. Only those with passion and lifelong dedication to their crafts could be remembered through the ages.

The next day, Zhang Yuwen picked himself up and took the subway to observe the weary faces of the corporate slaves. Then he went to the shared houses in Jiangnan and watched the people coming and going.

Separated by the Liujin River, Jiangnan and Jiangbei were two completely different worlds. He understood that to pay attention to reality, he first had to step into it, get close to it. Tall and handsome, he carried himself with poise and class, so while he was observing the street food stalls outside the filthy buildings in Jiangnan, many others were also watching him in curiosity, thinking he looked out of place here.

Zhang Yuwen had indeed lived in the Jiangnan District for a period in his childhood. It had been a long, long time since he last returned; so long he almost didn't feel like he belonged here anymore.

He plucked up the courage to strike up casual conversations with the people, but it felt so awkward that he eventually left in a hurry.

Then, he came up with a bold idea—

I can rent out the house! There are six rooms in total. I'll take one for myself and rent four out to observe the tenants' lives.

This brain wave motivated Zhang Yuwen. The next day, he tweaked this idea to "rent out the house to men with the same sexual orientation as himself." After all, for the sake of their personal safety, most girls wouldn't want to be roommates with unfamiliar men.

And if he was going to rent to men only, then it wasn't much of a step to limit his tenants to gay men. Being gay was just one aspect of their identities, after all.

A man of action, Zhang Yuwen put his listing up on a local rental website the next afternoon. To keep people from finding out just how wealthy he was, he posed as a sub-landlord, claiming to be looking after the house for a friend who was abroad. He also limited the tenants to male homosexuals, which proved quite effective. After all, most straight men were homophobic and avoided gay guys like the plague. Letting them live among gay men would really trigger their persecution complex.

He wouldn't need to worry about girls, either. Even if the tenants were all gay, they were still guys, which posed a lot of inconvenience—even if a girl were to come knocking, he could simply dissuade them and send them away.

He set the rent at a rather low price. After all, the goal was simply to find a few samples for him to observe and gather material.

That same night, he received one hundred and twenty-seven messages.

He decided to simply screen them based on his intuition and select suitable roommates who would also double as observational subjects, turning No. 7 Riverbay Road into his own material-gathering site. He could collect ideas for his novel without leaving his house—so why not?

A T A TABLE in Sunny Days Cat Café:

"Your name's Yan Jun?" Having found his first tenant, Zhang Yuwen made the first move and sized up the guy sitting across from him. The guy was observing Zhang Yuwen right back.

Yan Jun was tall, slim, and well-proportioned, with deeply chiseled facial features and tanned skin. Dressed in a well-tailored suit, he exuded poise.

"Yeah," Yan Jun answered. "I work at Zhaoling Tower. You sure you didn't make a mistake with the rent?"

"Nope." Zhang Yuwen had already thought of an explanation beforehand. "This is my friend's property. I'm just helping him to look after it. As long as it's occupied, the rent isn't top priority."

Yan Jun nodded, and Zhang Yuwen cast another glance at him. "What do you do for a living?"

"Sales," Yan Jun answered succinctly. Half a minute later, he added, "Equipment sales."

"What's your position?" Zhang Yuwen asked offhandedly before realizing he might have sounded a little offensive. "Sorry, I'm just curious. I mean, are you a top? Or in other words, a 1?"

Yan Jun seldom found himself in situations where he was asked about his sexual role right to his face. He was closeted, and the question reminded him of his sexual orientation, hitting him with the abrupt realization—*"Oh, I'm gay. I almost forgot. Close call."* It also felt like he was being described as some new equipment, which made him uncomfortable.

But he needed lower-priced housing, and this sub-landlord didn't seem to be a troublesome guy.

"I...guess top?" he said. "I haven't bottomed before. You?"

Yan Jun surmised that this sub-landlord, who had yet to introduce himself by name, might be well-off. His fair complexion showed he'd never had to brave the elements and toil hard for a living, and his well-proportioned figure suggested he did not have to relieve stress by bingeing on food. The lack of dark circles under his eyes also indicated that he got enough sleep. He spoke and drank his coffee at a leisurely pace, too.

Slow-paced—this was an important point. It was also a key criterion Yan Jun used to estimate a client's financial status. People who weren't in a hurry were usually well-off.

"Me neither." Zhang Yuwen thought for a while before adding, "I was the top in my last relationship."

For some reason, perhaps because he didn't know any other gay people, Zhang Yuwen was always keen to talk to someone about his feelings.

"You single?" Yan Jun asked in all seriousness.

"Yup." Zhang Yuwen looked into his sincere eyes. "Would you like to look at the house?"

"I can do it now," Yan Jun said. "I took half a day off today. Are we going by car?"

"It's just next door." Zhang Yuwen took the bill and went up to the counter to pay. "Let's go."

Yan Jun said nothing and followed Zhang Yuwen with strong, purposeful strides. Before he headed out today, he'd tidied himself up so that he looked neat and spirited. He'd also done an online search and learned that No. 7 Riverbay Road was a fairly lavish villa.

"It's right here." Zhang Yuwen unlocked the door with his fingerprint. "You can't bring dates home to stay the night."

"How about friends?" Yan Jun asked.

"Better not, but they can occasionally come over for a visit." Zhang Yuwen didn't want a stream of people coming and going; he didn't need that many observation subjects. "Try to make yourself the only tenant for your room. That's one of the reasons the rent is lower."

Yan Jun stepped into the front yard, a neat and well-maintained garden with flowerpots stacked together and a water vat in the corner filled with blooming water lilies. "Anyone doing the cleaning?" he asked.

"Yeah," Zhang Yuwen replied. "Two housekeepers will be here every day; one to do the grocery shopping and prepare the meals, and another to clean up the common areas. The homeowner doesn't want them to touch the stuff inside..." He opened the main entrance and stepped past the foyer to a large, two-story, high-ceilinged living room. A dining room to the side held a long table that could seat twelve people.

Yan Jun glanced at the stairs and offhandedly touched the corner of the coffee table. The furnishings were old but well-cleaned, and there was no dust even on the decorations.

"There are three rooms on the ground floor." Zhang Yuwen led Yan Jun to view them. Each was about 375 square feet in size, with one facing south, one north, and one east.

"There are three on the second floor too," Zhang Yuwen continued. "I'm staying in the master bedroom. If you're interested in moving in, you can choose your own room."

Yan Jun didn't reply, but after a moment's pause, he asked, "Can children come over occasionally?"

"Huh?" Zhang Yuwen shot Yan Jun a puzzled look.

"My...niece," Yan Jun explained. "My older brother's daughter. They have to work, so when something urgent crops up, they occasionally leave her with me in the evenings. When I'm babysitting, I have to pick her up from the childcare center, then take her home after ten."

This came out of the blue to Zhang Yuwen; he hadn't anticipated this at all.

"How old is she?" Zhang Yuwen asked.

"Just turned eleven months old," said Yan Jun, "but don't worry, she doesn't cry or fuss, and she won't be here every day, just occasionally."

Zhang Yuwen didn't reply. Thinking that felt like a tacit approval, Yan Jun waited patiently for several seconds before prompting, "Is that okay?"

"Yeah, that's fine." Zhang Yuwen thought about it. He couldn't hold it against a baby. "It's okay if she cries too. It's only natural for babies to cry."

Yan Jun felt a weight lifted off his shoulders. "Thank you. Thank you for your understanding."

Zhang Yuwen thought Yan Jun could have waited to bring this up until he'd already moved in. After all, it wasn't that big a deal to look after an infant for a couple of hours. This showed that Yan Jun was an honest person, but this wasn't a useful quality to have in a salesperson, since salespeople who were too honest rarely made money.

"I'd like to rent this place," Yan Jun said. "I'll take the east-facing room downstairs."

"Okay." Zhang Yuwen hadn't expected Yan Jun to decide so quickly. "Don't you need to go back and think about it?"

"Nah," Yan Jun said. "It's a direct line from the Riverbay Road subway station to my company. Very convenient. I was just thinking of looking for a new place nearby. How much for utilities and internet?"

Zhang Yuwen was about to say that it was included in the rent, but the price was already so low that making it too good of a deal might come off as a scam. "Two hundred a month if you don't use a lot of electrical appliances," he said. "Any excess, and we'll have to split the cost."

"That's cool with me." Yan Jun looked around. The room was spotless, and the bedroom he'd chosen had its own en suite bathroom. Close the door, and it'd look just like a studio apartment.

"You're pretty handsome," Zhang Yuwen remarked offhandedly. This was a habit from his days in film, when he habitually complimented the actors to drop them a little unexpected joy.

"Huh?" At this compliment, the polite and satisfied smile on Yan Jun's face disappeared, replaced with a more genuine one, tinged with the bashfulness of a young man being praised. "You're very good-looking yourself."

This wasn't just a return compliment made out of courtesy. Zhang Yuwen did have a composed, aristocratic air to him. If you were to match with someone like Zhang Yuwen on a dating app, you'd be in for an unforgettable night.

If Zhang Yuwen were to extend an invitation to him now, Yan Jun might really just follow him to the master bedroom and get to know him up close and personal. When was the last time he'd done it? Yan Jun couldn't really remember.

Of course, that was assuming Yan Jun got to be the one to take the initiative: Life had been fucking him over every day to the point of despair lately, and he didn't want to be fucked again in bed.

But Zhang Yuwen simply said, "Thanks."

"You work out often?"

"Every day or every other day. I run and do cardio."

"You have a great physique."

Zhang Yuwen smiled. "Thanks."

The second thanks got the point across. He didn't lift his T-shirt to flaunt his abs or anything, which hinted to Yan Jun that there would be no further development, at least not today. Yan Jun could naturally understand the subtext in the words of another adult.

Just earlier, he'd been moved by something Zhang Yuwen said. What was it, again? Which statement had cemented his notion that the young man before him was friendly and gentle?

Not his compliment on his appearance, or his demeanor, but when he'd said, *"It's only natural for babies to cry."*

These words were a lifeline to Yan Jun, casting a warm ray of light into the darkness in his life.

Next, Zhang Yuwen took Yan Jun to see the back garden, which was slightly larger than the front yard. There was a small pond with a tall ginkgo tree next to it, which had a swing hanging from its branches.

Looking at Zhang Yuwen's back, Yan Jun guessed that he was probably not this man's type.

"So..." They both spoke at once. Yan Jun gestured for Zhang Yuwen to go first.

"When are you moving in?" Zhang Yuwen asked. "Shall I send you the lease first?"

"I still have twenty days left on my current lease," Yan Jun said, "and my money is tied up in wealth management products. One month deposit and three months' rent, right? Can we delay the rent by a few days? I promise to pay it off within twenty days."

"Sure thing. Let's make it a quarterly payment," Zhang Yuwen agreed. "I'll send you the contract first."

Zhang Yuwen took out his mobile phone, adding Yan Jun to the instant messaging app and emailing the lease to him. Yan Jun noticed Zhang Yuwen looking at him again.

"What?" Yan Jun asked with a raised brow, flashing a professional smile. This was the trademark half-genuine smile he often used when he was trying hard to sell a product. He knew it was a smile people found hard to say no to, one that would leave a deep impression on them.

"You really don't have a partner?" Zhang Yuwen was actually wondering about something else. This tenant had the physique and the looks, and he hoped the guy's private life wasn't a promiscuous one.

"I'm too busy to date," Yan Jun explained. "Why? You gonna introduce me to someone?"

Zhang Yuwen waved his hand, accepting his explanation. Anyway, there was a clear clause on this in the lease. If he breached the contract, Zhang Yuwen would just kick him out. "All right. But let me know if you need help moving or anything."

The two of them returned to the living room, passed through the foyer, and stepped out through the front yard.

Yan Jun stopped in thought for a while. "I still don't know your name," he said at last.

"Oh, yeah." Zhang Yuwen was embarrassed. "My name is Zhang Yuwen."

Under the setting sun, Yan Jun happily waved goodbye to Zhang Yuwen and headed for the subway station. He'd gotten himself a great bargain. The rent for this room was only two-thirds the price of similar listings in the area, and it also saved him half an hour of commuting time. Now he'd be able to set aside more money to send to his mother in the countryside.

He treated himself to a restaurant set meal he was usually reluctant to splurge on. While he ate, he scrolled through the matches on the gay dating app on his phone. He wasn't looking for a partner, just browsing—as if by looking at these people's photos he could feel like he was in a relationship. Then he walked over to the childcare center to pick up the eleven-month-old Xiao-Qi.

It was less than a mile away from No. 7 Riverbay Road on foot, and he only had to cross the bridge to get to the childcare center. This was truly a prime location.

"Papa's here—" The childcare worker was cross-stitching when she saw Xiao-Qi standing up, holding onto to crib railing for support. That was when she knew the last parent had arrived.

"Papa's here early today, isn't he?" The lady smiled.

She was happy for Xiao-Qi. The last child to be picked up always tugged at her heartstrings. At the same time, she was also happy for herself, because Yan Jun's arrival meant that she could finally get off work.

"Pa-pa!" Xiao-Qi had learned to speak early, and her first word was "Papa." Aside from that, she would just make meaningless sounds.

Yan Jun picked up Xiao-Qi with practiced ease and thanked the childcare workers. He touched her diaper to make sure it wasn't wet, then strapped her in a baby carrier, facing out. Xiao-Qi babbled and waved her hands as he took her out of the childcare center and into the subway station to take the train. Leaning against the gangway, he scrolled through his phone, while Xiao-Qi smiled at a girl nearby.

A handsome man carrying a baby—this was a frequent sight on Subway Line 4.

"She's drooling," someone informed him.

"She has a rash," another whispered.

Yan Jun wiped her with a soft tissue. Xiao-Qi always had rashes on her face, and Yan Jun always felt terrible for not taking good care of her.

"Pa-pa!" Strapped to Yan Jun's chest, Xiao-Qi looked up and squirmed. Yan Jun turned away, not wanting others to gawk at her.

They arrived at their destination, and Yan Jun walked home with Xiao-Qi. Back home, he bathed her and changed her clothes, fed her powdered milk, and applied cream for her rashes. Then he carried her around the little room and did squats to lull her to sleep. The neighbor was still up watching a comedy, and the roars of canned laughter proved to be Yan Jun's nightmare.

But finally, Xiao-Qi fell asleep. At 9:30 p.m., Yan Jun opened his laptop to forty-two emails left on hold in his inbox since he had taken the afternoon off to view the house. The lease was among them.

Yan Jun set about clearing his work. Twice, Xiao-Qi woke up and cried, and twice, he fed her, changed her diaper, and carried her to soothe her. Fatigued, he fell asleep as soon as he hit the pillow at 2 a.m. Waking up at 5:40 a.m. to an already awake Xiao-Qi, he hurriedly prepared milk, changed her diaper, and went to work, completely exhausted as he plunged himself into a new day's toil.

Riverbay Road
MEN'S DORMITORY

ZHENG WEIZE was stunned when he arrived at No. 7 Riverbay Road. Such a wonderful house, going for just ¥3,700 a month?! But he made sure to feign composure and adopt an aloof display, nodding from time to time to show his approval.

Zhang Yuwen saw through this young man's pretense at a glance, but being a mild-tempered person, he didn't take offense. He had nothing against this guy's personality either. In fact, the more eccentric the potential tenants, the better the material he'd be able to gather for his novel.

"I have exactly the same dining table as you do," Zheng Weize said with a smile.

"Are you a bottom?" Zhang Yuwen asked in passing. He could see that the guy had light makeup on, and there weren't that many guys in this city who wore makeup regularly.

"I'm a top!" Zheng Weize was quick to clarify.

Twenty-two years old this year, Zheng Weize had fair, delicate skin and dressed like an internet celebrity bottom. Zhang Yuwen was half a head taller than him.

Zhang Yuwen smiled at him again. "Are you studying or working?"

"I'm in university," Zheng Weize lied. In truth, he hadn't made it into university—or rather, he hadn't wanted to continue with his studies after graduating from high school.

Zhang Yuwen hummed in reply. The nearest university was five stations away, but there was nothing out of the ordinary about renting a place off campus if your studies weren't too demanding.

"I'll take this one." Zheng Weize chose another room on the first floor. "That room's taken, right?"

"Yeah," Zhang Yuwen replied. "He'll move in later."

"What kind of person is he?"

Zhang Yuwen was very protective of his tenants' privacy. "A tenant just like you. It's not my place to reveal more about him. When you become friends with him, you can ask him yourself."

"Can you make it cheaper?" Zheng Weize asked.

"It's already the lowest it can be."

A 345-square-foot bedroom in a wealthy neighborhood with convenient access to transport and utilities included in the rent—and he still wanted to bargain? Zhang Yuwen was astounded, but he knew some people haggled out of habit. Instead of getting angry, he found Zheng Weize interesting.

"All right then," Zheng Weize said. "I'll move in tomorrow, but can I pay you a few days later? My salary for the month isn't in yet."

"Sure," Zhang Yuwen agreed. "Are you working part-time while you study?"

"Oh." Zheng Weize, lacking in social experience, had accidentally given himself away. "I'm working on a project for my senior, and there's funding."

Zhang Yuwen only asked in passing, but he noticed Zheng Weize was constantly sizing him up. This guy's efforts to uphold his image and persona reminded him of his ex-boyfriend—a young man who was always all bluff and bluster, not wanting to be seen as the weaker party in their relationship.

Zhang Yuwen informed Zheng Weize of some things he ought to keep in mind, while Zheng Weize absently listened, nodding occasionally. He showed no objection to the rule prohibiting tenants from bringing their partners to stay overnight.

When he was done, Zheng Weize asked, "Any parking space here?"

Zhang Yuwen was surprised. "You can reach the underground garage from the side road. There are two parking spaces there. Do you need parking?"

"Oh…" Zheng Weize didn't have a car or a driver's license. "Never mind."

Zhang Yuwen felt puzzled.

"It's nothing." This was just one part of Zheng Weize's bluff.

"Need help moving?" Zhang Yuwen asked.

"Nope. Give me the keys, I'll move in myself."

Zhang Yuwen took Zheng Weize to the main entrance to record his fingerprints, and with that, Zheng Weize's new residence was decided.

Starting today, Zheng Weize needed to pay his own rent. ¥3,700 a month—he would have to scrimp and save to afford it. He walked a short distance along the river to catch the bus, as it was two yuan cheaper than the subway. After a shaky ride, he arrived at his destination, a sixth-story apartment building. He fished out his keys and opened the door.

"Where have you been?" asked his former colleague, who was eating takeout at home. The living room was a mess, with heaps of drink cartons and instant noodle cups strewn everywhere. A Korean drama was playing on the television.

"I've found a new place to live," Zheng Weize said with cool indifference. "I'll move out soon."

"Eh!" His former colleague was a straight guy who lived with his girlfriend. He used to work with Zheng Weize at the same cosmetics counter selling lipsticks. At first, being the senior, he took good care of the newcomer, Zheng Weize. Not only did he personally guide him in his work, but he even allowed him to stay in his rented apartment—a move that touched Zheng Weize, who was on his own in the big city.

Innately and instinctively unable to resist the protective nature and indiscriminate flirting of straight men, Zheng Weize developed a deep attachment to him, at one point thinking he could turn this former colleague gay. He cooked for him, bought him clothes, and took meticulous care of him, trying his best to nurture feelings that weren't destined to blossom. The result was inevitable. Not only did he fail, he also incurred significant sunk costs. What was more, after he boldly confessed his feelings, he also saw the straight guy's cold-hearted side, as the guy quickly got himself a girlfriend and made a clean break with him.

Then there was also the exhaustion of his job, and the dual disillusionment of both work and love had left Zheng Weize despondent; in the end, he quit his job at the cosmetics counter.

However, he still hadn't found a satisfactory place to live after his resignation, so he shamelessly continued to stay in this straight guy's house for five days. These five days were so torturous, it had worn down the last bit of feelings he had for the guy. Zheng Weize didn't even want to look at him as he made a beeline for his room to pack his stuff, all the while calculating the money he'd get next month and wondering how to pay rent to Zhang Yuwen...

At the same time, he heard the discussion in the living room. The straight guy's girlfriend had been unhappy with Zheng Weize for quite some time, and even on his departure day, she was still criticizing him for not paying his share of the utility bills and for things like not cleaning the common areas... Zheng Weize threw things around his room, making some noise to remind her he still hadn't left yet.

The closet was full of cheap, low-quality impulse buys he had only worn once. When he opened it, these musty-smelling clothes came tumbling out like an avalanche, and he was almost buried underneath them.

Under the bed lay a heap of wigs, cosmetic samples, and stuffed toys. The desk was a mess too, and beside it was his live streaming equipment: his lighting setup, a ring light, and a small fabric backdrop.

Zheng Weize pulled out two large suitcases. He didn't know how to pack them, though, nor did he want to fold his clothes; instead, he simply shoved everything into the suitcases and kneeled on them to close the latches.

When he'd packed half of his belongings, he dragged the suitcases out of the house and left under the watchful eyes of his straight ex-colleague and his girlfriend. Struggling, he carried them down to the ground floor of the elevator-less building and dragged them to the bus stop, where he boarded a bus. By noon, he was back at No. 7 Riverbay Road.

Zhang Yuwen was having lunch, and the sight of Zheng Weize with his two huge suitcases startled him. He hadn't expected him to keep his word and move in today. Putting down his chopsticks, he went over.

"Have you had lunch?" Zhang Yuwen asked. "Want a bite?"

"I already ate," Zheng Weize said. "No worries, I can manage. Thanks."

Zhang Yuwen signaled to the housekeeper with a glance, and the woman said, "Let me help you."

"Thanks." Zheng Weize was moved by her offer of help, but he turned her down. "I can do it myself."

"This is Auntie Liu," said Zhang Yuwen. "She's the housekeeper here. Just ask her if there's anything you need. The other is called Xiao-Chen. She helps with the cleaning."

"Hello," Liu Jingfang said in greeting. "Let me do it."

Liu Jingfang used to do the cleaning at Zhang Yuwen's maternal grandfather's clinic. She looked after Zhang Yuwen, too, then a child himself. Ever since the clinic closed down, she'd taken care of No. 7 Riverbay Road, as well as Zhang Yuwen's meals and daily living needs.

Zhang Yuwen was just as good-tempered as his grandfather. He rarely got angry, but when he did, he became hostile and merciless, digging up every past grudge and grievance to settle the score. He had a great memory, and while he wasn't easily offended, it took only one offense for him to send the offender packing. Liu Jingfang understood the personalities of this grandfather and grandson pair well, so she never played the seniority card and was always tactful.

"Thanks!" There were even housekeepers here, Zheng Weize marveled. Just what kind of TV drama plot was this?

The villa and all that it came with made him feel like he was marrying into a wealthy family, and Zhang Yuwen's affability further fueled his fantasies, making him dream up a story where a rich heir guy took a fancy to him and posted a private message on a forum visible only to himself, luring him to a big villa where he began his life as the pampered wife to a high-powered, domineering CEO.

"I can clean it myself, thanks!" Having said thanks for the fourth time, Zheng Weize opened the door to his room, pushed in his suitcases, and closed the door softly, not wanting to show this high-powered, domineering CEO and housekeeper his messy belongings and the moldy smell that defined his life.

Taken by a sense of relief, he spent a moment admiring the view outside the window. Zhang Yuwen had renovated this place three years prior, installing in every room a large floor-to-ceiling window that opened to a balcony or garden with neatly trimmed greenery and deck chairs, resembling a beautiful vacation guesthouse.

Even now, Zheng Weize still felt like he was dreaming. He couldn't believe he had rented such a wonderful room for so little money. The dazzling afternoon sun shining on his bed, the fluttering, sheer window curtains, and the backyard filled with the beauty of autumn—living in a place like this improved his mood.

Zheng Weize opened his closet and carefully organized his clothing, hanging up his wrinkled-as-raisins clothes one article at a time. The live streaming platform would pay out a portion of his earnings the next month, so if he could just find a way to use his credit card to get cash, he'd be able to scrape together enough money for the rent and deposit.

It would all hinge on live streaming. Zheng Weize was confident he could make money as a live streamer. After all, he'd mastered the most advanced makeup techniques and had a face that could almost be called stunning after he applied makeup to it.

The only problem was that his top fan on the live stream platform hadn't shown up in a long time. Thinking about this made Zheng Weize sad again.

Having done a simple tidying of his room at three o'clock in the afternoon, Zheng Weize dragged his two suitcases back out so he could go get the other half of his belongings.

Zhang Yuwen was working out on the treadmill while watching TV. He was wearing a gym tank top, all drenched in sweat, looking very sexy with his attractive arms and side muscles on display. The most precious legacy his maternal grandparents had left him was good lifestyle habits. Children who grew up in a family of doctors had self-discipline and excelled at managing their own health. Even more commendably, Zhang Yuwen never used his physique to seduce people.

Zheng Weize couldn't help but stare when he passed by the gym. Zhang Yuwen waved a greeting to him from the other side of the glass window, and in that moment, Zheng Weize felt his heart flutter a little.

Zhang Yuwen moved to get off the treadmill, but Zheng Weize waved his hand to indicate that he still had something to do and left in a hurry.

He left Jiangbei and returned to Jiangnan. The scenery changed again, but Zheng Weize's mood was massively different, because he was now a resident of Jiangbei. He fantasized about Zhang Yuwen's looks and physique. Might sparks fly between them next?

Zheng Weize was a hopeless romantic, a lazy young man who also wanted to have it easy. He initially started live streaming to make some extra money. Working a regular job was too hard, and without academic credentials, he couldn't find an easy, well-paying job that matched his capabilities. He soon realized that being a live streamer wasn't easy either, so he revised his life goal: to find a rich boyfriend through live streaming, marry him, and live the life of a high-society gay wife.

This was, in his opinion, a simple yet pragmatic ambition. Unfortunately, his biggest obstacle to achieving this goal was his nature as a hopeless romantic. He wanted someone rich and handsome, young and energetic, with a great physique, who would be devoted and loyal. Also, that particular body part couldn't be shorter than six inches. His criteria for this and that were like a huge filter, and so far, no one had made the cut.

His lack of social experience made it hard for him to discern potential mates, and his chronic loneliness made him want to pounce on any decent-looking man he saw. *Is that Zhang-something-wen guy...single? He's such a catch, he couldn't be a player, could he? He must be a scumbag, yeah?* Reasonable concerns nagged at Zheng Weize's thoughts.

"Back already?" His straight ex-colleague's voice interrupted his reverie.

Zheng Weize simply hummed an acknowledgment and went about packing the other half of his belongings, all the while assessing the possibility of marrying a tall, handsome, and rich man by moving into No. 7 Riverbay Road, thereby realizing his life goals. His straight ex-colleague had already lost all his charm and become repulsive to him.

"Since you're leaving, how 'bout grabbing a meal together?" the straight guy suggested.

"Nah, not now." Zheng Weize entered his room, and his ex-colleague followed him in. During their brief, six-month "honeymoon period," Zheng Weize had spent thousands on him, and now that he was leaving, his ex-colleague remembered just how nice he'd been to him.

"Where are you staying?" The straight guy sat on the bed and watched Zheng Weize pack up his live streaming equipment.

"Riverbay Road," Zheng Weize answered, omitting the number.

"Whoa!" The straight guy was a little astonished. "A rich neighborhood! The house ain't cheap, right?"

"It's a friend's house," Zheng Weize said simply, leaving him to fill in the blanks.

"Oh." The straight guy obligingly pieced together the rest of the story, sitting silently on the bed for a long time. "Actually, I..."

The straight guy still had more to say. Zheng Weize placed the mobile phone stand he used for live streaming and a bag of clothes by the door and turned back to push his suitcases out.

He was going to say "see ya," but he didn't want to see him ever again, so instead he just said, "Bye-bye."

The straight guy followed him to help carry the suitcases, but Zheng Weize suddenly had the urge to vent his pent-up feelings. Just like Nora Helmer in *A Doll's House* embarking on a new phase in her life, he slammed the door shut in his face.

CHAPTER
4

THE THIRD TENANT was a busy-looking guy named Chen Hong, a twenty-nine-year-old fitness trainer who was currently standing at a crossroads in his life. He was practically glued to his phone, sending voice memos on his instant messaging app throughout his entire conversation with Zhang Yuwen about renting a room.

One moment it was, "Okay, okay, I got it. Just go there and look for him..."

The next, it was, "I've seen your BMI. It's a little high, but I can come up with a detailed plan for you..."

Then it was, "Okay, okay, sure. I got you. It's fine, no worries. Let's take it slow..."

The frequency at which Zhang Yuwen's speech was interrupted by the notification alerts from Chen Hong's two cell phones turned their conversation into a sampling of Chen Hong's busy and exciting work life.

"Sorry," Chen Hong said again. "¥4,000, right?"

"Yeah," Zhang Yuwen said earnestly. "There are three rooms left. The one downstairs costs ¥4,000, while the ones upstairs are ¥3,300 and ¥3,600. The ¥4,000 room also comes with a bathroom."

"I run a fitness studio," said Chen Hong, "and there's a promotion right now, so there's a lot going on—" Then both of Chen

Hong's phones chimed at once, and he hurriedly responded to the messages.

Zhang Yuwen nodded in understanding. Chen Hong looked up, still distracted, and asked, "Do you usually work out? It's important to keep yourself in shape."

"I occasionally do some cardio," Zhang Yuwen replied. "Would you like to see the house?"

"Oh! The house! Right, right! I was just thinking about that. Riverbay Road is a great location!"

Chen Hong had very short hair, strong facial features, and a well-built physique. He wasn't shy about showing off his muscles—a common trait among fitness trainers. Even in autumn, he still wore gym tank tops. He picked up his gym bag and followed Zhang Yuwen out of Sunny Days Cat Café to the villa next door. Along the way, he introduced Zhang Yuwen to his business: He had started a fitness studio in the Jiangbei area and employed several people, and business was booming. Many high-profile clients went to the trouble of traveling long distances to his studio every day to get in shape, and his clientele included multi-million-dollar businessmen, influential political figures, and movie superstars.

Zhang Yuwen nodded with sincerity, having gathered a lot of interesting gossip. He also spotted at least fifty plot holes in these stories. "You can't bring clients here to work out," Zhang Yuwen reminded him.

"Yes, yes, of course," Chen Hong said. "I want to keep work and personal life separate too. Eh... This is your house? W-T-F?! It's *so* big?!"

"Of course not." Following his prepared script, Zhang Yuwen stressed to Chen Hong that he was only a sub-landlord, and a broke one at that—a hint that he wouldn't be buying a gym membership.

Chen Hong was shocked. Such a wonderful place for only ¥4,000 in rent? He only took one glance at the room before deciding: "I'm renting it."

"Okay." Zhang Yuwen was already used to these kinds of astonished expressions and decisive attitudes from prospective tenants. He was a little concerned about renting to this fitness trainer, but he still had basic trust in the promises made between people. He added, "There's a simple fitness room here. You can watch TV while you work out or play games in the entertainment room."

"I'll give you lessons, free of charge," Chen Hong offered.

Zhang Yuwen laughed. "Let's talk about it again after you move in."

Chen Hong's phone chimed again. "I have to go," he said quickly. "There's a members' salon this afternoon. Wanna come along?"

"No thanks."

"Come on. I'll introduce you to some friends."

Zhang Yuwen did his best to fend Chen Hong off from grabbing his wrist, tactfully refusing this overzealous fitness trainer. "I'll send you the contract now," he said as he saw him out the door.

"It's fine!" Chen Hong called for a ride at the entrance. "I'll move in as soon as I can. Let's work out together tomorrow?"

Zhang Yuwen didn't dare answer. Four minutes later, the car arrived, and Chen Hong waved at him and got in, on the phone all the while. Zhang Yuwen decided to go back and highlight the breach-of-contract terms for emphasis. Any ideas Chen Hong might have about entertaining members at No. 7 Riverbay Road needed to be nipped in the bud.

While Zhang Yuwen revised the contract at the café, the fourth tenant arrived as scheduled. He felt like an HR rep, interviewing two tenants on the same day.

The fourth tenant carried a camera bag. About six foot one, he was stylishly dressed and had meticulously coiffed hair. Of the four tenants, he was the most handsome, with a high nose bridge, fair skin, thick brows, and large eyes.

"Hi, my name is Chang Jinxing," the young man said.

Zhang Yuwen shook his hand. Despite Chang Jinxing's outstanding looks, he seemed weary, and his lips were so dry they were peeling. He also kept yawning, as if he'd just woken up. He sat down across from Zhang Yuwen, snapped his fingers for the waiter, ordered himself a sandwich, and dug in.

"Where's the house you're renting out?" Chang Jinxing asked. "Can I go for a viewing later?"

"It's right next door," Zhang Yuwen replied. "Are you a photographer?"

"Yeah, I graduated from Jiangliu University's Department of Photography and I have my own photography studio. Sometimes I help film crews with promotional stills."

"Oh—?" Zhang Yuwen was surprised. "How old are you again?"

"Twenty-seven," Chang Jinxing replied. "You?"

Zhang Yuwen gave him a puzzled look. Realizing that Chang Jinxing was looking at him, he quickly explained, "I'm the same age as you."

The Department of Photography had been right next to Zhang Yuwen's department, the Department of Drama Studies. In his second year of university, students in his program had to take several classes with the Department of Photography for courses like storyboarding and set design, so he knew a lot of students from the Department of Photography. He was sure he'd never seen this guy before.

"What did you study?" Chang Jinxing asked.

"I went to school in the countryside," Zhang Yuwen said, "and now I'm working as a proofreader for a publisher."

Chang Jinxing nodded, cracked his knuckles, yawned, and stood up, having already finished his sandwich. Zhang Yuwen went to foot the bill, but Chang Jinxing stopped him. "Let me. It's our first meeting. I can't let you pay for me. I still haven't decided if I'm going to rent the place."

"It's fine," Zhang Yuwen said breezily. "Consider us friends."

Chang Jinxing hesitated, but the words "consider us friends" won him over in no time. He smiled, dispelling the hint of gloom lingering around him from all those late nights.

This photographer had such great looks that Zhang Yuwen was sure he would have been the department hottie even at the film academy. There was no way he could have been a senior—Zhang Yuwen would have at least heard of him.

"Wow!" Entering No. 7 Riverbay Road, Chang Jinxing couldn't resist taking out his camera, placing his fair, slender finger on the shutter. "Can I take a couple shots?"

"For the common areas, yes."

"Such a great house going for such low rent?" Everyone had the same question. Zhang Yuwen explained it again, and Chang Jinxing grinned. "I see. So does that mean you won't bring anyone home either?"

"Of course."

"Wouldn't your partner want to come over?"

"I'm single," said Zhang Yuwen. "I don't have a boyfriend. And even if I did, I wouldn't bring him back to stay for the night."

"You? Single? How's that possible for someone of your caliber? You a top?"

Zhang Yuwen didn't know which question to answer first, so he simply said, "Yeah."

"Oh." Chang Jinxing smiled and took a photo of the garden, then turned back. With a serious air, he looked Zhang Yuwen in the eye. "Actually, I'm bisexual. That bother you?"

Zhang Yuwen felt a rare twinge of nervousness at his gaze. *It's not like I'm dating you,* he thought, *I'm just renting you a room.* "Of course not."

But now Zhang Yuwen had new material.

With another smile, Chang Jinxing sat on the bed in the empty room upstairs and basked in the autumn sunlight. After a while, he lay down.

"Is it liberating, being bisexual?" Zhang Yuwen asked out of curiosity. "After all, you have a lot of options."

"Yeah." Still smiling, Chang Jinxing closed his eyes. "But I prefer dating guys."

This guy was most likely a player, a thought that excited Zhang Yuwen. Photographer, handsome, and bisexual—Chang Jinxing hit all three fuckboy checkboxes.

"Let me show you." Chang Jinxing turned on his camera and motioned for Zhang Yuwen to sit on the bed too. "This is someone I dated, but we've already split up."

The photo was of a pretty girl. Zhang Yuwen hummed in appreciation, and Chang Jinxing continued, "She dated another guy after we broke up, but her boyfriend liked me. I didn't reciprocate, though."

What kind of plot twist...? Zhang Yuwen thought. *Truly an eye-opener.*

Chang Jinxing then showed Zhang Yuwen his male lover. There were only two photos of him, a vibrant guy standing with Chang Jinxing. It was hard to tell who topped and who bottomed.

"Handsome guys always date handsome guys," Zhang Yuwen remarked, tossing Chang Jinxing a compliment.

Chang Jinxing looked at Zhang Yuwen and laughed. "You're handsome yourself."

"So have you decided if you want to rent the room?" Zhang Yuwen asked.

"Sure. I can stay here for a while."

He said it as if Zhang Yuwen was the one who invited him to move in. Zhang Yuwen didn't mind, though; this would make for excellent material. As a reminder, he added, "You can't take private photos here."

"What kind of person do you think I am? Why would I take private photos?" Chang Jinxing laughed and reached out to pinch Zhang Yuwen's ear, but Zhang Yuwen had seen plenty of players in the film industry; he was already on guard against this kind of casual touch. Thus, the player's first move against the director missed its mark.

Zhang Yuwen raised a finger at him in a gesture that said, *Behave yourself.*

"I can cook. How about I make dinner for you tonight?" said Chang Jinxing. "Where's the nearest supermarket? I'll go grocery shopping later."

Zhang Yuwen smiled. "Let's talk about it again after you've moved in. Need any help?" Chang Jinxing waved his hand, declining the offer, and Zhang Yuwen got up to leave the room. "I'll send you the lease contract," he said on his way out.

"Sure thing."

Zhang Yuwen went downstairs, revised the contract, and sent it to Chang Jinxing.

It was dangerous for a guy to be single for too long, especially when he encountered this sort of flirt who swung both ways. While

Zhang Yuwen liked his men handsome, he had no intention of dating his tenant. Besides, Chang Jinxing was obviously a top, and Zhang Yuwen wasn't quite prepared to bottom.

But unbeknownst to Zhang Yuwen, all was not as he thought.

Chang Jinxing lay on his side on the bed, facing the sunlight as he took photos of the view beyond the balcony. What he hadn't told Zhang Yuwen was that, while he was bisexual, he wasn't like most bisexuals.

The majority of bisexuals were like those dual plugs that fit both European and American sockets and could be switched freely between the different types of outlets. But Chang Jinxing was both a plug and a socket: He was equally compatible with other sockets and other plugs.

The cultivation of this talent could be traced back to his short-lived first love at university. A fujoshi poisoned by BL novels, she tirelessly experimented with her boyfriend's body and mind with electric and battery-powered toys. Chang Jinxing, unable to turn her down and fueled by his curiosity for new, thrilling experiences, found it both shameful and pleasurable—so much so that he sometimes even looked forward to it. Eventually, he reached the point of no return, and a whole new world opened up to him.

A pity Chang Jinxing's first love broke up with him after "training" him for less than a month. Those thirty days and nights left Chang Jinxing with many short but mind-boggling *What My First Love Taught Me* stories with which to regale others. Years later, he became accustomed to switching between roles, whether as a top or bottom, or even with women. But when he slept with men, he could last twice as long and get double the pleasure from the relationship.

Chang Jinxing had been single for a while now, but he suddenly felt something indescribable toward Zhang Yuwen, his sub-landlord. Perhaps it was because Zhang Yuwen treated him to lunch at their first meeting; although it was only a thirty-five-yuan sandwich, Chang Jinxing felt a little touched by the gesture.

He had lied to Zhang Yuwen about his education and work. He wasn't a Jiangliu University graduate or the owner of a photography studio. His father was a chef in a small city, an alcoholic who had, in Chang Jinxing's childhood, abused him and his mother. Unable to put up with it, his mother left home. Chang Jinxing's grades were far from stellar, and after he graduated from high school, he took his camera with him to the big city to make a living.

His father had been a womanizer, so Chang Jinxing followed in his father's footsteps and became one too.

The culinary skills that he picked up from home won him the hearts and affection of gentle girls. Even as Chang Jinxing relied on his handsome looks to live off these women, he did his best to maintain his persona as a talented photographer. His ex-girlfriends and ex-boyfriends occasionally gave him pocket money to try to preserve whatever bit of self-esteem he had. Chang Jinxing knew very well what they wanted: They were infatuated with his looks and body, and in return, he asked them to cover his living expenses.

Fair enough. Everyone had their own needs.

After a breakup this year, Chang Jinxing decided to live on his own for a spell instead of depending on other people. He tried taking on some photography jobs. Although he struggled to make ends meet, he no longer needed to provide emotional value to others or subject himself to their whims and fancies. He was poor, but a lot freer. He still had something to look forward to in life.

Now that he'd found this new place to live, he could start fresh. He wanted to find a partner, someone he was in genuine, mutual love with, who he could fuck and get fucked by. They would depend on one another and earn money to support the household together. This was almost his entire life goal.

It was hard for a leopard to change its spots, though, and he couldn't resist flirting a little with the sub-landlord. Fortunately, Zhang Yuwen was experienced enough to nip it in the bud.

So it was that Zhang Yuwen gathered four observational subjects, each with their own stories, from whom he could gather material.

Just the thought of it was fascinating.

NOW THAT HE thought about it, though, Chen Hong, the fitness trainer, had yet to make much of an impression. Zhang Yuwen contemplated going back on the decision to rent to him and finding another tenant instead, lest the guy drag him into signing up for a gym membership.

He hadn't received the rent yet, anyway. In fact, he hadn't seen money from any of the four rooms he was renting out. Everyone was slow to pay him, but that was normal in today's society; when it came to payments, it was common practice for people to drag their feet. It would actually be weirder if they paid on time.

Looking intently at his computer screen, which displayed a new potential tenant, Zhang Yuwen made a call to Chen Hong. "When are you moving in?" After all, Chen Hong hadn't signed the contract or paid the rent. Zhang Yuwen suspected he hadn't even looked at the contract.

"Oh!" Chen Hong exclaimed. "Oh! I'll be there today. The contract is already signed. I'll bring it with me."

"All right." Zhang Yuwen had no choice but to send the backup candidate an instant message: *All rooms have been rented out.* There was nothing to be done about it. A man had to keep his word.

Over at the fitness studio, Chen Hong was packing his personal belongings. He hung up the phone, searched through his email for the lease, and located it among a bunch of spam. He quickly printed it out, grabbed a pen, and then, using a flyer as a makeshift writing surface, skimmed the contract and signed and dated it.

Chen Hong was standing on the precipice of the big 3-0, waiting for time to tick down and punt him mercilessly into the life of an unaccomplished thirty-year-old. Contract signed, he looked around at the almost-empty fitness studio, suddenly feeling a bit sad. The studio's lease was up this month, and its future was uncertain. He still owed his partners tens of thousands, and in a few days, he would have to bite the bullet and call them up to tell them the hard truth: The studio was in the red. They had to declare bankruptcy and file for liquidation.

But he refused to throw in the towel. He thought it was a test from heaven. He'd always been tenacious, a rare and commendable quality. Some people saw it as perseverance, while others saw stubbornness.

When he'd come into this life, he allocated all the skill points the system gave him into physical strength. Born in a remote county, he weighed an astonishing 9.9 pounds at birth. He was sturdier than most of the other infants, and had a louder wail. This strong physique stayed with him through infancy, childhood, and adolescence, giving him an edge in most sports that didn't require brainpower. His one tiny regret was that his nutrition hadn't been up to scratch during his adolescence; as a result, his height was barely passable, a mere 5 feet and 10 inches. Among East Asians, however, it was perfectly adequate.

At the sports-focused college, he learned quickly that the talent gap between athletes often dwarfed the species difference between humans and earthworms. The bona fide prodigies eclipsed the athletic prowess that he was so proud of, and when it came to competitive sports, his barely passable stature made him look like a clumsy hobbit on the college's basketball court. In short, he realized early on that he couldn't make a living from sports.

He preferred to live a healthy life than to retire with a body plagued by injuries, so having lost all faith that he could make it as a sportsman, he turned instead to rehabilitation and training. Eventually, he wound up at the regular haunt of most jocks: the gym.

While he was in school, he worked at the gym distributing flyers and occasionally filling in as a part-time coach, giving pointers here and there and selling protein powder on the side. Figuring he'd mastered the ins and outs of the trade, he came up with the idea of launching his own lucrative fitness studio after graduation. But new gyms were all over the place these days, putting the trainers in fierce competition, and the influx of new entrants eroded the industry's ethical standards, giving fitness trainers a bad name. These newcomers behaved either like popular streamers, relying on flirtation and innuendo to sell training sessions, or like financial advisors who earnestly went door-to-door seeking business. Chen Hong, it seemed, fell into neither category.

His only advantage was the physique that he'd trained so hard for. Working as an escort could, in theory, net him a pretty penny. Male clients paid better than female ones; he could potentially rake in an astounding daily income of ¥4,000, and if he were to bottom—a far more lucrative role—he could also have received additional allowances. But Chen Hong never considered moving in that direction. He couldn't bring himself to take off his pants, nor could he swallow his pride.

His first gym was in business for less than half a year before it closed its doors. During his subsequent unemployment, he worked as a fitness trainer again and finally caught the eye of a trust fund baby who developed real feelings for him and dedicated himself wholeheartedly to pursuing Chen Hong.

Chen Hong's sexual orientation wasn't set in stone at first. After all, he came into contact with men's bodies every day, and a lot of his studies revolved around the aesthetics of male muscles and physique. But while he saw himself as a straight guy, he thought he wouldn't mind giving same-sex relationships a try, like an amphibious creature who could live on land or in water. It was just dating, no big deal. Try everything once, right? Besides, this young man was both rich and attractive, showering Chen Hong with gifts and taking him to see the world. Burdened with mixed feelings, but nonetheless moved by these gestures, Chen Hong reluctantly yielded to him.

During their honeymoon phase, they enjoyed the most extravagant candlelight dinners and stayed at the most luxurious hotels. In this opulent, romantic atmosphere, Chen Hong ran the gamut from resistance to reluctant acceptance to acclimation to addiction in only twenty-eight days.

In this one month, they made love in a variety of ways every day, so Chen Hong also became something of an expert in that regard. But never in his wildest dreams did he anticipate that while the rich guy's feelings were genuine, so was his tendency to be fickle in love.

Some people were like that. They fell head over heels into every relationship, only to lose interest a couple weeks later and turn back into a stranger. With the turn of a calendar page, everything abruptly ended.

Chen Hong felt like he'd been in a dream when he got the news that it was over. He'd had no idea that the other guy was only using him for a change of scenery. He didn't know that he was like a gacha card in a romance game, liable to be cast aside to await his fate—getting dismantled into crystals—once the novelty wore off. Perhaps he was just one of many from the rich guy's "bedding men from all professions" collection or "dating men from every zodiac sign" challenge... Whatever it was, he had met a specific criterion and happened to be decent-looking, and that was why he was "blessed" with this fleeting, heaven-sent romance.

He took a month to bounce back and move on. His healing period took two days longer than the romance itself, which was uncommon. Of course, he didn't cause a scene, even if he could have gotten compensation by doing so; he still had his pride as a top.

His rich ex-boyfriend knew the current market well. He didn't gift Chen Hong a house or a car, but instead discreetly assigned a daily usage price to Chen Hong's body, arbitrarily giving himself a discount like he'd subscribed to a monthly package. In the end, the value of the gifts he gave Chen Hong totaled exactly four thousand yuan a day.

Chen Hong kept some gifts as mementos and sold the others for a small sum to start a new business. At twenty-eight, he was a different man. His experiences with so-called high society, courtesy of his ex-boyfriend, had changed his mind about changing the world. No longer limited to philanthropic ideas about helping other people get healthy, he set his sights on a fitness salon.

He planned to start a private fitness studio and take on high-end clients and government employees as members, acting as a facilitator, middleman, and errand-runner for them, like a mama-san at a nightclub. The difference was that, on top of selling fitness services, he'd also organize social events for his members.

High-end! That was the key. That was the only way he'd be able to survive and rise above the fierce competition. But no matter how Chen Hong tried to hypnotize himself, reality insisted on following its own rules. Chanting "high-end" over and over didn't magically make his business high-end; his fitness studio had very few members, most of whom were ordinary folks struggling to make a living. He turned to his ex-boyfriend for help, and the guy introduced him to a few people, but then, fearing that Chen Hong would embarrass him in his social circles by boasting about their relationship to his clients, he cut off all contact between them.

Chen Hong was forced to take matters into his own hands. He found a job as a fitness trainer teaching group classes for a government department. It didn't pay well, but it gave him access to "high-end individuals," which was a good start. He hired two employees to take care of the gym while he went around networking, occasionally offering personal training sessions to a few rich members.

In that period, he adjusted the membership renewal price a few times, causing the already fragile relationship between supply and demand to collapse. Almost all of his members left, and also during this period, one of his trainers hooked up with a regular gym-goer, a wealthy woman, and left with her. Chen Hong accepted his resignation with mixed feelings and turned his sights on the remaining wealthy members.

Strangely, girls didn't show much interest in him, perhaps because he was no longer fresh young meat. Or maybe it was that he was too prim and proper around women and never flirted or joked with them. The gays at the gym, meanwhile, seemed to be obsessed with him. It was possible that he gave off different energy after the unique experience of that one-month fling with his ex-boyfriend. Out of habit, he still wore the same clothes and hairstyle as he had during that ill-fated relationship, which might well have been catnip for gay men.

He didn't want to date men anymore, though; he had to return to the world of heterosexuality, lest he disappoint his parents. On his twenty-ninth birthday, he started dating an online girlfriend, pouring out his woes to her every day. In their relationship, he found diversion in times of loneliness and understanding in times of hardship. Suddenly, life seemed bright. His business was running at a loss, but Chen Hong was willing to do whatever it took to give his girlfriend a good life. He agreed with what people said about settling down, and started to think there might be something to starting a family first before establishing his career.

Optimistic that this new romance might change his luck, he arranged to meet the girl he so deeply loved...only to find out that "she" was a boy who habitually wore a wig, applied lipstick and makeup, and used a voice-changer to deceive straight men online. This boy was surprisingly generous and open-minded, inviting Chen Hong to sleep with him and record a video as a keepsake. After Chen Hong turned him down, he threatened Chen Hong with the private photos and videos that Chen Hong had previously sent "her" at "her" request.

Chen Hong was shocked to realize that this person was a repeat offender who used cybersex to get the other party to masturbate on camera, then sold the video recordings to adult websites for extra cash. So Chen Hong beat him up, threatened to call the police, and demanded that he delete the videos completely. His "lover" panicked and pleaded for mercy. Thinking about the many nights "she" had comforted him and kept him company, Chen Hong couldn't bring himself to follow through on his threats, and in the end, he let him go.

In this way, the twenty-ninth year of Chen Hong's life swooshed past like the waters of the Liujin River. Chen Hong knew very well that time was continuous and linear, and his circumstances wouldn't change at the stroke of midnight on his birthday. But seeing the mess he was in as he approached his thirtieth, with his career at a dead end, his studio on the precipice of filing for bankruptcy and liquidation, and his assets sold off to repay his debts...

He couldn't help but panic.

CHAPTER

6

LET US REVIEW:

The first person to move into No. 7 Riverbay Road was Zheng Weize. He brought his many belongings with him and made quite a racket as he squeezed them into his room. The next day, he crammed the washer and dryer in the garden so full of his eccentric clothes that the machines gave up the ghost.

It was the first time the laundry had tripped the circuit breaker. Being familiar with the house, Zhang Yuwen rolled up his sleeves, got behind the washer, opened the cover, and fixed the problem in no time.

"Sorry," Zheng Weize said.

Zhang Yuwen wiped his sweat. "It's fine. When the load is too heavy, the water can't drain properly, and if it splashes onto the socket, it'll cause a short circuit. I've already fixed it."

Zheng Weize looked at him gratefully, thinking that men who could repair household appliances exuded powerful pheromones. His fondness for Zhang Yuwen clicked up several notches.

Chang Jinxing, the photographer, moved in the same day. His luggage comprised only a backpack and a suitcase. He bounced over to greet them, finding Zhang Yuwen on one knee before the washing machine and Zheng Weize nearby. His looks knocked Zheng Weize on his ass, but Zheng Weize was realistic: An Adonis of this caliber would never be interested in him.

"Hi." Chang Jinxing held out his hand with those long, fair, slender fingers and shook hands with Zheng Weize.

"Done." Zhang Yuwen turned on the circuit breaker and glanced to the side, but Zheng Weize's attention was no longer on him; he was transfixed by Chang Jinxing, staring up at him with blatant yearning. "Ahem."

This little hint from Zhang Yuwen snapped Zheng Weize back into reality.

Chang Jinxing, long accustomed to such gazes, was unfazed. He flashed them both a smile alluring enough to make a person fall in love with him on the spot. "Have the others moved in?" he asked Zhang Yuwen.

"Let me think... Another guy will be moving in later this afternoon, so there's one left after him, I guess."

Chang Jinxing nodded. "Why don't we hang out together on the weekend, once everyone has moved in?"

Zheng Weize seconded this idea. "Sure. Where should we go?"

"Up to you guys." Chang Jinxing grinned. "I'm good with escape rooms, murder mysteries, fishing, or board games."

Chang Jinxing was a gregarious person. Zhang Yuwen hadn't even known him for two days and they were already well on the way to becoming close buddies. As the landlord, he was curious about the other two tenants, so he readily agreed. "Let's wait for Yan Jun to come, then I'll ask."

"Is he the homeowner?" Zheng Weize whispered to Zhang Yuwen.

"No, no," said Zhang Yuwen, snapping back out of his thoughts. "He's a tenant, just like you."

"Oh."

At first glance, Zheng Weize found Chang Jinxing tall, handsome, and vibrant. Sure, he wore overalls and a jacket, but carrying a camera, he looked like he was born with a silver spoon in his mouth. Only rich people could afford a hobby like photography. *The quality of the guys in this place is so high,* Zheng Weize thought, wondering what the other two tenants were like.

Having fixed the washing machine, Zhang Yuwen returned to his desk and worked on his manuscript until Liu Jingfang brought him his lunch. Zhang Yuwen ate simply every day: a small plate of vegetables, a portion of meat, sometimes steamed fish, and a bowl of soup from the same pot that was used to prepare both dinner and lunch. He had inherited these eating habits and brought them with him from his grandparents' house. Liu Jingfang and the other housekeeper arrived every morning at ten and left at seven in the evening, taking care of all aspects of Zhang Yuwen's daily living: from shopping to picking up deliveries, from cleaning to doing the laundry.

As Zhang Yuwen ate, Chen Hong moved in too, bringing with him bags of odds and ends and exercise equipment from his defunct gym. He greeted Zhang Yuwen.

While Chen Hong passed by the dining room, Zhang Yuwen extended an insincere invitation. "Have you had lunch? Join me?"

Chen Hong declined the offer, also insincerely. "No thanks. I've already eaten." In truth, Chen Hong hadn't eaten, and his stomach was growling in protest. "I'm trying to burn fat at the moment, so I can't eat too much. What are you having? Let's see... Refined carbs? Nope, glycemic index is too high. Don't eat too much of that."

Zhang Yuwen nodded. "Makes you feel sleepy after lunch." He eyed Chen Hong's belongings, hoping the guy wasn't about to start recruiting members at home.

In fact, Chen Hong had been living in his gym all this time, and now that he couldn't afford its rent, he had to find another alternative. He had lots of belongings that he planned to bring over and take his time sorting through.

"The washing machine is in the garden," Zhang Yuwen said. "Weize will teach you how to use it."

"Who's Weize, the housekeeper?" Chen Hong asked, carrying the dumbbells into his room.

"Huh?" Zheng Weize's voice rang from the garden. "Did someone call me?"

Chen Hong went over to greet him. By the time Zhang Yuwen finished his small plate of steamed fish, he could hear them laughing heartily from the garden; they must have gotten acquainted. And when he began drinking his soup, they were playing with water, so presumably they were now good friends.

After lunch, Zhang Yuwen took his laptop with him and left for the publishing house to receive another round of admonitions. He had a car parked in the underground garage, though he rarely drove. He wasn't a skilled driver and was afraid of scratching the car, and there were always traffic jams in Jiangnan. Driving just wasn't as convenient and fast as taking the subway, where Zhang Yuwen could put on his headphones and think about plotlines.

It was a fine, sunny day, and Zhang Yuwen was sitting across from the deputy editor at the publishing house.

"How should I put it... Your novel is very..."

"Contrived?" Zhang Yuwen asked the deputy editor sincerely. The bespectacled deputy editor looked to be no more than thirty and had the air of a sadistic, ascetic elitist. He was also blunt with his words.

"Very...arrogant." The deputy editor found the right word. "Right. Arrogant and haughty. Your writing is uncomfortable to read. It's like you're up on a pedestal, looking down at a bunch of animals."

Zhang Yuwen humbly accepted the critique. He'd learned his lesson this time and sent a preview to the publishing house instead of a completed work, just in case his effort was wasted again, but the beginning of the novel still received harsh criticism.

"It's a kind of unsympathetic, mocking attitude," the deputy editor continued. "Reading through this opening, it feels like you're making fun of people with disabilities, using the hardships of your characters to flaunt your supposed wit. Have you been reading Maugham recently?"

Startled, Zhang Yuwen quickly distanced himself from Maugham. "Nope, not a fan. I don't read Qian Zhongshu either," he added.

The deputy editor flipped through the printed copy of the first 30,000 words again and sighed. "Compassion and empathy are essential if you want to write a good book."

"I understand. I'll reflect on it when I get back."

The deputy editor pushed up his glasses, which glinted deviously. "You're going to keep submitting manuscripts?"

"Of course. I want to be a writer."

"Then start by understanding the hardships of others. It sounds simple, but it's easier said than done."

Zhang Yuwen thanked him and left the publishing house. Camus won the Nobel Prize in Literature at forty-four, and Kafka published *Metamorphosis* at thirty-two. He still had plenty of time.

He also had dinner plans today with his childhood friend, another unapologetic fuckboy. This childhood friend, Liang Zheng, had known Zhang Yuwen for over twenty years and was his desk mate from elementary to high school. He now worked in the government sector.

Some guys didn't stand out in looks or height but still possessed a strange aura that seemed to project: *I'm looking for a partner.*

Potential mates threw themselves at guys like this in droves. Liang Zheng was one such guy. In the player circle, his overall score was only about 80 out of 100, and when they were in school, he ranked at "second-tier handsome guy"—the kind that wasn't considered especially physically attractive but still held a certain appeal.

Liang Zheng was a habitual womanizer and had been since primary school. Fortunately, fate intervened when a girl dragged him by the ear down the aisle. Now, while he might've still had the inclination, he no longer possessed the guts to go around terrorizing respectable ladies.

He was as straight as they came, and Zhang Yuwen had never harbored any intention of changing that. They were too close for him to be interested in trying, and the types of moves Liang Zheng made on girls didn't work on him.

Liang Zheng was dumbfounded when he heard Zhang Yuwen's latest plan. His sunglasses slid down. "Are you serious?"

"The tenants have already moved in."

"Are you out of your mind?"

Ignoring Liang Zheng's incredulity, Zhang Yuwen went on, "If the tenants start getting suspicious, I'll need you to make a guest appearance as the homeowner. Just say you occasionally return from abroad to stay at home for a day or two."

Liang Zheng erupted into laughter. "Ha ha ha ha ha!"

Zhang Yuwen looked at him expressionlessly. "Be serious. This plan is key to my transition."

"What?" Liang Zheng didn't catch it the first time. "Transition? Transition to what?"

"I want to be a writer."

Liang Zheng had heard something even funnier now. "Ha ha ha ha ha!"

Zhang Yuwen remained silent, not knowing quite what to say to that.

Liang Zheng laughed so hard his stomach hurt. Trailing Zhang Yuwen out of the restaurant, he apologized.

"Can I meet your tenants?" Liang Zheng asked.

"No!" Zhang Yuwen blurted. "At least not now. I've already gotten a scolding. The publisher said I lack empathy, so I need to reevaluate my views of other people."

Liang Zheng, who had wanted for nothing since childhood, possessed a modicum of empathy, but not much. He opened the car door. "You're already doing them a huge favor renting the place to them at such a low price. What more do you want?"

"To respect them from the heart, I guess," Zhang Yuwen said. "Honestly, the deputy editor is right. I'm too arrogant, and that's not a good thing."

"You're overthinking it. Other people don't necessarily respect you, either."

"Well, they're not trying to become writers..."

Liang Zheng got into the driver's seat and drove Zhang Yuwen home.

Over at No. 7 Riverbay Road, Zheng Weize, Chen Hong, and Chang Jinxing introduced themselves to each other and became friends. Chang Jinxing made coffee by hand and shared it with the other two, and Chen Hong offered a few serious comments. Zheng Weize was interested in Chang Jinxing, but determined not to make it too obvious.

"Where's Yuwen?" Chang Jinxing called out, topping up his fourth mug of coffee.

Housekeeper Liu, having already changed into casual clothes, replied, "He went out for a meal with friends. I'm getting off work now too."

"Bye, Auntie."

"See you tomorrow."

The three guys bade her farewell. Everyone was very polite.

Zheng Weize was the first to share his opinion. "The landlord's so rich. What does he do?"

He looked at Chang Jinxing expectantly, assuming, from Chang Jinxing repeatedly calling him Yuwen, that they were close with each other.

Chang Jinxing dodged the question. "You'll have to ask him yourself."

"He's the sub-landlord," Chen Hong put in. "The house isn't his. He's just looking after it for someone else. The original homeowner is the one who hired the two housekeepers, too."

"Oh." Zhang Yuwen's charm as a rich young master dropped several notches in Zheng Weize's eyes. "Doesn't he need to work, then?"

"He said his primary job is proofreading for a publisher," said Chen Hong. "He just has to correct typos and grammatical errors in manuscripts when he gets them."

"I saw him go out earlier with some manuscripts. He must have gone to the publishing house," Chang Jinxing said as he made more coffee. "The other tenant hasn't moved in yet. How about we go out to celebrate and have fun together once he's settled in?"

"Sounds good!" Zheng Weize said, even as he tried to work out how much money he had left. Guys like him would have their fun even if they had to skip meals. At worst, he'd just have to survive on instant noodles the rest of the month.

"Sure," Chen Hong said. "What about hiking? I know a few scenic trails."

"My friend runs an airsoft arena in the suburbs, like real-life *Counter-Strike*," said Chang Jinxing. "It's pretty affordable, and there are a bunch of us, so we can have a match."

"Okay, let's go with that. We'll play airsoft first," Chen Hong said. "Is the landlord coming?"

"He's—" Just then, Chang Jinxing heard a noise outside. "Oh, is he back?"

Because Riverbay Road was a quiet place with few vehicles passing by, the sound of anyone talking was audible. Liang Zheng dropped Zhang Yuwen off at the intersection. Zhang Yuwen declined his request to see the gay tenants and refused to let Liang Zheng walk him to the door; if his roommates saw Liang Zheng, it'd be harder to pass him off as the homeowner later.

Zhang Yuwen got out of the car at the intersection. He spotted a figure carrying a packaged piece of furniture and walking toward the end of the road, where Zhang Yuwen's house was.

The figure in question was Yan Jun, who by now was feeling pretty nervous. He had come by in the past few days to observe on the sly, which was how he learned that Zhang Yuwen was more active during the day and retired to his room early at night. Usually, he did not appear again in the living room after dinnertime. The photographer typically returned after 10 p.m., and the other one, who seemed to be a live streamer, holed himself up in his room from seven to ten. He hadn't figured out the fitness trainer's routine yet, but he couldn't wait until the middle of the night to move because he needed to pick Xiao-Qi up later. He had to take a chance.

Then someone tapped him on the back, startling him. "Hi!"

Yan Jun realized with mixed feelings that it was Zhang Yuwen. "Hi." He forced a smile in the darkness.

"Need help?"

"Nah, it's fine." Then, on second thought, Yan Jun said, "Actually, you can help me with the suitcase."

"Are you moving in today?"

"Just moving some stuff over first. What about the others?"

"They've all moved in. What's that?" Zhang Yuwen asked in passing, referring to the object Yan Jun was carrying on his shoulder. It looked like a bookshelf.

Yan Jun thought about it and decided to tell the truth. "It's a simple baby crib."

Zhang Yuwen was taken aback at first, but then it dawned on him. "Oh yeah, for your niece."

Yan Jun nodded. His plan had been to move in secretly while no one was around. He couldn't let anyone see this crib. But just as he feared, he ran into Zhang Yuwen on arrival. At times like this, Yan Jun knew he had to be honest—sure enough, Zhang Yuwen readily accepted it.

"I still have to go to my brother and sister-in-law's place later," Yan Jun told Zhang Yuwen. "I'll move in a few days after."

"Are you staying at their place?" Zhang Yuwen asked.

"Yeah. They're in Jiangnan..."

Zhang Yuwen scanned his fingerprint to open the door and was greeted by three people sitting on the sofa and drinking coffee.

"Hello!" Chang Jinxing, Chen Hong, and Zheng Weize chorused in unison, catching Yan Jun off guard. Once again, his crib was exposed under the bright lights of the living room.

"Whoa, what's that?" Chang Jinxing asked.

Everyone hurried over to help Yan Jun unload. Abandoning himself to despair, Yan Jun was forced to let them scrutinize him and the socially humiliating crib.

"Are you having a baby?" Zheng Weize asked, sounding curious.

"Ahem!" Zhang Yuwen tried to hint to him not to dig deeper, but Zheng Weize, who had low emotional awareness and zero social experience, didn't get it. He shot Zhang Yuwen a confused look.

Yan Jun shook hands with them and realized he hadn't introduced himself. "I'm Yan Jun. Nice to meet everyone."

"What were you guys chatting about?" Zhang Yuwen asked, changing the subject.

"Hanging out," Chang Jinxing said. "It's Thursday today. How about we play real-life *CS* this Saturday? Yan Jun, are you free?"

The question mystified Yan Jun. He'd never met anyone so convivial. Instinctively, he threw Zhang Yuwen a glance: *Did you guys plan this beforehand?*

Zhang Yuwen's first impulse was to agree to Chang Jinxing's proposal. After all, it would be a great opportunity to observe his subjects and gather material for his novel. But then he wondered if he needed to maintain his own façade. "How much per person?"

This question reminded everyone: *You haven't paid your rent yet.*

Chang Jinxing automatically bypassed the subtext about the rent. "One hundred, and that includes dinner."

Yan Jun, who had by then retreated to his room with his belongings, listened to the discussion outside. Since the crib had already been discovered, he figured there was no point in continuing to be secretive, so he set about assembling it.

So cheap? Zhang Yuwen thought, but he couldn't make his reaction obvious, so he nodded. "I see." Turning to Yan Jun, who was doing his own thing and not taking part in the conversation, he asked, "Yan Jun, are you going?"

"Are you?" Yan Jun returned through his partially opened door. "I'll go if you are."

Eh? Everyone looked at Zhang Yuwen. *What kind of maneuver is this?* Zhang Yuwen thought.

"All right," Zhang Yuwen said, "then let's go together?"

So it was that the group came to a consensus. Come Saturday afternoon, they would play airsoft and have dinner together after.

Chen Hong put down his coffee mug and went over to help Yan Jun assemble the crib. "Let me help you!" Yan Jun didn't have any tools, not even a screwdriver or a wrench, so Chen Hong retrieved some from the odds and ends he'd brought over from his bankrupt gym. Everyone pitched in with suggestions, and finally, Xiao-Qi's crib was set up.

"I have to babysit my niece sometimes, just for the time being," Yan Jun explained to Chen Hong, "but I won't bring my brother and sister-in-law here." Chen Hong nodded in understanding.

Yan Jun thanked everyone and left without telling anyone where he was going. He didn't return the entire night.

Zhang Yuwen found it intriguing. Why would Yan Jun say, "I'll go if you are?" He sensed a barely perceptible undercurrent. Was it because Zhang Yuwen was the only one in this house Yan Jun was willing to trust? Or was Yan Jun just giving him face?

This was a subtle emotion that Zhang Yuwen had rarely touched on in his writing.

Riverbay Road

MEN'S DORMITORY

YAN JUN HADN'T GIVEN HIMSELF a day off in a long time. He worked six days a week and spent the remaining day doing chores and keeping Xiao-Qi company in the morning, then taking her to the park to sit and gaze at the scenery in the afternoon. Not only did he have to find ways to earn money, but he also had to take care of a baby. Living this way, he was teetering on the verge of losing himself.

He requested a shift change this week and swapped with a colleague. Then he dropped Xiao-Qi off at the childcare center. With a promise to pick her up at nine that night, he bade her farewell and left for his appointment.

Meanwhile, Zheng Weize carefully applied his makeup. He'd been looking forward to this since the previous night, hoping chemistry would spark between him and Chang Jinxing. After all, he was the one who invited everyone. And no, Zheng Weize was no longer as interested in Zhang Yuwen. The reveal that Zhang Yuwen was only the sub-landlord had automatically downgraded Zhang Yuwen's rich young man appeal to an ordinary proofreader at a publishing house. He wouldn't consider Zhang Yuwen even if he was interested in him. After all, there were no benefits to being with him, beyond maybe saving on rent.

By contrast, Chang Jinxing appeared to be well-off, especially with that DSLR camera he carried around every day. He might as well have worn a T-shirt that said *I'M RICH*. Moreover, he was handsome and warmhearted, and he had a smile in his eyes whenever he looked at Zheng Weize. Zheng Weize thought he was a great catch.

What Zheng Weize didn't know was that the camera was a gift from one of Chang Jinxing's ex-boyfriends, and this warmhearted, handsome guy had only ¥120.30 left in his savings. His next month's rent was still up in the air.

Chang Jinxing had to make money, fast. Maybe he could take on a part-time job as a wedding photographer, or perhaps do cosplay shoots for a few rich ladies. Just a few days ago, it occurred to him to set his sights on Zhang Yuwen, thinking he could woo him to save on rent—but Zhang Yuwen didn't seem to be interested in him. That only spurred his competitive nature. The more Zhang Yuwen refused to take the bait, the more he piqued Chang Jinxing's interest.

It was true that his friend ran a *CS* outdoor arena and that the prices were low. The business owner, with whom Chang Jinxing was acquainted, was struggling with poor business, and since the place would be empty anyway, the owner agreed to waive his fee and throw in a low-cost meal if Chang Jinxing could refer players. It was a way to make some chump change.

He decided to use the opportunity to hit on the sub-landlord.

Chen Hong, on the other hand, was bored and idle. He still had some savings left, so he was in much better financial shape than the other three. After all, when he declared bankruptcy and liquidation, all that lost money belonged to the investors. But he'd been overwhelmed with stress lately, and he needed to relax a little—and hopefully this would be an opportunity to get to know his roommates. Who knows, maybe he could net himself some new clients through them?

He also had a personal motive. He had suspicions that one of his clients was gay, and based on his observations, this client was a somewhat wealthy small business owner. A single man who led a disciplined lifestyle, he had spent tens of thousands on memberships at Chen Hong's fitness studio.

Chen Hong wanted to introduce this client to a handsome guy. If they hit it off and became a couple, he might earn himself a red packet for playing matchmaker. His initial candidate of choice at first was Chang Jinxing. In fact, he thought Chang Jinxing might even offer himself up as tribute. But now, having known him for a day, he suspected Chang Jinxing was rich and promiscuous. Chen Hong's plan would backfire if Chang Jinxing were to cheat on his client, so instead, he temporarily shifted his sights to Zhang Yuwen.

It had been a long time since Zhang Yuwen took part in this kind of group activity. He used to occasionally shoot films in remote areas, but he'd never played airsoft in the suburbs, and the anticipation of fun overtook all thoughts of observation and material-gathering for his novel.

And so, everyone set off with their own agendas. They waited outside the subway station for Yan Jun, who arrived in a hurry and blended into the group once he'd greeted them. Aside from Zheng Weize, who wore casual clothes, everyone was in sportswear for ease of movement.

Sportswear suited this group of tall, handsome guys, who resembled a boy band strolling down the street. They were young, too, and each had his own distinctive presence and demeanor. Chang Jinxing was the most eye-catching of all of them.

"Don't we look like a group of guys from a dorm going out together?" Zhang Yuwen smiled; fate really did work in mysterious ways. He never imagined he might befriend a group of strangers this way.

"More like a bunch of bodyguards taking their young master out to experience life," Chen Hong teased.

Chang Jinxing grinned. "Who's the young master?"

Everyone looked at Zheng Weize, the only one in casual wear. "Oh, you guys—!" Zheng Weize quickly adopted a shy expression to conceal his inner delight.

They boarded the subway car. Yan Jun kept quiet, leaning against the door and observing his roommates, while the other three traded banter. Zheng Weize, speaking to Chang Jinxing, was the most animated, while Chen Hong stood in the middle like an EOD container.

The topic of conversation turned to the best part of the countryside to live in. "Where's your hometown?" Chang Jinxing asked Yan Jun.

"Guangze County."

"Oh," Zhang Yuwen chimed in, "the place where they grow sunflowers. It faces the sea and it's backed by mountains. There are lots of indigenous people there too."

"Yup," said Yan Jun. "There are a lot of sunflowers planted behind my family's house."

"Guangze is a surfing paradise," Chen Hong said. "Can you surf?"

"A little," Yan Jun replied. He used to be a sports enthusiast, and enjoyed almost all outdoor activities from basketball to badminton to surfing.

"What about Yuwen?" asked Chen Hong.

The subway pulled into a station, and the guys turned sideways to make way for the people entering and exiting. "I'm a local from Jiangdong," Zhang Yuwen replied.

"Then you should be familiar with the place," said Chang Jinxing.

"I went to university out of town, though," Zhang Yuwen explained.

None of them except Zhang Yuwen were local. They all came to Jiangdong City to work and make a living.

"Which university did you go to?" Zheng Weize asked Chang Jinxing.

"Jiangliu University, Department of Photography."

"Ohhh." Everyone nodded. In truth, Chang Jinxing had never even set foot on the campus.

With a smile, Zhang Yuwen shifted his gaze away and happened to meet Yan Jun's eyes. Thinking Zhang Yuwen was smiling at him, Yan Jun raised his eyebrow in an inquiring expression.

"How about you?" Chang Jinxing asked Zheng Weize.

"Chonghan University of Finance and Economics. Major in International Economics and Trade." In fact, Zheng Weize had never attended university either. He'd run away from home at eighteen after a fight with his family.

Everyone nodded, and Chen Hong volunteered his own answer. "I did my postgraduate at Changling. Changling Sports University." He had actually only completed a vocational college education.

"I envy you guys," Yan Jun said. "I didn't go to university."

His words left his boastful friends at a momentary loss for words. Fortunately, Zhang Yuwen came to the rescue. "You can consider a vocational degree."

"Too busy to study," Yan Jun said. "Once I entered the workforce, I realized that educational qualifications are indeed important."

"Sometimes, but sometimes not so much," Zhang Yuwen said, hoping to comfort him. "Still, it's never a bad thing to find time to upgrade your credentials."

"You're right."

"We're here," Chang Jinxing announced. "Let's get off at this station."

They swarmed off the subway car and exited the station under the gaze of everyone around them, then transferred to a bus to the suburbs. While they were waiting for the bus, Chen Hong noticed that Zheng Weize had latched onto Chang Jinxing. They were both so engrossed in their conversation he couldn't get a word in. Yan Jun and Zhang Yuwen seemed more approachable, so he turned to them.

Chang Jinxing picked up the camera hanging around his neck and started taking photos of his roommates. As one, Zhang Yuwen, Yan Jun, and Chen Hong looked at him and burst into laughter.

"What are you laughing at?" Chang Jinxing asked, a little shy.

Zhang Yuwen pointed behind him. "Someone's secretly taking photos of you."

It wasn't the first time that the photographer found himself being photographed on the sly. Chang Jinxing looked back to see a few high school girls waiting for the bus and taking stealthy snapshots of them with their phones. A pack of handsome guys together was indeed a pleasing sight.

They showed no embarrassment at being discovered. Instead, they approached Chang Jinxing to shoot their shot. "Can I have your phone number, handsome?" Chang Jinxing just smiled and waved them off, and one of the girls turned to Zhang Yuwen. "How 'bout you? Our bestie wants to ask if you'd be friends with her."

"I'm gay," Zhang Yuwen said candidly.

"Whoa!"

At their astonished and disappointed voices, Zhang Yuwen quickly added, "But they aren't. How about asking this guy?" He pointed at Chen Hong, who promptly gave Zhang Yuwen a light smack and told him not to talk nonsense.

The bus came, and the five of them got on. Chang Jinxing generously paid the ten-yuan fare. The bus wasn't too full, and there were four empty seats. Everyone traded looks, and they were about to offer each other the seats when Zhang Yuwen sat down and patted his thighs. "Whoever wants to can sit on my lap."

Chen Hong got Zhang Yuwen to move over and gestured for Zheng Weize to sit on his lap instead. Rather enjoying this, Zheng Weize took him up on his offer with a smile, feeling like a bottom going out with four doting tops.

Meanwhile, Chang Jinxing and Yan Jun sat in the back row, away from the other three. In a rare moment of initiative, Yan Jun asked Chang Jinxing, "You get asked for your phone number a lot, don't you?"

"Not that often," Chang Jinxing said, smiling.

"You seem used to it."

Chang Jinxing nudged Yan Jun with his elbow and gestured for him to look ahead. "That girl's pretty."

Yan Jun glanced over and nodded. "Yeah," he said, looking back at Chang Jinxing.

"I suspect you're straight."

"I'm not, but in certain situations, you can treat me like I am."

Chang Jinxing laughed and picked up his camera to take a close-up shot of Yan Jun. Yan Jun reached out to block the lens with his broad palm, but Chang Jinxing pulled it away. Inexplicably, Yan Jun felt his heart rate pick up a little when their fingers touched. It had been a long time since he last held hands with a guy.

He was trying hard to be himself today, to put aside his role as a father and forget about his job and responsibilities. He wanted to recapture those feelings from the good old days of his youth.

"We're here," Chang Jinxing announced. He led everyone off the bus.

The fresh, invigorating countryside air and the lush sight of nature, away from the city, pushed their worries—like empty wallets and never-ending rent obligations—to the backs of their minds.

"Wow." Zheng Weize stretched. "It's so nice out here."

Chang Jinxing called the owner over, and everyone willingly made the payment with their phones.

"Shall we begin?" asked the owner. "Are there any first-timers who need an explanation? Come, sit here. I'll keep your phones so they don't get dropped or lost while you're playing, and I'll take photos for you during the match."

Everyone turned off their phones and handed them over. Zheng Weize spotted a mahjong table nearby. "We can play mahjong too?"

"Yup," said the owner. "Once the match is over, you can come back here and play mahjong." He spread out a map. "Look at the map and remember as much as you can."

The owner explained the rules: They would split up into a red team and a blue team, then walk to the two bases and advance toward the central hill. Everyone would have a virtual infrared gun, which they could aim at the opposing team. Each successful hit netted them points. If you were hit, your gun would become unusable for fifteen to thirty seconds, so you'd need to find a place to hide during this period. This was like a respawn cooldown.

There were three treasure caches hidden on the middle hill. If they found one and used their gun muzzle to press the button with the corresponding color, they could capture a flag for their team.

However, a flag captured during the respawn cooldown was considered invalid and wouldn't score the team any points even if they pressed the button.

Victory was determined by the team's total respawns and captured flags, and the winner would receive a mysterious grand prize.

"This place is too big," Zhang Yuwen said. "It's hard to remember the routes."

"Don't worry, there are markers along the way," said Chang Jinxing.

"How should we split the teams?"

The owner held out a box to them. "Come over here and draw lots."

"But there are five of us," Zheng Weize protested. "How are we going to make even teams?"

"No worries!" said the owner. "I'll get someone from my end to join you. Just draw the lots!"

Everyone took turns picking a ping-pong ball from the box. Zhang Yuwen and Chang Jinxing got blue, and Yan Jun, Zheng Weize, and Chen Hong got red. Zheng Weize regretted that he wouldn't be in the same group as Chang Jinxing, but having sat on Chen Hong's lap on the bus, he was starting to feel like muscular guys had their own special charm. You could feel secure with a big, strong guy, too. It'd be a pleasant change of pace.

The owner called over a man with a fair complexion who wore a sports jacket, a pair of cargo pants, and a fisherman's hat. He put away his fishing rod and walked over.

The man, who the owner called A-Chen, nodded. "Sure, I'll join."

Chen Hong looked surprised to see A-Chen. "Eh?"

A-Chen greeted him and came over. They shook hands and patted each other on the shoulder.

"You know each other?" Zhang Yuwen asked.

"We're friends." Chen Hong smiled and exchanged glances with A-Chen. Everyone said hello to him, wondering if he might be some experienced player.

"It's my first time playing this," A-Chen said.

He took off his fisherman's hat. His hair was slightly messy, but overall, he was quite handsome. He looked a little younger without the hat, perhaps in his late twenties. He received his firearm and sensor vest and joined Zhang Yuwen and Chang Jinxing's team.

"I'm Sichen," he said by way of introduction. "Huo Sichen."

Zhang Yuwen and Chang Jinxing briefly introduced themselves. Then they put on their off-road jackets and took their submachine guns, which made them look even cooler.

"Take the two of them over!" the owner said to Huo Sichen. "I'll take the other three!"

"Okay."

Huo Sichen drove Zhang Yuwen and Chang Jinxing along a winding path to the blue team base. Smiling, Chang Jinxing asked, "Do you come here often?"

"I come here occasionally to fish," said Huo Sichen. "You're acquainted with Lao-You?"

Mr. You was the owner of the arena. "I helped him take some photos for a promotional brochure once," Chang Jinxing explained.

Huo Sichen and Chang Jinxing chatted for a bit, and Zhang Yuwen tactfully declined to butt into their conversation. This new guy wasn't exceptionally handsome, and his fashion sense wasn't all that great either, but despite his casual dress, he was clean and carried himself well. He had the air of a knowledgeable, mature, and sedate person.

Even his name, Sichen, sounded pleasant. Perhaps the person who named him was educated and well-read. Add the surname Huo, and it sounded just like it had been transliterated from another language—very exotic. Zhang Yuwen took note, planning to steal this name (with a change of surname) for a character in his novel.

"Are you guys from the university dorm?" Huo Sichen asked Zhang Yuwen as he drove.

"Hm?" Chang Jinxing glanced at Zhang Yuwen, ready to spout nonsense out of habit, but Zhang Yuwen laughed and cut him off.

"No, but we're roommates."

"I see." Huo Sichen nodded. "No wonder you didn't invite any girls."

"If we had, we wouldn't come out here to the open country," said Zhang Yuwen. "It'd be pretty tactless to bring a date somewhere so remote."

Finding this idea amusing, Huo Sichen nodded again. He stopped as they arrived at the woods. "We're here," he announced. "We'll go up from here on foot."

The camp was just slightly over a mile away, but the moment they stepped into the woods the place transformed into a deserted wilderness, so silent it was unsettling. The late autumn mountain wind howled through the forest, chilly enough to make them shiver.

"Just follow the markers on the trees," Huo Sichen said, "and don't pin your hopes on me. I can't remember the map either."

"You've played this before, right?" Zhang Yuwen asked Chang Jinxing. "So lead the way."

"Just once, and I was on the red team. Why is this route so difficult? We have to climb rocks and everything?"

"The red team's route is usually more challenging," Huo Sichen explained. "Most of the time, they assign people who've played before to the blue team. Also, heads up: You can't go beyond the areas blocked off by barbed wire."

Chang Jinxing was starting to worry. He was the one who'd recommended this place, but it was cold and desolate, and so far, it seemed boring. If the others found it dull, then even if they didn't say anything to Chang Jinxing, they might silently grouse about wasting money.

There was almost no walkable path on the northern side of the hill, but Zhang Yuwen could handle it; he used to traverse terrain like this when he went to look at filming locations with the crew or inspected sites with the director.

They came to a slightly steep slope with no way forward. Suddenly, the three of them were startled when Zheng Weize's shout rang out in the distance.

Zhang Yuwen laughed. "So the teams are pretty close."

"I'll go up and take a look," Huo Sichen said. He attempted to climb the rock.

Zhang Yuwen was adjusting the electronic submachine gun in his hands when a playful impulse overtook him. He fired a shot at Huo Sichen's back, triggering a *beep beep beep* that indicated he'd been hit.

"Hey!" Huo Sichen thought he was being ambushed, but he looked back to see Zhang Yuwen aiming at Chang Jinxing. Chang Jinxing exaggerated a yell and made to retaliate, and Zhang Yuwen darted behind a tree.

"Stop fooling around and get up here," said Huo Sichen.

Zhang Yuwen leapt and clambered up the rocks, with Chang Jinxing in hot pursuit and looking for revenge. Huo Sichen aimed his gun at Chang Jinxing, who froze, but Huo Sichen was just joking. The two guys pulled him up.

"Watch out for snakes," Chang Jinxing cautioned.

Zhang Yuwen, scouting ahead, responded offhandedly. "Aren't they all hibernating this time of year?" From time to time, he pressed the reload button on his gun, making noises that sent nearby birds scattering.

Following Huo Sichen, Chang Jinxing asked, "You work in Jiangdong?"

"Yeah," Huo Sichen replied. "I work at a foreign trade company. What about you?"

"I do photography." Chang Jinxing mimicked pressing a shutter, all the while keeping an eye on Zhang Yuwen, who was attempting to navigate a large thicket. Ahead, an open area was visible through the sparse trees.

"Mind your clothes," said Huo Sichen.

Zhang Yuwen almost got stuck in the middle of the thicket, but he managed to make his way over. Suddenly, he stopped pressing the button.

"I see them!" Chen Hong called out. "Quick, fire!"

All three of them dashed for cover. It turned out the open area had been set up as the battlefront for the red and blue teams. There were plenty of makeshift shelters made up of tires and wooden crates. Zhang Yuwen quickly ducked behind one and provided cover fire for his team-mates. Huo Sichen raced over, keeping his head down, and from the other side, they heard Zheng Weize yelling. Chen Hong opened fire as he dragged Zheng Weize toward one of the makeshift forts.

"Don't bother with Weize!" Zhang Yuwen said. "His aim is off! Watch out for the sniper, Yan Jun!"

With his gun mounted on a crate, Yan Jun took aim at Chang Jinxing as he darted out of the thicket. He fired, hitting him right on target. Chang Jinxing let out another exaggerated shout and scrambled for cover.

"**L**EAVE CHEN HONG TO ME!" Chang Jinxing yelled. "You handle Yan Jun!"

"I don't know their names," said Huo Sichen.

Zhang Yuwen made two standard hand signals used by the special forces: *crouch down* and *gather here*. Huo Sichen understood and ducked over from another cover, while Zhang Yuwen popped his head up and traded gunfire with Yan Jun. Neither hit the other, but it bought Huo Sichen time.

"Were you in the military?" Huo Sichen asked in disbelief.

"Nope." Zhang Yuwen laughed. "I learned it from TV. You handle those two over there, I'll keep watch over the sniper. Jinxing, circle over there and scare them!"

"I've been hit!" Chang Jinxing yelled.

"You'll respawn by the time you run over!"

"Why is there another player?" Chang Jinxing cried. "Lao-You, this isn't fair!"

The owner's laughter rang out from the woods. "Your team's battle prowess was unbalanced to begin with!"

The fight got a lot harder with the owner joining in, but Zhang Yuwen stayed calm. He popped up, intending to shoot Yan Jun, who opened fire and ducked behind his shelter—but the ball was now in Zhang Yuwen's court. He mounted his gun.

"It's useless to aim for the head," Huo Sichen reminded him as he reloaded from behind his cover. "You can only hit the body."

"Got it. Where's Jinxing?" Zhang Yuwen asked. "Get ready to flank them."

Huo Sichen made an OK gesture and dashed over with his head down to support Chang Jinxing.

Now that they'd encountered their opponents, everyone quickly got into the game, fighting with such gusto that they forgot ever thinking that it was boring. Zhang Yuwen remained locked in combat with Yan Jun the entire time, neutralizing the other team's strongest player and even trading shots with the owner a few times. Meanwhile, Huo Sichen and Chang Jinxing worked together to ambush Chen Hong and Zheng Weize, successfully putting them into a cooldown period of thirty seconds.

"Argh! I've been shot!" Zheng Weize seized his chance to fall into Chang Jinxing's arms.

"Get up!" Yan Jun shouted. "He's the enemy!"

Amused, Chang Jinxing turned Zheng Weize around and held him with one arm while pointing the gun at him with his other hand, effectively holding him hostage. Zheng Weize even played along. Yan Jun had no choice but to leave Zhang Yuwen and go over to assist.

"Where's Huo Sichen?!" Zhang Yuwen looked around. Huo Sichen whistled at him from behind a tree. "I'm going to take Yan Jun down. Keep an eye on the bodies."

"Who's Yan Jun?" Huo Sichen asked.

"The tall one!" Zhang Yuwen darted out to charge him from behind. Yan Jun, who had been on guard against Zhang Yuwen all this time, whipped around at once. They opened fire, hitting each other. Their vests started flashing, and they ducked for cover. Yan Jun even somersaulted, his movements elegant and beautiful.

On the other side, Huo Sichen caught up with Yan Jun. Despite valiant attempts, he was unable to dodge and found himself hit again after he respawned. As Huo Sichen chased him, Yan Jun shouted, "Backup! Requesting backup!"

The owner came to his aid, only to be ambushed and gunned down by Zhang Yuwen.

Chang Jinxing, still holding Zheng Weize hostage, was engaged in a fierce battle with Chen Hong.

"Stop being so cooperative!" This was driving Chen Hong crazy.

"But I've been shot!" Zheng Weize said.

Chen Hong was speechless. But Zheng Weize was just stalling for time—Chang Jinxing was so engrossed in his fight with Chen Hong that he forgot to reload. Zheng Weize ambushed him, and Chang Jinxing was hit. Yelling, Chen Hong unleashed a barrage of shots and then charged over and rescued Zheng Weize.

The red team was nearly wiped out, and the blue team successfully drove them off. Yan Jun led the remaining people up the hill.

Chen Hong's voice drifted over from a short distance away. "We need to change our tactics..."

Zhang Yuwen, Huo Sichen, and Chang Jinxing all gathered, and Zhang Yuwen laughed, shouting, "Say that louder!" Both sides cracked up, and the blue team quickened their pace and advanced toward the hilltop. At the top sat a deserted slide, a carousel, and bumper cars, resembling an abandoned amusement park.

The owner withdrew, making it three-on-three again. Another intense gunfight broke out. Zhang Yuwen thought the flags would be well-concealed, but to his surprise, they were placed in several conspicuous spots. Unprecedented chaos broke out as they fought to snatch the flags. Everyone was running around the amusement park, flipping over fences and hiding behind the rides, firing wildly.

Zhang Yuwen knew there was trouble afoot when he realized he couldn't see Zheng Weize. "Watch out for Weize!"

Yan Jun appeared from nowhere behind Zhang Yuwen and pressed his gun into his back. "You've lost. Bang!"

Zhang Yuwen whipped his head around to see Yan Jun smile. He smiled too, and they both swiftly retreated. He knew Yan Jun had made a point of coming over to pay him back for the earlier ambush.

Huo Sichen dropped everything to save Zhang Yuwen, but it was too late. The sound of a flag being seized rang out from a corner of the amusement park.

Unexpectedly, the music that came with the first flag capture was "Happy Birthday." Zhang Yuwen was too busy trying to find the second flag to roast this bizarre choice, but it was pandemonium, and he had to hide under the slide with Huo Sichen. The other three kept advancing; if Zhang Yuwen and Huo Sichen so much as poked their heads out, they would get shot.

Amidst the chaos, Chang Jinxing managed to snag the second flag. The teams scattered again, trying their best to claim the third flag. In the end, Chen Hong was the one who seized it.

"Yay!" Zheng Weize, Yan Jun, and Chen Hong showed themselves. The final score was 2–1 in favor of the red team.

Zhang Yuwen and the others put down their guns. The game was over.

Everyone was sweaty. Chang Jinxing, who often stayed up late, had almost dropped dead several times during the match. This kind of competitive game was just too intense.

Huo Sichen high-fived Zhang Yuwen and Chang Jinxing.

"You guys are amazing!" Zhang Yuwen told them.

Zheng Weize laughed. Yan Jun even pointed a finger gun at Zhang Yuwen and winked.

The owner and Huo Sichen drove the starving guys down the hill. Back at the camp, everyone collapsed onto the sofa, physically worn out but still in high spirits. They chattered among themselves, occasionally cracking jokes and then erupting into laughter. The intense match, by transforming them into comrades in arms and adversaries, had drawn them all closer together. From a professional player's standpoint, the match was a mess—like kindergarten kids fighting over fruit—but the two teams were still able to appreciate each other.

Mr. You handed out the prize, a coupon for a free game on their next visit. The players grumbled about pyramid schemes, but they eventually accepted it. The owner knew they would take the coupon. He'd seen this happen many times—yes, business was poor, but those groups that did come to play were always bubbling over with enthusiasm and cheer after the game was done, their relationships all the stronger for having played.

The joy was contagious, and bringing people happiness was his business's raison d'être.

Zhang Yuwen noticed that one of his comrades in arms was missing. "Where's Huo Sichen?"

"He was still outside last time I saw him," the owner said.

But before Zhang Yuwen could go talk to Huo Sichen, he returned to say his goodbyes, wearing his fisherman's hat and carrying his fishing rod in a bag.

"I have to go back," he said. "I still have something on tonight."

"Aren't you staying for the food?" Chang Jinxing asked. They all agreed: It was a pity he was leaving.

"Can we exchange contacts?" Huo Sichen asked.

Everyone agreed readily. "Of course." Although the red team hadn't interacted much with him, they were happy to make a new friend. Huo Sichen added all the contact details, then bade them farewell. A moment later, they heard his car engine starting, and he was gone.

"Mahjong?" Chang Jinxing asked.

"Sure," said Zhang Yuwen. "The food isn't ready yet, anyway."

"It's been a while since I last played," said Chen Hong. "Come on, guys, let's win back our rent."

Everyone laughed. There were four seats at the mahjong table. Yan Jun initially said, "Count me out," but in the end he couldn't refuse them and was bullied into sitting down.

Zheng Weize sat behind Chang Jinxing, helping him with his tiles. Chang Jinxing was confident in his own skills. He had indeed thought he might offset the household expenses, but after Chen Hong joked about it, he found it harder to go ahead with the plan.

Zhang Yuwen was a bad player, mostly just going along with the others. He didn't mind; he'd be happy to toss out a bet of fifty or a hundred thousand yuan for fun, never mind five or ten.

But Chen Hong was different. He was addicted and played for an hour, despite his poor skills. Everyone felt awkward about winning money from the sub-landlord—winning from him when they hadn't even paid the rent yet, what kind of monster would do that?—so they set Chen Hong up as the fall guy instead. He became the whole table's target and suffered the greatest losses in the end, with a few hundred going to Chang Jinxing. Far from moping, though, Chen Hong was happy to lose and displayed extraordinary sportsmanship. He remained jovial throughout.

Meanwhile, Zhang Yuwen managed to maintain his dignity as the sub-landlord because Yan Jun kept giving him tiles. He only lost a bit of money to Chang Jinxing. Yan Jun, for his part, lost a little to Zhang Yuwen; debts reassigned, he paid Chang Jinxing instead.

Crediting Zheng Weize for his win, Chang Jinxing handed the winnings over to him for safekeeping and tasked him with buying groceries. That way, Chang Jinxing could cook for everyone when Yan Jun officially moved in the next week.

When dinner was ready, the dishes served were unexpectedly sumptuous, featuring ginger duck, poached chicken, braised pork, and a huge fish that Huo Sichen had caught that afternoon. The owner's wife was a great cook, and she prepared the fish three ways: braised fish belly, steamed fish head, and fried fish bones.

Even Chang Jinxing was shocked. "Why weren't there this many dishes the last time I was here?" he asked.

The owner laughed. "We have an extra fish today. A-Chen usually doesn't take home what he catches. He left it for everyone to enjoy. That's why it looks like so much."

The dinner was a perfect end to a joyful day. Chang Jinxing took lots of photos of their shared memories, and in the bus on the way back, Zheng Weize fell asleep against his shoulder. Aside from the small snag when they were assigned to different teams, Zheng Weize had fulfilled his wish: He spent all of his time with Chang Jinxing.

Chen Hong stood with Yan Jun and Zhang Yuwen, chatting with them off and on. Zhang Yuwen had one hand on Chen Hong's shoulder while he sent messages on his phone with his other hand. The light from the phone illuminated his face.

"Are you chatting with Huo Sichen?" Chen Hong asked.

"I was thanking him for the fish. How long have you known each other?"

"Not long. He's a member of my gym," Chen Hong lied. "Have you told him about our group's relationship?"

The question was a little odd, but Zhang Yuwen knew Chen Hong was referring to the roommates' sexual orientations. Maybe

Huo Sichen had picked up on it? "I didn't say anything. I don't know whether or not he could tell."

"I think he could," Yan Jun chimed in. "He was observing each of us pretty closely. I could just be overthinking it, though."

"What if he's gay? Don't we still have a room? Maybe we can ask him if he wants to stay there," Chen Hong joked.

"That's the landlord's room," said Zhang Yuwen. "It's not for rent."

In No. 7 Riverbay Road, there was one bedroom that was always locked. It had been his deceased grandparents' bedroom when they were alive, and their photographs were still inside. Zhang Yuwen always kept the room intact. Whenever he felt sad or happy, he would spend a little time alone in it.

"I don't think he's gay." Zhang Yuwen followed the information on the messaging app and found Huo Sichen's Facebook, which contained some landscape photos. "These scenery photos have no filters, and his selfies aren't retouched either. It's clearly a straight guy's work."

"I guess he's either a boss or a senior employee," Chen Hong said.

Zhang Yuwen didn't comment, just scrolled through the app a bit longer and then closed it. The bus arrived at the station. Chang Jinxing and Zheng Weize were sound asleep, but after the other guys woke them up, they groggily disembarked to transfer to the subway.

"I'm getting off here," Yan Jun said suddenly as they pulled into Jiangnan's Jinqiao Station. "I had a great time today, thank you."

Everyone said, "How polite," and burst into laughter again. Without saying another word or looking back, Yan Jun turned and got off the subway car. His goodbyes were always so abrupt.

Yan Jun got off one stop before Riverbay Road and had to walk some distance to pick up Xiao-Qi. He was late by an hour, which pricked at his conscience. He'd been having so much fun outside that he hadn't even thought about lonely Xiao-Qi waiting in the childcare center all afternoon.

The others rode one more stop to Riverbay Road. As soon as they set foot inside, Chang Jinxing and Zheng Weize perked up, each making a loud fuss as they went to take their respective showers. Chang Jinxing wanted to invite them to the bar, but Zhang Yuwen, utterly exhausted, vetoed the motion mercilessly.

Outside, it began to drizzle. Winter was just around the corner. The lights of Jiangnan District blazed as shops on the bar street opened for business. Saturday night was just beginning.

AFTER A FEW BOUTS OF RAIN, winter entered the game. Golden ginkgo leaves, damp from the rain, paved the asphalt road. When a resident of Riverbay Road woke in the morning and opened their floor-to-ceiling windows, the breath they expelled turned into white mist. Jiangdong always saw an unbroken spell of wet weather when the season changed, with only a few rare sunny days brightening the month. The Liujin River's water level gradually dropped as it entered the dry season, when the dried-up riverbed became prime real estate for idle schoolchildren to poke and dig around.

Yan Jun's lease expired in a week, and he had moved his stuff out, more or less. He decided to take Xiao-Qi to No. 7 Riverbay Road.

Recently, he'd been coming to the new house every day after work to observe the others' living habits. Zhang Yuwen retired to his room daily at eight in the evening like a grandpa. Zheng Weize often ate instant noodles in his room, and he, too, rarely went to the living room after eight. Yan Jun hadn't seen Chang Jinxing yet; allegedly, he never returned before two in the morning. Chen Hong was the only one who was sometimes at home all day, but other times he was nowhere to be found.

Yan Jun wasn't sure if he could avoid his roommates. He'd thought the coast was clear when he moved in the crib and accidentally made a grand entrance instead. *Forget it, just move in,* he told himself. The new house had a great vibe and Zhang Yuwen's attitude was reassuring, so Yan Jun opted to set off on Tuesday, carrying a backpack with the last of the diapers, bottles, medicines, and milk powder. With Xiao-Qi in a carrier on his chest, he made his way to No. 7 Riverbay Road.

"Today Papa is taking you to our new house," Yan Jun said to Xiao-Qi in hushed tones. She smiled, facing out at the house in front of them. "We'll be living here from now on, so be good."

He took a deep breath, unlocked the door with his fingerprint, and entered. Seeming to understand the gravity of the situation, Xiao-Qi behaved herself, simply casting curious looks around.

Yan Jun breathed a sigh of relief. There was no one in the living room, and the housekeepers had already left for the day. Xiao-Qi reached out to grab the decoration on the shoe cabinet, but Yan Jun stopped her and took her into his room.

"Pa-pa!" Xiao-Qi called out.

The room had already been cleaned. Yan Jun set her on the floor and smiled as he went to boil water to prepare formula for her. He'd gotten a kettle and all the baby supplies ready in the room so that he wouldn't need to keep going in and out.

He would get up at half past seven every morning and take Xiao-Qi to the childcare center, then bring her back after seven in the evening. That way, he wouldn't disturb his roommates.

Yan Jun carried Xiao-Qi back. "It's too cold outside, we can't go out!"

This room was much bigger than the other rented rooms, and he could use the remaining space to roll out a play mat, put out some toys, and set up a spot for reading picture books. He was pleased with the place.

So it was that Yan Jun moved in quietly. On the first day, no one noticed Xiao-Qi. The second day was the same. On the third day, however, when he was bringing her home, he ran into Zhang Yuwen, who was repairing the printer with ink-covered hands.

Anxiety gripped Yan Jun as their eyes met. Zhang Yuwen looked baffled when he spotted Xiao-Qi, but then he broke into a smile.

"Hi!" He hurried away to wash his hands. Upon his return, he asked Xiao-Qi, "What's your name?"

Xiao-Qi said, "Pa-pa!" Zhang Yuwen burst out laughing.

"Her name is Yan Yuqi," Yan Jun explained. "She calls every man she sees Papa."

"Papa!" Xiao-Qi looked up at Yan Jun again from her spot on his chest.

Zhang Yuwen helped Yan Jun take off his backpack. "Have you been sleeping here lately?"

"Mm," said Yan Jun. His fears, it seemed, were unfounded, and he was beginning to realize that Zhang Yuwen had a magical ability to instantly relax everyone who interacted with him.

He seized this chance to sound Zhang Yuwen out on his daily routine. "You haven't gone to bed yet? I thought you'd be asleep by now."

"Not quite this early," Zhang Yuwen said, "but soon. I grew up with my grandparents, and my grandfather was a doctor, so I inherited the habit of sleeping and waking up early. Aren't you going to put her down?"

Yan Jun unstrapped the carrier and put Xiao-Qi down at the side of the sofa. Zhang Yuwen clapped his hands at her and asked, "Want a hug?"

Xiao-Qi came over to let him hug her, but less than twenty seconds later she spread her arms out at Yan Jun and called, "Pa-pa!"

Zhang Yuwen handed her back. Surprised, Yan Jun said, "She never lets anyone other than me and the nanny hug her."

"Whoa!" Zhang Yuwen didn't catch the plot hole in his words, merely taking it as a polite remark. "Maybe she really likes me."

"Wow!" Zheng Weize exclaimed in surprise. He'd heard the conversation and come out of his room to investigate. "So cute! Oh my god!"

Zheng Weize came over for a hug, but Xiao-Qi started crying and tried to dodge him. Yan Jun quickly patted her to pacify her. "She's a little shy around strangers at this age," he explained.

Zhang Yuwen realized Yan Jun was telling the truth when he said she never let strangers hug her. "But I managed to hug her," he boasted to Zheng Weize.

Zheng Weize felt like crying. His self-esteem would never recover if she didn't let him hug her today. Eventually, a tearful Xiao-Qi permitted a half hug, and Zheng Weize took his chance to lean against Yan Jun. But Chen Hong returned not long thereafter, triggering another round of cajoling and another bout of crying.

It wasn't until Xiao-Qi wet herself that Yan Jun brought her to their room. He poked his head back out to ask Zhang Yuwen, "Will we disturb you?"

"Of course not!" Zhang Yuwen said quickly. He was drinking milk and chatting with Chen Hong at the dining table. "This house has great soundproofing. Even if she bawls, it won't disturb us."

Yan Jun had already tested the room's soundproofing, and it was indeed great.

"Is your niece spending the night here?" Chen Hong asked.

"I'll send her home later," Yan Jun said. "Her parents are very busy; they work overtime a lot."

"Man, that's tough." Chen Hong understood it all too well, though it was hard to say whether his comment was about Yan Jun or his brother and sister-in-law.

"Just call for us if you need help," Zhang Yuwen said. "We don't go to bed that early."

Relief washed over Yan Jun when he saw his roommates' enthusiasm. "I'm used to it."

He closed the door and filled the basin with water to bathe Xiao-Qi. Then he dressed her, placed her in her crib, and turned the TV on for her before he took his own turn in the shower.

The new house was a comfortable environment. No noisy neighbors, plenty of hot water, and no cold drafts in the bathroom. Zhang Yuwen had already turned on underfloor heating for the whole house, so he didn't have to worry about Xiao-Qi catching a cold. In fact, the house was even warmer than the childcare center. The room was clean, and the air was fresh and free of dust from the road outside.

Yan Jun was grateful to Zhang Yuwen from the bottom of his heart. Zhang Yuwen had saved him.

That night, he observed again, but the others soon went back to their own rooms, and he no longer needed to put up an act. With Xiao-Qi, he went to bed with peace of mind and slept through the night.

As usual, he didn't run into anyone when he woke up the next day.

The weekend rolled around, and Chang Jinxing kept his promise. He went to the supermarket with Zheng Weize and bought a lot of groceries so he could whip up a feast to celebrate everyone moving in and getting to know each other.

Yan Jun felt a little put on the spot. "I might have to take care of my niece today."

"Let's eat together!" Chang Jinxing still had yet to meet Xiao-Qi. "I can make her some baby food?"

"You can even make baby food?" Yan Jun was amazed.

"It's just mashed carrots and potatoes. Easy-peasy."

The kitchen was fully equipped with a variety of cooking utensils. As Chang Jinxing cooked, Chen Hong assisted him, commenting from time to time that his methods were unhealthy. Together, they made quite a mess of the kitchen. Zhang Yuwen didn't mind, though, and anyway, the housekeepers would be there the next day to put everything back to usual.

Overall, Zhang Yuwen was satisfied with his observational subjects. He was never bothered by any of them, though he didn't know if they bothered each other. Gradually, he was coming to see them as friends and not model dummies—and even beginning to like them a bit.

"You have the day off, right?" Zhang Yuwen asked Yan Jun. "Let Xiao-Qi sit here and eat with us. I'll go and borrow a baby chair from the café next door."

"I'll go," Yan Jun said hurriedly. "And in that case, I'll pick Xiao-Qi up later."

"Bye-bye," Zhang Yuwen said.

It was still raining outside. Yan Jun was wearing a black, knee-length trench coat and carrying a black umbrella. He was in a good mood. It had been a long time since he'd experienced such a heart-warming atmosphere. His roommates even felt a little like family...

He forced himself not to harbor any wishful thoughts. After all, the world was full of liars, and people often gave the illusion of warmth and tender affection before their disguises were ripped away. But even if it was just for one day, Yan Jun couldn't help but daydream. What if he was successful in his career? What if the house was his? What if he had a lover like Zhang Yuwen? And what if that lover was willing to raise Xiao-Qi with him...?

It was no easy task to start a new phase in life with so many what-ifs.

He abandoned his what-ifs. It was clear that Zhang Yuwen had no interest in him beyond friendship, and his observation told him that Zhang Yuwen's friendliness extended to everyone he met. Yan Jun was no different from the rest.

Winter had come, and a flu was set loose upon the city. Many people wore masks, coughing incessantly. Yan Jun worried about infection in the childcare center; many parents had already come to take their children home. He considered keeping Xiao-Qi home for a day. He could take another day off tomorrow, but how was he going to explain it?

The heating in the childcare center was turned up, and Xiao-Qi's face was flushed red. After he picked her up, Yan Jun shielded her from the drizzle with an umbrella as they walked back, trying his best to protect her from the chilly wind. They arrived home to chaos in the kitchen.

"You're back!" Zhang Yuwen was wiping up some borscht that had spilled on the floor. Earlier, Chen Hong accidentally scalded himself while bringing out the soup, adding to the mayhem. Yan Jun was struck dumb by the sight.

"Oh wow! Xiao-Qi! You're here!" Zheng Weize made a beeline for her. He adored the baby, though his fondness came partially from the heart and partially from thinking it was the right way to act when there was a baby around. "Still remember me?"

"Still remember Uncle Weize?" Yan Jun asked.

"I'm too young to be an uncle," Zheng Weize protested.

"I'll wipe it up," Yan Jun said to Zhang Yuwen as he set Xiao-Qi down to help with the housework. Zheng Weize brought out a stuffed toy from his room to play with her. She loved it, babbling happily and toddling around, holding onto the sofa with one hand for support and the toy with the other.

"Xiao-Qi's mom is working the night shift tonight. Can she sleep here for a night?" Yan Jun asked.

"Of course." Zhang Yuwen was fond of the little baby. "Can you manage?"

"It's no problem for me. I'm just worried we'll disturb you."

Yan Jun didn't meet Zhang Yuwen's eyes as he went to change the rags. The aroma wafting from the kitchen made him feel even more homesick.

"Chef." Yan Jun patted Chang Jinxing's arm as Chang Jinxing tasted the soup. He smiled at Zhang Yuwen when he came out of the kitchen again.

"What?" Zhang Yuwen asked, puzzled.

"We're friends," Yan Jun said.

"Yeah, we are. What about it?"

Yan Jun wanted to confess something to Zhang Yuwen. If Zhang Yuwen had just laughed him off, he would have dropped the idea, but Zhang Yuwen said "Yeah," which made him feel like maybe Zhang Yuwen could understand his difficulties.

However, this wasn't the best time for it.

Chang Jinxing's culinary skills were as good as advertised. The braised pork knuckles were tender, the huge platter of blanched seafood included springy prawns and smooth shellfish, and the piping hot steamed fish was perfectly cooked and seasoned with soy sauce. More than half of the fish was devoured as soon as it was served. Chang Jinxing flipped it over while he was serving the dishes, and by the time he went back into the kitchen for the vegetables and came back out to take his seat at the dining table, all that was left of the fish was bones.

"Oops, sorry!" Chen Hong said. "We didn't wait for you."

"The flavor of a dish starts changing the moment it leaves the pot," Chang Jinxing said with a smile. "If you want to taste it at its most delicious, you have to eat it as soon as possible. That's how you show respect to the chef."

He'd put a lot of thought into impressing his roommates, meticulously planning the meal so that the six dishes and the soup were served at almost the same time. This was the perseverance of a great chef.

"How long are you two going to keep wiping the floor?" Chang Jinxing said as he served up the last dish. "Let's dig in!"

Zhang Yuwen nonchalantly separated from an embarrassed Yan Jun. A group of gay guys living together would inevitably enjoy teasing each other, and the best way to avoid being teased was to strike first and tease someone else. Zhang Yuwen understood this well, but based on his observations, any two of these guys could easily make up a pair. There were so many possible combinations that he didn't know where to start.

When all the dishes were served and everyone raised their glasses for a toast, Zhang Yuwen chose a pair and launched his attack. "To Xing-ge's and sister-in-law's health."

Zheng Weize was teaching Xiao-Qi to say "thank you" when he heard this. "Hey! Hey! Don't talk nonsense!" he exclaimed, exaggerating his response in both embarrassment and excitement. "Who knew you could be so cheeky!"

Zhang Yuwen raised his glass. "Now you know."

Everyone roared with laughter. "Zhang Yuwen looks serious and decent on the surface," Chen Hong remarked, "but deep down, he's all mischief."

Zhang Yuwen approved of this evaluation and had no intention of refuting it, but he did interrupt to change the subject back to Chang Jinxing and Zheng Weize. They all started ribbing Zheng Weize about whether he waited for Chang Jinxing to return home every night, and what were they always doing in Chang Jinxing's room...?

It was true: Zheng Weize liked going into Chang Jinxing's room to lie on his bed and chat with him. Chang Jinxing never chased him away, either. Zheng Weize gave Chang Jinxing skincare products and face masks, and Chang Jinxing accepted them all. Chang Jinxing kept smiling, offering neither confirmation nor denial, which was probably a typical player strategy. Zheng Weize, however, was blushing hard from all the teasing.

Seeing that Zheng Weize was about to get worked up, Chen Hong stepped in to smooth things over. "You're the youngest here, so everyone sees you as their younger brother. We're just fooling around." He put an affectionate arm around Zheng Weize.

The joking finally stopped. Yan Jun, who had been seriously feeding Xiao-Qi baby food while everyone else roasted Zheng Weize and Chang Jinxing, occasionally laughed out loud at their interactions. He'd had a bit of the red wine that Zhang Yuwen had brought out for the occasion, and the lock on his heart was coming loose a little. He almost believed these were his friends now.

"Someone in your family must be a chef." Zhang Yuwen only had to look at Chang Jinxing's food presentation to guess. "These are truly remarkable culinary skills." Chang Jinxing winked at Zhang

Yuwen, partly teasing and partly hinting, and Zhang Yuwen let him off without probing further.

"Thank you, Yuwen." Chen Hong raised his glass again. "It's thanks to you that we could all get to know each other."

"Yeah!" Everyone set down their chopsticks and raised their glasses.

"That's the work of fate." Zhang Yuwen clinked glasses with them. As the group of good friends came together, drinking to their hearts' content, the crisp clinking of their wine glasses sounded just like the jingling of coins in a purse—a simultaneous reminder to all four tenants that they still hadn't paid their rent. Silence hung in the air for a few brief seconds before they awkwardly laughed it off.

After dinner, Yan Jun and Chen Hong chatted as they washed dishes in the kitchen. Xiao-Qi, who was learning to walk, toddled around the house, Zheng Weize close behind her. "What do you do for a living?" Chen Hong asked Yan Jun. "You always seem to be very busy."

"Equipment sales," Yan Jun replied.

"Introduce some clients to me when you have the time." Chen Hong handed the washed dishes to Yan Jun, who wiped them dry and put them away.

"Sure, I'll ask around," Yan Jun said noncommittally. "Where's your gym?"

"No gym, but I'll be happy to provide home fitness training," Chen Hong corrected himself. He only had the service, no longer the facility. Yan Jun hummed in acknowledgment, and Chen Hong added, "Business has been bad with the economic downturn."

"Yeah," Yan Jun agreed. "Our company has also seen a drastic drop in business."

Chen Hong had never talked about his business to his roommates before, but after all that wine, he felt like talking to someone. In his eyes, Zheng Weize was a kid, Chang Jinxing didn't seem like he had a proper job, and Zhang Yuwen might not necessarily understand him. Yan Jun was the only one who seemed like he might be on the same wavelength as Chen Hong.

Zhang Yuwen entered the kitchen. "You can leave the utensils. The housekeepers will be here tomorrow to clean up. They only have Saturdays off."

"It's fine," Chen Hong replied. "We're done washing up. Want a cup of coffee?"

"No thanks. I might not be able to sleep later. I'll play with Xiao-Qi for a while."

After clearing the dining table and cleaning up the kitchen, Chen Hong and Yan Jun stood in the backyard for a while, drinking coffee and chatting about how tough it was to make a living. Chen Hong had picked the right person. Yan Jun knew how it was: Life was tough and money hard to earn, especially now, when there seemed to be no end to inflation and the economic recession. Neither of them knew when things would take a turn for the better.

As they chatted, they began to lament the unfairness of the world.

"To be honest," Chen Hong said, "it's only when I'm back here that I feel like I can breathe and put everything to the back of my mind."

Yan Jun looked out into the night, lost in thought. "Me too."

No. 7 Riverbay Road was like a utopia, but what use was a momentary escape? Sooner or later, they still had to return to reality.

"Because the homeowner is rich." Chen Hong sighed. "In the end, you've still got to have money."

"We will." Yan Jun had never given up hope for the future. "I hope I can afford a house like this one day."

Coffee finished, Yan Jun returned to the living room, picked Xiao-Qi up, and took her back to his room. "She has to stay here and sleep with me tonight," he told Zheng Weize.

"That's great!" Zheng Weize smiled. "I can see her again tomorrow. I'll be sure to keep my voice down tonight."

"No need," Yan Jun said hurriedly. "I'll be thankful as long as she doesn't disturb you guys." It kept surprising him that his roommates were all kind people whose first thought was not to disrupt Xiao-Qi's sleep.

Xiao-Qi had been having a great time. This was the happiest she'd been over the past few months. Yan Jun daydreamed as he bathed her. He found himself overcome with the sudden urge to find a partner. He was caught off guard by the way the dinner's lively atmosphere had magnified his loneliness. Even after he coaxed Xiao-Qi to sleep, Yan Jun continued to toss and turn in bed.

But the night wasn't a good one. Xiao-Qi cried a few times in the middle of the night and vomited milk all over her pillow. Yan Jun sprang out of bed to hug her, hoping to soothe her, only to find that she was burning up—a fever.

Oh no, Yan Jun thought. She probably caught a virus at the childcare center.

Ever since she was born, Xiao-Qi had rarely been sick. Yan Jun turned on the lights and fed her medicine, but she resisted, and her cries grew louder as he struggled with her. Then Yan Jun applied a fever relief patch. Xiao-Qi was obviously very uncomfortable, leaving him no choice but to carry her around the room. It was almost an hour before Xiao-Qi fell back into a fitful sleep.

Yan Jun groped in the dark to clean up the vomit in the crib, then set the linens aside to wash by hand tomorrow. When he was finally done, he checked the time: already one in the morning. He couldn't send Xiao-Qi to the childcare center tomorrow. They wouldn't accept babies with fevers. He'd need to wait until she recovered.

He had to take another day off. Yan Jun thought about who could cover his shift and sent his colleague a message, then checked Xiao-Qi's temperature again. Her fever hadn't subsided. He panicked a little, wondering if he should go to the hospital.

Half an hour later, Xiao-Qi started crying. Her fever had worsened. Yan Jun carried Xiao-Qi in his arms and used a ride-hailing app to call for a car, but he couldn't find one on Riverbay Road at this time of the night, and the nearest hospital was four and a half miles away. He remembered Chen Hong had an electric two-wheeler, but he hesitated over whether to knock on his door.

"What happened?"

When Yan Jun came out to the living room, he ran into night owl Chang Jinxing, who was still up. He hadn't gone out that night, but he couldn't sleep before four in the morning because it felt like the day wasn't over yet. He was in the dining room putting up photos of everyone from the last time they went to play outdoor laser tag.

"Xiao-Qi's running a fever," Yan Jun said. "I'm thinking of..."

Chang Jinxing set aside what he was doing and came over to feel Xiao-Qi's forehead. "Damn, she's burning up. What's her temperature? Has she taken medicine?"

"104 degrees now," Yan Jun said, his brows deeply furrowed. "I gave her medicine, but it wouldn't stay down."

"I'll wake Yuwen up," said Chang Jinxing.

YAN JUN TRIED to stop him. "I can just borrow Chen Hong's e-bike."

"It's too cold outside, and her fever will get worse in the wind." Chang Jinxing headed upstairs. Yan Jun tried to yank him back, but he was already at Zhang Yuwen's door. "Yuwen! Wake up! Yuwen!"

Chang Jinxing knocked on the door, but there was no response. He tried the doorknob—it wasn't locked. Counting on his presumed familiarity with Zhang Yuwen, he went in and shook him awake.

Zhang Yuwen was hugging a pillow, deep in sleep. Startled awake, he sprang up, thinking there was a fire. He didn't blame them when he found out what happened, though, and merely touched Xiao-Qi's forehead. "Any convulsions?"

"No," Yan Jun replied.

Zhang Yuwen went to get his car keys, and Chang Jinxing called out a reminder to him. "Yuwen, put more clothes on."

"Yup, don't worry," Zhang Yuwen said. He headed to the garage to start the car and drive it out. "Which hospital?"

"The nearest." Yan Jun showed him the navigation steps.

"I know how to get there." It was the hospital Zhang Yuwen's grandmother had worked at; he was familiar with the route.

The two of them fell silent. Yan Jun didn't thank Zhang Yuwen, and Zhang Yuwen didn't probe any further.

Yan Jun watched the night scene outside the window. The whole city was asleep, and the yellow streetlights looked lonely. Cold rain was still coming down outside, and the wipers kept in constant motion, creating a halo of lights on the windshield that made Yan Jun feel like he was in a dream.

"If you aren't going to the children's hospital, you have to go to the A&E department here," Zhang Yuwen said when they arrived at the hospital's back entrance. "You take her to register first. I'll park the car."

"Okay." Yan Jun quickly got out.

"Just go through this corridor and you'll see the A&E," Zhang Yuwen added.

Zhang Yuwen parked the car and hurried over. It was flu season, and there were lots of patients at the hospital's accident and emergency department. Some were lying down, receiving intravenous drips, while others were coughing. Hearing Xiao-Qi crying from one of the emergency rooms, Zhang Yuwen knocked and entered. A doctor he didn't know was listening to her heartbeat.

Arriving at the hospital had alleviated Yan Jun's anxiety, as if he received an "immunity to death" buff the moment he set foot inside.

"A viral cold," the doctor said. "If you're worried, we can do a blood test."

Zhang Yuwen went to pay the fees while Yan Jun took Xiao-Qi to get her blood drawn. Xiao-Qi cried and, flustered, the two of them comforted her. Once that was done, they waited at the entrance for the test results.

Zhang Yuwen stopped an exhausted doctor who was passing by. "Can you give her something to bring her fever down?"

"If she's still the same after taking medication, giving her more isn't going to help. Besides, we can't increase the dosage any further." The doctor touched Xiao-Qi's little hands, his heart aching for her. "Since she already has a fever relief patch on, we'll just wait for her fever to subside."

They sat in front of the emergency room together, awaiting the test results. Yan Jun, exhausted, looked down at Xiao-Qi in his arms. She was drifting in and out of sleep, the fever making her uncomfortable and restless.

Zhang Yuwen kept wanting to ask Yan Jun why he wasn't notifying her parents, given how ill she was. Then he realized that Yan Jun had probably lied to him. Maybe there were no brother and sister-in-law, and Xiao-Qi was, in fact, his own daughter.

Zhang Yuwen was often deceived by sweet talk, but he rarely flew into a rage. Yes, some people were habitual liars, but he knew that the majority had their own difficulties, reasons to withhold the truth. Case in point: Yan Jun.

The test report came back: flu. The doctor sent them home with the advice to monitor Xiao-Qi and wait for the fever to subside naturally, although they would have to return if she worsened. If her fever was still over 100 degrees Fahrenheit tomorrow, they could give her an antipyretic injection, which was essentially a faster-acting version of the same medication Yan Jun gave her.

Zhang Yuwen knew the hospital's modus operandi. As long as the patient wasn't in critical condition (read: dying right now), the doctors remained calm. After all, there was always someone sicker than you, and infants' illnesses were harder to treat. Experienced doctors generally believed that these newcomers to the world could rely on their own immune systems to overcome a virus.

"Do you want to go to the children's hospital?" Zhang Yuwen asked.

"Nah," Yan Jun said. "Let's go home first. It's easy for infections to spread, given how many sick people there are here. Besides, going there won't immediately bring her fever down."

"Looks like it's gone down a little." Zhang Yuwen touched Xiao-Qi's neck. He wasn't sure if it was due to the cold weather outside or the fever relief patch, but she wasn't as hot to the touch.

Once they were home, Zhang Yuwen headed upstairs to go back to sleep. "Just come in and wake me if something crops up. My door's open."

"Thanks," Yan Jun said.

"You're welcome." Zhang Yuwen yawned, returned to his room without looking back, and collapsed onto his bed.

It was an agonizing night for Yan Jun. Xiao-Qi had never been so sick. From parenting courses, he knew, roughly, that fevers were common in babies, most of whom would have one around the age of one. He just hadn't expected it would come out of the blue like that, catching him off guard.

He measured Xiao-Qi's temperature with an electronic thermometer every half hour: 104°F, 104°F, 103°F, 103.5°F, 104°C, 102°F... It left him utterly exhausted. At 5:40 in the morning, he finally couldn't hold on anymore and fell asleep leaning against the headboard, Xiao-Qi in his arms.

Dawn came. Yan Jun heard someone talking outside.

Zhang Yuwen, who had already gotten up, was knocking on the door. "Yan Jun? Has Xiao-Qi's fever gone down?"

Blearily, Yan Jun got up and touched Xiao-Qi. She must have still felt uncomfortable, because she started crying.

"I think it's time for her medicine," Zhang Yuwen said. Having washed his hands, he touched her to gauge her temperature. "Doesn't seem to be as hot." The temperature on the thermostat read 102°F.

"I'll give her the medicine one more time," Yan Jun said. "If it still doesn't work, we'll go to the children's hospital."

"Come out for a while," Zhang Yuwen told him. "Let the house-keeper clean your room first."

Yan Jun's room was a mess and smelled of Xiao-Qi's vomit from the night before, so he carried Xiao-Qi to the living room. The two housekeepers were already there for work.

"Oh!" Liu Jingfang exclaimed, surprised. "Whose little precious is this? Are you sick?"

"Can you take a look at her?" Zhang Yuwen asked Liu Jingfang.

She took Xiao-Qi into her arms. Raising two sons and two grandchildren had honed and deepened her parenting skills, and she'd also gleaned a lot of nursing knowledge from the Zhangs. Every time her children and grandchildren fell ill, she'd consulted Zhang Yuwen's grandparents. Over time, she came to learn even more than Zhang Yuwen did.

As soon as Liu Jingfang took Xiao-Qi into her arms, she said, "She's got a fever. I'll give her a tuina massage, and the fever will go away. Give me a moment. You boys go make her some milk so you can give her the medicine later."

It was the first time Yan Jun had heard about the mysterious powers of tuina massage, so he was inevitably nervous, but Liu Jingfang moved with such practiced ease it left no room for doubt. First, she undressed Xiao-Qi down to her diaper and sent the other housekeeper to wash her clothes. Then she spread out a towel on the sofa and massaged Xiao-Qi's feverish body. After a full-body massage, she wrapped the baby in the towel and carried her face-down. Gently, she massaged the nape of her neck and the Fengfu acupoint at the back of her head.

Xiao-Qi's loud cries gradually tapered off to soft sobs. Finally, they came to a stop.

Milk at the ready, Yan Jun waited off to the side. When he took her temperature again half an hour later, it had gone down to 100. With a sweet and doting smile, Liu Jingfang carried Xiao-Qi in her arms and fed her some milk, then burped her in one smooth motion.

Another reading put her temperature at slightly over 100. "You can give her the medicine now," Liu Jingfang said. "I'll give her another massage after her afternoon nap."

Yan Jun gave her the medicine, and Xiao-Qi fell asleep. By that point, the cleaning was done too. Yan Jun returned Xiao-Qi to the crib and left the door ajar as he stepped out to thank Liu Jingfang.

"Auntie Liu can help you take care of Xiao-Qi. She's very experienced," Zhang Yuwen said. "Just go to the office if you can't take the day off."

Yan Jun finally had the time to look at his phone. His work group chat was full of snide remarks from his team leader, though they still approved his leave. Yan Jun thought about it, then decided, "I'll rest for a while before I go to work."

Zhang Yuwen kept yawning as he made two cups of coffee in the kitchen and handed one to Yan Jun. "I'm sorry," Yan Jun said.

"It's okay," Zhang Yuwen replied breezily. He'd been observing Yan Jun, this young man who spoke little and was already worn down by life despite his tender age. He wondered what kinds of responsibilities Yan Jun had on his shoulders and whether he'd made "father" part of his identity. This was a complex and contradictory character.

Zhang Yuwen thought Yan Jun was handsome. If he were to meet him in the countryside, he would have thought of Yan Jun as a vibrant guy with healthy, tanned skin who loved sports and life and playing basketball. He had chiseled features and a great physique, and his height of six feet and two inches made him a great fit for all sorts of clothes. With just a bit of hair styling, he could become a model.

But Yan Jun didn't seem cognizant of his own appearance, or maybe he just didn't care and chose instead to focus on work. His sense of responsibility gave him the air of a classic top, making him appear manly. But even the most masculine of men had moments of vulnerability.

"I mean, I'm sorry I lied to you," Yan Jun said tiredly.

Zhang Yuwen said nothing this time, just watched Yan Jun silently. Whether as a matter of mutual trust or a desire to continue living at No. 7 Riverbay Road, Yan Jun had to come clean; that much was clear. Yan Jun hadn't contacted Xiao-Qi's parents once since last night. If Xiao-Qi had a mother, you'd expect her to storm the house in an anxious rush to see her daughter. Given that Xiao-Qi called him Papa, she was Yan Jun's child, and there were only two possibilities: either he was divorced from or never married Xiao-Qi's mother in the first place, or she was a child he had taken in.

Instead of jumping to conclusions, Zhang Yuwen waited for Yan Jun to explain.

"She really is my niece." Yan Jun looked Zhang Yuwen in the eyes, and his own were full of pain. He was tired of pretending; he had to come clean.

Zhang Yuwen raised his brows, signaling for Yan Jun to continue.

"Her story is tragic. Her biological parents passed away." Yan Jun averted his reddened eyes and held a clenched fist under his nose as he started choking up. Trembling, he took out his wallet and pulled out a photo to show Zhang Yuwen. "This is my brother and sister-in-law. It happened...four months ago. They died and left Xiao-Qi behind. My mother still doesn't know about it..."

"Take a break first. Catch your breath; don't talk." Zhang Yuwen looked at the photo of the couple and understood immediately. The man in the photo bore a striking resemblance to Yan Jun, and the woman held a baby in her arms. Zhang Yuwen stood up, walked to the other side of the table to stand beside Yan Jun, and leaned down to hug him.

Remaining in his seat, Yan Jun turned slightly to hug Zhang Yuwen back, leaning into his waist as he sobbed with grief. The pent-up emotions that had been bottled up all this time finally found release.

Just then, Chen Hong returned from his morning run. The scene startled him, but he tactfully said nothing and trod softly back to his room. Some time later, Yan Jun regained his composure, and Zhang Yuwen let go of him.

Yan Jun was now able to tell his story calmly.

"My brother and sister-in-law ran a shop in Jiangnan. Back in July, they were on their way to make some purchases when they were involved in a multiple rear-end collision on the highway... My father passed away early, and my mother is old. She has cataracts, and her heart has always been weak. My sister-in-law had been on bad terms with her parents since she was a child. She ran away from home a long time ago and only got together with my brother later. We have no other relatives, and I don't want to hand Xiao-Qi over to anyone else to raise. I don't want her to end up in the system."

Zhang Yuwen nodded. "So you've been caring for her all this time."

Much more collected now, Yan Jun explained, "I send her to the childcare center in the day and pick her up in the evening."

Yan Jun had come to Jiangdong City two years ago to seek refuge with his brother and sister-in-law. He also found a job here. The devastating news came like a bolt from the blue, and his life, which had been modest but full of familial warmth, was torn apart. He took care of the funeral affairs and canceled the lease for the apartment that his brother and sister-in-law rented. He didn't want to be separated from Xiao-Qi; he was waiting outside the delivery room with his elder brother when she was born, and they had an emotional bond. He refused to hand her over to someone else to be abused or neglected.

He'd kept all of this hidden from his mother. Since her parents' deaths, he and Xiao-Qi only had each other. Not wanting Xiao-Qi to feel like she didn't have parents, he taught her to call him Papa. At least, this way, she would have a father.

"This is her birth certificate." Yan Jun showed Zhang Yuwen a photo on his phone. Yan Yuqi's biological father was listed as Yan Dai. "The original's in my room. If you—"

"No, no, no need," Zhang Yuwen cut in quickly. "I believe you. Unreservedly." They both fell silent. "Your mother doesn't call your brother at all?"

"I used my brother's phone to send her voice messages. We sound alike, so all I need to do is change my speech habits. She hasn't suspected anything so far."

Zhang Yuwen nodded and looked at Yan Jun's room again. Xiao-Qi was sleeping soundly, likely tired out by the hectic night.

"You going to work now?" Zhang Yuwen asked. "We can take care of her for you."

"Yeah, I'm going to the office," Yan Jun said. "Thanks."

He didn't ask what would happen to Xiao-Qi next. If Zhang Yuwen chased him out, he had no choice but to accept it. After all, Zhang Yuwen had never agreed to a child in the house. Yan Jun had deceived Zhang Yuwen, and now the ball was in his court. If Zhang Yuwen said, "Sorry, but you can't stay here anymore," or even dropped a hint to that effect, Yan Jun would move out that very afternoon.

But after a long silence, what Zhang Yuwen said was, "So when are you going to pay your rent?"

Yan Jun was taken aback. Then it dawned on him: Zhang Yuwen had accepted him and Xiao-Qi. "N-now," Yan Jun stammered. "Y-yes! Right now!" He transferred the money to Zhang Yuwen from his phone, claiming the title of the first tenant to pay the full rent and deposit.

Zhang Yuwen checked his account. "Okay, got it."

Yan Jun looked at him with gratitude and emotion, his lips trembling as he tried to convey his thanks. He couldn't find the right words. His eyes reddened again.

Finding himself abruptly at a loss for how to handle the situation, Zhang Yuwen borrowed Yan Jun's own technique. He said stiffly, "Go on. I'll see you later." Having ruthlessly cut the conversation off and halted the exchange of feelings, he cleared away the two coffee mugs and hurried back into his room.

CHAPTER

11

ON TUESDAY MORNING, Zhang Yuwen worked on the manuscript for his new novel, feeling a little depressed. His thoughts swirled, running wild one moment with his characters' relationships and predicaments before jumping in the next moment to the harsh blows of reality that life had dealt Yan Jun. The deputy editor's condescending critiques were tangled up in there, too: his characters were too fake, the story lacked empathy, the whole thing was littered with grammatical errors, and so on.

"What the hell have I been writing?" Zhang Yuwen, unable to get himself into the right frame of mind for writing, grew more irritable the more he wrote. He resisted the urge to toss his computer out the window.

"Trash" was right. Each time Zhang Yuwen looked over the masterpieces he had painstakingly written, he felt the truth of the deputy editor's verdict. The electricity he'd wasted creating trash would be humiliating enough on its own, but he'd also wasted paper printing his trash out.

He considered revising the draft to add some delightful wisecracks, like putting eyeshadow on an ugly child to brighten him up—but if other people didn't like your child, was it because he didn't have eyeshadow? No. It was because he was ugly. In the end, he would open a new document, create new trash, submit it, get rejected, and return to square one. Rinse and repeat. New day, new trash. But he didn't want to go through the same steps today, so he shut down his computer and allowed himself to take a breather.

Disheartened, Zhang Yuwen went downstairs to relax by making coffee and chatting with his subjects. The two night owls, Zheng Weize and Chang Jinxing, were asleep in their rooms. Yan Jun was at work, and Xiao-Qi, having recovered from her fever, was at the childcare center. Only Chen Hong was around at this time of day.

Zhang Yuwen found him in the gym, panting heavily with lifting straps wrapped around his wrists. He wore shorts but no shirt, revealing the gorgeous contours of his shoulders and back. For a muscular man, he had a very sexy physique, with broad shoulders and a narrow waist instead of bulky muscles all over. His pecs were well-defined, but not so defined that it made you think about breastfeeding. He was good-looking, too, with clearly defined facial features: a high nose bridge, large eyes, thick eyebrows, and a strong jawline—you name it, he had it. He was lying on the bench working out, offering a front-row view of an absolute unit of a bulge. It was so impressive, it single-handedly shattered the myth that muscular men were overcompensating for something. His face was flushed as he strained to lift the barbell, making strange gasp—a sound common in gyms and widely known as "power grunts."

Zhang Yuwen's arrival made Chen Hong self-conscious about how he looked. With some effort, he put down the barbell and sat up straight. "Wassup?"

"Nothing," Zhang Yuwen replied from the side. He just wanted someone to talk to.

Chen Hong assumed for a moment that Zhang Yuwen was there to remind him about the rent, but he sensed that Zhang Yuwen had something to say. This was the perfect opportunity to close the distance between them.

"Need help?" Chen Hong undid the straps on his hands. "I can help you work out. Cardio will make you feel better. Here, this is all yours."

"No, no." Just looking at the barbell made Zhang Yuwen tired. He thought about it, then added, "I'll just run for a while."

Zhang Yuwen changed his clothes, and it wasn't long before he broke out in a sweat. It soaked his white T-shirt, making it stick to his back and revealing the shape of his body underneath. As he got off the treadmill, he sensed Chen Hong's eyes on his back, so he glanced at him in the full-length mirror. Their eyes met.

Instead of averting his gaze, Chen Hong smiled. "Something on your mind?"

"Yeah," Zhang Yuwen replied. "Work stuff."

Although Chen Hong couldn't picture what kind of stress might befall a proofreader, whose job was just correcting typos and grammatical errors, he respected that every profession had its own difficulties. "That's how it goes. Those who fail to plan ahead find themselves beset by worries closer at hand."

"True." Zhang Yuwen found it easy to talk to Chen Hong, maybe because the two of them were the oldest residents of the house and had more life experience under their belts. They could understand each other without having to spell everything out in words. It felt good to have rapport right from the beginning.

"You're always holed up at home," Chen Hong said. He'd noticed that Zhang Yuwen didn't seem to have any friends and that, week after week, he only went out on Tuesdays. "Life becomes monotonous when there's only so much to do or look forward to. You should try to widen your social circle."

"Yeah," Zhang Yuwen lamented. "It's just that it gets tough at work sometimes. No matter how hard I try, I can't do it well, and that makes me want to fight with it."

"There's no job in this world that can be mastered with effort alone. Even with a barbell, you can't just use brute force," Chen Hong said. "But sometimes, you have to remember that other people's opinions aren't everything. Besides, you don't seem like the type to care what other people think."

That was true, but now that he'd switched careers from director to writer, Zhang Yuwen was a rookie again. Even the slightest criticism from an editor could make him doubt himself. "But feedback is important for fitness, isn't it?" he asked.

"Of course. You can get injured if you train indiscriminately. That isn't necessarily true about everything in life, though."

This statement was so broad as to be meaningless, but Zhang Yuwen understood what Chen Hong meant.

Chen Hong smiled at him again. "To me, only two kinds of opinions matter: the investors' and the customers'."

Zhang Yuwen nodded. Chen Hong was like an older brother the way he eased Zhang Yuwen's irritability. Or maybe it was just the cardio. Either way, he felt a lot better.

"You want to go out for a stroll?" Chen Hong asked. "It's a beautiful day out there."

Zhang Yuwen thought about it and looked down at his phone. "Okay. Thanks, Hong-ge." Chen Hong was actually asking Zhang Yuwen to come out for a stroll with him, but it flew right over Zhang Yuwen's head.

Zhang Yuwen went to shower. To a certain extent, Chen Hong's words had inspired him, and he felt like he should show his manuscript to other people and hear the readers' opinions. But who?

Zhang Yuwen didn't want to go looking for that frivolous childhood friend of his.

Wat r u doing? Zhang Yuwen messaged Huo Sichen.

His reply was instantaneous. *At the office getting ready to head out for a meeting later. Y?*

They'd been keeping in touch for a while by now. After they parted ways at the gathering that day, they got to know each other and chatted about marksmanship. As it turned out, they both enjoyed playing first-person shooter games like *Delta Force* and *Call of Duty*, and they'd both played a lot of them before. Gaming brought them closer together. Huo Sichen had even asked Zhang Yuwen out to the arcade once, but he was busy with work and only had spare time to unwind on Saturdays. As it happened, Zhang Yuwen had dinner planned with his tenants that Saturday, so he didn't go.

Huo Sichen never probed into Zhang Yuwen's private life. In fact, he'd never even asked if Zhang Yuwen had a girlfriend or whether he was married. Their conversations occasionally revealed a tacit agreement between them that real life was boring and only games could save them. It was this kind of mutual understanding that Zhang Yuwen liked. They'd become friends through games, so they only chatted about games and refrained from prying into each other's professions or family backgrounds while their friendship was so new.

Zhang Yuwen understood Huo Sichen's boredom and even suspected he might be married. That was what happened with his childhood friend, Liang Zheng. Now that he was married, he had very little time to himself, and he often fielded criticism for the hobbies he cherished in his youth. Even drinking a cola got him chastised by his family. Straight guys like these desperately needed friends who had nothing to do with their present lives, friends to whom they could call out longingly: *Come play with me.*

There would be no boundaries crossed. The idea would never even occur to Zhang Yuwen.

Every day, when Zhang Yuwen set about creating his trash, he logged into the instant messaging software on his computer. If he was using a computer at work, Huo Sichen did the same. They became the most frequent online contact on each other's list. Occasionally, they made small talk or shared news links, and just like that, they gradually grew familiar.

Zhang Yuwen: *nice weather tdy.*

Huo Sichen: *a shame I'm here wasting time on work instead.*

Zhang Yuwen dried his hair and asked, *whr r u going for ur meeting?*

Huo Sichen: *Nearby. Jiangnan.*

Zhang Yuwen: *Wanna hv lunch tgt?*

They settled on a place to meet. Zhang Yuwen called for a ride to get there. It was the first time in a week that he'd stepped out of the house to hang out with someone. He always felt like he was on familiar terms with Huo Sichen, but now that he thought of it, this would only be their second meeting. From chatting with him, Zhang Yuwen had gotten the sense that Huo Sichen was either the boss or the second-in-command of a company small enough that some matters had to be handled by Huo Sichen himself.

Huo Sichen was standing outside a street food stall with a number tag in hand, waiting for a table. Arriving late, Zhang Yuwen got to enjoy the fruit of Huo Sichen's labor without lining up himself. It was a work day, and though the weather was cold, the place was noisy and crowded. Huo Sichen wore a suit that made him look like a completely different person from the angler Zhang Yuwen had met in the open country. Zhang Yuwen almost missed him when he was looking around for him.

"Wow." Zhang Yuwen smiled. "Looking good."

"Seems like I made a poor first impression on you," Huo Sichen said as Zhang Yuwen sized him up. "This place might be noisy, but the food more than makes up for it."

"I know. I've been here before. Did you grow up in Jiangdong City?"

"I did my graduate studies here," said Huo Sichen. "The school is just behind this place."

"Chonghan University of Finance and Economics."

"Yup." Huo Sichen flashed him a handsome smile.

Mature, neat, and gentlemanly, Huo Sichen sure was easier on the eyes when he wore a suit. He had already ordered food by the time Zhang Yuwen arrived—all dishes Zhang Yuwen liked. Their tastes were so similar that for a moment, Zhang Yuwen felt as if he'd been set up on a blind date.

Zhang Yuwen, for his part, looked more laid-back in a casual suit. "Are you done with work?" he asked.

"It's all settled." Huo Sichen was clearly in a good mood. "Sales gave the wrong order and made a dumb mistake, so I had to apologize in person. What about you? What have you been busy with lately? I still don't know what you do."

"I'm a proofreader," Zhang Yuwen said, "sort of like a copy editor. I work for a publishing house, but I don't have to keep office hours." He felt a little guilty about the lie, but Huo Sichen knew Chen Hong, and Zhang Yuwen didn't want to expose himself.

Huo Sichen nodded. "There aren't as many people who enjoy reading as there used to be."

"Yeah." Zhang Yuwen found it a shame too. Electronic devices had eaten up so much of people's reading time. Books still had their uses, though.

"Are you doing novels or other types of books?" Huo Sichen asked.

"Everything. I proofread whatever's handed to me, but I'm also learning to write. I hope I can publish my own book one day."

"A novel?"

"Yeah." Embarrassed, Zhang Yuwen wondered if Huo Sichen would ask him for specifics and force him to share his mediocre work. Luckily, Huo Sichen was tactful enough not to pry, which made Zhang Yuwen feel like he was back on steadier ground.

"I like reading novels," said Huo Sichen. "When I was in elementary school, I skipped class to read the complete collection of Jin Yong's novels at the rental bookstore." Zhang Yuwen laughed, which made Huo Sichen look a little bit sheepish. "Is my taste too basic?"

"No!" Zhang Yuwen said. "I love Jin Yong too."[1]

They started chatting about wuxia novels, and Zhang Yuwen was elated to learn that he and Huo Sichen had another shared interest to discuss besides gaming. As they spoke, the topic gradually shifted to Zhang Yuwen's writing, and by that point, he no longer felt as awkward. This time, he opened up about his frustrations.

"It's already a feat that you can write a story at all," Huo Sichen said seriously. "I'd be at my wits' end if you told me to make one up myself. I couldn't write an 800-word story for love or money, much less sit in front of the computer and write 3,000 words a day until I finished a novel. That's impossible for me, no matter how much I read."

"Um, maybe," Zhang Yuwen said. "But I think it all boils down to skills. I wouldn't know where to start if you told me to manage a company. Everyone thinks writing is difficult, but to some people,

---

1   Jin Yong is one of the most famous authors of wuxia fiction, known for titles like The Legend of the Condor Heroes.

it's just a way to make a living." As a director, Zhang Yuwen occasionally had to write or revise scripts, so he knew this well.

The dishes were served, and Zhang Yuwen talked a little about his novel. The more he spoke, the more embarrassed he became, but Huo Sichen listened attentively the entire time. Zhang Yuwen was starting to think it might not have been a good idea to confide all this in Huo Sichen.

"The way I put it makes it sound dull..."

Huo Sichen considered this. "It'll be a lot more vivid on paper. I think your story is fascinating."

Zhang Yuwen perked up. "Really?"

"Show it to me when you're done."

"Sure thing." Zhang Yuwen didn't know if he could push on to the finishing line, but Huo Sichen's encouragement and anticipation might just have been the motivation he needed. Huo Sichen didn't share his opinions on the story beyond asking about what happened. Zhang Yuwen had to think back on the plot, and inspiration struck him as he spoke about it.

But he'd bore Huo Sichen to death if he made him spend a whole afternoon listening to his story, wouldn't he? Zhang Yuwen made to pay for their meal out of habit, but Huo Sichen had already settled the bill.

"Should I drive you home?" Huo Sichen asked. "You must be busy in the afternoon. I've got to get back to work, too."

"Thanks," Zhang Yuwen said. "Wanna hang out on the weekend?"

"Sure. Let's decide on the place later."

Finding a parking spot in a busy downtown area was difficult, and Huo Sichen had parked his car a distance away. They walked through a park, passing a group of high school students. The winter sunlight shone brightly, making them feel warm and cozy.

"Where do you live?" Huo Sichen asked.

"No. 7 Riverbay Road."

"Riverbay Road?" Huo Sichen sounded surprised.

"Yeah," Zhang Yuwen said, equally surprised. They got into the car. "Didn't Chen Hong tell you?"

"Nope." His surprise blooming into astonishment, Huo Sichen asked, "You own a house there?"

Zhang Yuwen smiled. Huo Sichen must not have asked Chen Hong about the arrangement. "I'm only looking after it for a friend. Chen Hong is his tenant," he explained.

Huo Sichen nodded his understanding. "Some houses and cars are completely out of reach if you weren't born into them. Doesn't matter how hard you work."

"Perhaps." Zhang Yuwen didn't quite know how to react. "Do you see Chen Hong often?"

"We used to meet up once a week." Huo Sichen, with his excellent driving skills, steered the wheel with one hand, occasionally glancing at Zhang Yuwen in the passenger seat. "But I've been lazy lately. It's been a month since we last met."

Huo Sichen drove a Mercedes-Benz, itself a luxury vehicle, but Zhang Yuwen had never been interested in cars. As long as he had a ride, he was happy with anything. Huo Sichen dropped him off and they cheerfully said their goodbyes; then Huo Sichen left. He didn't seem overly curious about the mansion on Riverbay Road.

"Out on a date?" Chang Jinxing asked. He'd woken up and was waiting for his food. Zheng Weize was cooking a pot of instant noodles with two eggs.

"Nope," Zhang Yuwen said. "I was with the guy from the outdoor laser tag game, Huo Sichen."

"I think he might be gay," Chang Jinxing said. "Maybe he's interested in you."

"Nah, just a casual chat. And besides, even if he's gay, it's not like we can't be friends." Zhang Yuwen cheekily sized Chang Jinxing and Zheng Weize up, ready to fight fire with fire. Sensibly, the two of them kept their mouths shut to avoid being teased.

Zhang Yuwen turned on his computer, ready for another round of trash farming, but his thoughts inevitably drifted to Huo Sichen. Their meeting had indeed felt like a blind date, or even just a regular date. But Huo Sichen was a little taller than Zhang Yuwen, and his interests and hobbies seemed more like those of a straight man. Even if he were gay, he'd probably be a top. Zhang Yuwen didn't hate the idea of switching roles between top and bottom, but he wasn't ready to try it just yet.

Meeting Huo Sichen for lunch made him want to fall in love, though.

It took him longer than usual to fall asleep that night. Maybe because it was winter, and humans were social animals who craved closeness and warmth from each other.

Riverbay Road
MEN'S DORMITORY

THE RENT WAS CURRENTLY Zheng Weize's most pressing concern.

He tried various methods of begging for money in his live streams, but none of them worked. The settlement date next month was fast approaching—the day on which the platform would disburse the proceeds of his live streaming earnings, minus service fees. As of today, the combined earnings for both his accounts were a measly ¥205.73. This number seemed to mock Zheng Weize for overestimating himself, and it was a harsh indictment of his looks.

He'd been eating nothing but instant noodles for half a month. Well, *almost* nothing: There was the one time he got to feast on Chang Jinxing's gourmet cooking. Zheng Weize considered borrowing some money from his roommates, but Yan Jun had a baby to care for and seemed to be hard up, and Zheng Weize couldn't bring himself to ask Chang Jinxing; after all, he wanted to woo the guy, so he had to keep up appearances. Borrowing money from Zhang Yuwen to pay the rent was pointless, so he set his sights on Chen Hong…until he accidentally discovered that his fitness trainer roommate was also living on instant noodles. Disheartened, he went back to live streaming.

Zheng Weize alternated between two accounts every night, one male and one female. The female account sold skincare products.

When he was logged in as the female streamer, he wore a wig and used a voice changer. The intention was initially to promote products to other women through his streams, but gradually, straight men who thought with their dicks came to outnumber his female viewers. In the end, he was forced to resign himself to it, and he switched tactics to humoring them for tips.

He couldn't get into the role, though, and he struggled to act cute. Playing a different gender went against his nature, making him feel restricted and ill at ease. Sometimes, he even slipped back into masculine speech and mannerisms.

The other account—a gay university student whose client base was gay men and fujoshis—was much easier. He felt more at ease being a guy. At night, he opened some books and read them bedtime stories, developing the persona of a gentle student and hoping his target audience would tip him generously for lulling them to sleep.

However, a gay without a boyfriend was like an over-boiled chicken breast: healthy-looking but dry and tasteless. Not even fujoshis, who could even ship a pair of Transformers, showed any interest in him. There were only a few dozen viewers watching his live stream, and at least half of them were views from the platform. Worse, Zheng Weize couldn't focus during his live stream because he kept straining for any sound of Chang Jinxing's return.

He was also a bit distracted. Sometimes, he thought he could bring in the money faster if he acted cute and asked for gifts, so he swapped to his female account, put on his wig, and hustled to keep the money coming. At other times, though, he worried he would miss out on a match made in heaven with a tall, rich, handsome gay man, so he switched back to his male account and waited for his destined one to fall into his lap. The constant switching between accounts made it even more likely that he'd slip up, and finally the day came when he forgot to turn on the voice changer as he swapped over to the female account, scaring away his few remaining horndog viewers. He spent that night in utter despair.

Zheng Weize sighed. *Hang in there,* he told himself. *Perseverance is crucial in everything you do, including live streaming.* But persevering was easier said than done. The only thing he'd consistently done all these years was charge his phone every day. Moreover, while some types of perseverance were commendable, others ought to be scorned. It was tricky to know which kind you were dealing with until the final moment of triumph.

Should he find someone to fake date? If he did that, no one would ever try to woo him through his live streams. Zheng Weize still held out hope that his ideal partner would check out his live stream, feel moved by his intellect and gentleness, and ask him out.

Today, he was eating instant noodles in the living room, reflecting on his career.

"Instant noodles again?" asked Chang Jinxing, who was back early.

He had a camera around his neck, having just returned from an outdoor shoot. A group of girls dressed in period costumes had rented a ride and hired him for a photoshoot in the early winter ginkgo grove.

These girls had met through an interest group and were close friends online, but in real life, they vied and schemed against each other. In addition to putting up with their bizarre demands, Chang Jinxing also had to navigate their overt and covert warfare. His good looks were useless in times like this; everyone was too busy with their imperial palace strife to pay attention to him. After playing the eunuch for the whole day, Chang Jinxing was exhausted, physically and mentally.

"I'll cook an egg for you," he offered.

"I'm almost done eating," said Zheng Weize. "Don't bother."

Chang Jinxing sat down at the table. "You can't keep eating like this."

"I don't know how to cook," Zheng Weize said with a smile, "and I don't want to cause Auntie Liu any trouble by using the kitchen."

With a hint of a smile playing on the corners of his lips, Chang Jinxing looked down at the photos he'd taken today on his camera. *So handsome...* Zheng Weize thought. From this angle, Chang Jinxing's side profile was even more attractive. He had a high nose bridge, great skin, and soft lips. His clothes fit him perfectly, too, making him look neat and trendy.

Zheng Weize's reliance on Chang Jinxing was genuine, but he didn't dare to make it obvious. Chang Jinxing would always flirt with him, but just as Zheng Weize was about to take him seriously and the others were about to make fun of them, Chang Jinxing would go back to his usual self. Their relationship oscillated between friends and something more, like a swing that couldn't stop but was bound by the pull of gravity, preventing Zheng Weize from flying high into the sky.

Chang Jinxing looked up at Zheng Weize and smiled. "Are you still live streaming these days?" Zheng Weize had told him about the live streams before.

"Yeah, just for fun. I don't have that many fans. Everyone's like a friend; we just chat."

"What have you been streaming lately?"

"Nothing much, just casual chats. You wanna join?"

He was just asking for the sake of asking, and in truth, he expected Chang Jinxing to decline. To his surprise, Chang Jinxing asked, "Now?"

Surprised but flattered, Zheng Weize said, "I'll call for you in a bit."

"What time? I might have to go out later."

"Now is fine. I'll go get ready."

Chang Jinxing was overwhelmed. It was only once he gave up on living off others that he'd realized just how hard it was to make money. Spending the whole day as a eunuch had only netted him ¥300, and once he deducted food expenses, he was left with ¥130. To pay the ¥4,000 rent, he would have to play a eunuch for thirty days—he'd be a eunuch for the rest of his life. It was miserable.

He thought about finding other alternatives. Who knew, maybe live streaming could help to supplement his income.

"Wait a moment," Zheng Weize told him. He tidied up his room, hiding the wigs and bras in his closet, then prepared two seats and turned on the ring light. Chang Jinxing entered uninvited. Zheng Weize often went to Chang Jinxing's room to chat, but this was the first time Chang Jinxing had set foot in his room.

"You shouldn't put the light here." Chang Jinxing took the light and changed its direction.

"Oh, okay."

"You can show the window in the back." Chang Jinxing pulled the curtains open. "The afternoon light is good."

"I usually stream at night," Zheng Weize explained.

"I see. Do I need to put on makeup?"

"Nah. There are filters, and besides, you're already gorgeous... Hi everyone, I'm Xiao-Tu. Welcome to my live stream, Xiao-Tu's Reading Room..."

"Is it starting?" Chang Jinxing leaned in out of curiosity.

"Yeah," Zheng Weize said, "no one's here. You see, at this time of—"

But no sooner did he say these words than viewers began to come online. Whenever Zheng Weize started a live stream, the software notified his followers. Today, he was streaming at a different time than usual, in the afternoon instead of late at night; that piqued his regulars' curiosity, and so they logged on to see what was happening.

"Say hi to everyone," Zheng Weize told Chang Jinxing.

Chang Jinxing glanced at the phone. While he was not exactly thrilled with his appearance today, he sucked it up and waved his hand. "Hi, I'm Star."

A barrage of comments flooded the screen: *So handsome!* Someone even asked, *Xiao-Tu, finally saying goodbye to singlehood?*

Zheng Weize watched the viewer count rise, hitting 80 percent of his usual late-night audience, and he marveled at the power of good looks. Attractive guys just seemed to fire people up with the urge to communicate. His fans, who were usually like zombies, dropped all reserve and dignity the moment they saw Chang Jinxing, typing furiously at the screen. They spammed him with questions about who he was, what his job was, and whether he was Xiao-Tu's boyfriend.

"'Handsome,' 'how are you so gorgeous'... Oh, thanks for the rose." Chang Jinxing started reading the chat screen aloud, thinking that was how live streaming worked, and thanked them for the gifts. "'What did you eat growing up to turn out like that?' 'What's your relationship?' 'Are you straight?' 'Is your real name Star? There are stars in your eyes.' Thank you, cuv3494, for the rose."

Zheng Weize was speechless as he sat to the side, caught in a complex emotional miasma. Chang Jinxing freed a hand and wrapped it around Zheng Weize, and the chat erupted into squeals of *omg wat is this flirting I cannot!*

"What should we stream?" Chang Jinxing asked Zheng Weize in all seriousness.

"What do you want to stream?" Zheng Weize returned with a grin.

Chang Jinxing flashed him a radiant smile. "I don't know either."

Apparently having gotten word of what was happening, a bunch of gays popped into the chat like a sightseeing tour group. Zheng Weize recognized one of the nicknames as an old regular of his stream. The others were users who occasionally came to show support.

You hoes! Zheng Weize screamed internally. *Hoes! Stop flirting with my Star!*

Chang Jinxing continued reading questions. "'Are you a top or a bottom?' Hm, take a guess... 'You must be a bottom.'" He laughed. "Baby, you guessed wrong."

"I'll get you a glass of water," Zheng Weize said.

Not even fifteen minutes into the live stream, Chang Jinxing had already received a ton of gifts. Zheng Weize's fans, usually as miserly as Grandet,[2] sent Chang Jinxing lots of roses because of his looks—one even gifted him a virtual sports car. When Zheng Weize sat back down, Chang Jinxing was saying, "Many thanks for the sports car, baby," which made the actual host of the stream so furious his face almost contorted in anger.

Chang Jinxing didn't respond to the comments about their relationship. When Zheng Weize handed him water, someone commented, *Wow! These two are definitely a couple!*

Struck by a brain wave, Zheng Weize wrapped his arms around Chang Jinxing's neck from behind, leaned against his back—the way he usually took liberty with Chang Jinxing—and looked into the camera alongside him. Chang Jinxing appeared as if he was used to this, and the duo received even more roses.

Calculating how many tips he'd raked in, Zheng Weize wondered if he should call it a day, like a lottery winner who instinctively

---

2   One of the main characters of Honoré de Balzac's La Comedie Humaine, Felix Grandet is an ungenerous penny-pincher.

scurried away after claiming their prize. But Chang Jinxing kept interacting with the fans with a smile on his face.

People often complimented his looks, but it was rare that they did it to his face. It was different on the internet, though. Everyone spoke frankly, no one held back, and they did so in packs, which inflated Chang Jinxing's vanity.

The viewer count rose from 200 to 2,000. The sudden influx of gawkers told Zheng Weize that he must have made it to the trending list and was now featured on the app's home page. What could be better than this sudden rise to the top? His popularity was still soaring, and the messages came in so fast Chang Jinxing couldn't even read them.

"Hm, what should I perform for everyone?" Chang Jinxing had been streaming for nearly an hour, and he was starting to feel dizzy. Live streaming was a job that required not only good looks, but also stamina. Many streamers became exhausted after focusing for a while and started babbling nonsense. Zheng Weize quickly herded him offline; they said goodbye to their fans and reluctantly ended the stream without ever answering the question about their relationship.

"That was fun." Chang Jinxing grinned. He was a little tired and, with this having been his first live stream, nervous too. Once the camera was off, he reclined on the bed to relax. Zheng Weize lay down beside him, and Chang Jinxing freed an arm for Zheng Weize to use as a pillow.

"The stream was so lively today!" Zheng Weize exclaimed, in part out of envy and in part out of jealousy. "The viewership was over 6,000 when it ended."

"Really?" Chang Jinxing felt a little pleased with himself, but he said, "That's only because you're so popular."

Zheng Weize didn't deny it. Chang Jinxing didn't know that Zheng Weize's viewership was closer to two digits without him, but after today, he had a strong sense that live streaming basically just involved meaningless babbling.

"I have to go out now," said Chang Jinxing. He said nothing about splitting the tips from the gifts they received; to him, the whole endeavor had just been about hanging out with Zheng Weize. In that moment, Zheng Weize was certain he really had fallen for him.

"Okay," Zheng Weize said. "You gonna be back for dinner?"

"Nah, I've got plans with a friend. Bye."

This conversation could so easily have been an exchange between a couple—it made Zheng Weize feel like they really were one. Then Chang Jinxing pinched Zheng Weize on the cheek, got up, and left. Zheng Weize lay on the bed and stared blankly at the ceiling, feeling melancholic.

For a while, when they were just starting the live stream, he really saw Chang Jinxing as his lover. He'd boldly hugged Chang Jinxing, which Chang Jinxing was gracious enough to allow, and they touched each other frequently, petting heads or holding hands like a couple. These suggestive gestures made Zheng Weize's heart flutter—until the broadcast ended, and he returned to reality.

Zheng Weize wistfully pulled up his earnings page and promptly sprang to his feet. ¥4,200! He was shocked. They had earned ¥4,200 from the live stream!

His hand trembled as he clicked the button to withdraw his earnings, but he received a final sum of only ¥3,000 in his account—which was still ¥700 short of the rent. He cursed those unscrupulous capitalists. At least he was one step closer to the rent, though. All he had to do was ask Chang Jinxing to do another live stream and he'd be able to pay the next month's rent. Maybe he could even pay off the debt on his credit cards, which he'd racked up paying off other bills.

But...Zheng Weize didn't want to ask Chang Jinxing to do another shipping live stream. He didn't want Chang Jinxing to feel like he was being used to boost Zheng Weize's popularity. He knew now that he was in love with Chang Jinxing, and if he wanted to confess his feelings, he would have to maintain equality between them, or at least the appearance of it.

If Chang Jinxing were his boyfriend, Zheng Weize could pull him into a live stream whenever he wanted.

He wavered for a while, then ordered takeout for dinner and got ready for a second round of streaming. When he went online again, even more gawkers and fans showed up to ogle the handsome Star, only to be disappointed when only Zheng Weize materialized. When they saw him reading a book like a monk reciting scriptures, they cyberbullied him and dispersed.

Zheng Weize was none too pleased, but he had to grit his teeth and bear it. Disgruntled with lecherous fans who made impertinent remarks about the man of his dreams, he ended the stream early and switched to his female account.

When all was said and done, most fans were unlikely to unfollow, so his follower count still increased by the thousands—an order of magnitude more people than before. While it wasn't precisely accurate to say that his popularity skyrocketed with it, at least he now had a glimmer of hope. Streaming with Chang Jinxing made Zheng Weize realize that he might be able to save the situation another way.

Thus, he set his sights on Chen Hong as his next target. He could do a fan service stream where he got someone to "service" his "fans" by having Chen Hong appear in a gym tank.

"What?" Chen Hong looked utterly bewildered.

He was pumping iron in the home gym. These days, he rarely went out other than to give lessons to a few members, supplementing his income with the meager hourly rates. At home, he read, worked out, and reflected upon himself, lest others accuse him of being all brawn and no brains. After all, he had to keep active mentally as well as physically.

Zheng Weize sat down beside him. "Have you heard of Sohee Lee?"

Chen Hong gestured for him to say no more. "How many followers does your channel have?"

"Uh... Over 20,000?" Zheng Weize said. In truth, he'd only had a few thousand until last night. More than half of the current number were horndogs Chang Jinxing had lured over the day before.

Hearing this gave Chen Hong a start. "Over 20,000? That many?"

Zheng Weize didn't dare tell him that they were mostly ghost followers. He came to Chen Hong intending to do a knowledge-sharing session and a casual chat with the fans. Chen Hong didn't even need to think about it; he agreed at once.

Chen Hong had tried shooting short videos on Douyin and TikTok to promote his classes, hoping to sell some lessons online, but few people went to the gym these days, much less took online classes. He was clueless when it came to short videos and streaming platforms, and had no idea that the key to boosting traffic was to shed his clothes—the more skin he showed, the more views he'd get. He couldn't cast aside his pride, either, and the videos he filmed in all seriousness raked in only a few dozen to a hundred, tops.

Now that Zheng Weize had offered him a generous opportunity, he readily agreed. That night, he changed his clothes and joined Zheng Weize's channel as a special guest.

Chen Hong's appearance elicited a chorus of catcalls. Zheng Weize wanted to play up the bromance with Chen Hong, but that turned out not to be feasible: The juxtaposition of a delicate bottom wrapping his arms around the neck of a muscular man under an array of touch-up and face-slimming effects wouldn't be as cute as Zheng Weize had thought. It might even make people uncomfortable.

Zheng Weize said, "This is—"

"Hi, everyone. I'm Labrador." Knowing the trick was to cutesify everything, Chen Hong gave himself a stage name. "You can call me Lab."

Zheng Weize renamed the channel: Xiao-Tu & Lab. According to Zheng Weize's script, they would start by playing up the "romance" in "bromance" and wait for their online popularity to soar before Chen Hong started dishing out tips on physique. But the fujoshis didn't buy it. Most of them weren't interested in muscular men, preferring pretty boys like Chang Jinxing, so they fled the stream, leaving behind a smattering of pervs to chat with them. The viewer count plummeted, but right as Zheng Weize began to worry, the gay army arrived to liven up the stream.

The language they used was a lot blunter and more explicit. At the viewers' request, Chen Hong generously removed his gym tank top and showed off his chiseled physique. Zheng Weize felt Chen Hong up on the fans' behalf, touching his chest one moment and pinching the back of his shoulder the next.

Suddenly, Zheng Weize understood the appeal of a compact muscleman. Not "compact" as in the size of Chen Hong's frame, but the way he'd sculpted his body into a more moderate figure with low body fat, so it didn't appear overly bulky. Zheng Weize started to think that Chen Hong wasn't all that bad, after all. Although his looks couldn't compare to Zheng Weize's Star, his years of self-discipline had left him with an enviable complexion and a body that looked slim when clothed and muscular when naked.

"'Gege, how do you usually take care of your hole?'" Chen Hong read. "Well, honey, gege don't need to do that..."

Zheng Weize mouthed a reminder to him that he didn't need to read every comment, especially not the obscene ones.

Lonely gays flooded the live stream in the middle of the night to flirt with Chen Hong. Slang and anatomical references flew across the screen, along with obscene comments and abbreviations. Yet there were no gifts. At first, Zheng Weize occasionally prompted them to send gifts to demonstrate their support for the skin show, but eventually, he gave up.

"'Wanna give u a prostate massage...'"

"'Gege's boobies...'"

"'...like a woman's boobs.'"

"'wat shld I eat to grow bigger tits...'"

"'ur dick...'"

Chen Hong skipped several comments before picking a normal one. "'How do you maintain such a good figure?' Well, it's important to stabilize your metabolism if you want to keep your figure. Having the appropriate muscle can increase your body's energy consumption." He explained with such earnestness that Zheng Weize's heart ached a little.

At the end, Chen Hong picked up the white sign he'd prepared and placed it before the camera. "Here's my contact info on the messaging app. You can add me for consultations, and feel free to follow my personal page. I regularly share fitness tips there."

"Please do follow Labrador!" Zheng Weize chimed in.

"'Where did you find so many handsome guys?'" Chen Hong read. "Huh? L'il tramp…'"

"That was for me," Zheng Weize explained as he clicked the button on the interface to post a link to Chen Hong's personal page. Chen Hong rose again to get some water. His pants were pulled low over his hips, revealing his beautiful Apollo's belt and finally winning a wave of gifts for Zheng Weize.

"All right, it's almost two," Zheng Weize said. "Sleep early, everyone. Good night." He blew them a kiss and ended the stream.

It was now the dead of night. It was raining in Jiangbei. Dressed in thick pajamas, Zheng Weize was tired and sleepy. Chen Hong went to the dining room and retrieved his fitness meal from the refrigerator; they both had yet to eat dinner.

Zheng Weize poured hot water into his cup of instant noodles. "We got ¥700 in gifts. I'll split it with you."

"No, no," Chen Hong said. "No need. I still haven't thanked you for helping me get more followers." Zheng Weize insisted, but Chen Hong turned him down and pointed upstairs, telling him to say no more lest he wake the others.

"In that case, I'll treat you to a meal someday," Zheng Weize whispered.

"Sure." Chen Hong smiled and checked his personal page on his phone. Based on the boost in his follower count, it seemed Zheng Weize's recommendation was working.

Waiting for his instant noodles, Zheng Weize said in hushed tones, "Some of my followers can be pretty abrasive in their language, sorry. Don't take it personally."

"It's nothing." Chen Hong was almost thirty years old, nine years Zheng Weize's senior. He understood the realities of the world they lived in and the desires that lurked deep in many people's hearts. He was also no stranger to seeing people hurt others because of those desires. So he didn't take it to heart. "You must encounter more toxicity online than I do. It's just that you're young and tend to get fixated."

Zheng Weize smiled at Chen Hong. "I was definitely bothered by the verbal abuse when I first started live streaming. But I'm all good now."

During the stream, there had been a few times when Chen Hong had noticed Zheng Weize clearly wanted to lash out but did his best to hold back. He reached out and patted Zheng Weize on the head.

"There were a lot of times when I thought I was used to it, but then a comment or two would leave me feeling terrible, even if I was in a good mood all day. It would totally ruin my night." They both fell silent. Then, still smiling, Zheng Weize peeled back the foil lid of his instant noodles and added, "You know? When I was in school, the boys in my class always bullied me, calling me a sissy..."

"They were just jerks," Chen Hong said. "Don't dwell on those memories. They'll get their comeuppance."

"Yeah," Zheng Weize said absently. "They threw my books into the toilet and even put their leftovers in my desk. My health wasn't very good, so I was slow during our runs, and they'd surround me and shout, 'Preparing for sissy launch, 360-degree spin,' and stuff like that." Even Zheng Weize found it funny now. He laughed.

Chen Hong didn't laugh, though. "If I were there, I would have beaten them to death," he said seriously. "People who bully others are scum." He'd never been the victim of bullying before and never participated in it himself. He was the kind of person who'd step in when he saw a pack of kids taunting cats and dogs, pulling them away and telling them not to bully the weak. His physique gave him a natural sense of justice and responsibility.

Zheng Weize dug into his noodles, and they both went quiet for a while. Zheng Weize's tears fell soundlessly into the noodle cup. Chen Hong remembered the day when, on returning home, he'd seen Yan Jun crying while hugging Zhang Yuwen. He felt he had to comfort Zheng Weize too, so he went over to his side and gently wrapped his arms around him.

Zheng Weize leaned his head against him, sobbing softly. His tears soaked through Chen Hong's flimsy gym tank top, revealing the alluring contours of his abdominal muscles.

His abs are so sexy... Zheng Weize thought as he cried.

He wanted so badly to find a boyfriend and pour all his woes out to him.

Zhang Yuwen could sense that something had happened between Zheng Weize, Chen Hong, and Chang Jinxing. There was a subtle improvement in their relationships. A few times, he'd seen Chang Jinxing and Chen Hong sitting at the dining table chatting when Zheng Weize came out of his room and hugged Chang Jinxing and then Chen Hong from behind. Neither of them protested; they behaved like it was normal.

This made him a little curious, and he thought he should warn Zheng Weize not to get too emotionally invested in Chang Jinxing, in case he got himself hurt. Judging by Chang Jinxing's daily routine of going out at night and returning at dawn, he was obviously not a reliable guy. Chen Hong was probably a better option.

But who could say? Maybe Zheng Weize could tame a playboy. Zhang Yuwen thought it better not to be nosy. His own love life was still up in the air, after all.

Yan Jun got off work a little earlier now. He no longer let Xiao-Qi have her meals at the childcare center. Instead, he would pick up a bento set from a convenience store, buy some vegetables and chicken to prepare meals in the kitchen, and feed Xiao-Qi baby food.

Every tenant was careful to keep the common areas clean out of fear that they wouldn't deserve such a wonderful house otherwise. Zhang Yuwen managed to catch a glimpse of their rooms when No. 7 Riverbay Road carried out a thorough clean-up of the house on

Tuesday. Chang Jinxing's room was still the same as it'd been when he moved in. Yan Jun's was neat and tidy despite the baby staying with him. Chen Hong's was slightly decorated with an additional bookshelf filled with books on self-help and success. Meanwhile, Zheng Weize's resembled a messy dog kennel.

But after the housecleaning, Zheng Weize called Zhang Yuwen to his room and surprised him into silence by handing him the month's rent.

"This is all I have on hand," Zheng Weize whispered. "I'll pay you the remaining two months' rent and the deposit next month, okay?" Zhang Yuwen said nothing. After a while, Zheng Weize added, "I lent a classmate some money. He'll pay me back next month."

Zhang Yuwen didn't have an opinion on the rent, but if the others were to find out that Zheng Weize was paying his rent in installments, they would probably decry him for playing favorites. After nearly a month of observation, Zhang Yuwen had discovered Zheng Weize never attended classes, even though he claimed to be a university student. In fact, he hardly went out. If the kettle he needed to boil water hadn't been out in the kitchen, he might never have left the room at all. Zhang Yuwen was beginning to have his doubts about Zheng Weize.

"Then tidy up your room," Zhang Yuwen said. "It's too messy."

"Sure, sure!" Zheng Weize promptly picked up the pile of clothes on the chair and shoved them into the closet, stunning Zhang Yuwen speechless.

That was how Zheng Weize became the second tenant to pay the rent—albeit not in full.

Chen Hong had been on the go lately, offering classes to members, and he managed to scrape together enough to pay off the rent without touching his savings. Chang Jinxing was the only one left, but Zhang Yuwen didn't plan to push him for it.

Chen Hong was in a good mood now his rent was paid. "Let's hang out this week?"

"Okay!" Zheng Weize wouldn't miss a chance to have fun, even though his pockets were practically empty.

"What about Yan Jun? Hey, Yan Jun!" Chen Hong called out.

Yan Jun was in the living room, accompanying Xiao-Qi as she tried walking without support. Usually, he treated their conversations as background noise and paid attention only when Zhang Yuwen was speaking. At the mention of his name, he looked up. "When?"

"Saturday?" Chen Hong said. "That okay for you?"

"Where to?"

"How about hiking?"

"Huh?" Zheng Weize blurted out. *Hiking? When it's so cold?*

Yan Jun looked at Xiao-Qi hesitantly. "You need some time for yourself," Chen Hong said. "If Xiao-Qi could talk, she'd tell you to go and have fun every now and then."

After a moment's consideration, Yan Jun agreed. "You're right."

Xiao-Qi had recently made some friends at the childcare center and often babbled with them through the bars of their cribs. Taking her to the childcare center for one day on Saturday was probably fine.

"What about Jinxing?" Yan Jun asked. "Still in bed?"

"He'll go for sure," said Chen Hong. "I'll tell him later. Should we stay overnight? I know a campsite. We can rent tents there, and dinner is provided too."

Everyone unanimously opposed this suggestion. Only a lunatic would abandon the comfort of home to brave the elements on the mountain.

Just then, Zhang Yuwen came downstairs to make coffee. Chen Hong told him about his idea, but Zhang Yuwen said, "I'll skip this week. You guys have fun."

"Do you have something on?" Chen Hong asked.

"Uh… I'm meeting Huo Sichen. The straight guy who treated us to fish last time."

Everyone looked astonished. "You've been keeping in contact with him?" asked Yan Jun. "Are you sure he's straight?"

"Yeah," Zhang Yuwen replied. He felt an inexplicable twinge of guilt at Yan Jun's questions, as if he were two-timing him. "I'm pretty sure he's straight. Ask Hong-ge if you don't believe me."

"I don't know for sure," said Chen Hong, "but I feel like he's straight, because his taste in girls is like a straight guy's. He mentioned once that Saturday is his personal time for de-stressing."

"Oh." Zhang Yuwen figured Chen Hong might have sounded him out at some point. If Chen Hong said so, then it was probably true.

"We don't talk much, though," Chen Hong reminded him. "He hasn't reached out to me in a long time. Tell him to come and use up his remaining sessions."

Even after they got to know each other, Zhang Yuwen and Huo Sichen's conversations still revolved around their common topics. They never asked each other about their private lives.

"Actually, I think he's handsome, and he has a good temperament." Having just returned, Chang Jinxing cut into their conversation, startling them.

"There's nothing between us beyond friendship," Zhang Yuwen explained hurriedly, noticing his roommates' odd expressions. "Straight or not, I have no feelings for him. We just hit it off talking about reading and gaming. We're going to hang out on the weekend.

We haven't decided where to go, but we'll probably go to the arcade to play some shooting games."

"Where?!" Chang Jinxing exclaimed. "I'll come too!"

The allure of the arcade had much more appeal than hiking. Even Yan Jun was a little tempted. Zheng Weize wasn't a fan of video games, but he could play the claw machines.

Losing face as his hiking plan began to crumble, Chen Hong cut in with an objection. "No! We should exercise! Forget the arcade!" Then he identified his perfect breakthrough point: Zhang Yuwen. Win Zhang Yuwen over, and the rest would naturally follow. "Ask A-Chen along too."

"But he's straight," Zhang Yuwen said. "Wouldn't it be awkward for him to join us?" With a straight guy tagging along, the group of gays would have to be careful when they joked among themselves. They also couldn't openly discuss which guys they thought were handsome or stylish.

"It's fine," Chang Jinxing said. "I like straight guys. They're very cute."

"Hey!" Zhang Yuwen's warning bells started ringing. He rounded on Chang Jinxing. "Don't try to turn him gay."

Chang Jinxing took this as a compliment. "You guys decide, then," he said, and left, whistling, to take a shower.

"Shall I invite him?" Chen Hong asked.

"I'll do it." Zhang Yuwen sent Huo Sichen a message.

The reply was fast: *Fine w either. I'll go if u r.*

That was how they dragged Huo Sichen, who had just wanted to play games, along on their hiking trip.

It was a bright and sunny Saturday. The weather report forecasted rain, but looking at the clear, cloudless sky, nobody was very worried.

Carrying their own backpacks with snacks and bottled water, they walked across the bridge to the visitors' bus stop half a mile away to meet up with Huo Sichen. It was true: Riverbay Road was a prime location with convenient access to everywhere.

"We should get matching team uniforms," Yan Jun commented. "We can buy them online and wear them when we go out together."

"Good idea," Chen Hong said. He used to organize hiking trips for club members to socialize and foster ties; the same idea was behind this suggestion for his roommates. They had all woken up very early today, however, and except for a spirited Zhang Yuwen, who was an early riser, the others at the back, Chang Jinxing and Zheng Weize, were still groggy with sleep.

Chang Jinxing, carrying his DSLR camera with him, downed a large flask of coffee. Zheng Weize had deliberately chosen a casual outfit similar in style and color to Chang Jinxing's, so they looked a bit like a couple. Chen Hong and Yan Jun were in sportswear, and Zhang Yuwen wore a jacket and a utilitarian ensemble that made his legs look longer.

"What time did you arrange to meet him?" Chen Hong asked.

"He should be here, I think." Zhang Yuwen looked toward the bus stop and waved.

Huo Sichen was dressed in utilitarian fashion too, complete with a simple belt bag slung across his shoulder. He had his hands in his pockets, looking suave and handsome. Zhang Yuwen wore beige, while Huo Sichen was in dark green. Surprised, everyone threw Zhang Yuwen impish looks, puzzling the still-oblivious Zhang Yuwen.

"Good morning," Huo Sichen said.

The group exchanged greetings. "Morning."

Zhang Yuwen had expected to find Huo Sichen decked out in full off-road gear, not wearing something so simple. "You didn't even bring a bag?"

"Isn't this a bag?" Huo Sichen asked. "There's tissues and a thermos inside. That's enough."

"I'm not going to share my snacks with you," Zhang Yuwen warned him. "If you didn't bring any with you, you must be planning to mooch mine."

Huo Sichen laughed. "You saw through me."

The bus came, and everyone boarded. Having an additional companion turned out to be a good idea; they were in pairs now, and no one would be left alone or need to sit on someone else's lap. Zheng Weize and Chang Jinxing leaned against each other and dozed off, and Chen Hong and Yan Jun sat together. Zhang Yuwen, of course, shared a seat with Huo Sichen.

Apart from Chen Hong, Huo Sichen was unfamiliar with the rest of the group and couldn't even remember their names. He asked Zhang Yuwen to refresh his memory in hushed tones. The gays had shown no interest in him at all after they swapped contacts at their last meeting, with only Zhang Yuwen reaching out to chat from time to time. Zhang Yuwen was basically Huo Sichen's only friend in the group.

"Chen Hong wants me to remind you to use up your remaining training sessions," Zhang Yuwen told him.

"I don't feel like it," Huo Sichen said. "His training sessions are exhausting, and I'm lazy. I just want to have fun."

Zhang Yuwen laughed, not expecting Huo Sichen to be so frank. "But you have a good physique."

"I was born with it." Huo Sichen raised an eyebrow. "I love to eat junk food."

"I can tell." Zhang Yuwen knew Huo Sichen bought a large cup of cola on his way to work every day and drank it at his desk. Carbonated drinks were strictly forbidden in Zhang Yuwen's family because they led to calcium loss and weight gain.

The bus arrived at Elephant Gorge, one of the most famous peaks on the outskirts of Jiangdong City. At an elevation level of more than three thousand feet, it had cable cars to transport visitors up and down the mountain. The scenery was picturesque, with the Liujin River flowing through the gorge and the peaks extending north and south. A naturally formed ridge resembling an arched spine connected the south and north peaks, evoking the image of an elephant's trunk spanning across the river—hence the name.

Elephant Gorge had cherry blossoms in full bloom in spring, provided a cool refuge from the sweltering heat in summer, and offered a display of maple foliage in autumn. It bustled with activity three seasons a year. Only this time of year—when the first snow of winter had yet to fall, and the view offered only monotonous dark green pine trees and no snowscape—was a rare tourist offseason.

"Brrr, so cold!" Chang Jinxing exclaimed exaggeratedly. He had slept for almost an hour on the bus, and the blast of cold wind that greeted him as he disembarked made him shiver even harder. Zheng Weize, meanwhile, seemed to be dazed by the frigid cold.

"Start moving and you'll warm up," Chen Hong told them.

"Let's go!" said Zhang Yuwen.

The group started hiking up the mountain at a leisurely pace. Their plan was to climb the mountain on foot, then take the cable car down.

Zhang Yuwen walked alongside Huo Sichen. "So you don't usually exercise?" he asked.

"I play two soccer games a month with my university classmates from Jiangbei Athletics Hall," Huo Sichen said. Not only did Huo Sichen enjoy playing and watching soccer, he also liked soccer video games. He had to be straight; most gay men didn't like intense, competitive contact sports like basketball and soccer. The ones who liked sports tended to prefer badminton or swimming.

"When are the matches?" Zhang Yuwen asked casually. "What position do you play?"

"Sometimes defender, sometimes goalkeeper," Huo Sichen said, "depending on whether the goalkeeper pissed his wife off the night before."

Zhang Yuwen laughed. He wanted to follow up and ask if Huo Sichen had a girlfriend or a wife, but that was a question that concerned his private life, so he prudently decided not to pursue the topic.

Huo Sichen had learned discretion from his time in the business world. Since Zhang Yuwen didn't ask him about his life, he refrained from asking any personal questions in turn. When, on occasion, Zhang Yuwen did inadvertently ask Huo Sichen something personal, Huo Sichen took the opportunity to do the same.

Zhang Yuwen and Huo Sichen walked ahead of the others, chatting as they went. Zhang Yuwen couldn't ignore Huo Sichen—he had invited him, after all—and besides, chatting with him was comfortable. Zhang Yuwen didn't have to keep guessing what he was thinking.

"Let me carry your backpack," Huo Sichen said to Zhang Yuwen when they reached a rest stop. The others, trailing behind them, were nowhere in sight.

"I'm not tired."

"I know, but if I carry it for you, you won't be able to refuse me when I ask for your snacks later."

Zhang Yuwen burst out laughing and handed him the backpack. Huo Sichen lifted it effortlessly; it wasn't all that heavy. They sat at the rest stop and waited for the others.

A group of female university students arrived, panting and sweating. They looked to be about eighteen or nineteen years old and probably from the same dorm. They took off their jackets and stood in front of the rest stop in their sweaters, fanning themselves.

"Where's the restroom?" a girl asked her roommate.

Huo Sichen answered. "Follow this path down. There's an entry sign at the rear entrance."

The girls laughed, and even Zhang Yuwen, who was in the middle of drinking from his flask, almost spewed the water out. Flabbergasted but realizing he hadn't made himself clear, Huo Sichen said, "I mean, there's a signpost directing you to the restroom."

The girl who had asked the question hurried, blushing, down the path. Zhang Yuwen teased Huo Sichen, who said nothing. When the girl returned, the group continued on their way, and Huo Sichen's gaze followed one of them.

"She's pretty," Zhang Yuwen commented.

Huo Sichen came back to his senses. "She reminds me of my senior from university," he said.

"Oh." Zhang Yuwen nodded, his suspicions confirmed.

"Are you married?" Huo Sichen asked suddenly.

"Nope. I'm single. I broke up with my ex a year ago, and I haven't dated since."

"Why not?"

"Too poor," Zhang Yuwen said simply. "Plus, I'm staying at a friend's place. I can't let the person I like live under someone else's roof, can I?"

"Having rich friends is enviable, but it can also make you insecure," Huo Sichen observed.

Zhang Yuwen smiled. "You're right. But the rich don't mind at all. Ultimately, it's all in our own heads."

"Everyone has pride," said Huo Sichen.

At last, the others caught up to them. Chen Hong and Yan Jun appeared normal. Yan Jun wore an outdoor jacket that was zipped up to his neck. He wasn't sweating much and looked to be in good spirits. Chen Hong had taken off his own jacket and tied it around his waist, exposing his T-shirt that revealed the muscular lines of his shoulders and back. Predictably, Zheng Weize was by far the most tired of the lot. He held Chang Jinxing's hand and kept stopping and looking up every three steps.

"How much further?" Zheng Weize asked.

"Almost there!" Zhang Yuwen said, perking up. "Twenty more minutes!"

"Lemme rest for a while," Zheng Weize pleaded, seeing that Zhang Yuwen and Huo Sichen were ready to continue with their hike. "We just got here!"

"You guys go on ahead!" Chang Jinxing said. "We'll catch up soon."

"It's okay. I was thinking about taking a break too," Yan Jun said.

Zhang Yuwen felt sheepish; they had walked too fast and left his roommates behind. He adjusted his plans and walked with them.

Hiking was like the journey of life. While everyone set off together, some might speed up without realizing it, while others gradually fell behind until they dropped out of sight entirely. They met new people along the way, walked a distance together, and parted ways again soon after.

But this path was really, really long. They'd chosen the north peak, which rarely had many visitors. The plank road was not only narrow and precipitous, but also steep. By eleven in the morning, even Zhang Yuwen was feeling tired and had to stop for the occasional break.

Chang Jinxing had his DSLR hung around his neck. Carrying both his backpack and Zheng Weize's, he stood high up on the horizontal steps to take photos of everyone—and especially to document his roommates at their most wretched moments.

"Enough already," said Yan Jun.

Chang Jinxing laughed. He'd shown himself to be boyfriend material today, carrying the bags and even taking care of Zheng Weize, who could barely move.

Zheng Weize repeated the question he had asked the most today: "How much further?"

"Almost there," Zhang Yuwen said. "Twenty more minutes."

Zheng Weize realized he'd been had. "That's what you said an hour ago!"

"It's really twenty more minutes this time," Zhang Yuwen said, serious as anything. People could rarely tell when he was lying with a straight face. All he had to do was look them directly in the eye with an innocent expression; it was impossible not to believe him.

"What if we don't get there in twenty minutes?" Zheng Weize asked.

"Then the ball's in your court," Zhang Yuwen said with a smile.

"You'll do anything I ask?"

"Sure, go wild. But you can't dawdle on purpose."

"Fine. Let's go." Not that Zheng Weize had anything to lose. This was a zero-cost deal.

Zhang Yuwen knew Zheng Weize wouldn't make any unreasonable demands. In fact, he remembered the day he went hiking with his ex. They'd had the exact same conversation, right down to the punctuation. His ex, like Zheng Weize, had also been too exhausted to move, and Zhang Yuwen had coaxed him all the way up. Did all bottoms think the same? Even the flirtatious atmosphere was familiar.

They were indeed only twenty minutes from the lunch break rest stop. Zhang Yuwen was sure he would win this time, but after his ex made the same bet, he'd whined and dawdled for the rest of the journey, dragging it out to twenty-two minutes. Zhang Yuwen was forced to admit defeat.

Then his ex made his demand: *I wanna top you once.*

A bet was a bet, so Zhang Yuwen accepted. Anyway, pleasure in the bedroom was all about spicing things up, and to Zhang Yuwen, who still loved him very much at that time, it was no big deal to let his partner top him occasionally. As long as they were in love, he could go with anything. Of course, when they finally reached the summit, the hotel was cold and damp, and his ex was half dead from exhaustion. Zhang Yuwen promised him he could take a rain check, but they broke up not long thereafter, and his ex never did get to top him.

This left Zhang Yuwen with the sense that he owed it to someone to bottom at least once. Now, hiking with his roommates, Zhang Yuwen found that he missed his ex a lot. He never thought his ex had let him down, and anyway, it didn't matter who let down whom; they were together for four years, and he still had feelings for him.

If only he were here. If his ex had been here, Zhang Yuwen thought, he'd act like Chang Jinxing. Zhang Yuwen would carry both their backpacks as they dawdled behind the rest of the group, listening to his ex gripe.

Indeed, having backpacks to carry and someone to boss you around was its own kind of happiness.

Huo Sichen's voice dragged him back into reality. "Zhang Yuwen, you're going to lose. How do you feel about that?"

Zhang Yuwen was speechless. They'd arrived at the waterfall to find a sign on the trail leading up the mountain:

Road ahead under maintenance.
Please take a detour.
Approx. 35 min walk to the lunch break rest stop.

1 2:10 P.M. Elephant Gorge rest stop, visitors' reception center, cafeteria.

"Let's come up with something for Yuwen to do," Yan Jun said teasingly as he took his seat.

Bracing himself, Zhang Yuwen got up. "I'll go buy some food for everyone..."

This was usually a restaurant where you could order stir-fried dishes, but since there were few customers in early winter and the roads were undergoing repairs, it had been converted into a cafeteria. Taking the initiative, Zhang Yuwen bought everyone fast food at ¥20 per person, including a meal for Huo Sichen, and waited at the counter for the food to be served. When he returned, everyone took one look at his expression and roared with laughter again.

Even so, they took out their phones and transferred the money for their meals to Zhang Yuwen. Looking confused, Huo Sichen retrieved his belt bag from Zhang Yuwen's backpack and fished out his phone to do the same.

"You don't have to pay me," Zhang Yuwen told him. This, of course, incited a wave of teasing from the gays. They were driving Zhang Yuwen crazy.

"Why doesn't he have to?" Yan Jun asked.

"You don't have to either," Zhang Yuwen said. "It was meant to be a treat for everyone!"

"It's not good to resort to bribery," Chang Jinxing joked. Zheng Weize looked at Chang Jinxing and beamed. Zhang Yuwen put his head in his hand, praying Zheng Weize wouldn't make any weird requests.

"Let's eat first, guys," Chen Hong said. "We can think it over later."

Zhang Yuwen was at a loss for words.

Huo Sichen jumped in to add his two cents. "I think we can have Zhang Yuwen—"

"Stop!" Zhang Yuwen was afraid Huo Sichen would give them weird ideas. "Just eat your food."

With Huo Sichen around, no one took their jokes too far. Zhang Yuwen was glad to have invited him; the guy was truly a lifesaver.

After lunch, Zheng Weize asked, "Are we going down the mountain now?"

"It's still early!" Chen Hong said. "We're only halfway up. We'll take the cable car down when we reach the mountaintop later in the afternoon."

Zheng Weize let out an exaggerated cry. "What—!"

"There's no point in giving up now," Chen Hong told him solemnly. "There are no cable cars here. If you give up, you have to walk all the way back down."

Zheng Weize was struck dumb.

An idea came to Zhang Yuwen in a flash. "How about I carry you up?"

Everyone jeered. "Bribery isn't going to work!"

Busted, Zhang Yuwen tried to defend himself. "This could count as his wish."

"Thanks, but no thanks," Zheng Weize said. "I can walk by myself. I'll think carefully about my wish later this afternoon."

Zhang Yuwen winked at Chen Hong: *Look, he's willing to keep going now.* Chen Hong nodded. The older, the wiser, just as expected.

"I'll go buy coffee for everyone," Yan Jun said. "Thank you all for looking after Xiao-Qi."

Everyone replied, "You're welcome," but nobody turned him down. Zhang Yuwen understood that when it came to treating others, no one wanted to be the first to initiate. After all, every time someone treated, someone else accepted, and the recipient felt obligated to return the favor. It created an endless back-and-forth of treating and reciprocating, which wasn't very kind on people with tight budgets. This was why everyone voluntarily transferred the lunch money to Zhang Yuwen and why, when Yan Jun treated them all to coffee, he offered the excuse of thanking them for "looking after Xiao-Qi." It meant they didn't need to reciprocate.

Zhang Yuwen sighed with feeling. His roommates were all such kind, gentle souls.

Yan Jun bought six cups of coffee, and Zhang Yuwen helped carry them. Yan Jun handed him a cup. "This is for Huo Sichen."

"Okay..." Zhang Yuwen's eyes met Yan Jun's, and they both went silent for a second. Zhang Yuwen looked back to see that Huo Sichen had finished his meal and was now outside on the suspended platform, facing away from the cafeteria. Zhang Yuwen sensed that Yan Jun had something to say, but was holding himself back.

"Sugar and milk?" Yan Jun asked.

"I take my coffee black," Zhang Yuwen replied. Yan Jun raised an inquiring eyebrow, asking about the guy out there, and Zhang Yuwen shrugged. "I don't know."

Zhang Yuwen took the sugar and creamer and went over to Huo Sichen, who was taking a phone call with a Bluetooth earpiece. Zhang Yuwen hadn't realized that at first; he didn't hear Huo Sichen's conversation until he got closer.

"Yeah... I'm hiking with my friends... Elephant Gorge." A pause. "The earliest I can be back tonight is 8 p.m." Huo Sichen turned around and saw Zhang Yuwen holding two cups of coffee. He reached out for one, put it on the railing, and added the sugar and creamer.

The others came out to the other side of the plank road leading up the mountain. Huo Sichen picked up Zhang Yuwen's backpack and joined them. He glanced at Zhang Yuwen, then said nonchalantly into the phone, "No girls. They're all boys." The person on the other end of the line seemed to be reminding him to be careful. Huo Sichen replied, "All right, I'm setting off now. Later."

It was 1 p.m., and the group, having eaten their lunch, spent more time walking together. They chatted about places they had traveled, and Chang Jinxing suggested finding time to go somewhere further away and stay the night there.

Out of nowhere, Huo Sichen said, "Let's play truth or dare."

"No way!" Zhang Yuwen exclaimed. "What kind of place is this for truth or dare? Are you misunderstanding something about the game?" In fact, Huo Sichen found it amusing to see Zhang Yuwen being teased today, and the bet earlier had given him the idea.

"Sure." Zheng Weize decided to veto whatever Zhang Yuwen supported and support whatever he opposed. This would be fun.

"Okay!" Chang Jinxing piped up. "Let's start with the person who suggested it."

Thus, Huo Sichen fell into the pit he dug with his own hands. He tried to back out. "No, no. I meant we should guess riddles..."

"He's right," Chen Hong chimed in. "It has to start with you."

Huo Sichen was speechless. Zhang Yuwen felt a little bad for him, but if he tried to help at times like this, he'd end up with a target on his own back, so he played along. "So what's your choice? Truth or dare?"

"No, that's not how you start it," Huo Sichen protested.

"Majority wins!" Yan Jun said, joining in. "You don't have a choice."

In patient tones, Huo Sichen tried again. "I'll give you a riddle first—"

"Truth or dare?" Chen Hong interjected, refusing to listen to him.

Seeing that the situation was too far gone and worrying that they might come up with something even crazier if he kept dragging it out, Huo Sichen gave up. "Dare."

Suddenly, the guys were stumped for what to make a straight guy do. Seeing his chance, Zhang Yuwen chose a dare that was embarrassing but not too humiliating. "Do a flip."

"What?" Huo Sichen was baffled.

Consummate tricksters, they all goaded him. "Can't do it? Then choose something else!"

Huo Sichen nearly fell into their trap, but snapped to his senses at the last moment. "I'll do it! I'll do it! But how do I do a flip?"

"How can you not know?" Yan Jun said. "Like...this." He took a running start and did a perfect roundoff backflip, executing it beautifully and with robust form.

"Daaaaaamn—!" Everyone was dumbstruck. The flip had even exposed Yan Jun's tanned abs.

"You have training?" Chen Hong asked.

"No," Yan Jun said expressionlessly to the sound of applause.

"You must have," Chen Hong said. "Did you use to do high jumps?"

Yan Jun redirected Chen Hong's attention to Huo Sichen, refusing to let him escape his task. Left with no choice, Huo Sichen took off his belt bag, ran a few steps, and did a front flip. It wasn't as beautifully executed as Yan Jun's, and he almost crashed into the railing.

Zhang Yuwen's face paled. "Careful!" Huo Sichen barely managed to make it through the dare.

"All right," Chang Jinxing said, "you can give us a riddle now."

Huo Sichen gave Zhang Yuwen a brainteaser, but Zhang Yuwen couldn't solve it. "Oh no, now I have to do two things."

"You can choose truth too," Yan Jun reminded him sympathetically.

"I think...I'll choose dare," Zhang Yuwen said. "Guys, please give me a quick one."

Everyone talked it over for a while, and they eventually settled on having Zhang Yuwen do a flip in front of the girls who were coming up the mountain trail behind them. This left Zhang Yuwen speechless, but he never objected when it came to truth or dare. They waited until another pair of hikers came along, then Zhang Yuwen successfully completed his dare, dying of embarrassment all the while.

As he returned to the group, Zhang Yuwen went on a rampage. "Who's next?!" He turned to Chang Jinxing, the one who'd come up with this whole awful idea. "You!"

True to his expectations, Chang Jinxing didn't manage to figure out Zhang Yuwen's riddle. "I choose truth," he said magnanimously.

"Is there someone you like right now?" Zheng Weize asked.

Chang Jinxing looked at Zheng Weize. "Such an easy question? You sure you don't wanna choose another one?"

Chen Hong had noticed the fleeting expression on Chang Jinxing's face. "Nah, this is it," he said. "Tell him to answer it!"

Chang Jinxing didn't say a word. Confused at what was happening, Huo Sichen looked to Zhang Yuwen. Zhang Yuwen didn't offer any explanation, however, so Huo Sichen didn't probe further.

This turn of events surprised Zhang Yuwen. Maybe something really was going on between those two?

But to Chang Jinxing, this was nothing new. He averted his gaze. "No."

"He's lying!" It was clear to everyone that this was a deliberate move meant for them to notice.

Exposed, Chang Jinxing changed his tune. "Oh, well then, yes, I do."

Zheng Weize's heart jumped to his throat. "Give us a name," he said, but Zhang Yuwen flashed him a signal with his eyes: *Don't be foolish! Huo Sichen is here—and are you sure you want to ask a question like that in the middle of a plank road?*

Chang Jinxing glanced at Zheng Weize with a smile before looking away. "That's another question."

"That's so cunning of you," Yan Jun remarked.

"I said no," Chang Jinxing said, grinning, "but you guys said I was lying." He put his hand on Zheng Weize's shoulder and continued walking.

Just give up already, Zheng Weize, Zhang Yuwen thought. *You and your star are in completely different leagues.*

They left the path and started crossing the huge bridge of Elephant Gorge. It was 2 p.m., and this was where the scenery was the prettiest. Chang Jinxing took a tripod from his backpack and shot a group picture, putting a temporary pause to their game of truth or dare. Zheng Weize stood in the center, with Chang Jinxing and Chen Hong to his left and Yan Jun, Zhang Yuwen, and Huo Sichen to his right.

Zheng Weize continued to pester Chang Jinxing about his "truth" even after they crossed the bridge. Zhang Yuwen thought it over, then led Huo Sichen ahead a little.

"Is there a rule in your dorm that prohibits dating?" Huo Sichen asked. He sounded puzzled.

"Oh, no." Zhang Yuwen was quick to improvise. "Anyone in a relationship will be fleeced into treating everyone to a feast."

"Oh." Huo Sichen got it now. He glanced back at Chang Jinxing; by this point, Zheng Weize was clinging to him. Zhang Yuwen figured that Huo Sichen probably didn't suspect a thing and merely saw Zheng Weize as an adorable teen.

"If he keeps changing girlfriends," Zhang Yuwen continued, "he'll have to keep treating us."

Huo Sichen turned back and smiled at Zhang Yuwen. "He certainly has the looks for it."

"Let's keep playing truth or dare!" Zheng Weize shouted from afar. "You two stop walking so fast!"

Zhang Yuwen wanted to howl in despair. "Let's not!" Huo Sichen, on the other hand, found it amusing.

Everyone stopped and took out the snacks in their backpacks. "Oh, finally," Huo Sichen said. "Let me see what goods you've got in there."

Zhang Yuwen laughed. "You've been eyeing them for a while, huh?" He found it interesting that Huo Sichen had been thinking about his snacks all this time. It kind of made him seem like a child.

Chang Jinxing called on Chen Hong for the riddle, but it didn't take Chen Hong long to figure it out. For the first time since the start of the game, someone had cracked one of the nonsensical brainteasers, and thus Chen Hong's bizarre brain won the day.

"Yan Jun." Chen Hong pointed, his target clear.

"I can't guess anything," Yan Jun said. "Don't bother with the riddle. I choose dare. Just tell me what you want me to do."

"Ah!" Zheng Weize exclaimed. "Monkey!" A monkey was looking at them quizzically from the branch of a tree, interrupting their game. "Can we feed it?"

"Better not," Zhang Yuwen warned him. The last time he was here, he saw monkeys attacking the visitors. No words could ever describe that sight.

The color drained from Chen Hong's face. "Pack up and leave now! Quick! Don't provoke them! If you get scratched, you'll need to get rabies shots!"

The monkey ran off not long thereafter. There wasn't much for the monkeys to eat in the wild come winter, and there were few visitors to feed them, so they scavenged. Everyone thought they were out of the proverbial woods when the first monkey left, but before long, it returned with reinforcements.

Zhang Yuwen exclaimed in surprise. Tensing up, everyone packed their stuff and prepared to run.

"Drop the snacks! Let the monkeys have them!" Chen Hong yelled.

Chang Jinxing, whose camera was expensive, was the most anxious of the group. The monkeys jumped onto the guys, and utter mayhem broke out. No one wanted to be the first to run, because that would mean abandoning their friends to save their own skin. Even Zheng Weize only ran a few steps before he felt compelled to turn back and save the others.

"Watch out for the big one!" Huo Sichen warned him, but a small monkey jumped onto his belt bag. Zhang Yuwen hurried over to give him a hand, and even more monkeys swarmed the pair of them. Then a loud *crack* rang out: Yan Jun was whipping his jacket around like a weapon, scaring two monkeys away.

Huo Sichen shielded Zhang Yuwen, swinging his belt bag to drive the beasts away. Chen Hong, for his part, was nearly knocked over by monkeys. Meanwhile, Chang Jinxing covered Zheng Weize as they fled—but he hadn't gotten more than thirty feet away when his occupational disease acted up, and he went into overdrive clicking away on his camera.

"Why are you still taking photos?! Go already!" Zhang Yuwen took off his jacket and threw it to Chang Jinxing, who used it to protect his camera. The group finally managed to beat a hasty retreat.

Everyone was panting hard by the time they neared the mountaintop and took a break at the last rest stop to regroup.

"Did anyone get scratched?" asked Huo Sichen, still worried. "Zhang Yuwen, come here and let me have a look."

Zhang Yuwen didn't know if he'd been scratched by the monkeys or if he'd scraped himself against the wooden railing while he ran away. The side of his rib cage burned painfully.

"You'll need to get a shot if you were scratched," said Chen Hong.

Zhang Yuwen lifted his T-shirt, revealing the fair skin and muscles of his abdomen. The side of his waist had been chafed red.

"Looks like you scraped against the railings." Yan Jun brought the medicated oil over. "I didn't see any monkeys going after you."

"Yeah," Zhang Yuwen agreed. "Don't worry. The skin isn't broken; it won't get infected."

Yan Jun poured some of the medicated oil onto his palm. He seemed intent on applying it for Zhang Yuwen, so Zhang Yuwen took his T-shirt off altogether, baring his upper body. His figure was fair and sexy; his skin's flawless complexion had pale, cool undertones.

The atmosphere abruptly turned weird, and Yan Jun felt too awkward to apply the medicated oil himself, so he handed it to Zhang

Yuwen. As Zhang Yuwen's shirt came off, Huo Sichen's Adam's apple bobbed ever so slightly.

Chen Hong, who was sitting at the side with Zheng Weize and Chang Jinxing, whispered something, and they all cracked up.

"What's so funny?" Zhang Yuwen asked, confused.

Chang Jinxing, still bowled over with laughter, picked up his camera and seized his chance to take a candid photo of Zhang Yuwen.

"Stop that!" Zhang Yuwen didn't know whether to laugh or cry, figuring Chen Hong must have made some kind of indecent remark.

"You've got a great figure. You should flaunt it more," Chang Jinxing said.

Everyone erupted into laughter again, blatantly ogling Zhang Yuwen's half-naked body. Huo Sichen applied the medicated oil for Zhang Yuwen and gestured for him to put his shirt back on, lest he catch a cold.

By the time they reached the top, it was already 5 p.m. The sky was overcast, warning of rain to come. "Let's have hot pot tonight," Zhang Yuwen suggested.

Everyone concurred. There was nothing better than sitting in a shop with rain-speckled glass windows on a winter day when you were ravenous and exhausted, enjoying steaming hot pot with your friends.

"Do you have somewhere else you need to be?" Zhang Yuwen asked Huo Sichen.

Huo Sichen considered it for a moment. "Nope, I don't."

Zhang Yuwen gave him a knowing look, but Huo Sichen seemed confused by it. Having breathed in the air at the mountaintop, everyone was in better spirits, their exhaustion from the hike up promptly forgotten.

But in the next moment, fate dealt them a merciless blow:

The cable car is out of service.
No access down the mountain.

"WHAT—?!" Zheng Weize almost fainted.
Everyone stood before the signboard, shivering.

Riverbay Road
MEN'S DORMITORY

"**S**ORRY," SAID THE STAFF MEMBER, a young girl on the verge of tears. "I'm so sorry. The cable car broke down around 2 p.m. Repairs are underway, but we can't operate after 5 p.m. because we aren't permitted to run the cable car after dark..."

The visitors gathered at the summit raised hell. "Then what'll happen to us? It's way more dangerous to walk down in the dark!"

Standing at the visitors' reception center, with a loudspeaker in hand, the staff member said, "Everyone, please hear me out. *Listen!* Ladies and gentlemen, please do not panic!"

On the periphery of the crowd, Zhang Yuwen and the others looked around.

"Food and lodging will be provided for everyone!" the employee continued. "I'm really sorry! The weather will be very cold tonight. Please do not try to descend on your own. It's dangerous, especially with how slippery the trail is on rainy days! The cable car will take everyone down tomorrow morning!"

The crowd kept on making a ruckus for a long time, but in the end, everyone begrudgingly accepted the proposal. Fortunately, it was Saturday, and they still had Sunday to rest. Besides, it was the offseason, with fewer than three hundred people at the mountain-top; there would be plenty of room for everyone.

"What should we do?" Zhang Yuwen asked, having gathered the others to talk it over. Most of them had no important matters to attend to, except for Huo Sichen and Yan Jun, who both needed to get back. Yan Jun, who had Xiao-Qi to take care of, was in a particularly tricky situation.

"I'll call the childcare center," Yan Jun said. "If worse comes to worst, I'll just have her stay there overnight."

Yan Jun went to make the call, and Chen Hong asked, "Can we make it down if we take turns lighting the way with our phones?"

"It's going to rain," said Chang Jinxing. "Let's not. It's too dangerous."

Zhang Yuwen, too, knew better than to fight nature. The mountain during the day was a completely different beast from the mountain at night, when the cold was biting and the trail perilous to navigate. If their body temperatures dropped while they were halfway down, they wouldn't just need to worry about whether they could reach the bottom; they might not survive the trek.

Before long, Yan Jun returned from his phone call and made an "okay" gesture, surprising his roommates. Perhaps, with the situation having no ideal solution, Yan Jun understood that grumbling wouldn't help anything and didn't want to inconvenience everyone. "It's okay," he reassured them. "It's not Xiao-Qi's first time spending the night at the childcare center. I'll video call her later."

Huo Sichen stood by and listened silently, letting them discuss the arrangements between themselves. Zhang Yuwen turned to him. "What about you?"

"I'm cool with it," Huo Sichen said.

"Then let's stay for the night," Chen Hong said decisively. "We can play cards and chat."

That their hiking trip had taken an unexpected detour into an overnight stay wasn't that bad, all things considered. Chen Hong, who'd been screwed by fate more than his fair share of times, had developed the habit of giving in and enjoying the moment. At his words, the others gradually cheered up.

"In that case, we'll join the queue," said Zhang Yuwen. "You guys go on ahead and find a place to rest and get a cup of hot milk tea."

"Sure," Chang Jinxing agreed readily. "*You guys* go queue up; *us guys* will take a break. That's settled, then!" Zhang Yuwen threw him a menacing look at this blatant bit of teasing.

Huo Sichen and Zhang Yuwen collected everyone's IDs and went to join the queue. There weren't many people ahead of them, and their turn came quickly.

"You really have nothing on at night?" Zhang Yuwen asked as he accepted the hotel room cards and meal vouchers.

"Actually, I do," Huo Sichen said, "but it's nothing important. Can I share a room with you, though?"

Zhang Yuwen laughed and shot him a quizzical look, but when Huo Sichen made a "phone call" gesture, he understood.

Zheng Weize was resting in the visitors' cafeteria, all bundled up in Yan Jun's jacket, while Yan Jun himself stood by the railing and looked down at the scenery below.

Zhang Yuwen asked the obvious question: "How are we sharing the rooms?"

Just as he expected, Chang Jinxing and Zheng Weize took one room while Yan Jun and Chen Hong shared another. "Brace yourselves," Zhang Yuwen reminded them. "The accommodations up here won't be great."

They had three adjacent rooms, each with a large double bed. Zheng Weize, perking up at the prospect of sharing a bed with Chang Jinxing, started fussing about the state of the room. Once they'd agreed on a time for dinner, he closed the door.

"Have you stayed here before?" Huo Sichen asked.

"Yup, with my ex." Zhang Yuwen touched the bed—it was icy cold. Since there was only one large bed, he'd have to sleep with this straight guy. He took off his jacket.

"You should keep it on," said Huo Sichen. "It's not very warm in here." He looked around and turned on the TV, but the picture wasn't clear, so he turned it off again.

"You can watch TV if you want." Zhang Yuwen wanted to change his clothes, but he hadn't brought an extra set with him. Fortunately, the hotel had toiletries.

"It's just my ADHD. I always have to check out everything I come across." Huo Sichen fiddled with the air conditioner's remote control but couldn't get any warm air out of it. Then he asked, "What's that?"

There was a rusty heater set into the wall at a corner. If Huo Sichen hadn't asked about it, they would have never found it. Like a wallflower at a party, it hid in a secluded corner, occasionally trying to liven up the atmosphere. Zhang Yuwen went over and touched it. "It's even colder than I am."

Once they'd examined all the room's amenities, they sat side by side on the bed, the mood becoming a little awkward. Their phones were running low on battery, so they had to take turns charging, but with one of them unable to use their phone, it would have been rude for the other to take out his.

Zhang Yuwen went over and parted the curtains, revealing floor-to-ceiling windows that offered a view to the bottom of the mountain. "Wow!"

"Is it snowing?" Huo Sichen stood behind Zhang Yuwen as they gazed through the unobstructed glass window.

"Looks like it." As Zhang Yuwen watched, the sky outside grew darker and darker until all he could see was Huo Sichen's reflection on the glass. Their eyes met in the reflection, and they shared a smile.

"Yuwen! Sichen!" Chen Hong knocked on the door. "Dinnertime!"

"Coming," Zhang Yuwen replied.

"We need to ask for another blanket," Huo Sichen reminded him.

It was one thing to share a bed with Huo Sichen, but sharing a blanket would have been really weird. Zhang Yuwen went to the front desk to ask for another blanket, then waited for the other guys to assemble.

When he arrived, Zheng Weize looked so listless that Zhang Yuwen touched his forehead, concerned that he had fallen ill. "You okay?"

Chang Jinxing answered for him. "He's hungry. He'll be fine once he's eaten."

For dinner, the visitors' center provided individual self-serve hot pot. But there were so many visitors and families dispersed throughout the place that the seating arrangements were a mess, and it was impossible for the six of them to sit together. Spotting a single empty seat, Zhang Yuwen gave the others the paired seats. "I don't care. I'm hungry too. I'm taking this seat." Off they went to find their own seats.

Zhang Yuwen glanced at Huo Sichen, who was looking at his phone as he ate at a table a short distance away. Chen Hong, Chang Jinxing, Yan Jun, and Zheng Weize had better luck and managed to get four seats together.

Zhang Yuwen went to get his food and returned to find that the person beside him had left, and Yan Jun shifted into the seat next to him. Zhang Yuwen shot him an inquisitive look.

"I don't want to be the third wheel, so I brought my pot over here," Yan Jun explained. "And Chen Hong keeps nagging about how this isn't healthy or that has too many calories." Zhang Yuwen laughed, and Yan Jun asked, "What do you want to eat? I can get some meat for you, if you want."

"No, thanks. This meat is tougher than my great-aunt."

Yan Jun roared with sudden, exaggerated laughter. Not far away, Huo Sichen glanced at them.

Yan Jun started a video call to Xiao-Qi, who was drinking milk but paused when she saw Yan Jun. "Pa-pa!"

"Look who's here!" Yan Jun turned the camera to Zhang Yuwen.

Xiao-Qi still hadn't learned to address anyone other than Yan Jun, but she recognized Zhang Yuwen and smiled at him. Yan Jun spoke to the caregiver at the childcare center next. They were already starting to put Xiao-Qi to bed, so Yan Jun disconnected the call.

"That must have added to their workload," Zhang Yuwen remarked.

"They have full-time childcare services in case the parents have an emergency to attend to," Yan Jun said. "I just have to pay for the additional service when it happens. I can't do this all the time, though."

"Yeah…" Zhang Yuwen felt for Xiao-Qi, but staying with Yan Jun was so much better for her than being sent to an orphanage. Yan Jun was doing everything he could to give her all the love he had to offer. Zhang Yuwen knew Yan Jun thought the same, so he offered him some comfort. "You need to have your own life too, even if you only carve out little bits of it. You have to be in a good frame of mind to care for her. Her emotions depend on yours."

"Yup, I've noticed that too," said Yan Jun. "I can't take good care of her unless I take good care of myself."

Yan Jun had sweated a lot during their hike, and he smelled slightly, but not unpleasantly, of sweat tinged with the aggressive testosterone unique to athletic men. It reminded Zhang Yuwen of the flip he did earlier. "Did you specialize in sports in school?" he asked.

"Not exactly. I trained in high jump for a couple of years, but then my father passed away. So instead of going to university, I followed in my brother's footsteps and joined the workforce," Yan Jun explained. Zhang Yuwen nodded. "What about you? You've never mentioned your parents."

"They're divorced, and they have their own families now. My grandparents raised me, but they passed away while I was still in school."

Yan Jun hummed in acknowledgment and picked out some food for Zhang Yuwen, who ate it.

"What did your grandparents do?" Yan Jun asked.

"They were doctors."

"Sorry, should I not have—"

"No, no," Zhang Yuwen said, amused. "I've already eaten it, see? Let me get you some vegetables."

"I know children from doctor families are..." Yan Jun trailed off.

"Not me," Zhang Yuwen assured him. Zhang Yuwen knew what Yan Jun wanted to say. It was true he rarely ate from someone else's bowl; he grew up in a household fastidious about cleanliness, after all, and they never ate food that had been in contact with someone else's utensils. Teasingly, Zhang Yuwen said, "The hot pot would have killed the germs anyway, and prohibiting the sharing of food has no real significance other than psychological reassurance."

Yan Jun laughed, with a look on his face like a shy high schooler's.

"No wonder you and Chen Hong have so much to talk about," Zhang Yuwen added.

"Yeah." Yan Jun reverted to his usual serious expression. "He's a jock too, so we get along well."

That wasn't all: Another thing Yan Jun and Chen Hong had in common was that they were more mature than the others, having firsthand experience of the hardship of making a living in this society. They could act as each other's dumping ground for negative energy, and also encourage each other from time to time.

"I guess I must come across as a boring person," Yan Jun said.

Huo Sichen came over, and they both looked up at him. "I'm done eating," he told them. "I'll go back to my room first."

Zhang Yuwen was a little embarrassed about having left Huo Sichen to eat alone. "I'm almost done too."

"No, no," Huo Sichen said hurriedly. "It's fine. Take your time." Yan Jun waved goodbye to him, and Huo Sichen patted them both on the shoulders before leaving.

"You just don't like to talk," Zhang Yuwen said, picking up the thread of their conversation. "But you're a very gentle person once people get to know you better."

"I'm boring. You don't need to reassure me."

Zhang Yuwen could tell that Yan Jun wanted to fit in with them, to joke around without holding back and burst into hearty laughter with everyone else, but he just couldn't find the right way into the conversation. Talking about work was dull and wouldn't resonate with anyone, and Xiao-Qi... Well, it would be better not to overdo it. Everyone liked Xiao-Qi, but they didn't necessarily want to listen to Yan Jun monologue about the art of parenting.

Yan Jun rarely paid attention to the pop culture the rest of them were into, and when it came to joking, he just didn't have Zhang Yuwen's comedic timing, and things sometimes ended in awkward silence. But Zhang Yuwen could tell from the flip Yan Jun did earlier that he wanted to have fun with them.

"You're very cool," Zhang Yuwen said softly. "You know? Cool guys are very attractive. When I was a kid, I tried to act cool by not talking for several days..."

"And?"

"And then I was taken to the psychiatric ward for evaluation and ended up getting a beating."

Yan Jun didn't quite know what to say.

"Let's go see the snow," Zhang Yuwen suggested.

Having eaten their fill, they put on their jackets and went to the platform at the top of the mountain to take in the snowy view. Outside, the cold wind howled. It was really freezing out there.

"Are you cold?" Yan Jun asked.

Zhang Yuwen waved his hand. In truth, he was shivering from the chill, but it was bearable. Sleet swirled in the sky, the snowflakes yet to fully form. At the side of the platform was a wide—and slippery—marble surface.

A thin layer of ice had formed on the ground. "You can ice skate here," Zhang Yuwen said. He stepped onto it and made a skating motion, and Yan Jun followed close behind him. "Be careful," Zhang Yuwen said, but just as the words left his mouth, he slipped.

Yan Jun reached out to pull him up, but he was dragged down with Zhang Yuwen instead. Panicking, Zhang Yuwen tried to get up, and he ended up tripping Yan Jun a second time in the process.

The others came outside. "Are you guys wrestling?" Zheng Weize asked.

"Stop taking photos!" Zhang Yuwen was mortified with all the visitors watching him, yet there Chang Jinxing was, snapping away.

"Why do you always have your camera?" asked Yan Jun.

"I thought it was Huo Sichen," Chen Hong said from his position off to the side.

Everyone was taking in the sorry sight they made, but no one came over to help. "Give us a hand, here!" Zhang Yuwen pleaded.

At last, Yan Jun had almost made it to the steps... Then he slipped into a split, startling everyone for a moment. Then they broke into applause. Yan Jun was speechless.

"Wow!" Zhang Yuwen blurted out. "You're so flexible!"

Finally, reaching the edge of the ice, Yan Jun said, "Let's go back! It's too slippery here." He half carried, half dragged Zhang Yuwen to safety.

With his pants and jacket soaked through, Zhang Yuwen fled to his room. He slipped and almost fell again as he went, eliciting another round of laughter.

Back in the room, the extra blanket had already been delivered, and Huo Sichen was on a call. He glanced at Zhang Yuwen, who made a beeline for the bathroom to take a shower. Vaguely, Zhang Yuwen heard Huo Sichen saying, "The cable car won't resume operation until tomorrow morning... Yeah."

Probably explaining where he is to his girlfriend, Zhang Yuwen thought as he showered. *Brrrr, the water's freezing!*

It was so cold, in fact, that his teeth were chattering when he got out of the shower. He put his wet pants, jacket, and T-shirt on the miserable heater, which now had to shoulder more than it could take. Then he got into bed, wrapped himself in his blanket, and continued shivering.

Huo Sichen disconnected the call. Zhang Yuwen blurted out, "It's really too cold!"

"Put this on." Huo Sichen removed his jacket and handed it to him, before going to take a shower of his own.

"No, no. No need..." Zhang Yuwen said. "Oh, well, if you insist. This feels so much better."

He was naked apart from his underwear, but the jacket still retained some of Huo Sichen's body heat, which was better than nothing and gave him some warmth in the freezing night. It even smelled a little like Huo Sichen.

The winter night was so frigid that even the straight guy couldn't help but wail. "Brrrr! So cold!"

After his shower, Huo Sichen put on a T-shirt, which was one layer more than what Zhang Yuwen was wearing. He tossed his pants aside and, just as Zhang Yuwen had done earlier, jumped into bed.

Zhang Yuwen was just starting to feel warm and, fearing that Huo Sichen would fight him for his blanket, he quickly motioned for Huo Sichen to use his own. "That blanket's yours!"

They huddled under their respective blankets and traded blank looks.

Meanwhile, in another room, the actual sports jocks were very calm. Chen Hong had showered and was watching TV when Yan Jun came over, drying his hair.

"Aren't you going to video call Xiao-Qi?" Chen Hong asked.

"I did," Yan Jun said. "She's in bed already." Then he sat on the bed to watch TV with Chen Hong.

Chen Hong offered him the remote control. Yan Jun took it and surfed through a few channels before settling on a dating show. It was the kind of wacky entertainment show meant purely for killing time, and it was pretty attention-grabbing, so they each wrapped themselves in a blanket and leaned back against the headboard to watch.

In the third room, Zheng Weize had his eyes on Chang Jinxing's phone, which was plugged into the charger and kept lighting up with notification alerts. He wanted to ask who kept messaging him, but it wasn't his place. Instead, he said, "Do you have something important going on?"

"Nah, just friends," Chang Jinxing said dismissively.

"Oh?"

Zheng Weize tried to peek at his phone out of curiosity, but Chang Jinxing closed the chat screen, placed the phone on the bedside table, and patted him on the head. "Aren't you going to sleep? I thought you were tired."

Chang Jinxing had recently found a way to make money—by working as a personal photographer and acting as a temporary boyfriend for others online. In other words, still playing the eunuch. He rented himself out to girls, going shopping with them, carrying their bags, dining and chatting with them, and even helping them scout for places to take pretty photos they could post on social media. He earned a daily fee, and if he served them well, they'd even tip him. Apart from kissing and sex, Chang Jinxing would fulfill almost any of their requests, although, to avoid gossip, he drew the line at appearing in their photos. Occasionally, he would hold their hands as a little treat.

This business brought him quick cash, and it was easier than taking on a job from the studio. And he was less likely to be humiliated out of left field, too. After all, he was attractive, and even if customers had complaints about him, they tended to let it slide because of his good looks. He had repeat customers, too. One girl had purchased his services three times in a row, hoping to flirt with him and start a relationship.

It couldn't be helped; he was too handsome. People tripped over themselves to fork out money for that face.

After a week with these girls, though, Chang Jinxing was a little fed up with it. To a bisexual, dating different genders was like eating different meals. Too much Western fare and you'd miss home-cooked food, but too much Chinese cuisine and you'd want to try steak. Right now, he just wanted to date a guy.

He hadn't taken a job today, and several customers were asking him if he had time tomorrow or next week and if he had plans for Christmas. Chang Jinxing thought that maybe his roommates would have something planned for the holiday. He wanted to join them—it'd be relaxing and enjoyable—but he was a little reluctant to miss the chance to make money. He'd already made enough money over the past half month for the first month's rent. If he kept working hard until the end of the year, he'd be able to cover his rent and food expenses.

Having tried several alternatives, Chang Jinxing concluded that living off women was the fastest way to make money, though he viewed his current job as using his physical stamina and skills to take photos for his customers. He didn't want a relationship with them; after all, if he started dating one of them, he'd have to face a never-ending stream of requests. He wanted a boyfriend with the personality of a straight guy; someone straightforward like Yan Jun who didn't talk much, wasn't argumentative, and wouldn't try to control him.

But Yan Jun didn't meet Chang Jinxing's standards either in looks or finances, and he came with excess baggage—a troublesome combination. The only thing that met Chang Jinxing's expectations was his physique. From the looks of it, he probably had good stamina and a decently sized cock...but Chang Jinxing wouldn't consider anything but a hookup.

Better not get involved with the roommates, Chang Jinxing reflected. Even casual sex could make things awkward. But the truth was, he'd really felt tempted to do just that when he saw Yan Jun do that flip earlier.

Zheng Weize hugged Chang Jinxing from behind, interrupting his thoughts. Chang Jinxing turned slightly, wrapped his arms around him, and patted him, telling him to sleep peacefully. He knew Zheng Weize had feelings for him. If he were to pull Zheng Weize's pants down now, the guy might put on a slight show of resistance, but he'd accept. It had been a long time since Chang Jinxing had sex with a guy. The powerful thrusts of a top and the sensitive moans of a bottom were both very seductive to him. The fair, delicate bodies of skinny boys had their own charm compared to the firm breasts of voluptuous girls.

Aside from the muscular Chen Hong, Chang Jinxing found his roommates decently attractive. Zhang Yuwen's ascetic top vibe appealed to him, and Zheng Weize's tendency to wrap his arms around his neck and blow into his ear could make him hard too. In any case, Chang Jinxing wasn't a picky eater. The only thing holding him back from making a move was Zhang Yuwen's warning: *Don't mess with your roommates, or I'll kick you out.*

Chang Jinxing let Zheng Weize hug him as much as he liked. He was so tired that all he could do was lie on his side and play with his phone.

In another room, Chen Hong was again playing the role of a caring older brother. "You can't go on like this."

Yan Jun knew what he meant. "What else can I do? Are you going to introduce me to someone?"

Playing matchmaker for Yan Jun had indeed crossed Chen Hong's mind, but this time he was serious about it; he wasn't angling for a matchmaker fee. Yan Jun was a good guy. Chen Hong believed that, with time, he could overcome his difficult circumstances.

"I couldn't do what you're doing, in your shoes," said Chen Hong.

Yan Jun thought about it. "Yes, you could," he said calmly.

Then Chen Hong threw him a curveball. "Do you like the sub-landlord?"

The color drained from Yan Jun's face. Flustered, he jumped out of bed and gestured frantically, reminding him that Zhang Yuwen was right next door!

"They're across the hall," Chen Hong said. "Xiao-Ze and Jinxing are the ones next door."

Yan Jun breathed a sigh of relief and returned to bed, no longer in the mood to watch TV. After a while, he glanced at Chen Hong, feeling caught out. "No," he said flatly.

Chen Hong only smiled.

"Really," Yan Jun insisted, his tone serious. "Hong-ge, please don't talk nonsense. It's awkward."

"I guess I must have been mistaken."

Yan Jun sighed. "Maybe you misunderstood because of the way I act? I'm really not interested in him."

"I know," said Chen Hong. "You just feel like he understands you, so you can't help but want to get close to him."

Yan Jun's complicated feelings showed on his face. How did he feel about Zhang Yuwen? He felt relaxed with him, like a weary person who had been healed.

"What's your type?" Chen Hong asked. "I'll look around for you."

Yan Jun thought for a moment. "On the mature side—his personality, I mean, not his age. Someone who can accept Xiao-Qi. After all, she's the most important person in my life. He has to be willing to help me take care of her. Hm... Preferably someone who's not too busy with work. I can be the breadwinner. It's like the traditional family. You know?"

"Why don't you find a girl?" Chen Hong asked. "You can date women, right? I feel like you're more bisexual than Chang Jinxing."

"I could, but I don't want to."

"Huh?"

Reverting to a heterosexual lifestyle, getting married, and starting a family seemed like it would be the ideal course of action for Yan Jun.

"If I marry a girl, we might end up having a child, which would divide up the love we shower on Xiao-Qi. It hasn't been easy for her, so I don't want... The way it is now is just fine."

"What made you realize you were gay?" Chen Hong asked.

"My desk mate in high school," Yan Jun said. "You?"

"A client," Chen Hong replied.

A few short words, but a sea of heartache.

"In short," Yan Jun said, "he has to be truly willing to accept Xiao-Qi. Everything else is negotiable. I like people who read and people with white-collar jobs. Fair-skinned, too."

"All the better if it's fair with cool undertones," Chen Hong quipped.

"I have dark skin," Yan Jun said, "so I like people who are fair and handsome. Ideally with a sensitive body, the kind who would get hard with just a touch of the nipples..."

"Which part gets hard? The nipples or the little buddy down there?"

"Both. And my spouse and daughter can rely on me. I don't mind. I'm willing to earn money to support my family and give it all to them."

"You aren't that dark, actually," said Chen Hong. "That's a healthy skin tone."

"The muscles shouldn't be too obvious," Yan Jun went on. "Yeah, no musclemen."

"What did muscles ever do to you?!" Chen Hong exclaimed, slighted.

Yan Jun laughed and grabbed Chen Hong's pecs. Chen Hong held him down and tried to pull his pants off, but Yan Jun fended him off. They struggled briefly before Chen Hong realized that Yan Jun was stronger than he looked and might actually overpower him, so he wisely withdrew.

"A guy who's gentle but resilient. Like a designer, writer, cartoonist, pianist... Someone who's intelligent, sensitive, and creative." Yan Jun knew that a guy like that was out of his league. "I have absolutely no resistance against people like that, but of course they wouldn't be interested in me."

"Don't be so sure. As long as your hardware is impressive enough, you can still make it impossible for them to leave you." Yan Jun laughed, and Chen Hong thought it over and added, "But doesn't that still make the sub-landlord the ideal guy? He's refined, good-tempered, emotionally stable, educated, and he has lots of time on his hands. Yeah, his salary is a little low, but you guys can work hard together."

Yan Jun was taken aback.

"Go after him if he suits you," Chen Hong said. "Why limit yourself? If you manage to woo him, maybe you can even persuade him to lower our rent."

Yan Jun remained silent.

"I'm going to take a shower," Chen Hong said.

Yan Jun, remote in hand, channel surfed until Chen Hong returned from the bathroom. Having thought about it for a while, Yan Jun said, "You know, Yuwen and I... I've contributed nothing from my end. Never had the opportunity to. All this time, he's been the one helping me."

Chen Hong understood, and he couldn't argue. Yan Jun had nothing to offer Zhang Yuwen, who lacked for nothing. Zhang Yuwen was emotionally resilient and financially independent. Worse, they were both tops.

Love was a two-way street. Both parties needed to possess that spark to make each other happy; that was the only way the relationship would last. Having been on the receiving end financially in his own past relationship, Chen Hong understood Yan Jun's feelings all too well. Thinking of his own past made him sad, and he fell silent too.

"Huo Sichen would be suitable for Yuwen if he weren't straight," said Yan Jun. "They're well-matched."

Chen Hong sighed. "Let's go to sleep. We're just rambling on meaninglessly."

In the room across the hall, Zhang Yuwen and Huo Sichen were like a pair of grandpas with their sleeping habits. By ten, they were both sleepy. However, the room was still cold, perhaps because of the direction it faced. It felt to Zhang Yuwen like the window was letting in a chilly draft.

"Let's put these two blankets together and cover ourselves with them," Huo Sichen suggested.

"Okay."

Zhang Yuwen was so tired he could barely open his eyes. Huo Sichen arranged the blankets, and they huddled underneath them. Zhang Yuwen felt much better. Their bodies were both warm, but the thin blankets had been making them lose heat; now, it was finally warm. Zhang Yuwen fell asleep just as Huo Sichen plugged his phone into the charger.

A few minutes later, Huo Sichen yawned and said, "Yuwen?" Receiving no response, Huo Sichen fell asleep too.

Zhang Yuwen slept restlessly. At home, he liked to sleep hugging a bolster, so when the temperature dropped further during the night he instinctively hugged Huo Sichen, taking him as his bolster and thinking he was still at home. He was naked, save for his underwear, and when he turned over to hug Huo Sichen, his thigh pressed against a particular part of Huo Sichen's body. Several times, Huo Sichen woke up and struggled to shift his waist so that Zhang Yuwen wouldn't rub against or press down on his stiff little friend.

Out in the winter night, the rain gradually turned to snow. It fell harder and heavier, fluttering and swirling down all over the mountain forest.

Riverbay Road
MEN'S DORMITORY

CHAPTER 15

MORNING CAME.

Huo Sichen woke from the cold night with one arm around Zhang Yuwen, Zhang Yuwen's legs around him, and both of them, naturally, sporting morning wood.

In another room, Zheng Weize opened his eyes to find himself alone, though the bedding was still warm from Chang Jinxing's body. It had gotten colder in the night, so they, too, stacked their blankets and slept together under them. When Zheng Weize woke once, around dawn, Chang Jinxing was sound asleep. Pretending to be asleep too, he'd snuggled into Chang Jinxing's arms, feeling bliss like he'd never felt before.

Yan Jun and Chen Hong, meanwhile, didn't feel the cold at all. They slept separately and didn't even combine their blankets. Yan Jun got up early in the morning to brush his teeth and get dressed, then went to knock on his roommates' doors.

"You guys up?" Yan Jun asked.

Still relishing the last bit of Chang Jinxing's warmth, Zheng Weize rubbed his eyes and yawned.

Yan Jun knocked on Zhang Yuwen's door next. Huo Sichen almost jumped out of bed, gripped by an unaccountable sense that he'd been caught red-handed. "Who's there?" he asked warily.

"Me," said Yan Jun. Huo Sichen rolled out of bed, put on his pants, and went to open the door, his hair still a mess. "Still sleeping?" Yan Jun asked. "Get up. Why's your room so cold?"

"I don't know," Huo Sichen said. "Yours isn't?"

Bleary with sleep, Zhang Yuwen sat up in bed, hugging the blanket like a child who had just woken. After a moment of eye contact with Yan Jun, he plopped back down.

Yan Jun checked the windows. "You guys didn't close the ventilation window!"

Huo Sichen was lost for words. There was a ventilation window at the top corner of the floor-to-ceiling window that they hadn't noticed. Cold wind had kept gushing into the room all night. Yan Jun closed the window for them, and the temperature indoors finally began to rise.

Zhang Yuwen came fully awake. Seeing Yan Jun lying beside him, playing with his phone, he asked quizzically, "Did you sleep here last night?"

"Yeah," Yan Jun said, a smile quirking his lips.

Baffled, Zhang Yuwen's mind flooded with questions. He couldn't comprehend how the person sleeping beside him had gone from Huo Sichen to Yan Jun. Seeing Huo Sichen walk out of the bathroom after washing up only mystified him further. "The three of us slept together?" he asked, bewildered.

"Yup," said Yan Jun.

"Yeah," Huo Sichen chimed in. "You slept in the middle."

Zhang Yuwen didn't know what to say.

Zheng Weize, meanwhile, was searching for Chang Jinxing room by room.

"He's downstairs taking pictures," Chen Hong told him. "Are you done packing? If so, let's go."

Everyone went down and gathered outside the mountaintop platform. "Wow!" they exclaimed in unison.

Fate had brought them together to see the first snow on Elephant Gorge—a rare experience. After all, no one knew when the first winter snow would fall, and to happen to stay overnight on the mountaintop on that very night was serendipitous.

Chang Jinxing had gotten up early, and he was on the platform, snapping away. As the sun rose, its golden rays cast a gilded glow over the mountain's snow-covered pines. A few tourists were out enjoying the snow as well. Chang Jinxing found a perfect spot to set up his tripod and take a group photo of the guys standing in front of the railing.

A reporter from the TV station was there too, going around interviewing people and filming. When the cable car started running, the number of visitors swelled. Everyone finally managed to get tickets to return to the city.

The TV reporter interviewed them one by one. "Looking at this snowy landscape, are you happy?"

"No, I'm Yuwen." Zhang Yuwen covered his face with Huo Sichen's fanny pack, not wanting to be on camera.

After a night of heavy snow, they were all shivering and worn out as they got off the tour bus. It was just too cold.

"Are we getting breakfast?" Zheng Weize asked. "I'm so hungry! Hey!" He shook Chang Jinxing, who kept sniffling and looking at his camera.

"Okay, okay," Chang Jinxing said. "Let's go."

"I'll pass," said Huo Sichen. "I have to get home."

Zhang Yuwen laughed. "Due for a scolding for staying out all night, huh?"

Without responding to him, Huo Sichen forced a smile and said his goodbyes.

"The temperature dropped so suddenly," Chen Hong said. "It's freezing out here."

"I have to pick Xiao-Qi up," said Yan Jun.

"I'll go with you," Zhang Yuwen said, surprising Yan Jun.

But Chen Hong had an idea. "Let's all go together. We can grab breakfast on the way. It's nearby anyway."

They ate steaming hot porridge and fried dough sticks in a ground-level shop in the same building that housed the childcare center, and all of them felt much better after a hot meal. Then Yan Jun took them to the childcare center. Just as he'd said, there were a few children who had stayed overnight, with caregivers on rotating shifts looking after them.

When Xiao-Qi saw Yan Jun, she broke into aggrieved tears. Yan Jun was very busy, but it was rare that he had to leave Xiao-Qi in the childcare center overnight. She wasn't even a year old, and already she seemed to understand some things.

The others' hearts ached a little at this sight. But Yan Jun only had to pick her up, pat her, and say some comforting words, and Xiao-Qi stopped crying.

"Didn't I tell you?" Yan Jun let Xiao-Qi lie on his shoulder, gently soothing her. "Papa was stranded on the mountain, but I'm here now."

Xiao-Qi just hugged Yan Jun tightly around the neck and refused to let go.

"Stop taking photos already." Yan Jun didn't know what to do with Chang Jinxing. Even here he was trying to take a backlit narrative photo.

Under the beautiful sunlight of the early winter morning, the group strolled back to the warm and idyllic haven of No. 7 Riverbay Road. The moment they arrived, they each heaved a sigh of relief; they'd never realized just how wonderful a place home was.

"Home sweet home!" Zhang Yuwen said, heading directly to the kitchen to brew coffee.

"Oh, by the way, Yuwen." Chang Jinxing set down his camera and put an affectionate arm around Zhang Yuwen's shoulders. "I've got something good for you."

Chang Jinxing transferred the money, and Zhang Yuwen received the rent in full, minus the deposit. Chang Jinxing's luck had been good this past month; between his boyfriend-for-hire business and cash advances on his credit card, he'd gotten enough for the rent, although three months' rent was already his limit.

"So, you finally remembered?" Zhang Yuwen asked.

Chang Jinxing grinned, still trying to act cute even though he'd gotten away with it. "Heh heh heh. You didn't remind me, either. Want coffee? I'll make it." He took the coffee pot from Zhang Yuwen.

Zhang Yuwen glanced at Zheng Weize, who was returning to his room, and then back at Chang Jinxing, a warning look in his eyes. Chang Jinxing pretended not to notice and reached out to pinch Zhang Yuwen's face, and Zhang Yuwen promptly retaliated.

"Careful!" cried Chang Jinxing, who was holding the pot of boiling water. "Hot water!"

"Don't fool around if you want to be with him," said Zhang Yuwen.

"No idea what you're talking about," Chang Jinxing said. "Don't talk nonsense."

"You can't lead him on, either, even if there's nothing between you." Zheng Weize may not have had a great deal of emotional intelligence, but he was a kindhearted kid, and Zhang Yuwen didn't want to see him get hurt. Moreover, everyone in the house was on harmonious terms, and Zhang Yuwen didn't want that balance to be upset. "You hear me?" he told Chang Jinxing severely.

"Yes, sir!" Chang Jinxing replied loudly. He flashed Zhang Yuwen his handsome, innocent smile and looked him in the eye. "Then what if I want to date you, Yuwen-gege?"

Chang Jinxing was a few months younger than Zhang Yuwen, and the cute act he was playing left Zhang Yuwen defenseless against this flirt. Zhang Yuwen put his hands in his pockets and kicked at him. "Shoo, shoo, shoo."

He sat down and looked at Chang Jinxing's camera. Having made coffee, Chang Jinxing came to stand behind the sofa and leaned over to touch the camera, moving his handsome face close to Zhang Yuwen's.

"What a player." Zhang Yuwen was long used to these tricks. "Stop flirting. Your moves don't—work—on—me!"

Chang Jinxing burst out laughing. Zhang Yuwen put down the camera. Hearing some noise from Zheng Weize's room and not wanting to cause any misunderstandings, he took the coffee and stood up. "Thanks."

"I paid the rent," Chang Jinxing said. "Are you gonna give me a little reward?"

"I'll treat you to a meal sometime," Zhang Yuwen said.

"Just the two of us, or with everyone?" Chang Jinxing asked. Zhang Yuwen ignored him and walked away.

Chang Jinxing could be both endearing and exasperating. He always behaved so suggestively, and he would flirt and run, but no one could get mad at him because of his good looks. Zhang Yuwen wasn't bad himself, a solid seven out of ten if Chang Jinxing was an eight, so it wasn't like Chang Jinxing was out of his league.

He had no interest in Chang Jinxing, but he longed to be in love again. It had all started when he thought of his ex out of the blue during the hike yesterday, and it just got worse when he slept in the same bed as Huo Sichen. It had been a long time since he last shared a bed with someone else. Then, after they got home, Chang Jinxing's teasing seemed to awaken something inside Zhang Yuwen, and he suddenly wanted very much to be in a relationship.

He wanted someone to like, to pursue passionately and splurge on, to please and pamper without complaint. He wanted to be staring at his phone, waiting for messages that could come at any time, and to feel his spirits lift when they arrived. He wanted someone who would only have to say the word, and he would drop everything just to be with him.

He wanted to make love anywhere and everywhere, just like the time five years ago when he and his ex were head over heels for each other. He had banged his ex in the fire escape of the school building one spring night like they were two animals in heat. That was a sublime experience.

Zhang Yuwen heard Chang Jinxing leave again, so he took his laptop and went to the dining room to continue generating trash. But between the series of blows he'd been dealt and his current restlessness, he couldn't get a single word onto the page. Writing such bland words every day made Zhang Yuwen feel like a programmer clocking in on time, day in and day out, to create bugs. Flipping through his earlier chapters, he began to doubt himself. What kind of nonsense was this? It was like the shitty pile of legacy code in the Google–Android codebase.

He finally shut his laptop, deciding to give up.

"Hong-ge, I want to date," Zhang Yuwen said suddenly, startling Chen Hong and interrupting his lunch.

Thinking Zhang Yuwen had taken a fancy to him, Chen Hong was flattered. "What? You...you wanna..."

Zhang Yuwen ate his lunch, finding everything flavorless. His fledgling career was showing no progress either. Life was like a pool of stagnant water; he was repeating the same few things day after day. When he was eighty, he'd be buried with that pile of unfinished trash. Just the thought of it made him despair.

"Do you know anyone you can introduce me to?" Zhang Yuwen asked.

"Oh..." Comprehension dawned on Chen Hong. He sat at the dining table, looking suspiciously at Zhang Yuwen, who raised an inquiring eyebrow in return. Chen Hong couldn't resist teasing him. "You couldn't have fallen for that straight guy, could you?"

"Absolutely not!" Zhang Yuwen said reflexively.

When he met Chen Hong's eyes, though, something seemed to occur to him. It was a barely perceptible thought, one that had been floating around in his mind ever since he met Huo Sichen. Like a thread from a spiderweb fluttering in the wind, it was hard to spot.

"Maybe a little," Zhang Yuwen admitted reluctantly.

Chen Hong was stunned by his honesty but managed to maintain a nonchalant expression. "I knew it."

Zhang Yuwen still hadn't quite figured out his feelings yet—whether he wanted to fall in love or if he'd already fallen for a specific person. "You know anyone suitable?" he asked. "You have a lot of friends, right?" Of his four roommates, he knew Chen Hong had to have the most contacts.

"I'll look around for you."

"If I get together with someone you recommend, I'll waive your rent for a month."

Chen Hong sat bolt upright. He got up and hurried back to his room, grabbed a notebook, and returned with it to sit at attention. He had to take this seriously. "What's your type?"

"No specific type," Zhang Yuwen said. "Maybe tall and thin. Better if he's a bottom, but I don't mind if a vers wants to try switching. Hm... This time around, I want someone a little more mature. I don't mind if the top is the younger one."

"Oh, so you like a younger top? How about a golden retriever guy? The cute, innocent sweetheart type?"

"I'm not looking for someone to top me!" Zhang Yuwen corrected. "I'm the top! I'm the younger one!"

"Oh, I see," said Chen Hong. "So you want a mature guy."

"Yeah, guys who are mature are less likely to pick quarrels. Not too mature, though. I don't want anyone over forty. I'm looking for a spouse, not a sugar daddy. I'm all good as long as he has a stable job."

"Then Chang Jinxing is out. I heard he doesn't have a regular job."

"No roommates! What are you thinking?"

"Okay, then I'll voluntarily withdraw from the competition too," Chen Hong said. Zhang Yuwen blinked blankly at him. "What do you like for appearance? Like, any celebrity comparison?"

"Uh..." Zhang Yuwen had seen his fair share of celebrities, and some of them had faces that made him weak in the knees. Chen Hong posed a good question, though. What kind of guy did he like?

All that came to mind was his ex's gentle gaze, which was a bit reminiscent of his grandmother's. Perhaps because of his family background, Zhang Yuwen was inclined to choose a partner who shared some similarities with his maternal grandparents. After a simple reorganization of his thoughts, Zhang Yuwen realized the guys he liked fell into two broad categories: the gentle, caring, and understanding bottom, and the steadfast, optimistic, and assertive top.

The gentleness and thoughtfulness came from his grandmother, qualities that Zhang Yuwen also found in his ex. His ex had been thoughtful and understanding, at least when they first got together. On the other hand, steadfastness, shouldering family responsibilities, and giving everyone a sense of security were all qualities that his grandfather had. He was a doctor and a former surgeon. His hands were steady, and his emotions rarely fluctuated. He was like a mountain: reassuring and reliable. His grandfather often smiled, and he was optimistic about life.

Zhang Yuwen didn't explain that to Chen Hong, though. He just listed some qualities briefly. "A little gentler...and steady... Cancer. Right. I like Cancers."

"Okay, I got you," Chen Hong said. "Are you sure you wouldn't consider one of us? Yan Jun's a Cancer."

"If you suggest that again, the matchmaking fee will be halved."

Chen Hong got to his feet and left.

"**T**HIS STORY OF YOURS... How should I put it?"

On Tuesday, Zhang Yuwen returned to the publishing house for spiritual reform. Once again, the young, bespectacled deputy editor was assigned to him; he still had that sharp glint in his eyes.

Leaning against his desk with a cup of coffee in hand, the deputy editor somberly critiqued Zhang Yuwen. "Your story isn't interesting. That's it: uninteresting. Maybe you, too, find this story lackluster, bland, and lacking that"—he made a gesture like fireworks—"emotional intensity. Feelings that resonate with people. Maybe you find it boring yourself..."

Zhang Yuwen wanted to explain, but he decided to drop it.

"...Or maybe you find it interesting and think it's not all that bad," the deputy editor continued. "Either way, you're so disconnected from most of your readers that they can't relate to your writing. The storyteller narrates with gusto, but the listener finds it boring."

Zhang Yuwen humbly accepted his criticism.

"No offense, but you're single, right? You're not in a relationship?" the deputy editor asked.

"No," Zhang Yuwen answered numbly. It wasn't the first time the deputy editor had asked him this.

"So, when you write about feelings, you're conjuring them entirely from your imagination. Take, for example, this whole chapter of 20,000 words." The deputy editor circled a large section with a red pen. Zhang Yuwen rubbed his face and nodded earnestly, preparing himself for a serious discussion over this plot point. "It's completely unnecessary."

"All right," Zhang Yuwen said. "I'll reflect on it when I get back."

"Mundanity—that's the most pressing issue you need to address," the deputy editor said meaningfully.

Mundanity was an issue everyone had to address, not just Zhang Yuwen. Most people led uninteresting lives, toiling on like Sisyphus, day after day, year after year. The occasional fleeting moment of joy was but a mere reflection of dew on a tiny flower along the path where the boulder was being pushed uphill. When the sun rose, it would all vanish.

Zhang Yuwen reflected on himself. He thought he'd been living a fulfilling life, but at some point, that had started to change. Perhaps his one relationship had exhausted all his sense of romance and left him bland. He'd once hoped to travel the world with the person he loved, but now he was alone, and traveling was just aimless wandering. He couldn't dredge up any enthusiasm for it. Everyone had moments like this in their life. Games that had kept Zhang Yuwen up all night abruptly became boring, and drama series he was once hooked on now seemed meaningless. He didn't want to attend gatherings because it was too much trouble, and he didn't want to participate in activities because he was tired. He felt mired in a long period of listlessness.

Huo Sichen: *Hows ur day?*

Zhang Yuwen: *I showed the editor the manuscript. He called me bland, boring.*

Huo Sichen: *U r not boring at all. U hv an interesting soul.*

Zhang Yuwen: *I'm reflecting on myself. Maybe he's right. My life is bland, and the cause is my personality.*

Huo Sichen's status remained as "Typing..." for about three minutes before he sent his thoughts. *Mayb ur novel's got too many certainties. Bland is just another word for predictable. Everything's set in stone even b4 it happens.*

Zhang Yuwen suddenly saw the light. *Ur right, thx, I think it's bc theres no thrill, too few surprises in life.*

Huo Sichen: *So u gonna create something thrilling?*

Zhang Yuwen: *Nah. I'm not one for seeking thrill. Mayb there was a time I was, but now, nah. Hm...lemme think abt it.*

Zhang Yuwen was staring blankly at the computer when he heard the door open. It was Yan Jun—which, given the timing, took him by surprise, but he didn't pry. "Have you had lunch?" he asked.

"Yup." Yan Jun set down his bag and sat at the dining table. "I went to the market today and passed by Riverbay Road. I felt like slacking off, so I came back for a break."

"You're not dressed for the weather." It felt to Zhang Yuwen like Yan Jun was emanating cold air that he had brought in from outside. No matter how cold the weather was, Yan Jun always wore a sweater over a shirt with the collar turned up, complete with a long, black body-fitting trench coat, never a down jacket.

"It's fine." Yan Jun smiled and got up. "I'll make coffee."

Zhang Yuwen looked at his back. He seemed a little different today. "Did you learn to make coffee?" Zhang Yuwen asked.

"Yeah, Jinxing taught me. What did you do today? Working on your manuscript at home?"

"Yeah. I went to the publishing house."

"How's progress on the manuscript?"

Yan Jun made two mugs of coffee and placed them in front of Zhang Yuwen. Then he sat beside him and moved closer to put a hand on the back of his chair. Astounded, Zhang Yuwen laughed. "What did that playboy teach you?"

"Huh?" Yan Jun froze for a moment. "Playboy? Who?"

"Just kidding." Zhang Yuwen had a sneaking suspicion that Yan Jun had picked up bad habits from Chang Jinxing. The prospect of Yan Jun looking at his manuscript made him nervous and embarrassed, so he quickly closed the document, revealing the chat window with his conversation with Huo Sichen. He closed that one as well.

"Do you need any material?" Yan Jun thought for a moment. "I could share some of my experiences with you when I have the time."

"Sure, but I need time to organize what I already have first. I'll ask you again when I'm ready, okay?" Zhang Yuwen had been thinking about that "interesting" question, and when his eyes met Yan Jun's, a curious thought popped into his head. "You aren't Han Chinese, are you?"

"You can tell?" Yan Jun asked, surprised.

"Yeah." Zhang Yuwen hesitated. "You have some indigenous characteristics." The highland indigenous people had slightly deeper facial features and a higher nose bridge, and their skin tone was darker in comparison to the average Han Chinese person's.

"My father is indigenous," Yan Jun confirmed.

"Oh, no wonder. I thought you were a bit different when I first met you."

Yan Jun's hometown, Guangze County, had a large population of highland indigenous people. They intermarried with the Han Chinese, and their descendants possessed characteristics of both groups.

"So you're mixed-blood," said Zhang Yuwen.

"Pretty cool, isn't it?" Yan Jun laughed.

Zhang Yuwen laughed too. "You must be very good at singing."

"I'm okay, I guess? The highland people like singing and sports. I used to live by the sea, and they all loved singing. But I only spent a lot of time with them when I was studying in the countryside. Once I started high school, those cultural distinctions evaporated." Yan Jun held the coffee mug with his broad hands, looking lost in thought. "My brother was a wonderful singer when he was alive."

"My grandma was a good singer too," Zhang Yuwen said.

In a voice that was warm and magnetic, Yan Jun spoke about the time when he first came to Jiangdong City to find work. His first job was in telemarketing, where his voice proved to be an asset. In those days, he was poor, naive, and ignorant of the way society worked, but he was happy. He lived with his brother and sister-in-law and went to work every day with drive and enthusiasm, hoping for a better life.

Zhang Yuwen listened quietly without interrupting. When Yan Jun came to the car accident, they both fell silent. Just then, Yan Jun's alarm went off.

"I have to get back to work." Yan Jun cleared away the coffee mugs and went to wash them in the kitchen.

"Work hard," Zhang Yuwen said. He decided to spend the afternoon working hard, too, on his manuscript.

Zheng Weize arrived, having just woken up. He yawned. "Can I have a cup of coffee?"

"Sure." Zhang Yuwen got up. "I'll pour a mug for you."

Zhang Yuwen didn't know how to make coffee by hand, so he used the coffee machine to make two mugs and handed one to Zheng Weize. Zheng Weize was resting his head on the table, looking at his phone while keeping an eye on Chang Jinxing's movements, but Chang Jinxing never got out of bed. Zheng Weize finished his coffee and returned to his room.

Chang Jinxing finally woke up at 3 p.m., when he emerged to make coffee, including a mug for Zhang Yuwen.

"No, no. No thanks," Zhang Yuwen said. "I've already had two in a row."

Chang Jinxing's expression could only be described as heart-breaking. "You'll drink coffee someone else makes but not mine?"

He was so handsome... Zhang Yuwen had no choice. He added lots of sugar and milk to make short work of it.

Chang Jinxing leaned against Zhang Yuwen ingratiatingly. "Does your publishing house have any photography jobs?"

"Ran out of cash?" Zhang Yuwen asked.

Every day, Chang Jinxing straddled the line between riding women's coattails and standing on his own two feet. If he continued like this, he'd end up returning to his old ways. His clients' unrea-sonable demands were grating on his nerves, too. Even after the job was done, those rich ladies wanted him to keep chatting with them late into the night and sympathize with their sorrows about their husbands' infidelity. It irritated him that the only way to keep from offending his regulars was to serve as their emotional dump-ing ground, and he feared that the husbands would suspect they'd been cuckolded and come and beat him up. That would be one hell of a mess. He decided to cool it for a while and find another job to keep himself fed with.

"I'd like to build up some savings," he said.

"I'll ask around for you," said Zhang Yuwen.

Chang Jinxing snapped his fingers and went to change clothes. Then he went to the fridge, grabbed and pocketed Chen Hong's gym prep meal—a sandwich made with whole wheat bread—and left. Zhang Yuwen glanced at Zheng Weize's room and sighed inwardly.

Chen Hong returned just as Chang Jinxing left. He'd been out and about, giving his gym members private home lessons. It was so frigid outside he kept shivering as he lingered in the foyer, finishing up a phone call. Once he was done with his call, he entered the house. Seeing his tenants come and go daily, Zhang Yuwen felt like he was watching the ebb and flow of life.

Chen Hong had been too busy to eat, but now he returned, famished, to find the last bit of his spiritual comfort gone. "Where's my lunch?!" he howled.

"Jinxing took it," Zhang Yuwen told him. "There's leftover rice from my lunch. You can eat it with some sauce."

Chen Hong was too hungry to even care about carbs. He gobbled up a few mouthfuls and then went to make coffee.

Zhang Yuwen paled. "I really can't take any more," he said. "I already had three mugs of coffee."

But Chen Hong insisted on handing him a mug. "It's decaffeinated. I bought the beans separately." Zhang Yuwen was forced to accept it. Chen Hong continued, "I found you a suitable match. You wanna meet him?"

Zhang Yuwen whipped his head up. He hadn't expected Chen Hong to find someone so quickly, and he suddenly felt nervous. "What does he look like?"

"Uh, he's one of my clients," Chen Hong said vaguely. "He's a little shy and would rather not share his photo. I didn't give him your photo either. I just said that you...have lots in common."

"Huh? Not even a photo? Are you telling me to go in blind?" Zhang Yuwen asked. "Isn't that a bit much?"

"Well, it's important to have some excitement in your life."

A day ago, Zhang Yuwen might have disagreed, but now he was wondering if his life was too predictable. Maybe he did need a little thrill. "Then I'll add his contact for a chat."

"He's...also too shy to add you as a contact," Chen Hong said, shutting Zhang Yuwen up instantly. "Look on the bright side. If you meet and he's no good, you can just pick up and leave with no concerns whatsoever, right?"

"What the hell?!" Zhang Yuwen was torn between laughter and tears.

"He's willing to have a meal with you so you can have a conversation and get to know each other. If you guys think it's a good match, you can exchange contact info."

"How old is he?"

"In his twenties, the same as you," Chen Hong said. "Whether he's a top or bottom, I have no idea. I didn't ask."

"What type of guy is he? And how tall?"

Chen Hong shrugged. "All I can say is that he basically meets your requirements. No, actually, he's your ideal type, aside from not being a Cancer. You'll be satisfied with him. Whether or not he'll be satisfied, I can't say. After all, I know you better."

"Is he a lively and bubbly younger guy?" Zhang Yuwen asked. He could go with it. He didn't mind if they didn't get together in the end; a fling would be fun too.

Chen Hong changed the topic. "So, will you go? I promise I didn't tell him much about you, but he told me once that he likes your type." Zhang Yuwen gave him a skeptical look. "He's already made a reservation at this restaurant. You decide if you want to go or not. If not, I'll tell him to cancel it."

Chen Hong showed Zhang Yuwen a website on his phone. Zhang Yuwen had been to the restaurant before. It was pretty expensive. "At such an expensive place?" Zhang Yuwen asked, a little surprised.

"He said he'd treat you. You can drive the landlord's car."

Zhang Yuwen's car was a Bentley coupe. It was even more expensive than Huo Sichen's car, but he had told everyone that it was the landlord's property and that he only took it out for an occasional spin.

"Are you going to go?" Chen Hong asked again.

"You haven't told me anything about him!" Zhang Yuwen said. "I'm totally going in blind?"

"He's also going in blind. It's fair."

"Well, I guess I'll go, since he already made the reservation. Is he still in school?"

"I think he's working already. Seems like a young talent?" Chen Hong said. "I'll reply to him, then. It'll be on Wednesday—tomorrow night."

Filled with uncertainty, Zhang Yuwen agreed. This blind date was as nerve-wracking as the first time he joined a film crew and participated in a shoot. He hadn't felt this kind of thrill in years.

He couldn't help but imagine what his blind date might look like. He couldn't sleep after the four mugs of coffee he'd drunk in the afternoon, so he was tossing and turning in bed when it dawned on him: Maybe this was the "uncertainty" he had been seeking. But man, this was a bit too much excitement...

Oh! It was already five in the morning! Zhang Yuwen felt like going out for a run, but, like, seriously, did he really have to jump from extreme boredom to extreme excitement *so* abruptly?

Zhang Yuwen finally got up in the afternoon. His stomach was churning over his impending blind date, but he didn't plan to turn to his roommates for comfort. Wasn't this anxiety what he'd been looking for? Having finally captured that fleeting feeling, he sat down to put it to page, but when he opened his laptop and saw the mountain of trash that had accumulated over his days of work, he didn't know where to start.

Left with no choice, he opened another document to start a new story, writing in fits and starts. He couldn't focus, though, and his thoughts drifted to how he should present himself that coming night. A little more mature? Or younger? Some bottoms liked the gentle, cheery big brother type, but others preferred mature and steady tops...

Huh? Was it already four in the afternoon? Zhang Yuwen hadn't taken his lunch except for a mug of coffee, but he wasn't hungry. He got up and went to change his clothes, wondering if he should drive to the blind date. He wouldn't want to walk to the subway on such a cold day, and he didn't want to wear too many layers of clothes and end up looking bloated, either.

Chen Hong was back, taking off his shoes in the foyer. "Going out already?"

"Yeah," said Zhang Yuwen, unsurprised to find Chen Hong there. He'd heard the motorcycle earlier.

"Good luck." Chen Hong was very calm, as if he had no doubt that Zhang Yuwen would succeed, and his matchmaker fee was already in the bag.

"I didn't sleep last night," Zhang Yuwen said tiredly.

"Go now. Don't be late."

Zhang Yuwen lingered. He made one last attempt. "At least give me his number, in case something unexpected crops up."

"That won't happen," Chen Hong said. "Go, go. You can call me anytime."

Zhang Yuwen wore a casual linen suit. When he'd seen Huo Sichen dressed like this, he thought it looked cool, so he emulated the look and topped it off with a scarf. But all the crowding and jostling on the packed subway during peak hour messed up his carefully curated outfit and his hair, making him look like a tired office worker.

The closer he got to his destination, the more nervous he became. He remembered how amused he'd been to see his ex get flustered in front of him. He was used to being the dominant party in the relationship, even if one relationship was all the experience he had. How had he become the weaker one?

Maybe the other guy is nervous too? Zhang Yuwen thought, calming himself down a little.

He needed to talk to someone, or he couldn't relax. He thought it over, then sent a message to Huo Sichen. *I'm going on a blind date tdy.*

Huo Sichen: *?*

Zhang Yuwen took a selfie in the subway car and sent it to him.

So handsome, Huo Sichen said. When Zhang Yuwen started ranting about the literally blind date, he noted, *It's normal for Chen Hong not to tell u too much abt his clients.*

Zhang Yuwen: *He said they're my ideal type.*

Huo Sichen: *wats ur ideal type?*

Zhang Yuwen: *thats not impt. I was 2 nervous last night 2 sleep much.*

Huo Sichen: *u can do it.*

Zhang Yuwen: *wat if it doesnt work out?*

Huo Sichen: *Then u better sit down and finish the meal. Its such an expensive restaurant.*

Zhang Yuwen: *The other person's paying.*

Huo Sichen: *Rly? get me takeout while ur thr.*

Zhang Yuwen laughed despite himself.

Huo Sichen: *If u do end up tgt, I mean IF, will u introduce ur partner to me?*

Hesitating, Zhang Yuwen didn't reply immediately. He didn't quite understand what Huo Sichen meant by that and carefully thought it over. This "partner" would be a guy, and in introducing him, he would be essentially coming out to Huo Sichen. Could he do that? Maybe. A moment later, though, it dawned on him that this was Huo Sichen asking about their friendship.

Huo Sichen assumed Zhang Yuwen was straight. When a straight guy introduced his girlfriend to another straight male friend, it came at a risk. The grass was always greener on the other side, and introducing them might increase the odds of being cheated on.

Effectively, Huo Sichen was saying: *Zhang Yuwen, we're buddies, right?*

It was a little late by the time Zhang Yuwen worked this out, but he still replied candidly. *Ofc, we can hang out together. I swear I wont ditch u even if I'm dating.*

Huo Sichen didn't reply.

Zhang Yuwen exited the subway station and entered the bustling commercial district by the river. The area was full of upscale shopping malls and office buildings. The tallest building, Hengxin Tower, was a Jiangdong landmark. Impeccably dressed pedestrians thronged the streets, their spending limits off the charts. Lights illuminated the huge store facades of Hermès, LV, and Tiffany spanning three or four floors, making them look like crystals on a crown. Coming here felt like stepping into a futuristic movie, where skyscrapers intersected, and neon lights flashed through the night.

The restaurant his blind date had booked was on the 105th floor of Hengxin Tower. He had to go through a security check when he entered the building. Neon colors glittered on all sides of the lift as it carried him toward the faraway unknown, causing his nervousness to hit through the roof on his way up.

Zhang Yuwen stood before the restaurant reception counter. The waiting area was already packed with people. "Table forty-seven."

"Please follow me," said the handsome waiter, politely leading Zhang Yuwen inside. Zhang Yuwen's nerves reached a crescendo.

Across a quiet table for two in front of the floor-to-ceiling windows, he finally saw his blind date:

Huo Sichen.

Riverbay Road

MEN'S DORMITORY

CHAPTER
17

HUO SICHEN LEANED IN slightly. "So is this exciting enough for you?"

"Way too exciting," Zhang Yuwen replied. "I'm going to kick Chen Hong's ass when I get home." In just a few seconds, he'd gone from confusion, to shock, to a mix of anger and amusement as he pieced together what was happening.

Obviously, these two were in cahoots! And Huo Sichen wasn't a straight guy at all! There were no other explanations!

"It wasn't his idea," Huo Sichen said. "I told him not to tell you because I was nervous too, and I didn't know how to explain it to you...about this. Will you sit down? You aren't going to punch me in front of all these people, are you? I'll be blacklisted from the restaurant."

Zhang Yuwen sat down, and Huo Sichen breathed a sigh of relief. With the sly grin of a man whose evil plot had succeeded, he motioned for the waiter to come over and pour them some water.

"So," Zhang Yuwen said, "we're on a blind date?"

The waiter glanced at them. Huo Sichen's response came very naturally. "Yes. And an honor it is."

A tsunami of complaints swelled forth in Zhang Yuwen's heart, enough to sweep away Huo Sichen and the entire restaurant. "Give me a moment to calm down first." He drank some water and looked away to take in the restaurant's decor: the crystal chandeliers, the diners, and the pianist tinkling away on the piano, producing quiet music that added to the romantic ambiance.

Huo Sichen looked intently at the menu, then called the waiter to order. "We'll get the couple's set."

"Certainly, sir. Would you like some wine?"

"Go ahead," said Zhang Yuwen.

But Huo Sichen declined. "Not today. I need to stay sober to drive you home after dinner."

The waiter put in their order, then came back to light a candle that sat in a small glass on their table.

"A candle for you," Zhang Yuwen joked. "Rest in peace."

Huo Sichen smiled. He didn't retort.

Through the huge floor-to-ceiling window beside them, they could see a panoramic view of the city's dazzling nightscape, with its twinkling lights, ribbons of traffic, and luminous winter moonlight.

Finally calm, Zhang Yuwen sized his date up, his gaze aggressive and his thoughts written on his face as he rated Huo Sichen. First up, his appearance. They were both dressed fairly formally, especially Huo Sichen, who looked dashing and elite. In Zhang Yuwen's books, it was a pass.

Next up, his physique—i.e., his sex appeal. Zhang Yuwen had seen Huo Sichen's long legs when they stayed overnight on the mountain. He gave him a high score. Then there was his personality and character...

Zhang Yuwen curbed the fervor in his gaze and replaced it with his usual harmless smile. Huo Sichen felt certain that, in that half minute, he had been thoroughly catalogued and appraised.

"Should we go through the usual process?" Huo Sichen asked.

"Sure. On account of our intermediary."

It didn't take long for them to begin their usual back-and-forth banter. Huo Sichen made a "please" gesture to let Zhang Yuwen go first.

Zhang Yuwen used to write a lot of blind date scenes, which struck him as funny now that he thought about it. He laughed, then asked the classic question: "How much is your monthly parking fee?"

Huo Sichen laughed too. They couldn't stop laughing, and it made them look younger, like students. "I, uh, own my home," Huo Sichen replied. "A high-rise apartment at Franc Residences in Jiangbei. The parking came with the apartment."

"Oh, I see." Zhang Yuwen thought about it for a moment, then threw him another question. "What about mortgages?"

"There's still a twelve-year mortgage. Uh..."

"This is just standard blind date protocol."

"No objections from me," Huo Sichen assured him. "Ask away."

Zhang Yuwen grinned impishly. "You must have already gotten all the info on me from Chen Hong, anyway."

"No. I really haven't."

Zhang Yuwen looked at him skeptically but decided to believe him for the moment. Their appetizer arrived then, and they unfolded their napkins and set them on their laps.

Huo Sichen scooped some salad for Zhang Yuwen as he continued, "I work for a foreign trade company as the vice director. The boss is a friend of mine. I own a small number of shares in the company. Including my year-end bonus and share dividends, I take home an annual income of about five or six hundred thousand after taxes."

"Oh." Zhang Yuwen hadn't dealt with money for a very long time. After he achieved financial freedom, he'd lost touch with the salary benchmarks in various industries. All he knew was that a salary of

¥600,000 per year meant ¥50,000 a month, which fell within the range of a high-level executive.

"But I still have to pay off the mortgage." Huo Sichen started on the salad. "The car is paid off, though. How about you?"

Zhang Yuwen repeated what he'd told Huo Sichen previously. "I work at a publishing house. I just need to go in for half a day every week to pick up the manuscripts to proofread at home. I've been working on my own manuscript lately, and I hope to publish a book."

Echoing his own previous comment, Huo Sichen said, "That's very impressive." He looked at Zhang Yuwen expectantly, hoping he would volunteer more personal details about himself.

Zhang Yuwen thought it over and added, "My monthly salary is a little over six thousand, but with the year-end bonus, it's maybe around a hundred thousand."

"But you live in such an expensive house..." Huo Sichen trailed off.

"We aren't there yet," Zhang Yuwen said, displeased. "We haven't gone through the process, so how would you know where I live?"

"Oh, that's right. Yeah." Huo Sichen adopted a serious expression. "Where do you live?"

"No. 7 Riverbay Road," said Zhang Yuwen. Huo Sichen feigned shock, and Zhang Yuwen added, "I'm looking after the house for a friend."

Huo Sichen nodded.

"When my grandparents passed away, they left me a small shop in Jiangnan." Zhang Yuwen paused briefly. "I've rented it out."

"Collecting rent without lifting a finger. What an enviable position."

Even Zhang Yuwen was finding the routine funny. They fell silent again, and Huo Sichen gestured to him: Did he want a bite?

"I'm from Yuhai," Huo Sichen continued eventually. "I have an older brother named Huo Siting. He's two years older than me, and he lives in Los Angeles now. Our parents are quite old now, and they moved there to live with him. I did my undergraduate studies in California and returned to Jiangdong for grad school at Chonghan University of Finance and Economics. I majored in foreign trade."

"Oh." Zhang Yuwen nodded. "I majored in communication studies and graduated with a bachelor's degree. My grandparents raised me; my parents divorced when I was young."

"So your grandparents were practically parents to you," said Huo Sichen.

"I thought so. I've never felt like I was abandoned."

"Of course not! Folks from Yuhai tend to marry late, and many fathers have children in their fifties, so it's a lot like the relationship between a grandfather and his grandkids. The impression you give me is that of the youngest child in a large family."

Zhang Yuwen chuckled. "You think so too?" Zhang Yuwen had always felt like he had some personality flaws, but he wasn't sure if he should blame it on his divorced parents. The hardest thing for a person to know was themself, and even now, Zhang Yuwen still didn't fully understand himself.

"You have a great personality," Huo Sichen said earnestly. "Really!"

"Thanks."

The waiter cleared away the appetizers and soup and served the first course. "This restaurant is really expensive," Zhang Yuwen said.

"It's my first time here too," Huo Sichen admitted. "My bank account isn't crying yet; we should still eat more."

Zhang Yuwen cracked up, knowing that Huo Sichen was just joking with him. With his income, he could easily afford a place like this.

"Are we done with the process?" Huo Sichen asked.

"Let me think about it," said Zhang Yuwen.

"Can I ask a question?"

Zhang Yuwen looked at him. He seemed much more handsome than the first time they met. Maybe it was the lighting, or perhaps the effort he'd made to dress up today; Zhang Yuwen could tell he'd even gone to get a haircut.

"Why did you decide to come?" Huo Sichen asked.

"Because this restaurant is very expensive, and the other party is paying. It's always good to broaden my horizons."

They laughed again. Zhang Yuwen knew very well that Huo Sichen was sounding him out, but he didn't take the bait and kept deflecting Huo Sichen's questions with humor. Huo Sichen knew that he couldn't do anything about this.

But the next question was what Huo Sichen really wanted to ask. "If you'd known it was me beforehand, would you still have come?"

"Of course," Zhang Yuwen said. "A place like this, I'd come no matter who was treating."

Zhang Yuwen doubled over with laughter as Huo Sichen's face went red. No matter how many times Huo Sichen tried to feel him out, he could never get the serious answer he wanted. Instead, he'd revealed his own feelings for Zhang Yuwen and his intent to date him.

In truth, Huo Sichen's intentions had been exposed from the very moment he had Chen Hong set him up with Zhang Yuwen. There was a strange phenomenon that often existed in romantic relationships—whoever fell in love first lost. Huo Sichen had already lost the right to call the shots.

Zhang Yuwen didn't use it against him, though. He just said, "That's all for the formalities. Let's talk about something else. Is foreign trade tiring?"

"Easier than being a writer," said Huo Sichen. "But it's mentally exhausting with the economy going downhill these past few years, and the work environment is tough. I've been considering a career change recently."

Zhang Yuwen nodded. "I'm not very ambitious, so I can't really understand the work pressure other people deal with."

"Not struggling is the best kind of ambition."

As they joked with each other, a lithe woman in a black dress who'd just walked into the restaurant came over to greet Huo Sichen. "Hi, Mr. Huo, long time no see."

Huo Sichen looked surprised, not having expected to see an acquaintance here. He quickly put down the teapot he'd been pouring from and nodded at her. "Hello. It's been a while."

Zhang Yuwen glanced at the woman but didn't pry. The woman didn't linger and left after they exchanged a few pleasantries.

The main course arrived—a large steak. The waiter stood at the side and cut it for them.

"Why is his bigger?" Zhang Yuwen asked the waiter.

"Because I'm obviously the top," Huo Sichen said to Zhang Yuwen. "Tops have bigger appetites. Bottoms can fill their stomachs with just salad."

The waiter laughed so hard he could barely hold the knife steady.

The music in the restaurant turned into a lively saxophone melody. "Do you live alone?" Zhang Yuwen asked.

"Yeah," Huo Sichen replied. "Wanna come over to my place later for some fun?"

"What fun is there at your place?"

"I promise, everything at my place is fun. It all depends on what you wanna play."

Zhang Yuwen meant to ask him for game recommendations; he hadn't expected Huo Sichen to be such a consummate flirt. He wanted to ask Huo Sichen about his relationship history, like how many exes he had, but he held himself back. "You don't have pets?"

"Nope."

"I always thought you were straight."

The 180-degree turn in the topic came out of nowhere, but Huo Sichen steered skillfully around it. "That proves that you can be mistaken sometimes."

"I'm often mistaken, but I think you were definitely straight before."

"I'm not now, at least," Huo Sichen said. "What about you? I think you've always been gay."

"Yup. My ex and I broke up the year before last."

"Who's the lucky guy? Let me see if he looks like me."

"Not at all," Zhang Yuwen said. He scrolled through his phone for a photo to show Huo Sichen. Guys were usually pretty casual about discussing their exes. For a moment, while showing Huo Sichen the photo of his ex, Zhang Yuwen forgot he was on a blind date. He felt like he was just sharing with a friend.

"Indeed," Huo Sichen said.

Zhang Yuwen looked at Huo Sichen. "Shouldn't you reciprocate?"

"My ex was a woman. I don't think you'd be interested. And I've deleted all her photos anyway. I'll show you another day if I can find one."

There was Zhang Yuwen's answer. "Oh. Nah, keep it for yourself." He sized up Huo Sichen again. "You prefer women like the one who was here earlier?"

"She's my ex's best friend," Huo Sichen explained. "We've only met a few times."

"Oh." Zhang Yuwen nodded.

Huo Sichen's attention was still on Zhang Yuwen's past. "The boy in the photo—he's your type, right?"

"Yeah."

Dessert was served, a heart-shaped mousse with two spoons. Zhang Yuwen and Huo Sichen each dug into a side, mangling the heart.

"I remember you mentioning your ideal type earlier." Huo Sichen thought for a moment. "What's your ideal type like? Exactly like your ex?"

"Not exactly..." Zhang Yuwen was finding the mousse awfully sweet; he wasn't used to eating overly sweet stuff. "I don't have a fixed type, or rather, I have several. Like several sets, and if they overlap, even better."

Huo Sichen finally asked the question. "Am I in any of those sets?"

Zhang Yuwen sized him up again. "I guess? But I can tell you that someone like Chen Hong isn't in any of them."

"What? Repeat that first sentence?"

"I can tell you that someone like Chen Hong—"

"No, before that."

"You heard me."

"I didn't. Say it again?"

"I said, I guess!" Zhang Yuwen raised his voice a little.

Huo Sichen turned to the waiter. "Check, please!"

Surprisingly enough, Huo Sichen ordered takeout too. "For your roommates."

Zhang Yuwen accidentally glanced at the bill: ¥4,760—a month's rent. He was about to say something when Huo Sichen spoke up. "I get it now. You like two types of guys: the gentle, younger ones, and the mature, older ones. Both are your ideal types."

Huo Sichen had seen through him. "I guess that's it," Zhang Yuwen admitted.

"You also like guys who can act cute, right?" Huo Sichen asked as they entered the elevator. He was carrying the takeout bag.

"Yup." An idea occurred to him. "Act cute for me?"

"I don't know how to," Huo Sichen answered.

"What? How can you be gay if you don't even know how to act cute?"

"I can learn."

"Forget it."

They both burst out laughing simultaneously.

"So, tell me." Huo Sichen opened the passenger door when they came to the parking lot, placed the takeout bag inside, and gestured politely for Zhang Yuwen to get in. "What's your reason for putting me in that category?"

Zhang Yuwen buckled his seat belt. When Huo Sichen got in, he answered without hesitation. "You're rich."

At a loss for words, Huo Sichen drove the car out of the parking lot and took Zhang Yuwen home.

"You're rich, and I'm poor," Zhang Yuwen elaborated. "Freeloading off of you will allow me to improve my quality of life and widen my horizons."

Huo Sichen sang his praises highly. "Zhang Yuwen, you truly are a sincere person. Out of curiosity, can I ask if there's something you're lying to me about?"

"Of course there is," Zhang Yuwen replied. "What about you?"

"Me too." Huo Sichen kept his left hand on the steering wheel and waved his right hand to imply that it wasn't important.

"Mutual deception is one of life's little pleasures," said Zhang Yuwen. "I trust that you won't be angry."

"Of course not," said Huo Sichen. "But then again, what we consider important might not have the same significance to someone else."

"Absolutely," Zhang Yuwen agreed.

"So..." As they crossed the bridge, Huo Sichen finally asked his last question. "Do you think we...could give it a go? I mean, hang out together more frequently, and if it feels right, start dating?"

In a rare display of nerves, he glanced at Zhang Yuwen. The car stopped in front of No. 7 Riverbay Road.

Zhang Yuwen answered readily. "Sure, I'd love to, but don't pick such an expensive place next time. Now I need to hurry inside and beat up Chen Hong. I'll contact you again when I have time. Bye!"

"Don't forget the takeout." Huo Sichen handed him the food. "And don't swing the paper bag at him. It's not very sturdy."

Zhang Yuwen skipped to the entrance and leapt up midway to touch a leaf on the roadside tree. Huo Sichen whistled at him and drove away.

CHEN HONG WAS FACED with a dilemma.

He hadn't wanted to introduce Zhang Yuwen to Huo Sichen. He didn't want to see them develop a romantic relationship, either, especially when Huo Sichen was playing this exciting little romantic game—Chen Hong was certain that, provided Zhang Yuwen was amenable, the two of them would very quickly become a couple.

Chen Hong had really thought that Huo Sichen was straight. He didn't know why Huo Sichen had taken a sudden fancy to Zhang Yuwen. It came out of nowhere. Thinking back, the biggest change had come after their last mountain hike, when Huo Sichen suddenly booked a home training session with Chen Hong and asked if Chen Hong could reintroduce him to Zhang Yuwen.

"Why don't you just explain it to him yourself?" Chen Hong couldn't understand Huo Sichen's thought process at all.

"I can't bring myself to say it." Huo Sichen strained to speak as he did his final plank. "Just tell him you're introducing him to... a prospective match... Okay?"

Unable to hold on anymore, he rolled over and exhaled, perspiring profusely. He sat down to take a break.

"I'd like to reacquaint myself with him as a gay man," Huo Sichen explained expectantly, bewildering Chen Hong. Huo Sichen briefly outlined his plan. "Just do as I say."

"He'll get angry," Chen Hong said.

"He won't."

"Bro, do you like him? Have you turned gay?" Chen Hong hadn't talked much to him about their sexual orientations, but he knew Huo Sichen could probably tell from hanging out with them that they were all gay.

Huo Sichen glanced at Chen Hong, then averted his gaze with a hint of a shy smile. Grabbing a towel, he scurried away to mop up his sweat and shower. Chen Hong sat on the workout bench nearby and heaved a sigh.

"A-Chen." Chen Hong didn't care if Huo Sichen could hear it or not. "A piece of advice from me. This isn't an easy road to take."

If he had the choice, Chen Hong would prefer to be straight. Liking men inevitably made life a little harder.

Huo Sichen finished his shower quickly and emerged with a towel draped around his neck. He sat beside Chen Hong, fixated on the messages he was sending on his phone. Chen Hong glanced over and recognized Zhang Yuwen's profile picture.

"Right," Chen Hong said. "You're rich. It's not a problem." An elite like Huo Sichen probably didn't face the same challenges as he did.

"Then I'm counting on you," Huo Sichen said earnestly.

Now here Chen Hong was, dealing with a complex mix of emotions topped off with a twinge of jealousy. He'd thought he was more or less on the same level as Zhang Yuwen. To think that Huo Sichen would like him... Huo Sichen drove a luxury car, had a respectable job, and was courteous and manly. No matter how you sliced it, he was excellent husband material.

As Zhang Yuwen's friend, Chen Hong knew he shouldn't be jealous, and he still hoped Zhang Yuwen would find happiness. He didn't want his buddy to suffer; he just also envied his good fortune. Given a choice, he'd prefer to set Zhang Yuwen up with Yan Jun. As a friend, Chen Hong sympathized with Yan Jun, a young man with unwavering determination. Chen Hong quite liked him. In his opinion, Yan Jun and Zhang Yuwen were on the same social stratum and thus more compatible. Huo Sichen was in a different league, and he and Zhang Yuwen might not necessarily be happy together.

A worry nagged at Chen Hong, too: Huo Sichen wouldn't deceive Zhang Yuwen, would he? Chen Hong knew almost nothing about him beyond their trainer-trainee relationship. Huo Sichen rarely mentioned his job, his love life, or his family. He wasn't curious about other people's private lives, nor did he talk about his own. Their interactions were usually limited to the training sessions themselves. Because of that, Chen Hong didn't think that Huo Sichen saw him as a friend. Even when they did things together outdoors, be it hiking or playing laser tag, Huo Sichen hadn't acted chummy with him. Most of the time, he stayed close to Zhang Yuwen.

He couldn't be a playboy, could he? Or have some other character flaw?

Chen Hong pondered this, feeling like he had let Yan Jun down. He didn't want to offend Huo Sichen, though; he still needed to make money from him. After his gym closed down, a few major clients had become his primary source of income. He retained fewer than ten high-quality clients—wealthy gold-collar professionals with time to spare and the willingness to buy his training sessions. He just had to give them one class every week, and he'd earn enough to cover his basic living expenses instead of being reduced to sleeping under a bridge.

In the end, he resolved his dilemma by betraying Yan Jun.

Just as Huo Sichen predicted, after receiving a hammering from Zhang Yuwen, Chen Hong came to the realization that Zhang Yuwen also liked Huo Sichen. They had just been testing each other.

Those were the rules of adulthood: weigh the pros and cons, search for a reason, make plans, and draw deductions. Dating was less a revelry and more a cautious, cooperative advancement as each person tried to get what they needed—emotional value, economic strengths, social status, networking connections, and sex.

After his beating was complete, Chen Hong asked unwisely, "Aren't you both tops?"

"It's not that big a deal," said Zhang Yuwen. "Don't you think keeping me in the dark is a bigger problem than that?"

"Sorry, sorry!" Chen Hong held his hands up to plead for mercy. Zhang Yuwen finally let him off the hook, and Chen Hong opened the takeout bag and dug into the exquisite food. "Honestly, I don't know him all that well." His words were both a reminder to Zhang Yuwen and an abdication of responsibility.

"It's fine," Zhang Yuwen said. "I'm an adult. I'll take responsibility for my actions."

"Then what will you do when you're both tops?" Chen Hong was more curious about this than anything else.

"Talk it over, I guess... No, wait! I'm not planning to sleep with him just yet!"

Chen Hong finally showed his hand. "So you're okay with being the bottom?"

"Haven't done it before, but I don't mind trying. Why? Do I need to get a certificate to prove that I qualify to bottom?"

Chen Hong was amused. Zhang Yuwen actually was curious to try it. He was curious about bottoming. It was just a position, after all, and all that talk of prostate orgasms and full-body tremors sounded both stimulating and sinful to him. It piqued his interest.

As for the roles of top and bottom, Zhang Yuwen saw it more as a division of labor in a relationship. The top would also have moments when he was tired and needed comfort, when the bottom would need to take up responsibility. It wasn't a relationship where one was dependent and the other was the provider. His relationship with his ex, for example, had been unbalanced. With his new relationship, Zhang Yuwen hoped to try a completely new approach, more like the relationship between good friends.

As for the bedroom, they could always find opportunities to switch around. He was confident in his skills and technique. If Huo Sichen could accept bottoming once or twice, Zhang Yuwen was sure he could fuck him until he was hooked and wanted more.

That night, Zhang Yuwen finally had a good sleep. The next morning, he and Chen Hong kept quiet about the matter; it wasn't time to make it public just yet.

Dinner tonite? I'll come pick u up?

After the blind date, Huo Sichen's invitations became more frequent. Zhang Yuwen wanted to turn him down and wait until the weekend, but on second thought he decided it was be better to be proactive. They both had feelings for each other; there was no need to play hard to get.

Sure, Zhang Yuwen answered. *I'll go 2 u, no need 2 pick me up.*

Huo Sichen sent him several restaurant options, but Zhang Yuwen replied, *Too expensive. I'll pick.*

It was December, the busiest time on hot pot street in Jiangnan. Zhang Yuwen led Huo Sichen through the dazzling array of lights to a food stall and took a seat. Huo Sichen rarely ate at street food stalls, but Zhang Yuwen was well acquainted with them.

"Do you have any plans for Christmas?" Huo Sichen asked.

Zhang Yuwen thought about it. "Not sure yet."

"Another dorm group activity?" Huo Sichen had spontaneously started to call No. 7 Riverbay Road a dorm.

"Maybe New Year's."

"Okay, can I come?" Huo Sichen was unbothered by Zhang Yuwen saying he planned to spend New Year's with his roommates. He even asked to join them.

"Let me think about where to go first." He had promised to treat the guys once he'd collected all the rent, but he was trying to think of a way to do it that didn't seem too abrupt.

"I have to go away for a while, but I'll be back after a week since there's a company meeting at noon on New Year's Eve," Huo Sichen said.

"When are you leaving?"

"Next week. I'm thinking of going to Los Angeles to see my parents. It's been a really long time since I last saw them."

"Okay."

Huo Sichen noticed Zhang Yuwen's expression. "I haven't booked my ticket..."

"No, no!" Zhang Yuwen said promptly. "It's great to spend more time with your family. You should spend New Year's with them. I'll wait for you to come back."

Zhang Yuwen knew everyone had their own lives to lead. They weren't NPCs with no families or social connections. That went for his roommates, too.

After their meal, Huo Sichen habitually fished out his wallet to pay the bill. Zhang Yuwen wanted to tell Huo Sichen to let him pay instead, but after a moment's hesitation, he kept his mouth shut and accepted the gesture.

Am I in a relationship? What a surreal feeling. The situation was a lot like the way he and his ex had interacted, except the roles were now reversed. Back then, he would hurry to his alma mater after work to wait for his ex and take him out for dinner before returning to their rented apartment. Occasionally, his ex cooked for him, and he came home to a piping hot meal.

Just like that, with no prior discussion, Zhang Yuwen inexplicably became the bottom. There was no such thing as "negotiating." Huo Sichen's attitude made it all completely natural.

"Would you like a cup of bubble tea?" Zhang Yuwen asked.

"No," Huo Sichen replied. "Why do you ask? I don't want bubble tea. I'm already full."

"No, you want it," Zhang Yuwen insisted.

Huo Sichen smiled uncertainly. Then it dawned on him, and he said, "You can pay next time. I just think it's all the same."

"As long as you're aware." Zhang Yuwen smiled, thinking that usually, after a meal, the girl would buy bubble tea for the guy who footed the bill. People should always reciprocate, right?

Huo Sichen grinned at him, and they looked at each other in silence. In that moment, Zhang Yuwen felt a subtle emotion as natural as the night itself.

The car waiting behind them honked, and Huo Sichen turned the steering wheel, leaving the crowded Jiangnan street behind.

"Good night," Huo Sichen said to Zhang Yuwen.

"Nighty night," Zhang Yuwen replied.

He stood at his doorstep, watching Huo Sichen drive away before he entered the house.

Everyone was sitting at the dining table, having some kind of family conference. At the sight of Zhang Yuwen returning, they fell briefly silent.

"Went out with the straight guy?" Chang Jinxing asked.

Zhang Yuwen's heart skipped a beat. "Uh... Yeah." They couldn't be planning to interrogate him, could they? But it didn't really seem like it. Yan Jun was feeding Xiao-Qi baby food, Chen Hong was having his gym prep meal, and Zheng Weize was playing around with his phone.

Chen Hong probably hadn't mentioned the matchmaking session...

"What are you talking about?" Zhang Yuwen opened the fridge to get some milk. The hot pot from dinner had been very spicy.

"How we're spending Christmas and New Year's," said Chen Hong. "Are we gonna hang out together?"

Zheng Weize glanced at Zhang Yuwen with a slightly pitiful look in his eyes. "I don't have any plans for Christmas yet. What about you guys?"

"I have a job on Christmas," Chang Jinxing said. "An outdoor shoot. But I'll be back before the new year." He'd gotten a big job: a four-day, three-night cruise, taking photos for the cruise guests.

Oh, so that's why, Zhang Yuwen thought. No wonder Zheng Weize looked disappointed.

"I'm going back to my hometown to see my parents," Chen Hong said. "My clients don't have classes during the holidays anyway."

"Okay, go ahead," Zhang Yuwen said. "How about you, Yan Jun?"

"I'll be at home with Xiao-Qi."

"Will you spend the time with us, Yuwen?" Zheng Weize asked lazily.

"Yeah," said Zhang Yuwen.

"Not spending it with the straight guy?"

"Nah," Zhang Yuwen replied simply. "Are we spending the new year together? Let me organize it. All the rent has been paid, and I promised to treat everyone."

"Whoa!" Everyone perked up at the mention of a treat, so Zhang Yuwen made plans with everyone to get together again on New Year's Eve.

He wanted to organize an outing for everyone and invite Huo Sichen along, but where to?

The next day, Zhang Yuwen paid a visit to a film production company that he'd collaborated with before. The production company had prepared New Year's gifts to send to Riverbay Road, but Zhang Yuwen stopped them and made a trip down in person.

"I remember you sent me complimentary vouchers for a hot spring hotel, right?" Zhang Yuwen rarely had to be thick-skinned enough to ask for things like this. "Can you give me a few more?"

The vice president was flattered. "You really want them?! I'll get them for you. Now! As many as you want!"

"Oh, you're too kind!" Zhang Yuwen smiled, feeling relieved.

"Not at all, not at all. We should thank you for supporting us all this time." The vice president found a huge stack of vouchers, bowed, and handed it to Zhang Yuwen.

These were vouchers that the production company used to entertain their guests. They had shares in a hot spring hotel where they'd once shot a drama. One of their investors owned the hotel, so they often invited their partners to visit by handing out vouchers, but Zhang Yuwen had never thought of going before. His vacation time was precious, and he would rather pay out of his own pocket to travel.

"This is too many!" Zhang Yuwen exclaimed. "I'm just going with a few friends. Six is enough. Kids under two stay for free, right?"

"Yes, yes, that's right. And it's not that many at all. I'll reserve a family room for you. How many kids are going?" Embarrassed, Zhang Yuwen watched as the vice president stamped each voucher. "How many days are you staying?"

"Uh, is one voucher only good for one night?" Zhang Yuwen asked.

"You can stay as long as you want," the vice president said. "Or I can call and make a reservation for you, and then you can just go there with your friends."

"No, no. I'll use the vouchers. I...need these vouchers. I'll make the reservations myself. Speaking of which, are there any rooms available for reservation now?"

"You can try making the reservation first. If there are no rooms, I'll make a call for you! Here are the meal vouchers. Just bring them along and use them for dinner. Breakfast is free of charge."

"Three days and two nights it is, then," Zhang Yuwen said. "Thank you so much, and sorry for the trouble."

Zhang Yuwen was always careful not to inconvenience anyone else, and because of this, companies often struggled to find opportunities to connect with him. Their last collaboration had been a pleasant one, and the production company was eager to find more opportunities for collaboration. Zhang Yuwen coming in person to ask for a favor was a rare sight, so they quickly brought out a full set of Tiffany china, made coffee for him, and offered him snacks.

Zhang Yuwen accepted twelve accommodation vouchers and twelve meal vouchers, placed them in an envelope, and thanked the vice president profusely. The vice president was even more delighted than Zhang Yuwen. Carrying a luxurious year-end gift hamper in his arms, he politely escorted Zhang Yuwen to the door and put the fruit basket in his trunk. Then he complimented Zhang Yuwen's car, admiring his good taste.

Next, Zhang Yuwen went to another film production company to pick up his year-end gifts. He'd politely declined gifts from other companies, but as he had a favor to ask of these two companies, he had to make a trip in person.

The person who received him was the company owner, a young director in whom Zhang Yuwen had previously invested.

"President Wang is busy at the moment—"

"What could he possibly be busy with?" Zhang Yuwen interrupted the assistant and entered the office without even knocking on the door.

The director had gone on to become a producer and company president, and he'd been raking in the dough for the past few years. A man with a domineering presence in public, he came with his own personal whirlwind and lighting effects wherever he went. He was known in the industry as the Demon Director, and now the demon was on the phone in his office, furiously rebuking the producer for going over budget. Zhang Yuwen's sudden entry startled him.

"Yuwen-ge?!" The president quickly said into the phone, "That's all for now! My ge is here. Ge! What brings you here?!"

"Hey!" Zhang Yuwen was happy to see him too. This was his junior, after all. Zhang Yuwen went over and gave him a hug.

The young president called for someone to bring over snacks and quickly went off to personally make Zhang Yuwen coffee. Zhang Yuwen had eaten a lot at the last production company, though, and he really couldn't stomach any more.

"This mug's pretty," Zhang Yuwen complimented as he accepted the coffee. "Your taste is getting better."

"They bought Hermès mugs for clients as PR gifts last time. I thought they looked nice, so I kept a few. I have more here..." He started to climb the bookshelf to get the box.

"No, no, it's okay!" Zhang Yuwen was afraid he would inundate him with mugs. "I have some at home too. Keep them for your girlfriend."

"What have you been busy with lately?" asked the high-powered, domineering president, looking like a little rabbit.

"Nothing much. I'm writing a book."

"Can I read it?"

"It's really awful. I'm not even satisfied with it myself, but if it gets published, I'll give you a copy." He sat at the president's desk and started rummaging through his stuff.

"I want an autographed copy! What are you looking for?"

"Where's the script for your new movie?" asked Zhang Yuwen. He knew the guy was getting ready to shoot a new movie. Sure enough, the president pulled out a book.

"Here you go. Take it home and read it!"

"That's okay." Zhang Yuwen grabbed a pen and looked over the script for him. He was a little curious. It had been over a year since he last wrote a script, and on top of that, he was interested in this movie specifically. He mumbled to himself as he looked over the script. "Your last movie flopped at the box office, right?" he asked.

"Yeah, but I have a feeling this one will do better," the young president said quickly.

"It's fine." Zhang Yuwen smiled. "You can still live off your past gains for a while. Just do your best filming. Audiences are fickle. Cater to them if you can, but don't stress yourself out if you can't."

"Thank you, ge!" The president was touched. The times when Zhang Yuwen came to visit were the only moments he could truly relax.

Zhang Yuwen circled a few areas on the script and offered some suggestions, and the president turned on his laptop to note them down. "No one can be popular forever," Zhang Yuwen said. "You have to get used to it. The creation of a work is a gradual process of ups and downs. The important thing is to have a clear conscience."

"You're right," the president said.

"By the way, I have a good friend who studied photography and is currently looking for a job."

The young president understood immediately. "Is he a junior from our school? I'll call him once this movie starts shooting! He can be the cinematographer's assistant!"

"I think he is, but I didn't really probe. As for being the cinematographer's assistant... He might not be up to the task. I was just wondering if you could give him a chance to tag along and learn if there are any promotional shoots or something."a

"Got it." The young president snapped his fingers. "I'll arrange it now. Does he have a portfolio?"

Zhang Yuwen hesitated. "Just treat him as a newbie."

"No problem. Give me his number. The production department will call him in the new year."

Zhang Yuwen smiled. "Awesome! Just a heads-up: He doesn't know what I do, so don't mention anything about me. Just take it as a referral from a friend." The president made an OK gesture and grinned knowingly. Zhang Yuwen knew he must have gotten the wrong idea, but he didn't correct him. "It'd be a good idea to get a few more people to look over the script. Don't keep losing your temper every time someone gives you feedback."

"All right."

The young president walked him out, carrying the gift for Zhang Yuwen—a huge, extravagant fruit basket with some cigarettes, alcohol, and other items. "Ge, your car's always so cool," he said as he helped him put the hamper in his trunk.

Then he opened the trunk and saw the gift from the other company.

"Ge!" The young president blurted. "Why did you go to their company first?!"

Oops, he's jealous... Zhang Yuwen, who had completely forgotten about the other gift, was quick to placate him. "It was on the way. When I passed by their building, they just stuffed the hamper into my car. I won't accept it next time. All right now, work hard and make more money next year! Love ya, bye!"

The young president still wanted to throw a little tantrum, but unfortunately, a lot of his employees were standing nearby to see Zhang Yuwen off. Once Zhang Yuwen left, he turned and coughed twice, putting his cool and indifferent expression back into place.

"What are you looking at?! Get back to work! You're not on vacation yet!"

Next, Zhang Yuwen dragged the two hampers into the publishing house's elevator and carried them into the deputy editor's office.

"A...small token of appreciation for everyone," Zhang Yuwen said with sincerity and humility.

"That's so kind of you!" the deputy editor said.

"Not at all, not at all." Zhang Yuwen straightened up, taking on the complete opposite role from the one he'd been playing an hour ago. "I should thank you for all your help. I apologize for any inconvenience I may have caused."

The deputy editor looked at the two extravagant hampers and shook his head in resignation. He sighed. "Then...let's talk about your manuscript? The quality of the last one you submitted is worrying."

"Let's leave it for now. I won't take up your time. But you're right! I have a feeling the next one will be better." Zhang Yuwen was getting a sense of déjà vu from this conversation.

The deputy editor gave him a meaningful look and pushed his glasses up, flashing a devious glint. In that moment, Zhang Yuwen became the junior listening attentively to a lecture.

"Just do your best and put your heart into it," said the deputy editor. "Don't stress yourself out."

"Thanks."

"I'll make you some coffee." The deputy editor got up, went to the water dispenser for a cup, and brewed instant coffee for him. Zhang Yuwen smiled and accepted it with both hands.

"Then I won't bother you any longer."

"I'll see you out."

"It's fine," Zhang Yuwen said hurriedly. "It's the end of the year. You must be very busy."

"Yeah, man."

Zhang Yuwen left the office under the watchful eyes of a group of editors.

Riverbay Road
MEN'S DORMITORY

ZHENG WEIZE WAS A PERSON with a certain degree of self-awareness. He knew he was poor and not particularly handsome. He fell a little short in comparison to his roommates, who averaged an attractive 7.2. They were admired whenever they went out together, but he was still riding their coattails. Among this group of tops (or self-proclaimed tops), the only thing notable about him was his candid admission that he was a bottom who needed love and protection.

There were simply too many high-caliber men at No. 7 Riverbay Road. Yes, it was just four of them, but that was more than he had ever encountered at once in any environment growing up. And on top of their looks, they were all very stylish and had great personalities.

Of course, this was because Zhang Yuwen pre-screened potential tenants during the selection process and chose applicants who were good-looking, straightforward, and easygoing. But with everyone claiming to be a top, it was inevitable that territorial instincts would run high, so Zhang Yuwen brought Zheng Weize in to give everyone's protective instincts an outlet. His presence made the rest of them less likely to flex their muscles and release pheromones to show their dominance over the others.

Zheng Weize occasionally fantasized about being a princess and them playing the knights protecting him. He ranked them in his mind. Chang Jinxing was first, of course, followed by Zhang Yuwen and Yan Jun. At first Zhang Yuwen and Yan Jun were tied for second place, but eventually Zhang Yuwen's temperament won out, pushing Yan Jun to third. Chen Hong brought up the rear in fourth place.

Once he'd spent some more time with Chen Hong, though, Zheng Weize realized that muscular men had their own appeal. They gave you a sense of security and were packed with testosterone, offering an entirely different flavor from the pretty boys. Besides, Chang Jinxing was always playing coy; he refused to give Zheng Weize a straightforward response or rejection. Zheng Weize wondered whether he should choose a new chief knight.

But then he'd look at them and go *this one isn't bad* and *that one's quite handsome too.* Even Yan Jun, patiently feeding his daughter on a cold winter night, seemed to exude a special kind of charm. Zheng Weize had never been in a meaningful relationship in his life; his history was littered with unrequited crushes on straight men. When he moved into No. 7 Riverbay Road, where everyone openly discussed their sexual orientation and partners and took care of him like they would a little brother, a whole new world opened up for him—one in which he was so flattered and overwhelmed by the attention, he might just fall for 'em all.

"Where do you want to hang out today?" Zhang Yuwen asked Zheng Weize, sipping his iced coffee through a straw.

Although Zheng Weize had some complaints about Chang Jinxing's absence on Christmas Eve and the lack of explanation for his whereabouts, he was excited by the prospect of developing his relationship with Zhang Yuwen and Yan Jun.

"How did you guys usually spend Christmas when you were in school?" asked Zhang Yuwen.

"Nothing worth mentioning."

Resigning himself to Chang Jinxing's absence, Zheng Weize imagined himself as the protagonist in a dating sim. His main focus was on winning Chang Jinxing's heart, but that didn't mean he wouldn't spread his attention around and flirt with the others occasionally. Each had his own charm, after all.

Recently, a top fan with generous pockets had begun to show up on his female account's live stream channel. He tipped Zheng Weize daily, sometimes two or three hundred, sometimes five or six hundred. As Christmas neared, the top fan generously tipped him a whole thousand, so Zheng Weize wasn't as financially strapped as usual. He planned to get his roommates little gifts for Christmas. He couldn't spend more than a hundred on each of them, though, of course, or he'd have to spend the next month eating dirt again.

Meanwhile, Zhang Yuwen was browsing his phone for places to go on Christmas Eve, which was proving to be a bit of a headache.

"Are you not that keen on going out?" Zheng Weize asked.

"No, it's not that," said Zhang Yuwen. "I'm just...not very good with holidays and celebrations. I'm worried you'd be unhappy with my choices."

"How could I be?"

Zheng Weize didn't expect his opinion to be so important to Zhang Yuwen. He thought Zhang Yuwen must have been conditioned this way by his past relationships. If you failed to plan certain holidays and anniversaries to a partner's satisfaction, there'd be hell to pay, and some tops had holiday anxiety—a fear that they'd be given the cold shoulder if their plans fell through. This was normal.

"I'm really cool with anything," Zheng Weize told him. "Just the fact that you're hanging out with me already makes me super happy."

"How about a mall, then?" Zhang Yuwen suggested.

"Sure." Zheng Weize just wanted to have fun, and if Zhang Yuwen was willing to pick up the tab, all the better. The guy hadn't mentioned a word about expenses the whole time they'd been talking about it, so Zheng Weize's odds of freeloading today were high. He could mooch off a handsome guy and get himself a free Christmas dinner, so why not? "What are we having for dinner?" he asked.

He'd been surviving off instant noodles for several days, and his hunger debuff was chipping away at his health points. He just wanted to chow down on something delicious.

"Yan Jun said he'll make a reservation," Zhang Yuwen said. "He's getting off work early today. We'll pick him up together."

For once, Zhang Yuwen was driving. Zheng Weize settled into the passenger seat, and as he glanced at him, he discovered a whole new facet to Zhang Yuwen's charm.

"This car must be so expensive!" Zheng Weize had no concept of the lavish upper-class lifestyle.

"Yeah." Zhang Yuwen turned the steering wheel and drove out of the garage. "If only it were mine." He grinned and winked at Zheng Weize.

Zheng Weize's heart raced. He wondered where Zhang Yuwen had picked that up. Probably from hanging out too much with Chang Jinxing, goofing off and flirting. He laughed. "It's as good as yours."

"They're the same in the sense that these are all material possessions," Zhang Yuwen muttered to himself, "and yet they aren't all the same."

Zheng Weize didn't understand what he meant. "How much does this car cost?" he asked curiously.

Zhang Yuwen thought about it for a moment. "Two million? Two point six million, I guess."

This was a figure so astronomical that Zheng Weize couldn't even begin to fathom it. The cars he'd heard of that cost a little over a million already seemed extravagant. "It costs more than a house!"

It was enough to buy several houses in Zheng Weize's hometown, in fact.

"Yeah." Zhang Yuwen sighed and drove onto the bridge, heading to Jiangnan to pick Yan Jun up. It was Christmas Eve, and the streets were packed, creating traffic jams everywhere. "The roads are so congested. We should have taken the subway."

Zheng Weize was in familiar territory now. "You can take a right up ahead. There's a shortcut that isn't usually that busy."

Following Zheng Weize's directions, Zhang Yuwen drove the car around the back entrance of a shopping mall. "You seem familiar with this place," he remarked.

"Yeah." Of course he was. This was where Zheng Weize used to work, and he still felt nostalgic about the place. Coming back here more than a month later, to this narrow road with a row of small shops and food stalls lined up across from the shopping mall, his job here felt like a different lifetime. "I used to come here a lot with my classmates."

With some difficulty, Zhang Yuwen carefully maneuvered the car to avoid hitting the railing or the vehicles parked on the curb. Zheng Weize gazed at the street, full of nostalgia. He used to come here with his straight colleague for the ¥20 lunches.

Zheng Weize suddenly spotted someone—that very same straight ex-colleague. "Eh!"

"What's wrong?" Zhang Yuwen turned to look at him.

"That guy...is a friend of mine!"

With mixed feelings, he watched the straight colleague, who stood at the side of the road. He had left his counter to step out of the mall for a smoke, looking weary.

So ugly... So sleazy, man. How did I not notice before? Zheng Weize was shocked. *How did I ever like someone like that?*

Zhang Yuwen rolled down the car window, but Zheng Weize, not wanting to greet the guy, quickly intervened. "No need for that. He's just an ordinary friend." He was worried the guy might say too much and expose Zheng Weize's fabricated story.

Zhang Yuwen casually put on his sunglasses and whistled at the guy. "Hello."

This left Zheng Weize with no choice but to play along. He put his hand on the back of Zhang Yuwen's seat and plastered a cheery smile on his face. "Hi!"

When the guy saw Zheng Weize, his jaw dropped. Then he looked at Zhang Yuwen.

"Long time no see, man." Zheng Weize really did not like this straight guy anymore. Seeing him actually made Zheng Weize feel a bit nauseous.

"You guys..."

"We're going to celebrate Christmas Eve." After a moment, Zheng Weize added, "Happy holidays."

His former colleague waved at him, looking conflicted. Zhang Yuwen rolled up the window and glanced at Zheng Weize, who fell silent for a moment. He knew that Zhang Yuwen must have sensed something between him and the guy.

"He's straight," Zheng Weize explained. This time, his smile came from the heart.

"I see." Zhang Yuwen didn't ask how they met.

"He's pretty selfish. He knew I liked him, but he never outright rejected me so that I'd keep on sucking up to him. I'm really..."

"Hush." Zhang Yuwen drove onto the main road and, with a smile, gestured for Zheng Weize not to say another word.

"Huh?"

"Don't dwell on other people's flaws, and don't doubt yourself. Those memories also contain the past version of you. Forget what made you sad, remember what made you happy. Pick up the pieces and move on."

Zheng Weize nodded, not really getting it. He was still so young, barely over twenty—at his age, matters of the heart still befuddled him.

"We're here." Zhang Yuwen parked the car in front of Yan Jun's company building.

Yan Jun's colleagues were just getting off work, and the sight of the expensive luxury car gave them a start as they stepped out of the building. "Yo!"

Yan Jun bade them goodbye and happy holidays. Then, obviously in a good mood, he grinned and strode over to Zhang Yuwen.

Zhang Yuwen took off his sunglasses and grinned back. "Wow."

"Wow," Yan Jun mimicked, exaggerating his tone.

"Yo, look at you. A domineering CEO with your luxury car and chauffeur."

"Nah, I'm the CEO's kept boy. Baby, please move to the back."

"Why?!" Zheng Weize cried.

"The bodyguard sits in the passenger seat. The young master always rides in the back."

Just like that, Yan Jun relegated Zheng Weize to the back seat and occupied the passenger seat himself, adjusting it to accommodate his long legs with familiar ease before buckling his seat belt.

"You'll still need to move to the back later," Zhang Yuwen pointed out. "We're going to pick Xiao-Qi up now."

"Let's go have fun first before we pick her up for dinner. Look what we have here! A Bentley! This car really feeds the ego."

Zhang Yuwen was torn between laughter and tears. "It's not like it's your first time in this car!"

"It was late at night last time, it was dark," Yan Jun said, "and I wasn't in the mood to enjoy the ride. Even my boss probably hasn't been in a car of this caliber."

"And you want to abandon your precious daughter to enjoy it now?"

Yan Jun laughed. "I want to buy her some stuff, and it's tough to go shopping with a baby."

"All right then." Zhang Yuwen turned the car around to head for another mega shopping mall in Jiangnan, where they planned to spend Christmas Eve.

The festive atmosphere in Jiangdong City was cranked up to eleven during Christmas. Every shop was having a promotion, and they were all decked out with dazzling lights. To top it all off, the atrium had a hundred-foot-tall Christmas tree. Zheng Weize cheered and pulled the two of them in to take photos. Of course, most of them were of Zheng Weize and Zhang Yuwen, while Yan Jun was directed to get down on one knee to snap the photos.

As they shopped, Zheng Weize clung to Zhang Yuwen's arm and handed his phone to Yan Jun, ordering him follow them and take more pictures. From time to time, he looked back and made cute gestures for the camera.

Yan Jun didn't really want to keep taking photos of his roommates, so he plotted his escape. "I'm going to the baby store."

"I'm planning to head over there," Zheng Weize said, pointing out an adorable vintage-style shop. He took his phone back and began to compile the photos, feeling very pleased to have had his vanity indulged so thoroughly. "You guys go ahead. No need to keep me company."

Zhang Yuwen and Yan Jun stopped at a large baby store to find new clothes for Xiao-Qi. Babies grew fast; in a few months her clothes would no longer fit, and Yan Jun didn't want to buy her loose, oversized clothing.

"I'm thinking of getting Xiao-Qi a Christmas present," said Zhang Yuwen.

"I'll thank you on her behalf. What's it going to be?"

"I'm not going to let you choose. All you know is to buy pink stuff for girls."

"I was a jock," Yan Jun said. "My sense of aesthetics has never been good. The writer has the final say."

Zhang Yuwen followed Yan Jun around the store for a long time. Yan Jun picked some discounted baby clothes and bibs. Zhang Yuwen could tell that he was holding himself back from buying everything in sight. Occasionally, Zhang Yuwen saw a good deal on adorable clothes that he was tempted to buy for Xiao-Qi too.

In the end, he bought Xiao-Qi a stroller. Yan Jun tried to stop him. "It's too expensive."

"It's fine." Zhang Yuwen smiled. "This is my Rolls-Royce gift to her. When spring comes, you can take her racing around Riverbay Road."

Yan Jun was touched by the gesture. He smiled back. "In that case, thank you, Uncle, for the Rolls-Royce."

They deposited the baby stuff in Zhang Yuwen's car, then went to pick up Xiao-Qi. Yan Jun unpacked and assembled the stroller in the garage of the childcare center. Xiao-Qi clearly loved it. She kept playing with the toys built into the stroller. Then they returned to the mall to wait for Zheng Weize, who materialized with a ton of variously sized shopping bags in tow, and finally headed for the restaurant.

"I got you guys Christmas gifts," Zheng Weize told them, smiling. He lifted the shopping bags and, with his free hand, took a selfie with Zhang Yuwen.

"Let me take those." Zhang Yuwen relieved Zheng Weize of his bags. He knew that Zheng Weize would post photos of them on social media and pretend that they were gifts from Zhang Yuwen, so he was filling in the last piece of the charade. A man's top had to keep him company on a shopping trip, after all, and carrying his bags was the perfect touch.

The trio sat down at the restaurant. They opted for another all-you-can-eat hot pot, but with unlimited seafood and barbecue, it was a lot more sumptuous than the meal they ate on the mountain.

Zheng Weize was half delighted, half worried that they would have to split the bill after the meal. "This is too extravagant!"

Yan Jun gave the meal vouchers to the waiter. "These are from the company," he explained to Zhang Yuwen. "There were only two, so I bought another one from my colleague."

"All right, then I won't stand on ceremony," said Zhang Yuwen. "Thank you for the feast."

Zheng Weize revealed the Christmas gifts he'd bought. They were all soft scarves, like he'd bought them wholesale for each person in the same style but different colors. Remarkably, he'd also bought scarves for Chang Jinxing and Chen Hong, despite their absence. Even more remarkably, there was a children's version for Xiao-Qi. Most remarkable of all: He got one for Huo Sichen! He didn't leave a single person out.

Warm with gratitude, Zhang Yuwen took a photo and sent it to Huo Sichen.

After dinner, Zheng Weize was stuffed. Zhang Yuwen took them to the indoor amusement park. With tickets to the baby area purchased in advance, Yan Jun brought Xiao-Qi in to play, while Zhang Yuwen kept Zheng Weize company at the claw machines.

"Won't you get bored?" Zheng Weize asked.

"Nope!" said Zhang Yuwen. "Not at all. I'll get you more tokens. It's on me. We have to catch that duck."

Keeping Zheng Weize company was much more relaxing than keeping his ex company. Zheng Weize wouldn't lose his temper if he didn't get the toy or grouse about having to spend Christmas Eve playing claw machines. Zheng Weize's demands were simple: If he had a top to keep him company, he was okay with doing anything. If a top wasn't available, a straight guy would do in a pinch.

If it wasn't for Yan Jun and Xiao-Qi, Zheng Weize might have thought he was on a date. It would be even more perfect if Chang Jinxing were there in Zhang Yuwen's place... Even when he was already eating from the bowl, Zheng Weize couldn't help eyeing the pot for more.

Zhang Yuwen bought him a whole bunch of tokens, and as Zheng Weize accepted them, he was over the moon, feeling like the world was full of pink bubbles.

Before long, Yan Jun came out, and this time a contented Zheng Weize went in to play with Xiao-Qi. Yan Jun and Zhang Yuwen sat at the bar outside, their eyes trained on Xiao-Qi.

"She's grown so much," Zhang Yuwen commented. "It's only been a month."

"Yeah," Yan Jun replied. "I could hold her in one hand when she was just born. Kids grow up fast."

"She'll be a stunner when she grows up." Zhang Yuwen couldn't help but imagine a girl with Yan Jun's features. She would be a tall, long-legged classic beauty with chiseled features.

"Wanna play for a bit?" Yan Jun asked Zhang Yuwen.

"Don't you need to keep an eye on her?"

"It's safe in there, and I trust Weize. Let's go play some games."

The arcade zone was at the side of the amusement park. Zhang Yuwen and Yan Jun each got on a motorbike game machine and fired away at the screen. A few minutes later, they switched to a zombie game where they mowed down zombies with their machine guns.

"Silent Night" began to play, and suddenly the noise in the arcade seemed to recede into the distance. Yan Jun glimpsed Zhang Yuwen out of the corner of his eye. His profile was handsome. Very handsome.

Yan Jun kept readjusting his expectations, reminding himself that Xiao-Qi couldn't be his whole world. He needed his own time, his own life. These days, he was doing his best to make small changes, hoping to use his encounter with Zhang Yuwen to start life anew.

Zhang Yuwen's gaming skills were impressive too, a match for Yan Jun's. He was so engrossed in the game that he almost forgot about Yan Jun, but midway through, he realized his teammate was gone and whipped his head around in surprise.

"I'm already dead!" Yan Jun laughed.

Zhang Yuwen smiled at him. It made Yan Jun's heart flutter like the countless fine snowflakes dancing in the sky outside.

As they left the amusement park, a singer in a floor-length gown who'd been invited by the mall stood under the Christmas tree in the atrium and began to sing, her rich voice resonating in the visitors' hearts. "Silent night... Holy night... All is calm... All is bright..."

The light under the Christmas tree glimmered in the long night. Zhang Yuwen, Zheng Weize, and Yan Jun, who was pushing the stroller, paused for a moment as they passed the atrium to listen to her sing. Unable to help himself, Yan Jun sang along for a couple lines. His voice was deep and powerful, and it drew astonished looks from the people around them. He stopped singing, looking uncharacteristically shy.

"Encore! Encore!" Zhang Yuwen and Zheng Weize exclaimed in unison.

"Shhh... Xiao-Qi's falling asleep." It had been a long time since Yan Jun had sung. "Let's go."

"Drive slowly," Zheng Weize reminded Zhang Yuwen. "It's snowing, and the roads are slippery."

"Roger that." Zhang Yuwen smiled and glanced at the back seat, where Yan Jun held a sleeping Xiao-Qi in his arms. He drove through the city, taking them back to their heartwarming home.

Tonight, their fatigue was soothed and their unhappiness forgotten. It was just as Zhang Yuwen had said: "Forget what made you sad, remember what made you happy."

Riverbay Road

MEN'S DORMITORY

CHANG JINXING FELT like an object. No one understood how it felt to be objectified better than him. His wealthy female clients may have called him a photographer, but in their eyes, he was nothing more than a tripod with an automatic shooting function.

He was relegated to the lowest-class cabin, where he shared a quad room with two other male servants. He slept on an upper bunk, and the lower bunk was piled high with daily necessities. Of course, in essence, he was himself one of those supplies.

They made him work twelve hours a day. There was a quick breakfast at 9:00 a.m., and by 10:00, he was expected to be waiting outside the client's bedroom. Then he followed the girls and their boyfriends around, snapping photos. The day went on like this, broken up by only occasional breaks, until 10:00 p.m.

"Hey! Snap a pic over here!" That was how most of them addressed him. No one cared what his name was. The nicer ones called him "photographer" or just "bro." The less polite ones called him "cameraman." Most of the time, they called him "hey" or "oi." Honestly, it didn't make much difference what they called him; to his ears, it all sounded like, "That camera over there! C'mere!"

The Adonis-like face that Chang Jinxing was so proud of provided no advantage. Everyone on the cruise was gorgeous, men and women alike. Their eyelashes glittered with the sparkle of money, and their hearty laughter tinkled like gold coins scattered on the floor.

The people he served fell into two categories: the main clients, and their companions. The clients included men and women; most of the girls were fair-skinned, wealthy, and beautiful, and the guys were all scions of rich families.

The companions were a more diverse group. The men were young talents from securities firms or investment banks trying to curry favor with the girls' fathers or brothers, university classmates hoping to marry into wealth and skip thirty or forty years of hard toil, or small business owners masquerading as rich men who were actually on the brink of financial ruin. The women were mostly escorts and pretty Z-list actresses hoping to catch a break.

Every male companion was meticulously groomed. Masculine, handsome, and charming, they swirled their wine glasses in one hand while they held their girlfriends close with the other, whispering sweet nothings into their ears. Most seemed to have had good upbringings, and they came across as refined and cultured in front of those they were trying to ingratiate themselves with. The female companions were impeccably made up, considerate women with high emotional intelligence.

But the moment they turned to the waiters, cleaners, and other "objects," they showed their true colors. Cries of "hey," "oi," and "you there" filled the air, as if the servants were just stray mops or dirty plates that they wanted to kick away into the sea.

Squeezed among these gentlemen in suits, Chang Jinxing was, at best, a piece of equipment that was slightly more pleasing to the eye. His trendy outfit looked out of place against the servants' uniforms and the clients' custom-tailored suits, and the force of his presence was practically nil. He'd landed this gig thanks to a recommendation from a wealthy woman who had used his boyfriend-rental service, but the job was clearly beyond his capabilities. His photography still couldn't hold a candle to the work of real photographers. Most of the time he relied on coaxing and flattering, with a healthy dose of flirtation, to get the job done.

Now, as the group's photographer, he fielded constant criticism and nitpicking. Each day, he shot a never-ending stream of photos, shadowing clients during the day and editing selected photos in the middle of the night. Then he was woken early the next morning to repeat the process. The four-day, three-night tour left him drained and exhausted. Every time he felt an urge to swing his camera at the tourists like a meteor hammer, he silently repeated his mantra: *¥20,000, ¥20,000, just think of the ¥20,000.*

When he accepted the job, he hoped that a spark might ignite between him and someone else on the romantic cruise, male or female. He imagined that he might even be able to swing a memorable encounter. Now he was forced to face the facts: He had overestimated himself. The moment he boarded the ship, he'd transformed into a tripod. Nobody on the cruise, no matter how ravenous, would sleep with a tripod.

On the last day, Chang Jinxing was on one side of the deck, deleting photos on his camera, when he suddenly heard voices.

"No way, man!" one male voice said. "I thought you'd already slept with her a few times!"

"Nope," said a slightly younger male voice. "I can't do it. When I think about having to...I go soft. Oh well, whatever."

"Just close your eyes and get it over with. How 'bout I give you a couple pills?"

Chang Jinxing recognized the voices as belonging to two men from the group he was following around and photographing.

The one who said he couldn't get it up seemed to be an actor, and the other was an investor. Chang Jinxing rarely paid much attention to what the clients talked about; he was too exhausted to care about gossip, and if he got distracted, he'd be scolded.

"She likes your type," the investor continued. The two of them were out on the deck, smoking. "She's dated a few guys before, all gay. Some were even bottoms. She really likes your type, so you should seize the opportunity."

"I'll try again," the young man said.

They put out their cigarettes and left the deck. Chang Jinxing turned around and moved to the far side of the ship. Curious, he stole a glance at them as they departed. As he did so, the young guy turned back, and their eyes met. Chang Jinxing quickly averted his gaze, afraid they would realize he'd been eavesdropping. He wondered about the girl they were talking about: Who was she, and what was the relationship between them?

Later, during afternoon tea, he noticed the young man and his girlfriend and roughly put the pieces together. The actor, Kong Yu, had been introduced to the group by the investor. His girlfriend, who had a mature air to her and wore an expensive haute couture gown, was named Xixi. The group had cliques, and they were all chatting away in pairs and trios. Chang Jinxing's first impression of Xixi was that of an innocent young woman, one with whom he might actually stand a chance. From what he'd overheard, however, she wasn't someone he could tame. He made the prudent decision to keep his distance from her.

"Hey bro," Kong Yu called out. "Can you help me take a few photos?"

Chang Jinxing nodded and found a spot with good lighting. Kong Yu sat at the place where they'd had afternoon tea and posed for photos before the floor-to-ceiling window. "No influencer-style pics," Kong Yu reminded him.

"I know," Chang Jinxing replied, even as he thought, *But you are an influencer. Don't forget where you came from.*

Over the past few days, he had learned to take more photos of his clients and fewer of their companions. The clients were the ones paying him, the companions mere tools they brought along for emotional value. Chang Jinxing thought of it like this: They were all tools, so why make things hard for each other?

As a tool photographing another tool, Chang Jinxing did his best to make him look good.

When no one else was around, Kong Yu said, "Let's exchange contact info. Send me the photos later."

Chang Jinxing added Kong Yu as his contact, but he had absolutely no desire to sleep with him. He was exhausted, for one thing, and for another, Kong Yu wouldn't be interested in him. He hadn't realized it before, when he was still deep in the game, but being on the outside looking in gave him a new perspective, and he gradually understood that he'd been a bottom-shelf version of Kong Yu all along: getting by in life by social climbing.

Lots of people survived by leaning on their connections to people above them on the social ladder. There was nothing wrong with it, and being able to achieve success that way was a skill in and of itself. Chang Jinxing didn't judge anyone who lived that lifestyle, but he had decided not to live it himself anymore. He wouldn't go back.

The cruise drew to a close, and Chang Jinxing wanted to talk to someone. When he greeted his roommates over text, Zheng Weize was the most responsive, so Chang Jinxing showed him a few photos from the cruise. Zheng Weize's comments on the photos belied his envy; he felt inferior, like Chang Jinxing lived in an entirely different world from him. Chang Jinxing, realizing he'd gone too far with his bragging, had to comfort Zheng Weize by making up a story about tagging along with a group of old folks to take seascape photos.

When he showed the photos to Zhang Yuwen, Zhang Yuwen already knew what he'd been up to. He was unmoved, however, having always found cruise parties boring. Engaging escorts' services on a ship was no different from bringing call girls or rent boys on a joyride. It was all the same old thing: drinking and sunbathing by day, drinking and having sex by night. He preferred to just play video games at home.

Then Chang Jinxing texted the photos to Yan Jun, who was always busy caring for his daughter. Everyone experienced life's highs and lows differently, and Yan Jun just asked: *How much per night? Must be expensive, right?*

Dunno, Chang Jinxing replied, *probs tens of thousands.*

Chang Jinxing sent the photos to Chen Hong next. *So many rich ppl in the world. U think they hv a net worth of billions?*

Chen Hong had been on a trip like this before. His rich boyfriend once took him on a cruise, where Chen Hong was just one of the many escorts they brought along, so he had a rough idea of how much it would cost. He replied, *Nah, not that much. These peeps only booked 2 floors. If they were seriously rich theyd book the entire ship.*

That made sense to Chang Jinxing, who followed up by asking Chen Hong what he was doing. The answer: weeding the backyard of his childhood home back in his hometown.

Where u getting off? Chen Hong asked.

Lion Sands, Chang Jinxing replied. *Getting off tmrw. Gonna take the train back to Jiangdong City. U?*

Wanna come to my house? Just get off at Lanqiu County. We can head back to Jiangdong 2gether.

Chang Jinxing hadn't expected Chen Hong to invite him to his hometown. He couldn't be interested in Chang Jinxing, could he? From their usual interactions, it didn't seem like it. Chen Hong behaved just like any other roommate. He wasn't even as close to Chang Jinxing as he was to Zhang Yuwen.

It was on the way, though, so Chang Jinxing was fine with paying him a visit.

The next day, he sent several photos in a zip file to the email listed on Kong Yu's personal website, then packed up his stuff and disembarked. The domestic servant handed him an envelope containing his payment, plus a little extra as a tip, but they'd also deducted the cost of the five cups of coffee he had on board, each at precisely ¥60, and the three pieces of clothing he had laundered using room service, ¥160 apiece. It almost drove Chang Jinxing mad with anger. He had made a tidy sum of money, but he could tell from their attitude that they weren't satisfied with him. Chang Jinxing didn't like having his self-esteem trampled on, and he swore never to take a cruise job again.

He disembarked with a group of tourists to a dock full of waiting cars, where he sorted out the few pieces of luggage he had and bought a train ticket. The din inside the train and the homely, vibrant winter scenery outside quickly brought him back to reality. He was back in his own world.

When Chang Jinxing arrived at Lanqiu, Chen Hong was waiting on the train platform with two motorcycle helmets. The sight of Chang Jinxing's exhausted face startled him. "Wow, how long did they spend milking you?"

Laughing, Chang Jinxing gave him a playful punch. He took the helmet and rode pillion on Chen Hong's motorcycle through the cold wind to his house.

Chen Hong's family lived in the urban district, where they ran a printing shop that also offered simple advertising design services, helping nearby businesses make flyers. Occasionally, they produced blueprints for a few partner organizations. The shop faced the street, and the back side of the building served as their living quarters. The house was saturated with the smell of ink.

Chen Hong's parents were delighted to see that Chen Hong had a friend over. They were an older couple, already in their sixties, but they still worked hard in the shop every day. Chen Hong dropped off Chang Jinxing, then went to buy some ready-made food to prepare for the meal.

"I can do the cooking," Chang Jinxing offered.

"No, no, no." Chen Hong tied an apron around his waist. "You're a guest! We can't let you cook!"

Chang Jinxing was planted in the guest seat. The whole family treated him warmly. Chen Hong had a twenty-six-year-old younger sister who had been helping out in the shop since she graduated. Curious about Chang Jinxing, she peppered him with questions about everything from how he met Chen Hong to what he did for a living and whether he was a member of Chen Hong's gym. Chen Hong coughed and shot Chang Jinxing a warning glance, reminding him not to out him or get any ideas about his sister.

Chang Jinxing understood him, of course. In truth, he was dead tired, and all he could think of was sleep. When night came, Chen Hong laid out the bedding so Chang Jinxing could sleep in his room. They shared a bed surrounded by stacks of papers of varying sizes, Chen Hong's dumbbells, yoga mats, and so on.

"Why are there so few people in Lanqiu?" Chang Jinxing asked.

"They all went to work in the big cities. A lot of the young people have left. There are lots of old folks left behind, and the local economy can't develop." Chen Hong sighed. He'd once harbored a lofty goal of going to Jiangdong to make a name for himself and returning home in glory, but that plan kept getting pushed back. At this point it felt like a distant dream. Absently, he added, "I was the one who told my sister to stay here. She's idolized me since she was little. I don't want her to go out and work."

The printing shop was currently doing well enough to be self-sufficient. Chen Hong hoped his sister could marry and have children in their hometown instead of leaving to suffer the hardships of big city life. Here, she could take care of their parents for him, too.

"That's nice," said Chang Jinxing.

"What about you?" Then, noticing Chang Jinxing curling up like a worm, he asked, "Are you cold?"

"Not too cold." Chang Jinxing's eyelids were heavy with sleep. "Your room's a little damp."

Chen Hong turned up the temperature on the electric heater. "I haven't been back in a long time. Hey, do me a favor tomorrow. A friend of mine is holding a funeral at his house. Help me take a few photos, will you?"

I knew it, Chang Jinxing thought. *Of course you invited me over because you wanted me to help you.*

"Are there any superstitions where you come from?" Chen Hong asked. "About attending funerals?"

"Okay... Sure... Nope..." Chang Jinxing was so sleepy he was almost out of it. "We'll go tomorrow..."

Chen Hong's room was damp and cold, but Chang Jinxing slept much more comfortably than he had on the cruise ship.

It was nearly nine o'clock the next morning when Chang Jinxing yawned and got up, feeling rejuvenated after a dreamless sleep.

Chen Hong's sister was cleaning up in the living room. "Xing, you're up," she said when she saw him.

Chang Jinxing was the same age as her. He wasn't used to being addressed that way, but he just smiled. "Where's your brother? He asked me to help with taking photos today. I think he said it's for a funeral at a friend's house?"

"My brother and parents left early to go help out." Chen Hong's sister was very curious about Chang Jinxing. Chen Hong rarely brought his friends from Jiangdong back home. "I'll get you some breakfast. We'll go over around eleven. No rush."

"Oh, no, it's fine."

"I haven't had breakfast yet either, so…"

"I'll cook," Chang Jinxing said spontaneously. He entered the kitchen. "Noodles okay for you?"

He opened the fridge, took out the eggs, and began beating them with practiced ease. Just then, Chen Hong returned on his electric motorcycle. "Didn't I tell you to go out and buy something outside?" he said to his sister. "How can you let a guest cook?" Then he turned to Chang Jinxing. "What are you making? Give me a bowl too. I'm hungry."

"I don't have black clothes," Chang Jinxing told him.

Chen Hong put down his chopsticks. "I have an extra set that I used to wear."

Chang Jinxing changed into one of Chen Hong's black suits. To his surprise, it fit him well. "This definitely isn't yours," Chang Jinxing said, chuckling.

Chen Hong made a hushing gesture, reminding Chang Jinxing that his sister was still outside. Chang Jinxing went back to admiring the dashing figure in the mirror.

Chen Hong looked at him silently for a moment, then tied Chang Jinxing's tie for him with rough, quick movements, as if he had pent-up frustration to get out and Chang Jinxing was a punching bag.

"Choking... You're choking me... Hong-ge..." Chang Jinxing nearly suffocated.

"Done," Chen Hong said. He had such a deep voice. "Very handsome." Then he patted Chang Jinxing on the face and turned to leave. But Chang Jinxing touched his shoulder, prompting him to turn around, and when he did, Chang Jinxing cupped his cheek with one hand and moved in to kiss him.

Chen Hong made an indignant noise. "Stop fooling around!" he hissed, grabbing hold of Chang Jinxing's hand.

Chang Jinxing had done it out of mischief. He figured the suit must have belonged to Chen Hong's ex and that, through Chang Jinxing, Chen Hong was seeing his former boyfriend. He was more than happy to kiss Chen Hong so that he could relive a love once lost.

After the siblings finished Chang Jinxing's noodles, Chen Hong drove Chang Jinxing through town to the other family's home. He made his sister ride her bicycle.

"About that ex of yours," Chang Jinxing said. "How long were you with him? You've got good taste. How did you find such a handsome guy?"

"A month," Chen Hong replied calmly. "He's a far cry from you, but he's rich and dresses well."

Chang Jinxing wrapped his arms around Chen Hong's waist. They were both in suits and motorcycle helmets. Chen Hong accelerated and sped along the country road. "No need to be so modest..."

"I'm serious." Chen Hong turned his head slightly. "He's not as handsome as you or even Yuwen. No, he's leagues away from you guys. I don't know why I liked him."

Chang Jinxing didn't ask Chen Hong if he still liked him. His attitude toward the black suit said it all: He couldn't put his ex behind him.

The towns in Lanqiu County were underdeveloped: There was only one bus, which was now crowded with people coming to pay their respects to the deceased. The streets were full of funeral wreaths, and everyone seemed to know each other, exchanging greetings when they crossed paths and addressing each other by name.

Chang Jinxing was taken to the mourning hall. Chen Hong had already gone to greet people, so Chang Jinxing stepped forward, pulled aside the black drapes to let in some light, and started taking photos. The deceased person was an old man who had lived for exactly one hundred years. A hale and hearty man, he had declined any care or companionship offered to him.

There was heavy snowfall on Christmas day, though. When the old man went out for his usual stroll with his cane, he slipped and fell into the snow. No one noticed his absence, and he lay freezing in the snow for two hours before someone found him and brought him back. By then, it was too late. A few days later, he passed away quietly in bed during the winter night.

The guests wept, and the children of the deceased bowed in thanks. The eldest grandson held the old man's portrait in both hands, his face expressionless. Once in a while, he looked around. Chang Jinxing, who was snapping pictures, thought the grandson looked very handsome with the black clothes accentuating his fair complexion and solemn demeanor, so he took a few extra shots of him.

Chen Hong was popular. Everyone sought him out for a conversation. The older mourners also noticed his fair, slim, and stunning photographer friend, and they were curious about who he was. When Chen Hong glanced over at Chang Jinxing, he found him comforting the teary-eyed grandson, doing his utmost to play the gentle older brother. Concerned that Chang Jinxing would bang the grandson at the back of the mourning hall later, Chen Hong glared daggers at him and forcibly dragged him away.

After they paid their final respects to the deceased, Chen Hong said, "Let's eat. Thanks for your hard work."

"It's nothing." Chang Jinxing was used to doing things like this.

A feast had been laid out outside the mourning hall. After helping the host all morning, Chen Hong finally had his chance to come over and have a meal and a drink with Chang Jinxing.

The host came by to offer a toast. Chang Jinxing rushed through his meal and took his laptop off to the side of the table to export the photos, batch edit them, and email them to the host. "I don't think I'll live to a hundred," Chang Jinxing said suddenly.

"What's the point in living that long anyway?" Chen Hong asked. "What matters is a fulfilling life."

"I wonder how I'll evaluate myself when I'm old and looking back on my life."

They both fell silent and drank their tea. When evening came, all those who came to offer condolences left, one after another. A person could live for a full hundred years, yet it took only a few days to go from death to burial. Ashes to ashes, dust to dust. Friends and family joined together for a meal and dispersed, and just like that, it was over.

When they returned, Chen Hong handed Chang Jinxing an envelope. "Here, your payment from the host family."

Chang Jinxing refused it. "No. I'm not taking it."

"Just take it!" Chen Hong insisted.

Chang Jinxing refused it again, and Chen Hong tried to shove it at him. They began to push and shove each other. "You're my friend. I won't take the money."

"Are you going to accept it or not?!"

"Oh my god! Help! Ahhh!" Chang Jinxing cried as Chen Hong pinned him down on the bed and tickled his weak spot. "Gege! No! Daddy!"

Chen Hong might not have been able to overpower Yan Jun, but Chang Jinxing was much easier to subdue. Chang Jinxing's face turned red and tears welled up in his eyes as he frantically pleaded with Chen Hong.

Chen Hong had only intended to mess with him, but when he felt his little friend start to show interest in the proceedings, he stopped. He didn't want this to end with them rolling around under the sheets. Chang Jinxing was flushed and panting hard; he'd never been restrained so violently before.

"Take the money," Chen Hong said. "Don't force me to do something I'll regret. This is a warning."

Chang Jinxing took the envelope and collapsed back onto the bed, laughing hard. "Then I'll treat everyone to a meal when I get back," he said, figuring there was about ¥1,000 inside.

The exchange left them both feeling awkward. Accidentally awakening their lust had flipped a switch, but neither of them wanted to have sex with the other.

"Do you have porn?" Chang Jinxing asked. "Damn! You're so big!"

Chen Hong, who had just taken a shower, stepped out of the bathroom wearing only his underwear. He knew his figure was alluring, and he never shied away from flaunting it. "Sure I do. You wanna watch?"

"We jerking each other off?" Chang Jinxing asked.

Chen Hong couldn't say he wasn't tempted. That wouldn't count as a hookup with his roommate, would it? Then again, it was kind of awkward...

"Let me see the videos on your laptop," Chang Jinxing said.

"Keep your voice down. I watch them all online."

Chen Hong went to check the door and locked it, then used his laptop to access a website for Chang Jinxing. Chang Jinxing had been holding back for a long time, and now the urge was overwhelming him; he started to browse through the videos the second the website loaded.

Chen Hong sat down on the other side of the bed. Chang Jinxing picked a video, and Chen Hong began rubbing himself through his underwear. Chang Jinxing, who was less shy, had already taken off his pants, revealing his long legs. He wrapped his dick in the T-shirt he was wearing and stroked himself.

"Fuck," Chen Hong blurted. "The way you're sitting...is obscene."

Chang Jinxing spread his legs apart, stroking himself, and glanced at Chen Hong. "You want me to clamp my legs shut? Talk about obscene."

Chen Hong didn't know what to say to that. "Can we not watch this one? Watching this muscular guy being fucked makes me feel like I'm the one being fucked." This made Chang Jinxing, who was still pleasuring himself, laugh so hard he almost died. Chen Hong looked at him. "You like this kind of video?"

Chang Jinxing hadn't had sex while he was on the cruise, so he really wasn't picky as long as he got the relief he wanted. He pushed the laptop at Chen Hong and let him choose. Chen Hong picked a video of a beefcake pounding a long-legged hottie, and this time, Chang Jinxing felt like he was the one getting fucked. He wanted to protest, but the longer he watched, the more the video awakened a familiar, guilty thrill in him.

They watched for a while, their movements quickening and their breathing growing heavier as a sexual charge filled the room. When Chang Jinxing freed a hand to pinch and rub at Chen Hong's nipple, Chen Hong almost moaned aloud. He made a brief show of resistance but let Chang Jinxing do it. Eyes still fixed on the screen, Chang Jinxing let his hand wander southward. He pulled down Chen Hong's underwear, grabbed him, and jerked them both off.

Chen Hong was nervous at first, but that faded quickly enough, and before long, he shed his underwear altogether. Naked, he leaned back to watch the video, his hands free to play with his own nipples and occasionally tease Chang Jinxing's.

Chang Jinxing took off his shirt too, leaving them both fully naked. "Got any lube?" They were both on the verge of climax, and grasping Chen Hong's huge, scalding hot cock made him even more aroused. With his higher-order thinking temporarily AWOL, he really didn't mind the idea of getting fucked by Chen Hong.

"Nope," Chen Hong said, thinking Chang Jinxing just wanted to use lube to masturbate. "You think I keep lube at my parents' house? Focus, stop getting distracted..."

"Then forget it." Chang Jinxing's prostate was making some demands, but his brain would never consider letting a guy Chen Hong's size enter him without lubrication.

They stopped talking, and Chang Jinxing quickened his pace, rewarding himself at the same time he was servicing Chen Hong. A moment later, Chen Hong knocked Chang Jinxing's hand away and began to do it himself, jerking and braking, his breathing growing ever heavier.

Chang Jinxing glimpsed Chen Hong's cock, which was already at its limit. *He's going to come...* He reached over and gripped the base with one hand, pinching Chen Hong's nipple hard with the other. At the rush of pleasure from the two-pronged attack, Chen Hong ejaculated.

With his hand still slick with Chen Hong's cum, Chang Jinxing resumed beating himself off. With the warm cum as a lubricant, it felt better than ever. Chen Hong reached over to caress his chest, and before long, Chang Jinxing moaned, his face flushed, and came.

After ejaculation, rationality returned. It was time for post-nut clarity.

"Fuck," Chen Hong said. "That's sick."

Chen Hong wiped himself with some tissues, while Chang Jinxing held his own cock, worried that the cum would drip onto the bed. "Hand me the tissues, quick."

"Don't tell anyone about this," Chen Hong said, putting on his shorts.

"Duh." Chang Jinxing wiped himself clean, sat cross-legged on the bed, and turned off Chen Hong's laptop.

They were both sated, having found long overdue pleasure in getting each other off. This brief encounter hadn't turned their friendship awkward yet. Finally, everyone would be able to get a good night's sleep.

Chang Jinxing stretched out on the bed, playing with his phone. "What time is the train tomorrow?"

"A little after eight." Chen Hong yawned. "Let's sleep."

"You came a lot."

Sometimes Chen Hong found Chang Jinxing sexy, but at other times he felt disdain for him. Moments ago, when he used Chen Hong's cum as lube, Chen Hong had found it exciting and stimulating, but now, with post-nut clarity, he just found it a little gross.

Ignoring Chang Jinxing, he turned off the light and went to sleep.

HUO SICHEN: *Missed me?*

I guess so, Zhang Yuwen typed. He was a straightforward person, but for some reason, now that he'd entered the dating stage of his relationship with Huo Sichen, he couldn't help acting aloof. What was wrong with him? He retracted his *I guess so* and replaced it with *Missed you.*

Huo Sichen: *How did you miss me? Describe it in detail.*

Sitting at the dining table, Zhang Yuwen laughed. He had indeed been thinking of Huo Sichen over the past few days. He didn't know if this meant he liked him, but every time he ate a meal, he imagined Huo Sichen sitting across from him, talking to him about something interesting, or just about his day at work. When he was lying in bed playing games, he imagined Huo Sichen teaming up with him to help him beat the level. When he watched a movie at home, he even imagined the two of them watching it together and chatting about the plot.

There was one thing he still couldn't do yet, however, and it was the reason Zhang Yuwen couldn't be sure if he really liked Huo Sichen. He still hadn't fantasized about Huo Sichen in bed. To someone with a vivid imagination like Zhang Yuwen, liking someone meant fantasizing about them sexually—imagining making love to them while he got himself off. In the past, that was how he'd determined his feelings for other people, but he was still a little unfamiliar with Huo Sichen. He couldn't quite grasp Huo Sichen's role and position, or even imagine their interactions during sex.

Picture himself as a bottom? He had never tried it before, so it was hard to imagine being topped by Huo Sichen. Picture himself as the top? He'd never bedded this type of guy before, so he couldn't visualize Huo Sichen moaning and pleading for mercy beneath him. In fact, it felt kind of awkward to try.

Zhang Yuwen was so distracted that his trash-producing pace slowed down significantly. It was the end of the year, though, and the whole world was on vacation, so he was happy to give himself a break too. Huo Sichen would be back the next day...

He'd been away for a week, and given the time zone difference between North America and Asia, they hadn't been able to talk much. Zhang Yuwen wondered if things would be weird between them when they met again.

Seeing that his attempt at flirtation was going nowhere, Huo Sichen sent another message. *I dreamed of you last night.*

Oh? wat was I doing in ur dream? At the sight of the "Typing..." indicator, Zhang Yuwen realized too late: There was no way it was a decent dream. He spammed Huo Sichen with a bunch of emojis.

Seeing that his meaning had finally dawned on Zhang Yuwen, Huo Sichen replied simply: (❛‿˓❛) Then he added, *So did u dream about me?*

Not yet, Zhang Yuwen replied. *Trying harder.*

OK, said Huo Sichen.

Zhang Yuwen didn't understand what he meant and texted back a question mark. Suddenly, the doorbell rang, and he went to answer it. To his surprise, it was Huo Sichen!

"I thought you were coming back tomorrow morning!" Zhang Yuwen exclaimed.

"The meeting was moved up a day, so here I am."

Zhang Yuwen opened the gates and was amused to see Huo Sichen holding a bouquet of flowers. He accepted them.

"Wanna grab a meal?" Huo Sichen asked. "My car is parked outside. Where are your roommates?"

"Come in. Weize is the only one home today—Yan Jun took Xiao-Qi to get her shots."

This was the first time Huo Sichen had been invited into No. 7 Riverbay Road. "Let me see what a house worth hundreds of millions looks like," he quipped. Zhang Yuwen let him in and took a quick glance around, but Huo Sichen waved him off. "You probably don't have slippers in my size. Don't bother looking."

"Let me check this pair... What are you, size 10?"

"Yeah. It's fine, there's underfloor heating."

"I'll go change clothes, then. Make yourself at home." Zhang Yuwen put the flowers on the dining table. Hearing the noise, Zheng Weize opened his door a crack and peeked out. "The house is a little messy at the moment, since the housekeepers are on vacation until after the new year."

Huo Sichen nodded. Aware that the other rooms belonged to the roommates, he didn't investigate the place too thoroughly, he merely took a look around the living room, dining room, and backyard. Meanwhile, Zhang Yuwen went upstairs to get changed.

"Such pretty flowers!" Zheng Weize exclaimed, emerging from his room. "Can I take a picture?"

"Of course," Huo Sichen said, his mind very obviously elsewhere. All his attention was on the second floor as he waited for Zhang Yuwen to come down.

Zhang Yuwen's voice drifted out from his room. "Want to see the second floor?"

Huo Sichen walked up the stairs. "Can I come in?"

"Of course," Zhang Yuwen said, bewildered. He opened the door, and Huo Sichen stepped inside.

The bed was a little messy, left unmade after Zhang Yuwen's afternoon nap. A faint, masculine smell hung in the air. Zhang Yuwen opened the floor-to-ceiling window on the balcony to let in some fresh air. Huo Sichen saw the game controller Zhang Yuwen had tossed to the side and picked it up.

"That's very comfortable to use," Zhang Yuwen said, next to him. "It's custom-made." He paused for a moment. "Your hands are bigger than mine. That's an advantage if you play the piano."

Huo Sichen's hands were bigger than Zhang Yuwen's, and his fingers were longer too. They moved nimbly over the handles, rapidly tapping the buttons.

"The grip is too hard," Huo Sichen said. "I prefer something with a softer texture. It'd be more comfortable with a silicone case."

"I prefer it harder... Okay, let's not talk about this."

Huo Sichen laughed. Zhang Yuwen sometimes found Huo Sichen very prim and proper, almost too polite, but other times he seemed to speak in innuendos. It was easy for a guy to get the wrong idea.

Zhang Yuwen finished changing his clothes. "I'm ready."

"You wear glasses?" Huo Sichen asked, spotting a pair of black-rimmed glasses in the corner.

"Uh... I'm slightly nearsighted. Doesn't affect me much, but I wear them sometimes. Why?"

Huo Sichen looked at Zhang Yuwen. Zhang Yuwen had been about to ask, *Do you prefer guys with glasses or without?* but Huo Sichen's expression made the answer clear, so Zhang Yuwen took the black-rimmed glasses Huo Sichen passed him and put them on.

Huo Sichen whistled at him, a smile in his eyes. Zhang Yuwen took them off and set them aside, then went downstairs with him, wearing a small belt bag and carrying a paper bag of clothing. Huo Sichen took the bag from him.

"I bought you some shirts and pants," Zhang Yuwen said. "You can open them when you get back home."

Huo Sichen's car was parked just outside Zhang Yuwen's house. He put the items in the trunk, unable to refrain from peeking at Zhang Yuwen's gifts. Zhang Yuwen saw another paper bag in the back seat and guessed it was for him, but Huo Sichen said nothing about it.

"How did you know my size?" Huo Sichen asked.

"Yeah, how did I know your 'size'?" Zhang Yuwen parroted.

Huo Sichen laughed. "You know how big I am?"

"No idea."

"Then I invite you to measure me yourself when you have the time."

"I've already done a visual estimation. Enough talk, what are we having?"

Huo Sichen got into the driver's seat but didn't start the car. Instead, he said, "I'm fine with anything. What kind of hungry are you? Describe it."

Innuendo everywhere. "The normal kind."

"I can feel that," Huo Sichen said sincerely.

Zhang Yuwen aimed a playful smack at the back of Huo Sichen's head. Huo Sichen dodged him with a laugh, then fastened his seat belt and drove away.

His return today was unexpected, so they didn't have a restaurant booking. Instead they went to the mall to look for somewhere to eat—which proved to be a dilemma, since restaurants with great food had long queues, and those without queues were mostly not as good. Zhang Yuwen had to settle for a meal of roast duck.

"What are we doing tomorrow?" Huo Sichen thought for a moment. "I remember..."

"Yeah, I remember too. I've booked a hot spring resort."

Huo Sichen was surprised. "I'd love that. It's been a long time since I last went to a hot spring."

"But we're going with my roommates. You okay with that?"

"Of course. Are we splitting the cost? I'd like to pay for your share too."

"I have vouchers. They were year-end gifts from the publishing house."

"Looks like your publishing house made a lot of money this year," Huo Sichen remarked. "You must get a really substantial year-end bonus."

Zhang Yuwen downplayed it a little. "Nah, it's just because most of my colleagues are returning to their hometowns for the holidays, so they aren't using them. The vouchers have an expiration date, so some of my colleagues were selling theirs at a discount."

Zhang Yuwen always felt relaxed around Huo Sichen, even more than he did with his roommates. He could eat his meal and mess around on his phone at the same time, and he'd get a response to any topic he brought up. For some reason, though, Huo Sichen seemed a little preoccupied today.

Catching a fleeting moment in which Huo Sichen's brow furrowed slightly, Zhang Yuwen asked, "Something bothering you?"

Huo Sichen's mind had only wandered for a second, but he got caught. "No," he said hurriedly. "It's just the jet lag."

"Oh?" He must have gotten off the plane, gone to his meeting, and then headed straight to see Zhang Yuwen without going home first. "You'll be fine after some sleep."

Huo Sichen yawned obligingly. "Is there anything you want?" he asked after hustling through his meal. "I'll buy it for you."

"No thanks. There's nothing, really. Honest."

Zhang Yuwen knew the pain of shopping well, and he wasn't all that attached to material possessions. It was the same for Huo Sichen; he wouldn't even go to a store to browse around unless it was absolutely necessary.

Zhang Yuwen took the initiative to settle the bill. "Let's go home and get some sleep. We'll hang out again tomorrow." Huo Sichen perked up, nodded, and drove Zhang Yuwen home.

The streets were decked out in lights for Christmas and New Year's, like stars that had fallen to earth during the winter night. Huo Sichen was quiet on the way home, giving Zhang Yuwen an occasional glance.

"You can tell me if something's bothering you," Zhang Yuwen said. "I might not have a solution to offer, but I'm more than happy to listen."

Huo Sichen chuckled. "I will, but I'm fine right now. Nothing's troubling me."

The car stopped at No. 7 Riverbay Road. Night had fallen, and the colorful lights in the garden had already come on. They both fell momentarily silent.

Then Huo Sichen remembered something. "Oh, right. I got you a Christmas gift." He turned back to get the paper bag and handed it to Zhang Yuwen.

"Yeah, I got a gift for you too." Zhang Yuwen opened his bag and took out a small, wrapped box. Huo Sichen looked at him, surprised. "Well, then..."

Zhang Yuwen was about to say good night when Huo Sichen leaned in. Zhang Yuwen's heart started pounding. He didn't move; he knew what Huo Sichen meant to do.

Huo Sichen moved in and kissed him gently on the lips.

It was Zhang Yuwen's first kiss in nearly two years. He had almost forgotten how it felt. Even though Huo Sichen's looks were very masculine, his lips were soft and warm.

Huo Sichen tried to hold his aggressiveness back and keep the kiss gentle and patient. Zhang Yuwen closed his eyes, absorbing the feeling of Huo Sichen's warmth and the softness of the kiss. No matter how he defined his feelings for Huo Sichen, this kiss was romantic, and he couldn't bring himself to pull away.

Feeling like he needed to respond, Zhang Yuwen put his left hand on Huo Sichen's neck. It was an instant boost to Huo Sichen's confidence; emboldened, he unbuckled his seat belt with one hand while he wrapped the other around Zhang Yuwen, still kissing him.

Zhang Yuwen was already hard, and his rationality was taking leave of him. It was overwhelming, to be kissed so deeply and passionately by a top when that was usually his move... Just as Huo Sichen was deepening the kiss, his hand starting to wander, Zhang Yuwen called for a pause. He nudged the side of Huo Sichen's face with two fingers, and Huo Sichen let go.

They both breathed raggedly as they sat back in their seats.

"Sorry," Huo Sichen said.

"I'm too nervous," Zhang Yuwen said as he adjusted his pants. "It's been a while since I... You know. So it's easy to lose control."

Huo Sichen laughed, and Zhang Yuwen licked his lips, savoring the taste. Huo Sichen leaned in again, but this time, he just gave Zhang Yuwen a peck on the lips.

"Good night," said Zhang Yuwen. "See you tomorrow."

"See you tomorrow." Huo Sichen watched Zhang Yuwen go back into the house before he drove away.

This was progressing fast. Zhang Yuwen hadn't expected Huo Sichen to be so proactive in kissing him, but then again, it made sense; guys tended to be proactive when they were in a relationship, as long as it was with the right person. Zhang Yuwen himself typically wanted to confirm their relationship on the first day and sleep together on the second. No, scratch that: They could sleep together on the first day too, after they had dinner. On the second day, they could bring in the moving van.

That was the ideal scenario, anyway. In reality, there were a lot of misgivings and friction in life, so taking things slowly and making sure to understand each other was probably the better move. Guys were often driven by sexual desire, though, and when raging hormones collided, good sense went out the window, just like it had with Huo Sichen's sudden kiss. Even now, Zhang Yuwen could still feel the soft, warm touch of Huo Sichen's lips on his own. It had been too long since his last kiss, and being partially pinned down and ravished—being dominated like that—felt novel and exciting.

It was a totally different experience to be kissed by a top compared to a bottom. A bottom's lips were soft and fragrant, and once the kiss started, they stayed obediently still and let Zhang Yuwen tantalize them as he pleased. But the kiss of a top was firm, powerful, and protective, making Zhang Yuwen want to rise to the occasion himself...

Without meaning to, Zhang Yuwen licked his lips. He changed his shoes in the foyer and entered to find the living room brightly illuminated. All his roommates were sitting at the dining table, looking at him.

Chen Hong asked the obvious: "Where did you go?"

"Out for a meal," Zhang Yuwen said. "I just got back."

"With who?" Chang Jinxing pressed, grinning. He was hanging up a photo of the five of them hanging out. Zheng Weize was arranging the flowers Huo Sichen gave Zhang Yuwen, while Yan Jun sat at the table, watching.

"Huo Sichen," Zhang Yuwen replied. "Who else?"

"Are you two together now?"

"Not yet, but I want to try."

His roommates were shocked. "I thought he was straight?!" exclaimed Zheng Weize.

"Straight, my ass!" Chang Jinxing laughed. "Didn't you see how hard he swallowed that day on the hiking trip when Yuwen was changing his clothes?"

Everyone burst into laughter. Zhang Yuwen wouldn't have expected Chang Jinxing to remember a detail like that so clearly. Yan Jun laughed too, but he said nothing.

Chen Hong looked at the paper bag in Zhang Yuwen's hands. "What's that? A Christmas gift?"

"Uh..." Zhang Yuwen trailed off. "I haven't opened it yet."

"Gimme, gimme!" Chang Jinxing said. "I'm confiscating it!"

"Wait!" Zhang Yuwen protested, but they caught him off guard and snatched his gift away. He wasn't worried, though; he let them have it. "Where's Xiao-Qi?"

"Sleeping," Yan Jun said.

"Keep your voices down, guys!" Zhang Yuwen said. "Don't wake the little princess."

"Wow..."

"Quiet!" Zhang Yuwen hissed through gritted teeth.

Yan Jun sat up and looked at the bag. "Let me see. What is it?"

"A mobile phone!" Chang Jinxing said. "US version! Top of the line! Must have cost over ten thousand!"

Zhang Yuwen picked it up to take a look, hummed in acknowledgment, and placed it back on the dining table. Zheng Weize reached out for it, so Zhang Yuwen handed it over for him to play with.

Chen Hong was astounded at his reaction. "Aren't you touched?"

"Oh, yeah." Zhang Yuwen grinned. "So very touched."

Just then, Zhang Yuwen's new phone received a message. Everyone looked at it, but to avoid prying eyes, Zhang Yuwen refrained from opening the chat. Moments later, the phone vibrated, and the caller ID displayed, *The Fisherman*.

Zhang Yuwen didn't answer it, refusing to satisfy his roommates' lust for gossip. "Okay," he said instead, "what are you guys all doing here? Aren't you going to shower and sleep?"

Chen Hong said, "We were waiting for you. It's New Year's Eve tomorrow. What plans have you made?" He squinted at Zhang Yuwen. "You did plan something, didn't you? Or were you so busy with your dates that you forgot all about it?"

"I didn't forget! I promised to make plans. Don't worry." He went to the cabinet in the dining room and took out the stack of vouchers. "See? We're going to a hot spring resort tomorrow for three days and two nights."

This whipped them all up into a frenzy. "Wow!"

"Thank you, Mr. Zhang!" Chang Jinxing exclaimed. "Oh shit, meals are included too!"

"Shhh. Keep your voices down..." Zhang Yuwen couldn't handle this troop of monkeys.

"Papa!" It was Xiao-Qi's voice. Sure enough, they'd woken her. Yan Jun rushed back to the room, and her cries gradually tapered off into quiet sobs.

Zhang Yuwen shooed everyone off to bed, then cleared the coffee mugs from the dining table and sat down to reply to the messages.

Huo Sichen: *Too expensive. Whered u get it?*

Zhang Yuwen had known Huo Sichen would say that. He pictured Huo Sichen leaving Riverbay Road, driving for a while, and then, unable to resist any longer, pulling over by the curb to open the gift. If it weren't such an inconvenience to get out of the car, he might have even opened the trunk and taken out the clothes to look at each article in turn.

That was, in fact, what happened. As soon as Huo Sichen opened the package and saw the orange box, he messaged Zhang Yuwen. When he received no reply, he tried calling twice.

Huo Sichen: *This is at least 20–30k. Too expensive.*

Zhang Yuwen: *I won it at the publisher's annual dinner. It's not as expensive as u think.*

Huo Sichen: *U sure?*

Zhang Yuwen: *With my salary, I couldn't afford it even if I scrimp n save every penny. Relax.*

The "Typing…" indicator appeared. Huo Sichen still had more to say. Zhang Yuwen added, *Didnt u buy me a phone?*

Huo Sichen deleted what he'd been typing and replied, *All right, but dont buy such expensive gifts nxt time.*

Zhang Yuwen replied with a smile. *There wont b anything expensive nxt time.*

Huo Sichen had always felt inferior to Zhang Yuwen. He was handsome and had a great body, while Huo Sichen's only advantage was his financial status. He planned to sweep him off his feet, partially with his own charm and partially by buying his happiness. This was the most effective technique Huo Sichen knew. He'd never expected that flaunting his money would just get him one-upped by Zhang Yuwen, and he had conflicting feelings about it.

The wallet Zhang Yuwen gave him was a limited-edition men's item. Even at the specialty store, it went for at least ¥28,000 before tax. It was brand new, too, and looked like it was just recently purchased. It couldn't have been something someone else gave him... Huo Sichen recalled what Chen Hong had told him: Other than his dates with Huo Sichen, Zhang Yuwen hardly left the house. It was unlikely that he was two-timing Huo Sichen with a rich side piece.

Buying luxury goods came as naturally to Zhang Yuwen as drinking water. He just rarely used them. If the mood took him, he could have walked into a store and bought this wallet without a second thought. He could even outfit Huo Sichen from head to toe without breaking a sweat.

As he replied to Huo Sichen, he sipped some water and looked at the photos Chang Jinxing had hung on the wall. They documented many of the roommates' shared memories; the one of them being attacked by monkeys on their hiking trip was not only enlarged, but given pride of place.

Chang Jinxing had been using a tripod to take group photos, and the sudden appearance of the monkeys brought out different reactions in everyone. Zhang Yuwen had his jacket wrapped around his arm, about to shoo the monkey away. Yan Jun was trying to shield him and Huo Sichen was rushing over from the other side, while Chen Hong attempted to lure the monkeys away with the snacks in his hands. Zheng Weize was hiding behind Chang Jinxing, who held his bag up like a shield.

It was a hilarious picture. Zhang Yuwen had never expected to see the moment captured on film.

Another photo showed Huo Sichen protecting Zhang Yuwen as they fled to safety. There was also one from the rest stop. Zhang

Yuwen had taken off his clothes, revealing his beautiful figure. He was looking up at Huo Sichen, who held the medicated oil and looked incredibly nervous, gazing back at Zhang Yuwen like a loyal hound. The camera scene was backlit, too, lending a suggestive energy to the moment.

So that's how it was... Zhang Yuwen thought. Maybe Huo Sichen already liked him back then. No wonder Chang Jinxing was the first to see through him.

But that photo was too embarrassing to hang in the dining room. Zhang Yuwen took it right down. Next to it, another photo showed Yan Jun pulling him up after he fell down ice skating on the platform.

Having coaxed Xiao-Qi back to sleep, Yan Jun emerged just in time to catch Zhang Yuwen in the act of stealing the photograph. He didn't say anything, though, just sat at the dining table, staring blankly at Zhang Yuwen's back.

"Why does Jinxing always capture these embarrassing moments?" Zhang Yuwen complained.

"I don't mind," said Yan Jun.

Zhang Yuwen went through all the remaining photos and took away the one where Huo Sichen applied the medicated oil for him, leaving the others behind.

Yan Jun looked down at the hot spring vouchers. "I've been here before. It's amazing there's still water in the hot spring after so many years."

"It's really famous," Zhang Yuwen said. "It's been around for more than forty years. It used to be the best hot spring in Jiangdong."

A brief silence fell. Then Yan Jun asked, "You like him?"

Zhang Yuwen didn't answer. He sat down at the table and picked up the envelope, and Yan Jun handed him the vouchers to return to it.

"You really like him," Yan Jun said. "I'm talking about Huo Sichen."

"Yeah. What do you think of him?"

"He's great." After a moment's thought, Yan Jun added, "You guys are a good match."

"He was either straight or closeted before—"

"I thought so too," Yan Jun interrupted him. "But I keep getting this feeling that he's holding something back. Maybe he's hiding something from you."

"That's fine," Zhang Yuwen said breezily. "I'm hiding something from him too. Everyone has things they don't want to share."

"Yeah." Yan Jun smiled a little sadly. "That's just how you are, open-minded and magnanimous."

Zhang Yuwen knew Yan Jun was worried about him, that he would be hurt by Huo Sichen. When he thought about the situation rationally, Huo Sichen wasn't a magnate or a tycoon, but he was a gold-collar executive. He was tall and handsome. He could hardly have wanted for suitors. In dramas, people like him were usually seasoned womanizers, guys who'd seen everything and had no shortage of sexual opportunities. Even Zhang Yuwen found it hard to believe he didn't have colleagues, male or female, throwing themselves at him.

Yan Jun had been in the workforce for a long time and must have had a certain amount of experience with Huo Sichen's type. For him and Chen Hong, it wasn't hard to guess that Huo Sichen might be hiding something. Besides, Zhang Yuwen himself still didn't know much about Huo Sichen.

"Don't worry," Zhang Yuwen said. "If I feel something off... Hm, I can self-adjust. The best thing about me is that I won't get myself in too deep, emotionally speaking."

Yan Jun said nothing more on the matter.

"Xiao-Qi's coming with us tomorrow, right?" Zhang Yuwen asked.

"Yeah." Yan Jun smiled. "Sorry for the trouble."

Zhang Yuwen smiled back. "I'm looking forward to it."

That night, Zhang Yuwen wrapped himself in his quilt and rolled over in bed. As he lay on his stomach, he conjured up a sexual fantasy. That kiss seemed to have activated some sort of emotion in him. He pressed his cheek against the pillow and moved his hips; he was feeling very comfortable, so he wrapped his legs around his bolster and rubbed against it. Drifting between sleep and consciousness, he thought back to how Huo Sichen had behaved in the car.

What would have happened if he'd let things take their natural course? Huo Sichen's arm was around his waist, and then...

After a while, rubbing against the bolster wasn't enough. Zhang Yuwen had gone without for a long time, and that kiss had opened the floodgates. He stripped naked and clamped his long, fair, and well-defined legs around the bolster. He pressed his hard cock against it as he imagined Huo Sichen vying with him for dominance...

The long, cylindrical bolster was its own subliminal message. Zhang Yuwen was pretty sizable, but as a gay man, he had a bit of a phallus obsession. He wasn't satisfied merely knowing that he himself measured up; he also eagerly anticipated discovering how big his partner was. He especially loved it when a well-endowed bottom got uncontrollably hard when Zhang Yuwen entered him, a silent expression of praise and approval.

In his half-asleep state, images of a tender but thrilling scenario in which he and Huo Sichen ground their cocks against each other flashed through Zhang Yuwen's mind. Coupled with the soft stimulation from the bolster on his sensitive tip, those images activated his self-propelled rocket launcher; there was no stopping it.

Ugh, now I've got to wash the bolster tomorrow.

His mind cleared a little, and Zhang Yuwen wiped himself down efficiently. He was totally spent. As post-nut clarity set in, he found his cum on the bolster a little disgusting, so he kicked it off the bed and, without bothering to put on any pajamas, fell asleep.

CHAPTER 22

NEW YEAR'S EVE, 11:00 a.m.

When the doorbell rang, Zhang Yuwen sprang up, pulled on his pajamas at lightning speed, opened the window, and tossed his bolster down from the second floor, where it landed in the sink behind the washing machine. In one fluid movement, he vaulted down from the balcony onto the window ledge of Chen Hong's first-floor room, then used the momentum to spring and flip onto the garden grounds. He turned on the faucet and began to wash his bolster.

Sure enough, it was Huo Sichen. Yan Jun opened the door for him. Xiao-Qi, dressed in an adorable new onesie, was toddling around in the living room, and Huo Sichen waved at her. "Hello."

Leaving the bolster to soak, Zhang Yuwen glanced into the living room and saw that Chen Hong was up, too. He was talking to Huo Sichen, who looked a lot more re-energized after a night's rest.

"You're here," said Zhang Yuwen.

"Since when were you in the garden?" asked Yan Jun, startled.

Zhang Yuwen padded in barefoot. "Oh, just now. Huh? Where are my slippers? They were just here. Who took them? Sichen, you want some coffee?" He knew the house like the back of his hand, and no one batted an eye when he came and went like a shadow.

"I was early," Huo Sichen said, though they had agreed on 10 a.m.

"Nah. Coffee? You seem more alert today."

"I slept for ten hours." Huo Sichen rolled his neck. "I feel refreshed."

His roommates started emerging from their rooms. Chen Hong, drenched in sweat after waking up early to exercise, took a shower and emerged wearing a hooded tracksuit. A moment later, Chang Jinxing came down and greeted them, already dressed.

Then Zheng Weize emerged, yawning, from Chang Jinxing's room on the second floor.

"What—!" everyone cried in unison.

"We fell asleep talking last night," Chang Jinxing explained. "Don't jump to conclusions."

Zheng Weize stared at Chang Jinxing, looking displeased. Zhang Yuwen was shocked at first, but it did look like nothing had happened between them, so they said nothing more on the topic.

The boys put on their running shoes, looked for their stuff, and, carrying their duffel bags, crowded out of the door. The chaos reminded Zhang Yuwen of his university roommates, albeit with the addition of a stroller for Xiao-Qi. Their outfits weren't coordinated, but everyone wore the scarves Zheng Weize had given them, which gave them some important group cohesion.

"It snowed again last night," said Zhang Yuwen.

"Yeah," Huo Sichen agreed, "and the ground is slippery. Don't fall again."

They walked to the nearest train station. Chang Jinxing walked backward with his camera to take photos of the others, but he slipped and fell into the snow. Yan Jun reached out to give him a hand, but Zhang Yuwen cheekily shoved him down. Before long, everyone was tumbling around in a snowy heap.

"Watch out for Xiao-Qi," Zheng Weize said. "Stop horsing around in the snow, guys."

"I'm starving," Chen Hong said. "I can't win, you guys... Can we just grab lunch first?"

When they arrived at the train station, Chang Jinxing announced, "Lunch is on me."

"Oh?" said Zhang Yuwen, his tone rising skeptically.

"Looks like someone's been making bank," Yan Jun joked.

With a grin, Chang Jinxing went to buy boxed lunches for everyone to eat on the train, and then they boarded. It was Xiao-Qi's first train ride and she was enraptured, putting her little paws on everything she could reach and peering out the windows.

The suburban express train sped out of Riverbay Road station. It was the last day of the year, so there weren't many other people on board, and the vibe was very laid-back. Outside, snow blanketed the Jiangbei houses along the railway tracks, creating a tranquil vista.

Huo Sichen and Zhang Yuwen shared a row. Zhang Yuwen loosened his scarf and glanced sideways to where Zheng Weize and Chen Hong sat. Zheng Weize was gazing out the window. Over by Yan Jun, Chang Jinxing was taking photos of Xiao-Qi and ribbing Yan Jun occasionally.

Huh. Weird, Zhang Yuwen thought. Usually Zheng Weize would cling to Chang Jinxing, but that wasn't what was happening today.

Huo Sichen put a finger under Zhang Yuwen's chin and turned his face toward him. Zhang Yuwen looked at him wordlessly, and Huo Sichen raised an eyebrow, telling him to stop looking around.

"How did you sleep last night?" Huo Sichen asked.

This question was a little too close for comfort, and for a moment, Zhang Yuwen wondered if he'd been found out. He realized quickly, however, that Huo Sichen was probably asking because of the parting kiss they'd shared. "Hm... Not bad."

Huo Sichen flashed him a mischievous grin. "I dreamed about you again."

"Oh? What was I doing?" Zhang Yuwen asked reflexively, only to regret his words as soon as they left his mouth. With Huo Sichen looking at him like that, what else could the dream have been about?

Huo Sichen laughed, and Zhang Yuwen sensed that Huo Sichen was winding him up. After a moment's consideration, Huo Sichen said, "You strike me as the ascetic type."

"What else do you expect?" Zhang Yuwen countered. "Or am I supposed to go soliciting hookers when I'm single?"

This tickled Huo Sichen's funny bone, but in deference to the other passengers on the train, he suppressed the urge to laugh out loud. "I mean, you rarely have one-night stands, right?"

"Not rarely. Never."

Huo Sichen nodded. "As someone who was raised by doctors, I'm guessing you like things clean?"

"I don't know about that." Zhang Yuwen thought it over. "Maybe it's just a habit in how I live my life. Does that count as a hang-up about cleanliness?" He'd never been interested in casual hookups, and in fact, he found it hard to wrap his mind around the idea of two complete strangers having sex the first time they met. Wouldn't that be uncomfortable? He never made a big deal about his "clean" sex life, though, and he respected other people's approaches to sexual intimacy.

"How about emotionally?" Huo Sichen asked offhandedly.

"Nope."

Zhang Yuwen was unusually forthcoming, answering any question Huo Sichen asked him. He wanted to take this relationship seriously and invest whatever trust and feelings he had left. Maybe it was because he'd fantasized about Huo Sichen during the night, which amplified his attraction to him, or maybe it was just that self-reflection following his last, failed relationship had convinced him that he should be more honest. He looked expectantly at Huo Sichen.

"Me neither." Those two succinct words encompassed Huo Sichen's responses to all the questions he'd just asked Zhang Yuwen.

The train raced out of Jiangdong City, toward the endless stretch of mountains in the distance. A lot of the passengers were students returning to their hometowns. They chattered away, but Huo Sichen and Zhang Yuwen remained unusually quiet. Zhang Yuwen knew Huo Sichen's attention was fixed on him, though, because when he retrieved two bottles of coffee from his bag, Huo Sichen reached over to take them.

Zhang Yuwen snorted in amusement.

Huo Sichen was puzzled. "Hm?"

"I can open the bottles myself."

"Sorry."

Zhang Yuwen's heart softened. He glanced at Huo Sichen, several thoughts flashing through his mind at once. He was intrigued by this guy—physically, emotionally, and even sexually.

If he were to date Huo Sichen, they would look from the outside like more of a genuine gay couple than Zhang Yuwen's past relationship, which had in some senses been an extension of heterosexuality. He played the male role, his ex the female. With Huo Sichen, on the other hand, he was keenly aware of the other guy's masculinity. This also raised other issues: their dynamic, their positions in bed, and the attitudes they held toward each other.

Clearly, Huo Sichen had yet to think any of these matters through. A number of challenges still loomed ahead of them.

Xiao-Qi, who was learning to walk, toddled over to them.

"Eh, Xiao-Qi?" Zhang Yuwen said, picking her up just as Yan Jun followed her over. Zhang Yuwen gestured to Yan Jun not to worry; Zhang Yuwen could handle her, and Yan Jun deserved a break.

Xiao-Qi was still shy around people, but she didn't try to squirm away from Zhang Yuwen or complain about sitting on his lap. Huo Sichen politely played with her, but Zhang Yuwen could tell that he didn't particularly like kids.

"She's special to you," Huo Sichen remarked. It was clear he had been observing them.

"Yup." Zhang Yuwen adored babies. "A child's attitudes about other people comes from their parents'. Yan Jun trusts me, so Xiao-Qi's more comfortable being close to me."

"Ah," said Huo Sichen, understanding. "That makes sense."

"Have you ever thought about having kids?"

Huo Sichen snapped back to his senses. "No," he said. "Never. My older brother has two, and they're always so rowdy."

Soon, the train arrived at their station, and everyone disembarked. The resort shuttle bus was waiting at the train station to take them on a journey deep into the mountains, where the hot spring resort lay. Aside from them, surprisingly few guests seemed to be on their way to the resort.

When they reached their destination, they found the manager and the front desk staff waiting outside to greet them. They bowed. "Welcome."

"Wow!" Zheng Weize, vacationing here for the first time, was bursting with anticipation.

It was clear that the film production company that helped make the reservations had informed the hotel who Zhang Yuwen was in advance. He worried the staff might let something slip in their enthusiasm, but fortunately, they seemed to know not to go too far. He handed over the vouchers, and the resort arranged three rooms for them. The others divided the rooms among themselves while Zhang Yuwen accepted three wooden plaques, each with a key attached.

Zheng Weize reached for a plaque. "I want to share a room with Xiao-Qi."

"Sure—wait, what?" Zhang Yuwen looked at Chang Jinxing, but Zheng Weize had already taken the key away.

"Then I'll bunk with Jinxing," Chen Hong said.

Zhang Yuwen was dying to know what had happened between them. The rooms the resort arranged for their group were all next to each other, and there seemed to be no differences among them, so the room assignments ended up being Zhang Yuwen with Huo Sichen, Yan Jun with Zheng Weize, and Chen Hong with Chang Jinxing.

"Gentlemen, please come with me," the receptionist said, holding their bathrobes. "The hot spring for men will be downstairs during the night and on the mountain on the fourth floor in the day. Your accommodation is called Crane Hall; it's in a separate building. Follow the path…"

"Wow!" Everyone was suitably amazed.

Crane Hall had four bedrooms that faced each other in pairs, plus a common area in the center for drinking tea. Hot tea had already been prepared by the staff. The rooms were furnished with Japanese tatami mats. When it came time for bed, someone would come to set out the bedding for them.

"The dining area is across the path to the south," the receptionist said. "Here, please choose your robes."

"So comfy!" Zheng Weize entered his room and opened the tatami screen to reveal a terrace with floor-to-ceiling windows. Beyond that was a beautiful, wintry landscape dotted with mountain village houses in the far distance.

The fourth room was unoccupied; they had effectively booked the entire little building for themselves. Zhang Yuwen checked on everyone before returning to his room. By then, it was half past three.

The heating was turned up high. Huo Sichen had taken off his coat and was sitting at the low table in his black sweater, drinking matcha and admiring the scenery outside.

Zhang Yuwen smiled. "This is so much better than the last time." His memory of their stay at Elephant Gorge was still fresh in his mind.

"Your publisher is really generous," said Huo Sichen. The resort had taken him by surprise.

"Maybe? Or maybe they just upgraded our rooms because it isn't fully booked today."

Everyone had their doors open, perhaps not seeing the need to close them. Honestly, Zhang Yuwen would've started to feel awkward if the doors were closed. His relationship with Huo Sichen was no longer just friendship, but they weren't lovers yet, and somehow, anything they did felt inappropriate.

"What did you bring?" Huo Sichen asked.

"You want to rummage through my bag again?" Zhang Yuwen laughed.

"Just curious."

Zhang Yuwen had brought along a book on creative writing to read when he was bored. As he unpacked his belongings and put them away neatly, Huo Sichen flipped through the book with apparent interest.

"Don't force yourself," Zhang Yuwen said, guessing that Huo Sichen had zero actual interest in it. The book was commonly used by screenwriters, and it could be abstruse even for novelists. Huo Sichen stopped pretending.

Meanwhile, in the rooms across from them, the others had already changed into their bathrobes.

"Yuwen!" Zheng Weize called out. "Are you guys going to the hot spring?"

"Later! You all go ahead." Zhang Yuwen may have been the one who chose the hot spring, but he was still a little uncomfortable at the thought of being completely naked with his roommates.

Chen Hong came out of the room opposite theirs and pulled Zheng Weize back. "Come on, don't bother them..."

Zhang Yuwen and Huo Sichen exchanged a glance. The awkwardness between them intensified.

"Let's change into our bathrobes." Zhang Yuwen took a bathrobe, sat at the table, and removed his shirt. "Aren't you changing?"

Huo Sichen put the book down and hesitated for a moment.

"I'll see it all later anyway," said Zhang Yuwen, "so what are you shy for? Strip!"

Huo Sichen was unexpectedly hesitant. Zhang Yuwen came over and made to strip him himself. "Okay, okay," Huo Sichen said hastily.

He got up to close the door, but Zhang Yuwen said, "They're gonna see you later anyway. Does it make a difference?"

Huo Sichen was lost for words. Zhang Yuwen started laughing, and Huo Sichen closed the door partially. Trying his best to maintain his composure, he undid his belt.

Zhang Yuwen, now completely undressed, stood in his naked glory. Huo Sichen stopped what he was doing and turned to look at him. With one hand holding his bathrobe, Zhang Yuwen made a "What?" expression, openly allowing Huo Sichen to look.

Remarkably, Huo Sichen blushed! He looked at Zhang Yuwen, his Adam's apple bobbing, and took a sudden step toward him. Zhang Yuwen knew he wanted to kiss him, but the door was still open, so he made a "no" gesture. Huo Sichen stopped advancing and started stripping.

"Is the purpose of the hot spring to inspect the goods first?" Huo Sichen joked.

Zhang Yuwen was skilled at controlling the situation even at times like this. "It's to let *you* inspect the goods. So, are you satisfied?"

Zhang Yuwen was scrutinizing Huo Sichen right back, and he discovered to his surprise that Huo Sichen's physique was even better than his own. Slim when clothed, toned when naked, and he even had well-defined pecs!

Oh no! A certain part of Zhang Yuwen began to stir. He'd thought he'd be able to keep his cool today after he relieved himself the night before.

That was when he discovered why Huo Sichen had acted so bashful, and why he kept avoiding him when he was changing into his robe:

Huo Sichen was hard.

His cock looked even bigger than Zhang Yuwen's at its peak. That made sense; he was taller than Zhang Yuwen and had broader shoulders and longer fingers.

Zhang Yuwen's eyes curved in a smile. "You..."

Huo Sichen tried to make his disobedient little friend calm down, but it only became harder. "It's been a long time since I've... You know," he explained, wrapping himself in the bathrobe.

"So you were lying about dreaming of me last night?" said Zhang Yuwen, skeptical.

Huo Sichen's face turned even redder. He changed the subject. "We going to soak in the hot spring now?"

"I'll ask the guys?" Zhang Yuwen said. "Do you want to show it to everyone?"

Huo Sichen was lost for words, his face beet red. He waved his hand to tell Zhang Yuwen not to say any more. Sitting with his back to Zhang Yuwen, he did his best to calm himself. Zhang Yuwen found this adorable. He wouldn't have minded topping him.

A sexual stirring rose within him, Huo Sichen its target. Zhang Yuwen pictured, thrillingly, having this tall, long-legged, elite man panting under him.

Across from them, Zhang Yuwen saw Chang Jinxing changing clothes. Yan Jun was on a phone call in the common area. Zhang Yuwen sat down beside Huo Sichen. "Let's wait a while."

Huo Sichen was back to his usual self. "I found a chess set. Shall we play? Do you know how?"

The room had Monopoly and a chessboard. "Will you get angry if you lose?" Zhang Yuwen asked as he set the chessboard up.

"Nope. I'll go easy on you and let you take back moves."

"Oh, really? We'll see about that. I never take back a move."

"That's a good habit to have. Life is like a game of chess. No going back, no regrets."

Zhang Yuwen's grandfather liked playing chess, so Zhang Yuwen had been exposed to the game since he was a child. He was an adroit player.

But it took Huo Sichen only five minutes to trounce Zhang Yuwen, disgracing him utterly.

"I quit! Are you a professional or what?"

"A grade 5 chess player," Huo Sichen said. "Another game? I'll let you take back moves."

"Nah. Let's go soak in the hot spring."

Zheng Weize was on his way back, sipping iced cola, his face flushed from soaking in the hot water.

Zhang Yuwen arrived at the hot spring. Through the steam, the first thing he saw was Chen Hong's naked, chiseled body. He was talking with Yan Jun, but when Zhang Yuwen entered, they both went quiet.

"Hm?" After a moment's silence, Zhang Yuwen got into the water and squawked, "Whoa! Hot!"

Everyone burst out laughing. As he adjusted to the temperature, Zhang Yuwen exhaled sharply and shot Chen Hong and Yan Jun a surprised look.

"Where's Xiao-Qi?" Zhang Yuwen asked.

"Weize is keeping her company," Yan Jun replied. "Babies can't soak in hot springs."

"Where's Sichen?" Chen Hong returned.

"He's buying drinks at the vending machine."

Chen Hong smirked playfully. "Have you checked out the goods?"

Zhang Yuwen knew what he was asking. "Not as big as yours,"— Chen Hong wasn't even covering himself with a towel as he sat on the hot stones—"but not small either."

"Is it as big as mine?" Yan Jun asked, standing up from the water.

"Enough!" Zhang Yuwen laughed so he wouldn't cry. Yan Jun cracked up too, and Zhang Yuwen wondered, *What in the world is going on in those heads of yours?!*

But Yan Jun's was sizeable too, perhaps because he was tall and thin. From the looks of it, Chen Hong ranked first in size—S-tier, compared to the straight guys Zhang Yuwen had seen in porn. Yan Jun and Huo Sichen tied for second place with an A+, and Zhang Yuwen fell just below them with an A. As for Chang Jinxing...

Chen Hong seemed to read Zhang Yuwen's mind. "I've seen Jinxing's. More or less the same as yours, Yuwen."

Zhang Yuwen and Yan Jun both looked at Chen Hong. "Oh?"

Chen Hong chuckled but didn't elaborate. Zhang Yuwen was about to probe, but Chen Hong turned the tables on him. "So, Yuwen, between you and Sichen, who's the top?"

"We haven't done it," Zhang Yuwen said. "You don't need to worry about that kind of thing."

Huo Sichen finally appeared, and his naked form brought the conversation to an abrupt end. The high temperature of the hot spring caused everyone's blood to pump faster, and Huo Sichen had finally gone soft.

He handed iced drinks to Chen Hong and Yan Jun. "Whoa! Hot!" Huo Sichen howled as he entered the water, prompting another round of laughter. "I'm surprised there's still water in this hot spring, since it's been around for over twenty years."

"You've been here before?" Zhang Yuwen asked, surprised.

"Yeah. My parents brought me here when I was seven and my brother was nine. That was twenty-two years ago."

"I came here as a kid too," Yan Jun added. "That was when my dad was still around. Our family came to Jiangdong for a trip, and we stayed over in this resort for two days."

"This place must hold a lot of memories for so many people," Chen Hong commented.

"I really didn't think this was the kind of place you'd choose for New Year's Eve," said Yan Jun.

"It's because I've been here too." Zhang Yuwen laughed. "My grandpa loved coming here when I was a kid. We'd soak in these hot springs almost weekly in winter."

"I remember that most of the rooms in this resort were made of wood twenty-two years ago," Huo Sichen said. "Now all that's left is Crane Hall."

"Tortoise Hall and Kirin Hall have already been renovated," said Zhang Yuwen. He was still astonished that Huo Sichen had been to the resort before.

"This place was called Foothills back then, right?" said Yan Jun.

"Yeah!" Huo Sichen and Zhang Yuwen both replied at once. Now it was the Mid-Mountain Lodge.

"My brother used to take me down to the stream to fish," Yan Jun said. "There's a stream on the other side of the mountain that doesn't freeze."

"There were lots of deer on the mountain too," Huo Sichen added.

"Yeah! Yeah!" said Yan Jun. "I saw a few at the park halfway up the mountain. I'm thinking of taking Xiao-Qi there tomorrow for a walk."

Things got quiet again. Zhang Yuwen sat facing Yan Jun, and although Yan Jun's face was obscured by the steam, Zhang Yuwen knew he must be reminiscing.

"You have two boys in your family too?" Huo Sichen asked Yan Jun.

"Yeah."

Huo Sichen had never asked about Xiao-Qi's mother. Perhaps he was curious, but he knew better than to pry.

Chen Hong suddenly changed the topic. "Sichen, have you been skipping chest day?"

"It's enough already. I don't want it too big."

Everyone laughed again. "Stand up and let me have a look?" Chen Hong asked. Huo Sichen obliged. "Your abs are still there. It's been a while since your last session."

"It's not like I'm signing up for bodybuilding competitions," said Huo Sichen. "You shouldn't be asking me where I need muscles, though; you should ask the person who'll be making use of them."

Chen Hong and Yan Jun laughed. "What about Yuwen?" Chen Hong asked.

Zhang Yuwen stood up.

"Turn around," Chen Hong said, "I wanna see your glutes."

"Why didn't you ask to see his?" Zhang Yuwen protested. The others hooted with laughter again.

"I'm done soaking," Yan Jun said. "I can't take any more of it. I'm getting too dizzy." He got up and left the hot spring to put on his bathrobe.

"Me too," said Chen Hong.

This left Zhang Yuwen and Huo Sichen alone in the quiet hot spring pool. Huo Sichen moved closer to Zhang Yuwen, letting their thighs touch. Zhang Yuwen glanced cheekily between Huo Sichen's legs, then let his eyes wander over his body, landing on his abs, chest, and finally his face.

Huo Sichen reached out to stroke Zhang Yuwen's thigh. In that tranquil moment, they seemed to be in perfect sync as Huo Sichen tilted his head and leaned in. Zhang Yuwen turned to meet him in a kiss.

He stopped Huo Sichen from going further, though. "No messing around here. It's too easy to feel faint."

They left the near-scalding pool, their skin pink as shrimp. As they were putting on their bathrobes, Huo Sichen grinned at Zhang Yuwen. Zhang Yuwen raised an inquiring eyebrow.

"You're sexy," Huo Sichen whispered.

"You too," Zhang Yuwen whispered back.

Zhang Yuwen had a fair complexion with a cool undertone and a well-proportioned figure. Huo Sichen was tall and straight-backed, and his damp hair made him look even more handsome, like a meticulously styled model. Huo Sichen admired their bodies in the mirror. They looked like a perfect match.

Most importantly, they were both hard after the soak—their desires laid bare in their gazes, their pricks screaming, "I wanna make love to you," like a pair of desperate animals.

Guys were candid when it came to sex. It was pointless to play coy when their bodies betrayed their innermost thoughts. Zhang Yuwen didn't mind Huo Sichen's gaze on him at all, and he liked watching Huo Sichen too. At first, Huo Sichen had seemed flustered when he felt Zhang Yuwen's eyes on him, but by this point he was used to it.

"Your third leg is rock solid," Zhang Yuwen said, teasing.

"It hasn't gone soft at all today with you around."

Hearing noises from outside, they put on their bathrobes. Zhang Yuwen stopped to buy a drink as they passed the vending machine outside the pool, and a thought popped into his head: *Should Huo Sichen and I sleep together tonight?* Huo Sichen was clearly up for it.

But if they did, who would top? Huo Sichen clearly wanted to... Zhang Yuwen didn't mind bottoming this time, but once they'd established those roles, he was bound to be relegated to bottom status in the future; he'd only get to top occasionally. Zhang Yuwen was still not mentally prepared for that. He liked Huo Sichen, but not so much that he was willing to bottom *all* the time.

Two men dating was interesting for the sense of equality that came with it, but that was also where the trouble came in. It was sometimes hard to strike a balance when it came to sex.

Sipping his iced drink, Zhang Yuwen returned to his room and looked at his phone, killing time until dinner with his roommates later. Huo Sichen came over to sit beside him, so Zhang Yuwen put down his phone and looked at him. He suspected that Huo Sichen had the same question on his mind.

"What time is dinner?" Huo Sichen asked.

"Seven."

"What time is it now?"

"Four thirty. It's still early."

Huo Sichen wrapped his arms around Zhang Yuwen's waist. Zhang Yuwen thought about it. This time, he'd been proactive himself. It was as if they had their most honest communication while they were soaking in the hot spring.

So, with their bathrobes partially covering them, he straddled Huo Sichen's waist, savoring the taste of forbidden fruit.

"I have no experience with guys," Huo Sichen said in a small voice. "It's all purely instinct." He buried his face in Zhang Yuwen's chest, his breathing growing urgent. His eyes seemed to have lost all spark of rational thought, leaving only desire behind.

"But I think... Hm," Zhang Yuwen said, the hint of a smile in his eyes. "There's still something we haven't discussed."

"You mean the positions?"

"Do you want to be the top?" asked Zhang Yuwen.

"Can I?" Huo Sichen was a little nervous. "It's my first time, but I'll do my best to learn."

Zhang Yuwen thought about it for a moment. "So, did you bring it?"

"Bring what?" Huo Sichen asked, perplexed.

Zhang Yuwen stared at him. He let go and rolled off of him, wanting to laugh out loud. "You didn't bring anything, and you still want to top?"

"I really don't know. What do we need? I'll buy it now."

"Lube."

"Oh. I...don't have it," Huo Sichen said. "We need that?"

Zhang Yuwen held his forehead in one hand. "You really do have no experience," he deadpanned.

Huo Sichen put on his bathrobe. "Where do they sell it? I'll go now."

Zhang Yuwen motioned him over, and Huo Sichen gave him a questioning look. Zhang Yuwen had him sit in front of him without saying more.

He slipped off Huo Sichen's bathrobe, grasped his dick, and gently stroked it. Huo Sichen's body reacted instantly, stiffening and tensing up.

"Sleeping with a guy is different," Zhang Yuwen explained. "You need to use lube or it'll hurt, especially when you have such a big..."

Huo Sichen's lips parted as if he meant to say, *I had no idea,* but Zhang Yuwen kissed him before he had the chance to speak. Gradually Huo Sichen relaxed, relishing the taste of his lips.

An expert in sex Zhang Yuwen was not, but he was adept. As he kissed Huo Sichen's chest, sucking on and licking his nipples, he stroked him with his hand. Only the sound of Huo Sichen's urgent breathing lingered in his ears.

Huo Sichen shifted awkwardly, adjusting his legs to let Zhang Yuwen lie in his arms, and looked down at Zhang Yuwen with bewilderment in his eyes. When their eyes met, Zhang Yuwen felt the sudden pull of curiosity. Huo Sichen acted like a virgin!

Male or female, this guy couldn't have had sex more than ten times, and he's already twenty-eight or twenty-nine. How did he manage that?

"Does it feel good?" Zhang Yuwen asked him.

Huo Sichen's breathing was shaky, but he turned and pinned Zhang Yuwen to the floor.

"Hey..." Zhang Yuwen looked up at Huo Sichen, whose bathrobe he'd stripped off. Then Huo Sichen kissed him, rubbing his dick between Zhang Yuwen's legs.

What kind of innocent boy behavior was that? Zhang Yuwen found it funny. But the dry, burning, skin-to-skin contact of his naked body rubbing against another guy's felt good.

"I like you," Huo Sichen said in a low baritone. He spoke quickly, as if he was anxious to tell Zhang Yuwen his feelings. "No, I *love* you. Yuwen, I love you."

Zhang Yuwen felt unaccountably touched. He wanted to reply, "I like you too," but Huo Sichen kissed him, cutting off his words. Their breathing grew ragged as Huo Sichen pressed against him, rubbing up and down.

Obligingly, Zhang Yuwen spread his legs and wrapped them around Huo Sichen's waist like he was ready to bottom, but Huo Sichen didn't enter him. He couldn't anyway, not without lube; he could only rub himself against Zhang Yuwen's lower abdomen.

They tangled together, bodies and mouths. Zhang Yuwen had never had sex that was pure friction. If someone had suggested it to him in the past, he would've made them pay a forfeit. Yet Huo Sichen's actions felt beautiful to him, like the long-lost, golden innocence of youth.

A stream of heat sprayed Zhang Yuwen's abdomen. Huo Sichen stopped, panting violently, his handsome face flushed to the tips of his ears as he avoided Zhang Yuwen's gaze. Speechless, Zhang Yuwen looked down at himself, then at Huo Sichen, who seemed mortified.

"You haven't come yet," Huo Sichen said. "I'll clean it up for you."

What the hell? Zhang Yuwen thought. He motioned for Huo Sichen to sit against the wall with their bathrobes under them, had him hug him from behind, and began to pleasure himself.

He leaned his head back on Huo Sichen's shoulder and looked up slightly. Understanding him, Huo Sichen pinched his nipple with one hand and caressed his chest with the other, leaning in to kiss him. It was just like Zhang Yuwen's fantasy from the night before. Using Huo Sichen's cum as a lubricant, he stroked himself.

"You came so much…" Zhang Yuwen said in a husky voice between kisses.

Huo Sichen blushed even more. This was overwhelming. His cum was in Zhang Yuwen's hands, making slick sounds as he moved, as if they were having a full-scale, deeply intimate exchange through this gesture.

Zhang Yuwen felt Huo Sichen getting hard again—the guy's refractory period was barely three minutes! "You—"

"Hush," Huo Sichen breathed, then kissed Zhang Yuwen. Zhang Yuwen quickened his movements. Huo Sichen reached out to help, but after a while, Zhang Yuwen nudged his hand away and continued on his own.

Before long, Zhang Yuwen came. Unlike the previous night, it was a normal amount.

"Whew." Zhang Yuwen got up and went to the bathroom for a shower. A moment later, Huo Sichen joined him, fully naked. Zhang Yuwen smiled at him. Huo Sichen looked sheepish, like a high schooler.

"Is this how it is with men?" Huo Sichen asked. He plastered himself against Zhang Yuwen's back, pressing his erect member between Zhang Yuwen's legs.

"Yeah, but you can't," Zhang Yuwen replied, putting a stop to this inquisitive exchange. He was lathered all over in body wash.

"Hm?"

"Because it'll sting a lot if body wash gets inside. You can't use it as lube."

"All right, I get it." Huo Sichen politely shifted his dick away from Zhang Yuwen's opening, where it had been raring to go. "You're very experienced."

Under normal circumstances, Zhang Yuwen would've assumed that Huo Sichen was teasing him. Based on his performance today, though, he thought that Huo Sichen might really be a virgin.

"My ex and I tried it once," Zhang Yuwen explained. "He said it felt terrible."

Huo Sichen embraced Zhang Yuwen from behind, whispering, "You must have excellent technique."

Zhang Yuwen pinched Huo Sichen's cheek and smiled. "You wanna find out?"

Huo Sichen's expression clouded over, but Zhang Yuwen didn't say more. He just patted him, then stepped out, dried his body, and put on his clothes.

It was already past six, and his roommates were in the common area. Chen Hong, Chang Jinxing, and Zheng Weize were playing cards.

"What are you guys doing?" Zhang Yuwen glanced at his roommates, feeling a bit guilty. Everything seemed normal with them, though.

"Waiting for you two," Chen Hong replied. "Can we go eat now?"

"Dinner isn't until seven. Where's Xiao-Qi?" Zhang Yuwen asked.

Yan Jun had taken her outside to play and practice walking in the garden. Zhang Yuwen went looking for them. A moment later, Huo Sichen emerged from their room and came to the common area.

Zhang Yuwen glanced into the sitting room. They'd switched from cards to Monopoly. Huo Sichen looked like his usual self; nobody would be able to tell by looking at him that anything had happened.

While Zhang Yuwen was looking at Huo Sichen, Yan Jun was looking at Zhang Yuwen. Their eyes met, and they both started laughing.

"Why are you laughing?" Zhang Yuwen asked.

"Why are *you* laughing?" Yan Jun picked Xiao-Qi up and let her walk on the bench.

"I'm not laughing at anything," said Zhang Yuwen. "You seem happy today."

Yan Jun smiled. "It's my birthday."

Zhang Yuwen's jaw dropped. He'd seen Yan Jun's ID before—to think he'd forgotten! "No way. I thought it was... Oh! Your lunar birthday!"

"Yep," Yan Jun said. "Don't tell them."

"So, you're a Capricorn."

"Yeah, I am."

I T WAS YAN JUN'S birthday.

Yan Jun had first realized he liked guys in high school. At the time, the object of his affection was called Mu Zeng. They knew each other from the first year of junior high until their graduation. Mu Zeng was bright and soft-spoken, a first-rate guy, and he was careful not to reveal his true feelings for Yan Jun beyond being exceptionally nice to him. Beginning in the first year of high school, Mu Zeng bought him breakfast, took notes for him, gave him shoes, and went traveling with him.

Mu Zeng's parents were divorced, and he lived with his mother. A fair-skinned boy with pretty features, he was also sensitive, with emotions as delicate as a girl's. He liked to write stories in his notebook and listen to classical music. His sense of aesthetics was great too, and he bought clothes for Yan Jun, taught him to appreciate art and music, and even tutored him in his studies.

Yan Jun, in his adolescence, was at an age where his protective instincts ran high. He took naturally to the role of looking after Mu Zeng. The girls in their class often made fun of them, and after two years of being teased about it, their interactions began to resemble those of a young couple. If, at that time, Yan Jun had known to hit the brakes, things might have turned out differently. But he didn't; it never occurred to him. He saw his desk mate as a younger brother.

In high school, Yan Jun applied to share a dorm room with him. Once they started living together, Mu Zeng's feelings seemed to become even more fragile, and like a couple, they began to bicker, make up, bicker... Friends did that too, though, and Yan Jun still thought of it simply as brotherly possessiveness. His buddy just happened to be very sensitive, that was all.

Sometimes, he found Mu Zeng unreasonable. He didn't realize that Mu Zeng already considered Yan Jun his boyfriend and had just failed to make that explicit. In their sophomore year, Yan Jun was dealt a heavy blow: His father passed away due to illness. For almost six months, he was in extreme anguish, and in those dark times, Mu Zeng was there for him. Yan Jun's family was no longer complete, but Mu Zeng had been living with a similarly fragmented family for many years. They licked each other's wounds and sought solace in their companionship.

One winter night, just after his eighteenth birthday, Yan Jun got drunk. When he returned to his dorm, he somehow ended up in bed with Mu Zeng.

Waking up the next morning, Yan Jun thought, *Oh, fuck! What the hell have I done?!* He had no understanding of sexual identity. He considered Mu Zeng his buddy, not realizing that Mu Zeng had been eyeing his "little buddy" all along. It came as a great shock to him.

Mu Zeng didn't speak a word about what happened that night. After a few days, Yan Jun got over it, dismissing the episode of wild, bewildering feelings as an outrageous drunken romp and trying his best to return their relationship to what it was before. But before long, Mu Zeng launched another offensive. He was clever, while Yan Jun was clumsy and inexperienced. Yan Jun didn't want to continue that way, but he also couldn't bear to give up his five years of friendship with Mu Zeng.

They had sex again. Yan Jun was completely sober this time around, and could no longer make excuses to himself. Mu Zeng had been sulking in the dorm over a minor incident—Yan Jun didn't wait for him at mealtime—and he hid under the covers and cried. Yan Jun, trying his best to placate him, ended up hugging him, which led to kissing him. In the end, Yan Jun had to admit that he was gay. He had feelings for guys, especially guys with a gentle temperament.

Guilt-ridden, he kept denying himself, but at the same time, he indulged in Mu Zeng's tenderness... Mu Zeng had gotten what he wanted and went to great lengths to tie Yan Jun down. Yan Jun was a virgin, and Mu Zeng was his first love; after a show of reluctance, he agreed to be Mu Zeng's boyfriend. He was terrified that his classmates and teachers would find out, though, and was racked with apprehension and uncertainty about his future.

Fortunately, Mu Zeng took the initiative to end the relationship. In their junior year of high school, he left for the UK without so much as a word. Deep down, Yan Jun was relieved, but he also felt a sense of loss. This melancholy hit its peak when he prepared to visit Mu Zeng, only to learn that Mu Zeng had a white boyfriend now.

He was enraged, feeling deceived and betrayed. He wanted to tell Mu Zeng that he'd developed real feelings for him—and besides, whether his feelings were genuine or not, what kind of person ended things like that? Mu Zeng didn't even tell him he was going abroad. He simply stopped contacting him during the summer between their sophomore and junior years and vanished.

Down the line, though, Yan Jun reflected on himself and realized that he hadn't been forthcoming either. In the bedroom, Yan Jun was the top and Mu Zeng the bottom, but emotionally, Mu Zeng was the proactive one. Struggling with conflicted feelings, Yan Jun was always thinking about how to shake him off and resume a heterosexual—and conventional—lifestyle, one where he could date a girl, get married, have a child, and build a family, just like his older brother.

In the end, though, he didn't just fail to return to straight life, he lost interest in girls completely. The only thing he accomplished was breaking up with Mu Zeng. In his senior year, he found that he was no longer attracted to the opposite sex, only to gentle, fair-skinned, clean-cut guys. After his graduation, he went to Jiangdong City to join his older brother. His family urged him to find a girlfriend and get married, and Yan Jun endured it in silence.

He had no love life, and his career was nothing to write home about either. Every day, he grabbed a few steamed buns and squeezed onto the subway to get jostled around, feeling like the walking dead. Then, his brother and sister-in-law were involved in a car accident, leaving behind an orphaned Xiao-Qi with no one to rely on. Yan Jun finally found a direction. He decided that it didn't matter if he was single for the rest of his life. If he could raise Xiao-Qi into healthy adulthood, he would have fulfilled his purpose in the world.

Until, that was, he met Zhang Yuwen.

He was attracted to Zhang Yuwen from the moment he laid eyes on him. At first, this attraction was vague and hard to define, but it gradually sharpened and finally crystallized when they held their respective guns, aimed at each other across a vast expanse of forest, and looked into each other's eyes. It was as if the windows to their souls had opened to each other.

They shared a special kind of rapport that manifested in all aspects of their lives. Even after Huo Sichen entered the picture, Yan Jun still believed this. It was what his intuition told him. And before long, it became clear to Yan Jun that he was head over heels. Zhang Yuwen's striking looks, polite but not zealous temperament, open-minded and optimistic personality, and sense of humor... All of it had him hooked.

Yan Jun had an inferiority complex. Whether it was the low self-esteem of a country bumpkin in the big city, the inadequacies of his own shallow intellect against the erudite Zhang Yuwen, or the self-consciousness of his dull soul butting up against a charming one, his insecurities piled up until they crushed his unyielding heart. It made him too timid to express his feelings to Zhang Yuwen or pursue him.

And he had to admit that Huo Sichen and Zhang Yuwen were a good match. Huo Sichen was rich, good-looking, and interesting. If Yan Jun had been more like Huo Sichen, he would've pulled out all the stops to charm Zhang Yuwen. Sometimes, he even fantasized about being a social elite so that he could go wild pursuing Zhang Yuwen on equal footing. As it was, though, he had to hide his feelings carefully.

He was a little envious of Huo Sichen, but he also looked down on him. Intuition told him that Huo Sichen was devious. And at the same time, he doubted that Zhang Yuwen's affection for Huo Sichen would last.

Yan Jun had observed Zhang Yuwen and Huo Sichen on the train ride to the hot spring earlier. They sat together, engaging in simple conversation, but no matter how he looked at it, they didn't seem like a couple. The longer he watched Zhang Yuwen, the surer he was. It was only when Xiao-Qi walked over that he snapped out of it. When Zhang Yuwen picked her up, he looked over at Yan Jun, and they shared a smile.

These small interactions brought him an unprecedented happiness. They reminded him of his high school romance... No, this was even more soul-stirring than that. He hadn't loved Mu Zeng with such passion.

Yan Jun often found himself simmering with torment, and while it wasn't intense, it slowly eroded his self-control. Often, just as he thought Zhang Yuwen was about to pair up with Huo Sichen, Zhang Yuwen would take the initiative to walk over to him instead. Take just now, for example: He was outside playing with Xiao-Qi, and the first thing Zhang Yuwen did on leaving his room was come over to him.

"Let's go for dinner, Capricorn," Zhang Yuwen said.

Yan Jun made a hushing gesture, signaling him to keep it from the others. "I have social anxiety," he confessed. "For heaven's sake, please don't bring out a cake later."

"All right." Zhang Yuwen laughed. "I'll spare you that."

The dinner was a lavish feast of barbecue and hot pot. Since it was New Year's Eve, the resort also prepared some special dishes. Worried that the six of them wouldn't get enough to eat, Zhang Yuwen planned to add in some extra dishes, but the resort had accurately estimated their capacity for food. The portions were generous on top of the food itself being exquisite. Xiao-Qi even got her own children's special.

They all watched the New Year's Eve gala as they dug into their meal. Huo Sichen treated everyone to drinks, and they tactfully refrained from probing into his relationship with Zhang Yuwen. While the mood was lively, it was also a little odd. Chang Jinxing and Zhang Yuwen conversed nonstop, sitting so close they were shoulder to shoulder, while Zheng Weize entertained Xiao-Qi and chatted with Chen Hong. Meanwhile, Huo Sichen drank with Yan Jun, downing glass after glass.

Occasionally, Zhang Yuwen heard Yan Jun's voice. "You're pretty successful..."

Huo Sichen patted Yan Jun, a bit tipsy himself. "And how would you know?" Then something occurred to him, and he glanced at Zhang Yuwen, who was typing something on his phone to show Chang Jinxing.

It took a moment for Zhang Yuwen to glance over at them. "Go easy on the alcohol, you two," he reminded them. He didn't want to have to clean up the rooms if someone got sick later.

"We're good," said Huo Sichen. "This isn't strong stuff."

Zhang Yuwen was asking Chang Jinxing what had happened the night before, since it seemed like he had a falling out with Zheng Weize.

Chang Jinxing typed: *I showed him my new gf.*

Zhang Yuwen eyed Chang Jinxing skeptically, and Chang Jinxing pulled up a photo of a gorgeous girl to show him. Zhang Yuwen raised an inquiring eyebrow: Was it true?

Chang Jinxing waved his hand. She was only one of his clients. Zhang Yuwen understood then that Chang Jinxing had just wanted to stop Zheng Weize from getting his hopes up, so he wouldn't end up hurt in the long run.

Huo Sichen and Yan Jun began to play finger-guessing games as they drank, although they were restrained and didn't make too much noise. Xiao-Qi started to get sleepy around half past eight.

"Is it Xiao-Qi's bedtime...?" asked Zhang Yuwen. "Yan Jun! Huo Sichen! Why did you drink so much?"

There were several empty bottles in front of them. Huo Sichen was slumped over the dining table, and Yan Jun's eyes were glazed over as he replied, "S'fine. It's fine. I'll carry Xiao-Qi back now..."

Zheng Weize laughed. "Are we still watching the New Year's fireworks later?"

Zhang Yuwen suspected Yan Jun of deliberately trying to get Huo Sichen drunk, and he was a little angry with him. Of course, since his drinking capacity was about the same as Huo Sichen's, Yan Jun had ended up getting drunk too.

"I'll take them back," offered Chen Hong.

"Then I'll take care of Sichen," Zhang Yuwen said.

So Zheng Weize carried Xiao-Qi back to Crane Hall while Zhang Yuwen tried to pull Huo Sichen, who pushed him away, hollering. "I can still drink! Yan Jun! Yan Jun!"

Yan Jun, who Chen Hong was supporting back to his room, turned around when he heard the shouts.

"Let's go already!" Chen Hong said loudly. "You two are crazy to drink so much."

Chang Jinxing lent a helping hand. Zhang Yuwen thought it was fortunate they were all guys, or this situation would have been hell to manage.

Just as they were about to leave, the bill came: ¥3,000 worth of alcohol. Zhang Yuwen was speechless.

In the corridor, Huo Sichen shoved Chang Jinxing away and hugged Zhang Yuwen. "L-listen to me," he mumbled. Mischievously, Chang Jinxing grabbed a handful of snow and stuffed it into Huo Sichen's collar, eliciting a yell.

"Jinxing!" Zhang Yuwen said angrily.

Chang Jinxing ran off laughing, and Zhang Yuwen half-dragged, half-carried Huo Sichen, trying to make it back to the room. But Huo Sichen sank to his knees and clung to Zhang Yuwen's leg.

"I'm so sorry, Yuwen," he said, sounding sincere. "I didn't want this. I really don't..."

Zhang Yuwen was flummoxed. He looked doubtfully at Huo Sichen. Chang Jinxing, who was a distance ahead, suddenly looked back at them.

"Sorry about what?" Zhang Yuwen asked. Huo Sichen bowed his head, looking like he was going to lie down right there in the corridor. "It's too cold here. Let's go back to the room."

"I'm sorry..." Huo Sichen was acting like a child who knew he'd done something wrong.

Chang Jinxing slowly walked back toward them, but Zhang Yuwen waved a hand to tell him it was okay.

Meanwhile, Chen Hong helped Yan Jun into his room.

"I like Yuwen!" Yan Jun shouted. "Yuwen! I love you!"

"Shhh!" Chen Hong and Zheng Weize slapped their hands over Yan Jun's mouth in fear that Zhang Yuwen might hear him. That would have been embarrassing. This was the first Zheng Weize was hearing of this, and he looked at Chen Hong in shock.

"Xiao-Qi... Go look after her," Chen Hong said. They didn't just have to supervise Yan Jun, they also needed to take care of his daughter, putting them in a little bit of a predicament.

Yan Jun lay on his side on the ground, mumbling to himself, utterly wasted. "I like you... Yeah, I like you... I didn't have the courage to tell you..."

The commotion woke Xiao-Qi up, and the sight of her father dead drunk for the first time startled her so much that she began to bawl. Zheng Weize couldn't placate her no matter what he tried. Yan Jun, meanwhile, stared at Xiao-Qi without saying a word. After a while, Xiao-Qi crawled toward Yan Jun. Silently, he hugged her tight to his chest and closed his eyes.

Seeing this, Zheng Weize started crying instead. "Why are you crying?" sputtered Chen Hong, who had been preparing milk for Xiao-Qi.

"It's nothing." Zheng Weize just found it heartbreaking. There was someone else in the house who had a secret crush but didn't have the courage to confess. He understood Yan Jun's sorrow completely, and when he thought about his own situation, he cried even harder.

"Oh, dear." Chen Hong handed the bottle to Xiao-Qi, at the end of his rope.

Outside Crane Hall, Zhang Yuwen finally succeeded in getting Huo Sichen through the doors. "How's Yan Jun?" he asked the others.

"Yuwen!" Yan Jun snapped to his senses. "You... Take care of Xiao-Qi! I'll leave her to you!" Zhang Yuwen was speechless.

"Yan Jun's a little out of his head right now," said Chen Hong. "Don't engage him."

"Do you know how many bottles they drank?" Zhang Yuwen asked.

"No, how many?"

Yan Jun fumbled his attempt at lifting Xiao-Qi up. She looked confused. "Xiao-Qi...only recognizes you! Yuwen, help me take care of her."

"Six bottles of sake," said Zhang Yuwen. "Okay! I got you, go and sleep."

Zhang Yuwen took Xiao-Qi. She didn't cry this time, instead drinking her milk quietly as she looked at Zhang Yuwen.

"I'm exhausted," Chen Hong groaned. "Let's go and lie down already."

"I'll look after them both," Zheng Weize offered. "You should go and check on Huo Sichen."

Yan Jun lay in the corner, and Zhang Yuwen dimmed the light. Zhang Yuwen hugged Xiao-Qi until she fell asleep, then set her down on the other side of the bed so that Yan Jun wouldn't roll over and squash her.

"Leave the door open," Zhang Yuwen said. "Call me anytime if you need anything."

"Okay," Zheng Weize said softly. "Don't worry."

Zhang Yuwen returned to his room just as Chen Hong emerged from it. Chen Hong signaled that Huo Sichen was fine. "We'll leave our door open too," he said.

"Thanks."

He went in to check on Huo Sichen, who lay under the bedding with his long legs poking out. He reeked of alcohol. Zhang Yuwen was worried he might vomit, so he turned him on his side. But when he reached out to turn him by the shoulder, he realized Huo Sichen's eyes were wide open.

Is he crying?! Zhang Yuwen could hardly believe it. He understood how easy it was to get emotional after drinking, especially when a guy was under a lot of stress, but Zhang Yuwen had never been this drunk before.

Huo Sichen's tears streamed soundlessly down his cheeks. Zhang Yuwen wiped them off with the quilt.

"What's wrong?" he whispered.

Huo Sichen turned around and looked at Zhang Yuwen as if he didn't recognize him. Zhang Yuwen cradled Huo Sichen's upper body in his arms, and Huo Sichen hugged him tight, his breath hitching as he sobbed.

Zhang Yuwen didn't know what to say. He knew that Huo Sichen was hiding something from him, but surely nothing this dire, right? Maybe it was just work stress? Huo Sichen cried for a long time, leaning into Zhang Yuwen's arms without saying a word. He just kept weeping until he fell asleep.

This was the first time Zhang Yuwen had seen this side of Huo Sichen. Men didn't often show their vulnerabilities to anyone else, after all. Huo Sichen's emotional release stirred a strong sense of protectiveness in Zhang Yuwen. Everyone had moments of vulnerability, himself included, and everyone needed a gentle harbor in which to seek refuge.

That night, those who weren't drunk were very busy. Chang Jinxing volunteered to move to Yan Jun's room to help Zheng Weize look after him and Xiao-Qi, and Chen Hong came over a few times in the night to check on them. At midnight, New Year's fireworks began to light up the sky, but no one went out to watch them. Zhang Yuwen stayed quietly in his room, reminiscing about his childhood. His grandparents had once brought him to this resort for New Year's, and even after his grandfather passed away, Zhang Yuwen had come with his grandmother.

It hadn't been that long, but it felt like a lifetime ago.

He wondered what his grandparents would say if they were around to see the way he lived now. Would they accept Huo Sichen?

Huo Sichen turned around in the silent night and hugged Zhang Yuwen. Zhang Yuwen tried to adjust his position, but Huo Sichen had him in a vice grip, like a drowning man grasping a buoy.

Even at a time like this, Huo Sichen could get aroused... Zhang Yuwen didn't know whether to laugh or cry. He touched Huo Sichen through his underwear, but Huo Sichen didn't wake up. *So big,* Zhang Yuwen thought. *I can't let him be the top.*

He grasped Huo Sichen's equipment with one hand and his own in the other for comparison. Huo Sichen's was indeed bigger, and it was rock-hard too. The only fly in the ointment was that he came too fast—roughly ten minutes, based on today's benchmark.

Huo Sichen stirred. Zhang Yuwen withdrew his hand and patted him to let him continue to sleep.

Outside, the sounds of fireworks and the countdown filled the air. Everyone's phone screens lit up with congratulatory messages, flooding in one after another in the silent night, like fireworks blooming in succession.

Another year had passed.

Riverbay Road

MEN'S DORMITORY

YAN JUN'S FIRST THOUGHT when he awoke was, *Oh no, I blacked out.* "What happened last night?"

"Huh?" Zheng Weize glanced at Chen Hong, who was still fast asleep. "Nothing happened."

Yan Jun's head was buzzing. He hadn't been that drunk in a long time. "I didn't do anything weird, did I?" he asked, embarrassed.

"Nope," Zheng Weize said quickly.

Chen Hong woke up and blearily said, "I'm going back to my room now."

"I'm so sorry." Yan Jun felt terrible. Had he ruined everyone's New Year celebration?

"No, no. It's really nothing!" Zheng Weize insisted. "Oh yeah! Is it time for Xiao-Qi's milk?"

"I'll do it. Thank you, Weize." It looked like Zheng Weize and Chen Hong had taken care of him all night long. Yan Jun was touched.

"I didn't do much, actually. I was…sleeping. But Yuwen came over a few times," Zheng Weize said apprehensively. He wasn't sure if he should be telling Yan Jun this, but Yan Jun just hummed an acknowledgment, his expression unchanged. "Chen Hong and I fell asleep, but it seems like Yuwen didn't sleep all night."

Yan Jun looked out the open door to Zhang Yuwen's door, which was also open. It was quiet inside.

It was true: Zhang Yuwen had had a busy night.

He didn't understand it. Why did Huo Sichen and Yan Jun start drinking together? And Huo Sichen even cried afterward… Of course, that might not have been related; Huo Sichen's emotional release could have just been a consequence of his sake binge.

The whole night, Zhang Yuwen heard Chen Hong's snores from the room opposite. Zheng Weize also seemed to sleep like the dead. So once he'd taken care of Huo Sichen, he went over to check on Yan Jun and, more importantly, Xiao-Qi—in case Yan Jun puked on her in the middle of the night or crushed her in his sleep. While Xiao-Qi no longer needed nighttime feeding, she was still prone to waking during the night.

As a motherless child, Xiao-Qi was very sensible, possessing calm and maturity far beyond her years. She understood that crying was futile when she woke up in the night, because her exhausted father usually wouldn't stir. Her only options for entertaining herself in the dark were to keep her eyes open or crawl around. But that night, Zhang Yuwen came and sat down to hold her, lulling her back to sleep.

So Zhang Yuwen spent the night going back and forth between the two rooms, navigating around the unreliable Zheng Weize and Chen Hong, who were dead to the world. He only managed to drift off to sleep just before daybreak, and he hadn't even slept three hours when Huo Sichen woke up.

Zhang Yuwen rolled over in Huo Sichen's arms, and Huo Sichen hugged him from behind and watched him sleeping soundly, not daring to move or breathe. His heart pounded so hard it felt like the whole world was resonating with it. In his pajamas, Zhang Yuwen exuded the unique, clean vitality of youth. Hormones slowly diffused in the confines of the small room, acting like a peculiar boundary: This was another male's territory. It was a domain that carried the dignity of its owner even as it granted Huo Sichen entrance and tacit permission to run wild within. It was different from a woman's natural tenderness and unconditional inclusion and acceptance. This acceptance was conditional; the conditions made Huo Sichen tense and excited, and this stimulation transformed into a desire to explore deeper.

Zhang Yuwen stirred again. Huo Sichen, still half asleep himself, was pressed up against him. If this continued, Zhang Yuwen would probably wake up. Huo Sichen reeked of alcohol, and he knew he had to get going to clean himself up.

He got up, and before long, Zhang Yuwen woke. He held his blanket and sat up in a bleary daze.

"Didn't sleep well last night?" Huo Sichen couldn't remember what had happened at all. His last memory was of telling the waiter, "Bring me another bottle of this."

Zhang Yuwen yawned. He wanted to punch someone. "What do you think?" he retorted.

With a toothbrush in his mouth, Huo Sichen stepped out of the bathroom and raised a dashing brow at Zhang Yuwen. He went back to rinse his mouth, then said, "I didn't say anything strange last night, did I?"

Zhang Yuwen stared at him.

Now that he'd sobered up, Huo Sichen had reverted to his usual suave persona. "Hm?"

"No," said Zhang Yuwen, equal parts amused and exasperated. "Where's Yan Jun?"

"He got drunk too. Why did you guys drink so much?"

Huo Sichen spread his hands. He didn't know why either. "It just happened while we were talking. Maybe because we're both youngest sons from big families? We have common ground." Getting trashed was embarrassing, but it was usually also satisfying…though not for the person who had to play caretaker.

By ten o'clock, everyone was awake and in the common area, enjoying the breakfast the resort had provided. "Free time today?" said Zheng Weize. "We still have one more night."

"No more drinking today," Chang Jinxing said lightly.

As Huo Sichen observed them all, he noticed that Zhang Yuwen looked different. Everyone else was in high spirits, but Zhang Yuwen looked exhausted. It was the kind of exhaustion that made him look liable to flip the table and go berserk.

"Did you take care of me all night?" Huo Sichen whispered.

So you finally noticed, Zhang Yuwen thought. Out loud, he replied, "Nah. I fell asleep pretty quickly." Huo Sichen was puzzled, but he nodded. Yan Jun grinned knowingly at Zhang Yuwen. "No more drinking tonight," said Zhang Yuwen. "Because of you two, we missed the fireworks."

"I'll set off one for your eyes only." Huo Sichen made a suggestive gesture like fireworks going off, and everyone laughed.

"Shall we go to the park later?" Chang Jinxing suggested. "I checked the travel guide last night. There are plenty of places we can go to have fun in the mountains."

"Sure!" Zheng Weize was the most fun-loving of them all. Realizing belatedly that this might not be a good time to appear so enthusiastic, he cooled his expression and said, "Oh."

After a simple breakfast, the group set out together, taking the resort's shuttle bus to the park at the foot of the mountain. The sun was shining brightly on the first day of the new year, and with the rising temperature, the snow had melted. Green pines lined the roads on their way over.

Now that he'd had two cups of coffee, Zhang Yuwen finally felt like himself again.

"Deer!" Zheng Weize exclaimed in delight. "So many of them!" A herd of deer had appeared in the park. The place was packed with tourists, and numerous stalls set up at the side of the park sold crackers for the deer.

"Be careful," Zhang Yuwen warned him. "Don't underestimate these deer."

Chang Jinxing went over with his camera to take photos, and Zheng Weize looked for deer to play with. The deer here weren't skittish around people; when they saw visitors, they gathered to ask for food.

"Don't let Xiao-Qi get too close," Zhang Yuwen told Yan Jun.

"I know!" said Yan Jun. "I've been here before." He held Xiao-Qi in his arms to let her look at the deer.

The group dispersed in the park. Huo Sichen bought some crackers for the deer and handed them to Zhang Yuwen, who chuckled and said, "The deer here are mischievous. Greedy, too."

"They can be aggressive, especially the males," Huo Sichen said. "Be careful not to provoke the males."

Zhang Yuwen cautiously fed the crackers to a few fawns who had strayed from the herd. "I was attacked by one when I was little. It almost knocked me to the ground."

Huo Sichen laughed, "I was also... Eh?" He trailed off, seeming to remember something. He looked at Zhang Yuwen, then the deer.

"What's wrong?"

"I think...I made a friend in this park when I was very young," Huo Sichen said.

"Oh, really? Oh!" A memory surfaced in Zhang Yuwen's mind too. "Yeah, I remember! My grandparents brought me here, I think, when I was four... Yeah, that's right!"

Zhang Yuwen stopped feeding the fawns, but several more deer came over to join them. Huo Sichen drove them away.

"That year, I pestered my grandfather to bring me here to feed the deer," Zhang Yuwen went on, immersed in his memories. "He didn't want to leave the resort, though, so the couple in the next room over brought me here."

"Were there two brothers in that family? One nine years old, one seven?"

"I think so? Yeah! Was it in the spring?"

Huo Sichen gave Zhang Yuwen an earnest smile.

"Was it you?" Zhang Yuwen asked incredulously. "You and your brother?"

"My memories are hazy."

"What a magical coincidence, if that really was you," Zhang Yuwen marveled.

"I only remember that my father rarely took me and my brother out to play, so that day left a deep impression on me. I think...I think I was attacked, yeah."

"Yeah! The younger brother was knocked over by a deer when he tried to protect me."

Huo Sichen laughed. "Was I that weak then?"

"There were a few of them," Zhang Yuwen told him. "Yeah, it was two brothers. The older one came and chased the deer away. The younger one hit a rock and ended up bleeding from the head." He made Huo Sichen come closer so he could check his scalp, but sustaining an injury that young was unlikely to leave a scar.

"Find a scar?" Huo Sichen laughed. "I guess not."

Zhang Yuwen smiled, still absorbed in those memories. Every time he glanced at Huo Sichen, Huo Sichen was watching him with a smile in his eyes.

"So, fate is predetermined by heaven," Huo Sichen said. "I can't believe I met you when I was seven. But why didn't we write to each other after we went back?"

Zhang Yuwen's memory was fuzzy. It had been more than twenty years ago. "You said you didn't live in Jiangdong when we parted ways. I was only four, I didn't understand anything."

"Yeah." Huo Sichen thought about it. "After that trip, my father took us abroad."

"There should be photos somewhere."

"I'll ask my brother to go back and look for them. We moved house a few times, though, so it's possible we don't have them anymore." He took out his phone and sent a message to his older brother across the ocean. His brother replied with a promise to find them when he had the time.

More details were coming to Zhang Yuwen, but further away, chaos had erupted. A deer was tugging on Chang Jinxing's camera, and Zheng Weize was calling for help. It looked like the incident at Elephant Gorge was about to repeat itself. Zhang Yuwen and Huo Sichen rushed over to help and used the crackers to lure the deer away.

Elsewhere, in a sunny spot, Xiao-Qi was having a great time. Still in Yan Jun's arms, she petted a quiet, docile fawn.

Chang Jinxing took a lot of pictures. Afterward, the group set off for a nearby temple to pray for the new year. There were few people around at one in the afternoon. The main hall had paper slips for making wishes, and after they donated money for incense, each of them received a slip, wrote their wishes at the counter, and went to tie it to the tree outside.

"What did you wish for?" Huo Sichen asked.

"We aren't supposed to show each other," said Zhang Yuwen.

"But we can see it after we tie it up," Huo Sichen deadpanned. "Does your wish have anything to do with me?"

Zhang Yuwen gave in and showed it to him. "I wished for your career."

"How did you know?" Huo Sichen asked, looking stunned.

"Know what? Let me see yours."

Zhang Yuwen tried to get Huo Sichen's slip, but Huo Sichen wouldn't show it to him. "What did I say when I was drunk last night?"

"Nothing. Isn't it normal to make a wish for someone's career? Come on, show me," Zhang Yuwen insisted. Huo Sichen remained silent. "You must have wished for yourself..." He grabbed Huo Sichen's slip, took a look, and returned it to him, smiling.

"I made a wish for you too," said Huo Sichen. His wish slip said, *May Zhang Yuwen have a good marriage.*

What's that supposed to mean? Zhang Yuwen wondered. He figured that it probably made some kind of sense in Huo Sichen's mind.

As they hung up their wish slips, Zhang Yuwen's curiosity got the better of him. He peeked at his roommates' colorful slips—pink was for marriage, yellow for health, blue for career, and gold for wealth.

Yan Jun's was yellow. It said, *May everyone I love stay healthy.*

Chen Hong was for his career: *Here's hoping I can reach new heights next year.*

Chang Jinxing's: *Get rich overnight in the new year!*

And finally, Zheng Weize's: *I wish for all of us to live happily together forever.*

When they saw Zheng Weize's wish, a vaguely guilty silence fell over the rest of them.

"I'll treat everyone to lunch today," Zheng Weize announced, smiling.

"Sure!" said Chang Jinxing, bright despite the awkward vibe.

Zheng Weize treated them to pizza from the shopping street outside the temple, and afterward, they split up to walk around. Chang Jinxing had his camera around his neck, and he seemed to have made up with Zheng Weize, who kept getting Chang Jinxing to take photos of him. The others didn't intrude on them. Yan Jun and Chen Hong walked together, Xiao-Qi once again fast asleep in her stroller.

Zhang Yuwen, for his part, was too sleepy to walk around. He chose a warm, grassy spot near the garden and had Huo Sichen sit down so he could rest his head on Huo Sichen's lap and sleep.

"You didn't sleep last night, did you?" Huo Sichen asked.

Zhang Yuwen covered his face with his jacket to shield himself from the winter sun. "Is your career not going well?"

Huo Sichen thought for a moment. "I'm considering a job change. I can't work with my current partner anymore."

"A partnership is like a marriage. Over time, people change."

"An apt analogy. As expected of a writer."

Zhang Yuwen didn't answer. He was waiting for Huo Sichen to share more of his own accord. If they really wanted to be together, this level of mutual understanding was necessary. He decided he would eventually tell Huo Sichen about his real financial situation, too, but not just yet.

He could tell that Huo Sichen was proud. It wasn't obvious from his usual behavior, but a big part of his self-confidence stemmed from his career, wealth, and social experience. So Zhang Yuwen kept reminding himself to tread lightly so as not to step on his ego.

Eventually, Huo Sichen said, "When I think about my expenses, I find it hard to make a decision."

"You don't live extravagantly, though." Zhang Yuwen smiled. "Or is there someone else helping you spend your money?"

"I still have a mortgage to pay off. And I also want to give you a better life."

Zhang Yuwen was touched. He could tell that Huo Sichen's feelings were genuine, because Zhang Yuwen himself had said the same words to his ex. A man's love was, for the most part, pragmatic; it was mainly reflected in his considerations for the future, including how to give his lover a better life, what kind of family to build, and how to ensure they could stay together without the other suffering.

"I don't spend that much," said Zhang Yuwen.

"You lead a simple and frugal life. Your inner world is strong and rich, but I still hope... Anyway, I'm still thinking it over."

"Changing jobs?"

"Yeah. I don't want to speak ill of my partner. We've known each other for a long time, after all. No matter how bad the mess is, it's of my own making. It's pointless to pretend otherwise. All I want to do now is to split on good terms."

The way Huo Sichen thought was similar to Zhang Yuwen. They shared a lot of values. "If it really bothers you, you can consider giving up your shares. Is your company listed?"

"No. I've been thinking about that too."

"What are the shares valued at?"

"Nearly two million."

"Your partner isn't likely to buy out your shares with hard cash," Zhang Yuwen said. "The more you drag it out, the uglier it will get. It's better to give it up earlier."

"You know a lot," Huo Sichen commented.

"It's just common sense."

Huo Sichen held Zhang Yuwen's hands under the coat. "To most people, two million is not a small amount."

"Yeah, that's true." Zhang Yuwen's monthly investment income was over two million. Now he was wondering, *Was I too casual about that?*

"Another problem," Huo Sichen continued, "is that if I leave this company, I'll have to find a new job, and I can't get a satisfactory annual salary in CTO-level positions with the market how it currently is. You know, the economic downturn and all..."

"Oh? Have you been sending out your resume?"

"No, my position is usually filled through referrals from industry peers. The market rate is only approximately twenty-six or twenty-seven thousand."

"That's a lot!" Zhang Yuwen said quickly, trying to make up for his earlier composure. Then he added, "My salary is only a fraction of yours."

"It's different for you," Huo Sichen said offhandedly.

"Huh?"

"I mean, you don't have that many expenses. I still have a monthly mortgage of over ten thousand, and then there are the daily expenses too," Huo Sichen explained. Zhang Yuwen wanted to ask if he had any savings, but he held himself back. "Anyway, that makes it hard for me to decide."

"A new job at a new company won't necessarily be better than the old one," Zhang Yuwen said.

"Yeah, all crows under the sun are black."

At this point, Zhang Yuwen was so sleepy he couldn't keep his eyes open anymore. He rolled over and fell asleep.

WHEN HE WOKE UP AGAIN, it was already 5 p.m., and the sun was on its way down. Everyone gathered in the park again, each having bought their own souvenirs. Zhang Yuwen, who had Huo Sichen's coat around him, opened his bleary eyes to see Chang Jinxing taking photos of him, and Huo Sichen smiling and not stopping him. Zhang Yuwen made as if to get up to kick Chang Jinxing's ass, causing everyone to laugh and disperse.

When they returned to the resort, everyone went to soak in the hot spring separately. "I'll watch Xiao-Qi while you guys go enjoy the hot spring," Zhang Yuwen volunteered. Huo Sichen wanted to stay with Zhang Yuwen, but Zhang Yuwen shook his head. "You were exposed to the wind in the park without a coat. Don't catch a cold."

Yan Jun smiled. "Then I'll go take a bath."

Chen Hong moved his belongings to Yan Jun's room, and Chang Jinxing went over to share a room with Zheng Weize; something had definitely happened between them again today. And then everyone was gone.

The common area was strangely quiet, their game of Monopoly lying unfinished on the table. Xiao-Qi, no longer satisfied with exploring the furniture, was picking up the game money and looking at it curiously. "Don't tear it, okay?" Zhang Yuwen told her. He put the dice away in case she decided to eat them.

Zhang Yuwen was fond of children. If he'd had a daughter like Xiao-Qi, he probably wouldn't date again. He would devote himself wholeheartedly to taking care of her, showering her with all his attention; he'd spoil her and treat her like a little princess from the moment she was born—

Suddenly, Xiao-Qi looked at Zhang Yuwen and said, "Yuwen?"

Zhang Yuwen froze. For one wild moment he panicked, thinking something supernatural was occurring, but then he realized what had happened. "Are you calling me? Xiao-Qi, you can say my name?"

"Yuwen?" Xiao-Qi said again in her baby voice.

"What?!" Zhang Yuwen was stunned. As far as he knew, this was Xiao-Qi's second word, her first besides "Papa!" His name wasn't easy to pronounce, either—how had she learned it?

Xiao-Qi, who found Zhang Yuwen's reaction hilarious, came over to hand him the Monopoly money. "Yuwen?"

"Oh my god..." This was the first baby who had ever fully trusted Zhang Yuwen and called him by his name. He couldn't help the tears that sprang to his eyes. He wanted to pick Xiao-Qi up, but she refused.

"Yuwen! Yuwen!" Xiao-Qi said again, and toddled away.

"Is anyone here?" Zhang Yuwen was so worked up that he wanted to find someone to show this off to. Alas, everyone was gone. Light from the setting sun streamed through the doorway, casting everything in a golden glow, and Zhang Yuwen felt that he grasped the transient meaning of existence. He would remember this moment for the rest of his life! "Oh wow," he said. He was so moved he almost cried.

Yan Jun was the first to return.

"Sh-sh-she... She can say my name!" Zhang Yuwen exclaimed when he saw Yan Jun. "Yan Jun! Did you hear that? She can say Yuwen!"

Yan Jun wore a bathrobe, his hair still damp. His smile was striking. "Maybe she picked it up because of how often we all say it."

"Say it again?" Zhang Yuwen said to Xiao-Qi.

Xiao-Qi ignored him and opened her arms to Yan Jun, who picked her up. She was still grasping Zhang Yuwen's clothes, though, refusing to let him leave. "Yuwen."

Zhang Yuwen laughed delightedly. "You hear that?! How many words can she say now?"

"Three. This is the third. She can say 'auntie' too."

Zhang Yuwen was beside himself with joy. Gradually, the others returned, and when they heard Xiao-Qi could say names now, they took turns coaching her.

"That's not fair!" Chen Hong complained. "Hey! Yan Jun! Have you only been teaching your daughter Yuwen's name?" Except for Yan Jun, who was in his room blow-drying his hair and didn't hear them, they all erupted into laughter.

"Where's Sichen?" Zhang Yuwen asked.

"He's still waiting for you at the hot spring," Chang Jinxing told him. Zhang Yuwen quickly changed into a bathrobe and made his way there.

Huo Sichen was sitting on the stone area by the hot spring when Zhang Yuwen jumped in and splashed water all over his face. He watched Zhang Yuwen. "You're in a good mood."

Zhang Yuwen grinned but didn't explain.

"Feeling refreshed after your nap?" Now that Zhang Yuwen had arrived, Huo Sichen got back into the water—but Zhang Yuwen, noticing how red his skin was from the steam, made him get back out in case he fainted.

"No more drinking tonight," Zhang Yuwen said in a warning tone.

"Of course. I'd get a good beating if I wasted a beautiful night." Zhang Yuwen didn't reply, and Huo Sichen came closer. "Are you looking forward to tonight?"

Zhang Yuwen tried to dunk Huo Sichen's head into the water, but Huo Sichen was ready and fended off his attack. They wrestled in the water for a while, and Zhang Yuwen realized that Huo Sichen was much stronger than him; the guy almost upended him, but ultimately, he teased Zhang Yuwen playfully for a moment and then let him go.

Once they'd calmed down, Huo Sichen asked, "What do you think it should be like when two guys are together?"

"All I know is that they can soak in a hot spring together." Zhang Yuwen knew what he was trying to ask, but he refused to take the bait.

Huo Sichen laughed. "Uh-huh, that's one thing."

"You should get out of the water and drink something," Zhang Yuwen said. So Huo Sichen got up, naked, and sat at the edge of the pool to continue their conversation.

Zhang Yuwen sized Huo Sichen up. He was a bigger guy than Zhang Yuwen. In the natural world, larger animals often played the role of the "protector"—that is, the male. In same-sex relationships, this was maybe the top.

"By the way," Huo Sichen said, "can I ask to take the lead?"

"That's called being the top, or '1,'" Zhang Yuwen said. "I knew you'd been thinking about this."

Huo Sichen's breathing quickened, nerves setting in. He licked his lips and looked at Zhang Yuwen. "Just an idea... I'm just throwing it out for discussion."

Zhang Yuwen countered with a question of his own. "If I insisted on being the top, and otherwise, no deal, would you accept it? Or... take a step back and go back to being friends?"

"No, Yuwen," Huo Sichen said immediately. "I really do love you..." Belatedly, it occurred to him that a hot spring pool wasn't the most solemn place to profess his love. His face turned even redder as he tripped over his words, trying to explain. "I think...all of these things can be overcome. If you really can't agree to it, and it has to be me who...um... I'll be willing to give it a try, but..."

Zhang Yuwen watched Huo Sichen silently, feeling moved. It was clear from Huo Sichen's reaction that he had never done it with a man, and he was nervous and clumsy when it came to gay sex. It was also clear that Huo Sichen really liked him.

"It's just," Huo Sichen continued apprehensively, "I might not meet your expectations. I mean, it might not be totally harmonious..."

Zhang Yuwen gestured for him to stop talking. Generously, he said, "Okay, sure. It's just a position. No big deal. I want to experience bottoming too."

Huo Sichen's breath caught. His body reacted to those words, and Zhang Yuwen, seeing it, burst into laughter and splashed him with water. Huo Sichen blushed.

"Even if it feels uncomfortable," Zhang Yuwen rationalized, "there are still plenty of other ways to do it."

"Then that's decided!"

"Yeah, but I have a request." Zhang Yuwen looked Huo Sichen's naked body up and down. With his physique paired with that handsome, serious face of his, he really was gorgeous. "You have to let me top you once in a while. Can you agree to that?"

Zhang Yuwen *had* to have a taste of that glorious, fair, elite body.

"Sure," Huo Sichen said without so much as a second thought.

What a bizarre conversation. Who had serious discussions about sexual roles in a hot spring pool? But this was an issue two men who wanted to be together had to resolve. Zhang Yuwen wondered if two bottoms who fell in love would also bargain with each other like this.

When Zhang Yuwen decided to date Huo Sichen, his intent was to pursue a wholly new kind of same-sex relationship—one that was equal and mutual. There would be no big, strong top who had to care for and dote on the bottom, and no bottom relying on his top. But Huo Sichen was so inexperienced with this budding romance that he handled many of the details as if it were a heterosexual relationship. Sometimes he treated Zhang Yuwen as a girl.

But that didn't matter. People could change.

During dinner, the mood was much livelier than the previous night. Yan Jun and Huo Sichen didn't drink, and Zheng Weize and Chang Jinxing sat together again. Zhang Yuwen wanted to brag about Xiao-Qi calling his name, but she was engrossed in a cartoon on Yan Jun's phone.

"We haven't toasted yet!" Chen Hong said.

"Oh, yeah!" Chang Jinxing put down his phone and picked up his cup.

The moment the toast was suggested, Zhang Yuwen's social anxiety reared its ugly head. And sure enough, Chen Hong said, "Thanks to Yuwen for bringing us together."

"Yeah!" Zheng Weize chimed in. "Thank you, Yuwen, for taking us out to have a good time."

"It's the work of fate, I guess," said Zhang Yuwen, blushing.

"Thank you, Yuwen." Yan Jun raised his cup with a smile. "You know what I want to say."

"Thanks," said Chang Jinxing. "You've changed me a lot."

Zhang Yuwen dreaded situations like this more than anything, especially when people made genuine expressions of emotion. Every time it happened, he wanted to hide under the table.

"Yuwen is a wonderful person," added Huo Sichen. "It's truly a blessing to know you."

"Stop it, guys," Zhang Yuwen pleaded. "This is mortifying."

"Really," Zheng Weize continued, "my life has changed completely. I'm so much happier than I used to be."

Then I guess I won't be chasing you guys for rent, Zhang Yuwen thought. "Okay, enough. Let's toast," he said. "Let's all keep working hard in the coming year."

They clinked cups, and Zhang Yuwen felt a little ashamed. After all, his motive for bringing them all together at Riverbay Road was far from pure. If anything, he was the one who'd learned from his warm, kindhearted roommates. He used to think he could live perfectly happily as a recluse, but their presence made his life so much more vibrant.

He had nothing to give to them. All he had was a bit of money. Surrounded by his friends, for the first time in his life, Zhang Yuwen felt just how inadequate his soul was.

Thankfully, the adulation of the sub-landlord ended before long. They were having beef hot pot, and as soon as it was served, everyone exclaimed in delight and whipped out their phones to take photos. Chang Jinxing even used his camera.

"Man, I wish I could stay here forever!" said Zheng Weize.

"I'll bring you here again next time," Zhang Yuwen told him.

"Isn't home good, though?" Chang Jinxing laughed. "It doesn't have a hot spring, but home is also very comfortable." Thinking it over, Zheng Weize had to agree.

Hearing them speak about "home" made Huo Sichen look at Zhang Yuwen. Zhang Yuwen knew that he was thinking about how they would see each other in the future, whether they would live together, where they should spend the night, and so on. Those thoughts were a little premature. Yes, their relationship was progressing at lightning speed, but Zhang Yuwen still had no plans to discuss cohabitation just yet. Having sex while they were dating was one thing, but cohabitation meant sharing a life... But that didn't mean that Zhang Yuwen wouldn't tease him about it, seeing Huo Sichen lost in thought.

Huo Sichen sat across from him in the dining room laid with tatami mats. He was shoulder to shoulder with Yan Jun, who was chatting with Chang Jinxing. Listening to them joke around, Zhang Yuwen extended his foot, clad in a white athletic sock, found Huo Sichen's foot under the table, and stroked it.

Yan Jun stopped talking and glanced at Zhang Yuwen. Realizing he'd gotten the wrong person, Zhang Yuwen yanked his leg back. "Sorry!"

Yan Jun understood that Zhang Yuwen had meant to flirt with Huo Sichen, so he said nothing. Huo Sichen shot Zhang Yuwen a questioning look, but Zhang Yuwen couldn't try his move again; Huo Sichen would realize immediately what had happened. Instead, Zhang Yuwen sat in embarrassed silence. Luckily for him, Chen Hong made a joke about working out and beef, and everyone cracked up.

And then it was night. Dinner without alcohol always seemed to be missing something. When they returned to their room, Huo Sichen closed the door and embraced Zhang Yuwen from behind.

"What are you doing?" Zhang Yuwen said. "Keep your sneaky hands to yourself. I'm too full."

"But I'm not doing it sneakily; I'm doing it openly. I want to be intimate with you."

No sooner did Huo Sichen say these words than a voice outside interrupted his romantic wish. "Yuwen, what are you guys doing?" Chang Jinxing asked.

Zhang Yuwen laughed uncontrollably. Huo Sichen felt a little helpless. "Shhh," Zhang Yuwen said as he opened the door, "don't wake Xiao-Qi."

Yan Jun stepped out of his room into the common area. "She wouldn't wake up even if we played mahjong next to her. Want to come out and play?"

"Play what?" Huo Sichen stepped out too. "Monopoly?"

Chen Hong, Zheng Weize, and Chang Jinxing each took a seat in the common area. Everyone brought over cushions and sat around the low table. Huo Sichen's phone rang, and he went back to the room to answer the call. Zhang Yuwen reserved the spot next to him for when Huo Sichen returned.

"Let's play truth or dare," Zheng Weize suggested again.

Noooooo, everyone thought at the same time, but they were all waiting for someone else to object. Instead, the word that came out of each person's mouth was, "Sure."

"Okay, but let's set a theme," Zhang Yuwen said.

Everyone relaxed a little, thinking, *That's much safer than it was on the mountain.*

"Fine with me," Chen Hong said. "Dice? Or playing cards?"

"Lemme see..." Chang Jinxing said. "What topics are suggested online for a themed truth or dare?"

"Cards, I guess." Zheng Weize shuffled the cards. "We can use the Monopoly money and chips to play."

"Sure," said Zhang Yuwen. Thus, they made the decision for the absent Huo Sichen.

Zheng Weize dealt the cards, and Chen Hong distributed the chips. They started a six-person game. "One truth per round, a total of six rounds. The one who loses the most will do a dare."

"Okay," Yan Jun said. "What's the theme?"

"Lemme see... The first one is..." Chang Jinxing said. "This! Sexual preferences! What unspeakable fetish do you have? Let's talk about your kinks! You must describe it in detail, no less than three thousand words."

"Damn..."

Simultaneously, everyone thought, *This is too much!*

"Pick something else!" Zhang Yuwen said.

"We're better off choosing this one than the others," Chang Jinxing said. "Trust me."

"Damn, this is a good one," said Chen Hong. "I've been curious about your sexual fetishes for a long time." Zhang Yuwen stared at him.

"Do we drink?" asked Chang Jinxing. "It's no fun if we don't. Just don't drink too much."

"Hm..." Zhang Yuwen thought for a moment. "It's okay if it's just a little. Something with a low alcohol content. I'll go buy it."

Zhang Yuwen left to make the purchase, and Chen Hong said, "Let's all target Sichen. I'm curious as hell."

Huo Sichen emerged, his call finished, and everyone looked at him. "Hm? Where's Yuwen?"

"He went to buy some booze," Zheng Weize said. "Maybe you can help him with his cards."

Zhang Yuwen returned with a large bag containing fruit wine and milk wine in various flavors. The alcohol content wasn't as high as sake, but it wasn't low either. Everyone picked their flavor and started drinking.

Huo Sichen's phone rang again, and he apologized and stepped away to answer the call. For a while, everyone played their cards carefully, fearing that they would be targeted.

"Remember, we agreed on this theme, okay?" Chang Jinxing said.

Zhang Yuwen played dumb. "What theme?" He had two sets of cards; his own hand was almost done, but Huo Sichen's set was practically untouched.

Huo Sichen returned. "I'm really sorry. So much stuff came up tonight."

"No worries," the other guys said mischievously.

The card game was intense. They all knew that the moment of social embarrassment would eventually come calling, but they wanted to put it off for as long as possible.

Unexpectedly, the first round's loser was the person who'd suggested the theme—Chang Jinxing! At one point, he had only one pair of cards left, but the others were too fast, catching him off guard as they outmaneuvered him. He was stunned.

Everyone started laughing, not having expected Chang Jinxing to be the first to lose. "Spill it!"

But Huo Sichen, who was still unaware of the stakes, looked confused. "Is there a rule I'm missing?"

Doubled over with laughter, Zhang Yuwen gestured to Huo Sichen to just listen and find out.

"I..." Chang Jinxing just couldn't bring himself to say it. He could fabricate one, yeah, but this bunch of guys would see right through him.

"Don't make it up," Chen Hong warned. "We've been buddies for so long, you think we can't tell?"

Chang Jinxing glanced at Chen Hong, then braced himself and said, "I...kind of, like...um...wanna experiment with...P-spot highs."

"Oh, wow." Everyone was scandalized. Zhang Yuwen was surprised too, though it was entirely plausible.

Huo Sichen still looked clueless. "Are we playing truth?"

"But I'm a top," Chang Jinxing clarified.

"Aw, so what if you're a bottom?" Yan Jun said. "What's wrong with being a bottom? C'mere, gimme a kiss."

Blushing, Chang Jinxing pushed Yan Jun away. Huo Sichen whispered to Zhang Yuwen, "What's a P-spot high?"

Just as Zhang Yuwen was about to explain, Chang Jinxing clarified, "Prostate orgasm."

"Oh, yeah. Prostate orgasm."

Huo Sichen looked like he wanted to ask where the prostate was, but he wisely kept quiet.

Zheng Weize looked conflicted, as if the top he had a crush on was no longer pure. Chang Jinxing explained, "I had a girlfriend who I tried it with once or twice, and somehow, it became a bit of a kink. Of course, most of the time, I'm just fantasizing."

"A lot of straight men are into it," Chen Hong said. "I have a client who enjoys being rimmed by his wife."

Zhang Yuwen didn't find it all that shocking; instead, he was intrigued. The way Chang Jinxing looked as he composed himself and candidly discussed his preferences was actually a little sexy. It was a stark contrast to his playboy persona.

"Is a prostate orgasm really that good?" Zhang Yuwen asked.

"It's okay, I guess?" Zheng Weize said. "It depends on the top's technique. If you do it yourself, you can pinpoint the good spots more accurately."

Back when Zhang Yuwen was with his ex, he couldn't figure out if his lover felt good or if he was just playing along because he loved Zhang Yuwen. He believed that he did feel pleasure, but over time, the frequency of their lovemaking decreased.

"So it's an intense sensation?" said Yan Jun.

"You wanna try?" Chen Hong asked Yan Jun. Yan Jun waved his hand dismissively, and everyone laughed again.

"None of you have experienced it before?" Chang Jinxing asked.

"The three of them haven't," Chen Hong said. "I have, once."

"Whoa." Zhang Yuwen struggled to imagine Chen Hong as a bottom, but there was a sexy contrast in seeing an athletic man in that role. The positions weren't always set in stone among gay couples. Some people sought novelty and excitement, so they'd switch roles a few times to spice things up.

"Right?" Chang Jinxing said to Chen Hong, "It feels good."

"It hurt at the start," Chen Hong said, "but yeah, it does get kind of pleasurable later, I guess."

"Maybe you didn't find the right position," Chang Jinxing said. "Size and technique matter too."

"I used to hook up with a guy who had been a bottom before," Zheng Weize chimed in. "His technique was amazing. He made me come every time, like wave after wave of pleasure crashing into me."

"Then are you able to find the prostate with accuracy?" Yan Jun asked Chang Jinxing.

"Yeah. It's like a chestnut. You can't thrust at it too hard because it'll hurt, and you can't go too deep either, or you'll hit past the P-spot."

"What's past the P-spot?" Huo Sichen asked.

Everyone was struck speechless. Huo Sichen stared right back at them.

"It's deeper inside the body, and it'll hurt," Zhang Yuwen explained. "Doesn't matter if it's a man or woman. If it's too long, it'll feel uncomfortable." This knowledge belonged only to those with hardware of a certain size and sufficient experience.

"The prostate point is actually quite shallow," Zheng Weize added. "Five inches is usually enough. The rest depends on technique. Kissing and caressing are important too."

"Yeah, that's right," Zhang Yuwen agreed. Bigger wasn't always necessarily better when it came to hardware. At most, it just looked sexy.

"Then do you like being the bottom?" Zheng Weize asked.

"Actually, I don't want to be the bottom," Chang Jinxing said. "I just have this kink."

"Oh," Zhang Yuwen said. "So you're like a straight guy who likes being pegged."

"You can also play from the front," Chen Hong said. "You can reach the prostate by going the front route too."

"How do you know so much?!" Everyone was seeing Chen Hong in a new light.

"I've tried that," Chang Jinxing said. "It's more intense, but also easier to get an infection."

"What's the front route?" Huo Sichen asked.

Zhang Yuwen held his forehead in one hand. "Urethral play."

It was Huo Sichen's first encounter with this topic. He felt like he was in a cramming session before an exam, and his brain cells struggled to keep up.

"All right," Chang Jinxing said. "Let's continue?"

"Wait," Chen Hong said. "This doesn't count as a fetish, right? It's just something that any normal bottom likes!"

"But I'm a top!" Chang Jinxing insisted as he shuffled the cards.

Yan Jun caught on too. "He almost got away with it!"

"Really!" Chang Jinxing said. "I really only have this one kink. You have to consider each person's individual circumstances..."

Zhang Yuwen burst out laughing, and Chang Jinxing started dealing the cards again so that nobody would press further.

Huo Sichen started taking his cards seriously in the second round, but it was clear from his expression that he was still reeling from the previous conversation. "Does a prostate orgasm really feel that good?" he asked Zhang Yuwen with slightly furrowed brows.

Everybody heard the question. They chorused, "You wanna try?" and hooted with laughter, which finally woke Xiao-Qi up. Yan Jun quickly went into his room to pacify her, and everyone resumed their conversation with gusto. This time, instead of razzing Chang Jinxing, they moved on to Chen Hong's short-lived relationship from the previous year.

"All right, guys, shush," Yan Jun said. "Keep your voices down."

Playing cards flew across the table, and the fruit wine started to take its hold over them all. As the alcohol kicked in, their conversation became even more uninhibited, and Zhang Yuwen felt himself getting hard.

Chang Jinxing played his last card. "Your turn now, Yuwen!"

"Finally," said Chen Hong, who had forgotten all about targeting Huo Sichen.

Zhang Yuwen's hand this round had been terrible, and he knew he couldn't run from it, so he was ready. "I like it...outdoors. Outdoor sex, I guess."

"Oh." While not as shocking as Chang Jinxing's confession, it was still a relatively uncommon kink.

"Like, in school buildings," Zhang Yuwen continued. "On the rooftop, in the classroom, on the campus grounds...but you have to be very careful of security cameras."

Huo Sichen looked at Zhang Yuwen with surprise.

"What about the restrooms?" Yan Jun asked.

"Too dirty for me. The environment has to be clean."

"Then have you ever done it outdoors?" Zheng Weize asked curiously. "Uh, sorry for asking, Sichen-gege..."

"I don't mind," Huo Sichen said. "Not at all. I'd like to hear the answer too. Tell us."

Z HANG YUWEN RESIGNED HIMSELF to his fate. Huo Sichen didn't have a typical jealous mindset, so he wasn't at all jealous of Zhang Yuwen's ex; on the contrary, he was interested in knowing. He knew Zhang Yuwen was the top in his last relationship, but now that they'd defined their relationship, he was the bottom. The thought that his wife had fucked other people in the past instead of being the one getting fucked made Huo Sichen inexplicably excited.

"I guess places like the beach would be up your alley," said Yan Jun.

"Beaches are my favorite." Zhang Yuwen shuffled the cards. "It's sexy to be just wearing swimming trunks, and it's convenient to make love there, too."

"So do you want to be seen by others, or nah? Do you find that exciting?"

"No, no," Zhang Yuwen clarified. "We can't be seen. I won't do it in public. Those are two different things. I don't want a third person watching."

Yan Jun grinned. "I get it. It's the thrill of potentially getting caught in the act."

"Exactly." Zhang Yuwen laughed. "That's accurate. But no public exposure. It's not the same as exhibitionism."

"So," Chang Jinxing asked, "do you like wearing some kind of sex toy while you're taking the subway?"

"Uh…" Zhang Yuwen wanted to glance at Huo Sichen, but he held himself back. "If both parties are doing it, then yes, that'd be very exciting. Like a cage or something."

"Oh," everyone chorused, "got it."

Zhang Yuwen shared a little about his experience of having sex in the fire escape of a school building. Being a director, his language was expressive and precise, and his scene rendering was spot-on. By the end, everyone was blushing and had nothing to ask.

"So romantic," Huo Sichen remarked.

Everyone else rounded on him. "Seriously?!"

Zhang Yuwen dealt the cards. "At this rate, no one can escape!"

"You can, if you keep winning," Chen Hong said.

"When are we stopping?" asked Zheng Weize.

"When the fireworks start, I guess." Chen Hong glanced at the time. "Two more hours. There are fireworks at ten tonight."

This round, Yan Jun lost. Everyone stared at the devoted dad, and Chen Hong issued a reminder. "Let me make it clear: It can't be something like long legs or fair skin."

Yan Jun drank some wine and thought for a moment. "My sexual preferences are similar to Yuwen's. One is outdoor—"

The rest of the guys cut him off, exclaiming that his answer was unacceptable. Zhang Yuwen, for his part, said, "Right? Doing it outdoors is exciting."

Yan Jun went on, "I used to surf, and I only wore swimming briefs. It was at the beach, near naked… Let me finish; there's more!"

"Who's near naked? You or the other guy?" Chang Jinxing asked.

"Both. You know guys—less fabric. This is only one thing; I have more. The second is... You know the kind..." Yan Jun racked his brain for the right words. "Domestic guys."

Everyone was confused. Zhang Yuwen asked, "The kind that wears pajamas or casual wear?"

"Yeah. Kind of like a Japanese househusband. I really want to fuck them."

"Why do you want to fuck a Japanese house?" Zheng Weize asked, not quite catching all his words.

They all howled with laughter. Yan Jun tried again. "They give off a 'wife' vibe. A gentle man cooking, for example..."

All eyes turned to Chang Jinxing.

"No, no, not that sort," Yan Jun said. "Ideally, he would be wearing sexy, black briefs under his pajamas and have slight abs. After work, I could hug him from behind and start fucking him right there in the kitchen. If he had a thing for suits, even better."

"So essentially, a wife," said Chen Hong, summing it up for Yan Jun.

"A wife bottom, is that it?" Yan Jun said.

"Then you must like the plots in certain films." Huo Sichen had watched AV films before. "The guy wakes up and goes to work, while the girl wears only an apron..."

"Yes, exactly!" Yan Jun said. "But replace the housewife with a bottom wearing only an apron as he makes breakfast. The top steps out, having already changed into a suit. One in formal attire, the other naked, going at it on the dining table or the kitchen island. That's exhilarating. I could even skip work and stay home, fucking all day like rabbits..."

They erupted into laughter again.

"Uh... Okay." Zhang Yuwen thought this could also be considered a kink. Yan Jun rarely spoke, but he was brimming with vitality when it came to sex. Perhaps in his sexual fantasies, the scenarios were also full of sunshine.

"Let's see, who's next—"

They could barely hold back after Yan Jun's description and the others' never-ending additions. It was like a lights-out conversation in the university dorm, where everyone shared their sexual experiences without any restraint. The only difference was that all these dormmates were gay.

When Zhang Yuwen was in school, his roommates talked about girls every day. He couldn't just keep quiet, and he didn't want to come out to them either, so he'd had to pretend to be interested. This night filled in one of the missing pieces in his life.

It didn't matter anymore to the three who'd already lost the game, and they began to target the other three. Soon, Chen Hong lost too.

"Guess my fetish?" he said calmly as he shuffled the cards.

They all jeered at him: "How would we know? It's not like we've slept with you!"

Huo Sichen and Chen Hong were pretty familiar with one another, but Huo Sichen had to do some mental readjustment to adapt to the transition from being coach and client to their current relationship.

"I think...you told me before that you have a thing for suits?" Huo Sichen said.

"A little bit," Chen Hong said. "Actually, I have several kinks—wait, let me finish first. I think I'm a bit of an M, and I also have a fetish for socks and shoes... A mild one."

"Oh." Zhang Yuwen could have guessed that. Socks were a fairly common kink for gay guys, so maybe Chen Hong's was a little more intense. And feet were almost a universal fetish among men, gay or straight. Black stockings, fishnet stockings, high-heeled shoes—they came with inherent sexual connotations.

Everyone passed over the second thing, more curious about his masochistic tendencies. "Tell us more about this M thing."

"Like, I have to be in the role of a top as an M. Like, you know, in some films where a macho man is tied up... Uh..."

The guys began visualizing Chen Hong tied up.

"...And then I get a bottom to order me around and play with my dick. He can even step on it. If he's a gentleman in a suit, then it's perfect."

"Then all your fetishes will stack together," Yan Jun joked, sparking another round of laughter.

"Exactly!" Chen Hong wasn't embarrassed at all. On the contrary, he was very frank about everything. "I work out, right? So I want someone to abuse me and then, after he trains me, order me to fuck him."

"Your kink is like a straight man's," said Zheng Weize. "How is that different from being stepped on with high heels?" If the genders were switched around, Chen Hong would be the kind of straight guy who liked playing the submissive dog. Except his sadist partner would be an elite type instead of a queen.

"Right," Chen Hong said. "Seems like it. I wouldn't have realized that if you hadn't mentioned it."

"Do you like latex bodysuits?" Chang Jinxing asked, sizing Chen Hong up. "With your body type, I think people would drool if you wore a tight suit."

"Never tried it before," Chen Hong said. "Isn't that kind of gay?!"

Seeing that the discussion was about to cool off, Zhang Yuwen tossed Chen Hong a provocative line. "Would you let someone tie you up and penetrate you with a sex machine?" Everybody roared with laughter.

"No, I wouldn't," Chen Hong replied. "That's too hardcore."

"What's a sex machine?" Huo Sichen had too many questions.

Zhang Yuwen explained it to him briefly, then said to Chen Hong, "But you said you've been topped before."

"That was with my ex," Chen Hong explained. "I saw myself as his knight in shining armor, but he treated me like his dog. Well, not entirely a dog, but like, he taught me, trained me... Or rather..."

Zhang Yuwen found the right word. "Tamed you."

"Right! Tamed me! That was my first time. It was perverted, but I was addicted."

"Damn." Yan Jun was a little overwhelmed, but the matter-of-fact way Chen Hong talked about his doglike mentality was inexplicably captivating.

Huo Sichen stopped even answering his calls. He just pressed mute so he could listen attentively to Chen Hong.

"How about a dog tail butt plug?" Yan Jun asked.

Chen Hong patted Yan Jun on the head. Their relationship had always been good, so Yan Jun didn't have to hold back on his needling. "I don't like stuffing things into my butt."

"Then what about a ball gag?" asked Zheng Weize.

"That's fine with me," Chen Hong said, "but hey, don't start imagining it...and stop looking at me like that. Let's keep playing cards. Two more guys left, and we have half an hour to go."

Zhang Yuwen glanced at Huo Sichen's phone. "Do you have something important going on?"

"Same old crap from the company," Huo Sichen replied. Zhang Yuwen didn't press him further, and they resumed playing cards.

This time, Zheng Weize gave up resisting. All his roommates had been through a round of truth, and he couldn't just nope out of it. During the round, though, Huo Sichen left to answer another call, and Chen Hong immediately signaled to Zhang Yuwen. Zhang Yuwen played for Huo Sichen, unsure whether to laugh or cry.

"It's finally Sichen's turn," Chen Hong whispered.

But several seconds later, they heard Huo Sichen's furious voice from the room. "Can't you just let me have a vacation? What's so important that you have to say it now? You want me to go back now and sort it out with you?"

Everyone looked at Zhang Yuwen. "His business partner," Zhang Yuwen explained. "Sounds like a married couple, right? But that's how business partners' arguments go."

"As long as you're sure there's no problem," said Chang Jinxing, who was worried about Zhang Yuwen being deceived.

"I went to his house every time we had a training session," Chen Hong added. "He's been living alone the whole time. I can confirm that much."

"I work myself to the bone every day for you. Even on Christmas, I had to work overtime on the plane..." Huo Sichen's words dispelled everyone's doubts. Soon, his voice quieted a little, and in the end, he said, "I'm turning off my phone."

Then he stormed out, took two breaths, and composed himself. Back to his usual expression, he asked, "Whose turn?"

Zhang Yuwen was impressed. This was a self-possessed man who had not brought his anger out into the common area.

"Your turn," Chen Hong said, once he'd observed Huo Sichen's expression and satisfied himself that he wasn't about to start raging.

"I helped you lose," Zhang Yuwen chimed in. While Huo Sichen was on the phone, Zhang Yuwen had lost all his cards. Everyone laughed, and Huo Sichen looked astonished.

"Spill it!" Yan Jun said. "We're all ears."

"Uh..."

"You have to come up with one, even if you have to make it up," Chen Hong said. The guys doubled over with laughter.

Huo Sichen's face turned beet red. "What if I perform something instead?"

"Nope," Chang Jinxing said.

"Who cares about a performance?" said Zhang Yuwen. "Spill! You must have one!"

"I...I kind of want to try everything after hearing so much," Huo Sichen said. Everyone else erupted into laughter again. "I'm serious."

"That's such a diplomatic answer," Zhang Yuwen remarked.

He'd intended to let him off the hook, but Huo Sichen stammered, "I like little princes with black-rimmed glasses. I think... What's that word? The bottom conquering the top? Like what Chen Hong mentioned about the knight. Right, a knight who protects others. Oh, no, I just thought of one. I think I like...entering men from the back."

"That's what we call being gay, dude." Zhang Yuwen really didn't know what to do with him.

"Anal intercourse just makes me excited. It's very stimulating because—"

"Oh boy, you make it sound so clinical." Not even Zheng Weize could bear to listen further.

"—It hurts a little? Maybe?"

"It does," Zheng Weize said, "but it also feels good."

"Seeing someone I like that way makes me excited. Like, *very* excited. I might be a bit of an S. I was shocked the first time I saw them doing it from the back in a porno, but it also opened my eyes. Oh, yeah, and there's more."

Chen Hong had thought about getting him to drink as a penalty, but at this point, they were all realizing that Huo Sichen might really have been straight before. What was common to gay men, like penetrating each other, was, to Huo Sichen, a perverse act. But once he learned about it, he subconsciously turned it into his kink.

Homosexuality itself was just a sexual preference.

"What else?" Zhang Yuwen grinned. "We're listening."

Huo Sichen looked at him. "I used to be impotent."

"Huh?" Everyone looked flummoxed.

"What?" Zhang Yuwen had examined his goods earlier that day. He couldn't believe his ears.

"There was a time I couldn't get it up," Huo Sichen insisted.

"You probably just jerk off too much," Yan Jun said. "You'll be fine after a break."

"No, I rarely use my hands. It persisted for almost two years," Huo Sichen said. Zhang Yuwen gave him a skeptical look. "But I'm fine now. I've completely recovered."

He looked at Zhang Yuwen with a gaze that said, *You know what I mean.*

Zhang Yuwen promptly turned to the others. "Don't look at me! I've never tested it!"

"Uh-huh." The guys nodded sympathetically.

"Could be work stress," Chang Jinxing said.

"Maybe." Huo Sichen thought for a moment before turning on his phone. To Zhang Yuwen, he said, "Let me show you my last diagnostic report."

"Why would I want to see your erectile dysfunction diagnostic report?" Zhang Yuwen was laughing so hard tears were running down his face.

Red-faced, Huo Sichen explained, "Just so you know that for two full years, I basically didn't have...didn't... You know. It felt so terrible."

"So if you couldn't get an erection," Zheng Weize asked, "did you ejaculate in your wet dreams?"

"Yeah, but not very hard. I'd just inexplicably ejaculate in my sleep, and most of the time, I wouldn't even realize it. It wasn't wet dreams, either."

"Maybe you just didn't meet someone you liked," Yan Jun said.

"Even so, you can still get hard watching porn, right?" Chen Hong mused aloud. "And then there's also morning wood under normal circumstances."

"Yeah," Huo Sichen replied. "I just realized one day that I no longer had any reaction to girls' naked bodies, and later on, the morning wood stopped too."

"It must be psychological," Zhang Yuwen said. "In any case, it's all good as long as you're fine now."

"Maybe you were just too busy." Yan Jun could empathize with a fellow corporate slave.

Huo Sichen spread his hands, indicating that he was done talking. "Whose turn now?"

"Me," Zheng Weize said. "Might as well say it. I don't want to be left out." Everyone looked at him, grinning. "It's nothing special, actually. I like being sworn at and slapped in bed."

"Wow," Chen Hong blurted. "You're even more of an M than I am."

Not embarrassed at all, Zheng Weize quirked a smile. "And I also like being choked."

"Be careful with that, okay?" Zhang Yuwen said.

"I don't have a partner now, anyway," said Zheng Weize. "I think I'm a hardcore masochist. Being bullied and abused makes me excited."

Chang Jinxing grinned at Zheng Weize, looking like he had something to say but apparently deciding against it. In this brief silence, Chen Hong glanced at his phone. "It's time for the fireworks."

"So what's the tally? Who lost the most?" Yan Jun asked. "Look, it's time for the dare."

Flustered, Chang Jinxing tried to mix up the chips, but a sharp-eyed Chen Hong caught him by the wrist. "Hey! What are you doing? So you're it, then."

"Ha!" Zhang Yuwen counted the chips. The totals proved that Chang Jinxing was the one who'd lost the most, and surprisingly enough, Huo Sichen emerged as the top winner. The rule was that the winner would set a challenge for the loser. Huo Sichen hadn't really played all that seriously, though; Zhang Yuwen was the one who'd won money for him.

Chang Jinxing made a pleading gesture to Huo Sichen, telling him not to be too hard on him. Huo Sichen thought about it and glanced at Zhang Yuwen, who said, "Don't look at me. Our friendship is still going strong. Don't make me come up with the dare."

In the end, Huo Sichen said, "Choose one of us here and kiss him."

Chang Jinxing heaved a sigh of relief, and Zhang Yuwen shot Huo Sichen a slightly reproachful look.

"How about kissing Sichen?" Chen Hong suggested, ready to stir the pot. Huo Sichen crossed his hands in a NO gesture, looking flustered.

"Oh!" Zheng Weize exclaimed. "The fireworks are starting! Look!"

The sounds of the fireworks going off—*bang! bang!*—echoed outside. Fireworks shot into the sky from the side of the mountain, lighting up the first night of the new year. The guys stepped out into the back garden of Crane Hall and gazed into the night sky from the deck.

Chang Jinxing whipped out his camera and took photos of them all. When he got to Zheng Weize, the younger boy was staring at the resplendent fireworks, spellbound. Chang Jinxing snapped his fingers at him. Zheng Weize turned to him with a melancholic smile, raising a brow as he mimed taking a photo with his fingers against his face. Chang Jinxing took the photo, then leaned in and gave him a light kiss on the lips.

In that instant, fireworks bloomed, illuminating the long night and bringing the landscape below to life in a dazzling riot of colors, like a massive wish slip with everyone's New Year wishes on it, drifting in the wind toward that unreachable dreamscape far, far away.

CHARACTER & NAME GUIDE

CHARACTERS

Zhang Yuwen 张宇文

The owner of No. 7 Riverbay Road. A film director who dreams of being a writer, he decides to rent out his spare rooms so that he can spend time around people in real life to make his writing more realistic.

Yan Jun 严峻

The first of Zhang Yuwen's tenants. An office worker who takes care of his niece since his brother and sister-in-law passed away.

Yan Yuqi 严玉棋

Yan Jun's baby niece, usually called Xiao-Qi. Calls everyone "Papa."

Zheng Weize 郑维泽

An unsuccessful live streamer, the youngest of the tenants at twenty-two, and the only one who considers himself a bottom.

Chen Hong 陈宏

The third of Zhang Yuwen's tenants, a twenty-nine-year-old fitness trainer struggling to find clients after having to close his gym.

Chang Jinxing 常锦星

The fourth tenant, a self-proclaimed photographer. A bit of a playboy who's used to using his looks to get ahead.

Huo Sichen 霍斯臣

A rich, handsome friend of Chen Hong's who starts spending time with the group after he strikes up a friendship with Zhang Yuwen.

NAME GUIDE

Diminutives, nicknames, and name tags:

A-: Friendly diminutive. Always a prefix. Usually for monosyllabic names, or one syllable out of a two-syllable name.

DOUBLING: Doubling a syllable of a person's name can be a nickname, e.g., "Mangmang"; it has childish or cutesy connotations.

DA-: A prefix meaning big/older

XIAO-: A diminutive meaning "little." Always a prefix.

-ER: An affectionate diminutive added to names, literally "son" or "child." Always a suffix. Can sometimes be a fixed part of a person's name, rather than just an affectionate suffix.

Family:

DI/DIDI: Younger brother or a younger male friend.

GE/GEGE/DAGE: Older brother or an older male friend.

JIE/JIEJIE: Older sister or an older female friend.